WISH
YOU WERE
GONE

WISH
YOU WERE
GONE

Kieran Scott

GALLERY BOOKS

New York   London   Toronto   Sydney   New Delhi

G

Gallery Books
An Imprint of Simon & Schuster, Inc.
1230 Avenue of the Americas
New York, NY 10020

First Gallery Books hardcover edition November 2021

GALLERY BOOKS and colophon are registered trademarks of Simon & Schuster, Inc.

For information about special discounts for bulk purchases,
please contact Simon & Schuster Special Sales at 1-866-506-1949
or business@simonandschuster.com.

The Simon & Schuster Speakers Bureau can bring authors to your live event. For more information or to book an event, contact the Simon & Schuster Speakers Bureau at 1-866-248-3049 or visit our website at www.simonspeakers.com.

Interior design by Davina Mock-Maniscalco

Manufactured in the United States of America

10 9 8 7 6 5 4 3 2 1

Library of Congress Cataloging-in-Publication Data

Names: Scott, Kieran
Title: Wish you were gone : a novel / Kieran Scott.
Identifiers: LCCN 2020036578 (print) | LCCN 2020036579 (ebook) | ISBN 9781982153984 (hardcover) | ISBN 9781982153991 (trade paperback) | ISBN 9781982154004 (ebook)
Subjects: GSAFD: Suspense fiction.
Classification: LCC PS3619.C6744 S43 2021 (print) | LCC PS3619.C6744 (ebook) | DDC 813/.6—dc23
LC record available at https://lccn.loc.gov/2020036578
LC ebook record available at https://lccn.loc.gov/2020036579

ISBN 978-1-9821-5398-4
ISBN 978-1-9821-5400-4 (ebook)

For my mom

Your anger and damage and grief are the way to the truth.

—Anne Lamott

WISH
YOU WERE
GONE

EMMA

When Emma Walsh sat up in bed, the house still shook beneath her. Nuclear bomb. She was sure of it. Her eyes went to the panoramic window overlooking the woods, expecting to see a flash of blinding light. Ever since the nineties and the first Iraq war when some classmate had suggested that Saddam Hussein was going to smuggle a WMD—though no one was calling them that yet—into New York City and annihilate them all, this had been one of Emma's deep-seated fears. It had reemerged to niggle at her after the second war in the Gulf, after 9/11, at various moments in time when the Russians or the North Koreans had started acting all crazy, and had been present in the back of her mind ever since ISIS had become a thing.

Now, as she awaited her own incineration, she tried to remember where her kids were. Hunter hadn't been home when she went to bed. But Kelsey . . . what? God, how horrible was she that she couldn't remember? In her room listening to show tunes? Watching *Riverdale* for the thousandth time? It was James's fault that she couldn't remember. Because he hadn't shown up. He'd told her where to meet him and when, and she'd driven all the way into Manhattan to the Upper East Side and paid for parking and broken a sweat on the sidewalk and then she'd just sat there in the restaurant—alone. Full of adrenaline and righteous indignation—alone. So that when she finally came home she'd felt mind-bendingly idiotic and been so keyed up that she had to take an Ambien to fall asleep. Now, here she was, and the world was ending, and she couldn't focus.

That was when Emma realized James wasn't in their bed. She looked at the clock.

1:12 a.m. Well. This was a new low. Maybe this was the night he finally wouldn't come home at all.

"Mom?"

She'd never get used to Hunter's deep, authoritative voice. Of course, at that moment, her son didn't sound authoritative, but scared, and as her bedroom door swung open, she half expected to see him padding in wearing his SpongeBob pajamas, three-feet-nothing, thirty pounds soaking wet. It took a second for her eyes to travel up to his face along his six-foot-three frame. His dark hair stuck straight up from his head, and his skin was still tan from a summer of baseball tournaments, which had smoothly segued directly into the fall ball season. All baseball, all the time. He pulled a new Duke University T-shirt on over the chest that Emma still couldn't quite understand belonged to her offspring. She'd never been that fit. James had never been that fit. She wondered for the millionth time where the hell Hunter had come from.

"Mom? Are you awake?"

"Of course I'm awake." She was sitting up straight in bed, her heart trying to escape from her body by any means necessary. Thanks to the Ambien, her eyelids felt like tiny lead blankets, but she was slowly growing more alert. "Are you okay? Where's Kelsey?"

"She's sleeping over at Willow's, remember?"

Emma blinked. That did sound vaguely familiar, Kelsey asking to sleep over at the older girl's house, her cherubic face full of hope at the opportunity. But wasn't that supposed to be next weekend?

There was another, smaller crash. Emma flicked the blankets off her legs.

"What was that? What's going on?"

The idea of a nuclear blast was fading the longer she kept breathing. But that didn't mean there hadn't been a bomb. Or, shit, how close did they live to Indian Point again?

"I don't know." He adjusted the blinds on one of the back windows, which looked out over the patio and the pool, the vinyl cover socked in by fallen leaves. "I think something hit the house."

"Something *hit* the *house?*" Emma was out of bed and yanking a sweatshirt on over her white LBI T-shirt and cotton pajama pants, even though she was sweating. She still slept in the same uniform she'd slept in as a college student at UVA. But she also slept braless and her son didn't need to see that. "Like what? A meteor?"

Hunter glanced toward the door. He really did look younger right then. She noticed there was a scrape on his knee, a trickle of dried blood. "I don't know."

Glass shattered somewhere down below, and they locked eyes. Hunter crouched and pulled out the nine iron from under the bed where his father always kept it. The one James should have been wielding at that moment. Ire bubbled up inside her chest. Where the hell was the man of the house when the house needed protecting?

"Hunter, don't. Let's call the police."

But even as she said it, something inside her told her *no*. No police. A knee-jerk thing. Her throat felt tight.

"It's okay, Mom," he said. "I got this. Just stay behind me."

And Emma did. Because she was just that pathetic. She stayed *behind* her firstborn as they tiptoed down the long, carpeted hallway to the landing overlooking the foyer on one side, the living room on the other. The place was oddly silent, and even more strangely, nothing seemed amiss. The paintings still hung on the walls. The vase full of fresh seasonal mums she'd had delivered that afternoon still sat on the antique table at the center of the marble floor. No broken windows; not a knickknack out of place. Outside the wall of French doors off the living room, there wasn't so much as a wayward doe poking its nose where it didn't belong. The moonlight illuminated the empty flowerpots and tightly covered patio furniture. All the covers had been replaced after the recent hurricane—worse than Irene, not as bad as Sandy—and Emma had made sure the service had secured everything with top-of-the-line weights and ties this time, so that they wouldn't wake up and find another chaise lounge in the center of the pool.

After a breath, Hunter started down the stairs, and again, Emma followed. He first peeked his head into the den; nothing. Feeling braver, Emma crossed to the game room and glanced inside herself. Nothing. Together, side-by-side now, they walked to the kitchen. Every pot hung from its hook, every plate sat in its slot in the custom cabinet. The drawers were closed, the canisters lined up by height, the mixer clean and covered. A place for everything and everything in its place. Everything except for the broken front window, cardboard-covered, the tape already starting to peel back.

Was it possible they'd imagined it? A mass delusion of two people? A shared nightmare? When Hunter was young, there had been times that Emma woke up from a bad dream seconds before he called out to her, and when she'd arrived in his room, both of them bleary eyed, she was sure she'd taken as much comfort from cuddling up in his bed with him as he had in having her there. Hunter never wanted to tell her what his nightmares were about, but she always wondered if they'd dreamt the same thing at the same time. If it was possible to be that connected to another person.

Standing next to him now, together in their unease, she marveled that she'd ever felt that close to him. They still had their things—a shared sarcastic sense of humor, the ability to inhale entire pints of Häagen-Dazs while watching bad horror movies, yearly debates over which Christmas special is the greatest of all time—but in so many ways he was an enigma to her now. A grown man, practically. He was a good kid—good grades, glowing reports from coaches and teachers, nary a scandal about him in a private school with its share of scandals—but she barely knew him beyond that. He moved through the house with his own agenda—practice, school, workout, party, study, rinse, repeat.

Emma caught her ghostly reflection in one of the glass-fronted cabinets. Her skin looked pale, and she could see the bruise-like circles under her eyes. Her blond hair was a tangle at the back of her head.

Something groaned and the glasses in the cabinets tinkled. They looked at the door to the garage.

"Mom?" Hunter said.

This time, Emma went first, silently cursing James with every shaky step. Her feet were cold and clammy against the ceramic tiles and her hand shook as she reached for the doorknob. The door swung open soundlessly, but the garbled, gurgling, gaspy noise that issued from her throat was so odd it startled her.

For a long moment, Emma's brain couldn't process what her eyes were seeing. James's car—his brand-new, sleek, black, midlife-crisis BMW convertible—was in its spot in the garage, but it had been crushed. It was covered in brick and plaster and dust and random gardening tools—a rake, a shovel, a hose. Half the back wall of the garage was gone, collapsed over the vehicle, a massive hole lending a jagged view of the stars in the autumn sky.

The engine was still running. The headlights glowing softly from behind plaster shards. And her husband's leg—his pressed pants cuff, his Ralph Lauren sock, his shiny brown shoe—hung out the open driver's-side door.

EMMA

Emma had made it as far as the kitchen island before her legs gave out. Luckily, her son was there to catch her, having returned just in time from the bathroom, where he'd quickly and loudly thrown up. He'd deposited her on one of the less-than-comfortable stools that faced the marble countertop. Now, an hour later, she hadn't moved. Her bag was still there. The long brown envelope full of papers. Her keys. Everything she had tossed aside in anger when she'd arrived home hours earlier.

She remembered the texts she had sent her husband and wondered, in her haze, where his phone was right now.

The police had it, probably. The police, who had been here for the last . . . half hour? Forty-five minutes? She had no concept of time. Her face felt tight and her brain was made of pudding. The red and blue lights of the police cruisers pulsated all around her.

It was a good thing that their street was so private—only three homes on the cul-de-sac, and theirs at the very end—built way down in the valley. The neighbors would have noticed dozens of emergency vehicles, of course, but none of them were gauche enough to come out in the middle of the night, to stand at the end of the driveway gathering their robes at their necks and theorizing with one another.

How does someone drive his car through his own garage? Heart attack? Stroke? Or maybe he was on something. Maybe he was drunk. But James? James Walsh? Not possible.

No. In their town, their snug New Jersey town, tragedies happened in a vacuum. People didn't rush to help or to ask anyone directly involved what had gone down. They waited a respectable amount of time, and then, they started assuming; gossiping.

"Mom?"

Hunter stepped up behind her. He was clutching his own elbows. Behind him was a police officer. A young, nice-looking man, who seemed uncomfortable in his uniform.

"This is Officer Kim," Hunter said. "He wants to talk to you."

"Ma'am." Officer Kim held a stylus in one hand, an iPad in the other. Of course. No pads and pens for the Oakmont Police Department. They were keeping pace with the times. "I'm sorry for your loss, ma'am."

She stared at him. His black hair was cut very short and gelled into place. He had kind eyes.

"Mom?" Hunter said.

He'd moved off to the side and was hovering, chewing on the side of his thumb. She hadn't seen him do that since he was ten years old.

"Yes, I . . . thank you?" she said in the direction of Officer Kim.

"Can I get you anything?" he asked. Oddly, she thought, since this was her house and he was the interloper.

"Water, please," she answered, not wanting to be impolite. The officer looked at Hunter and, when Hunter didn't move, went to the Sub-Zero himself, extracted a bottle of Smartwater, and brought it back. Emma saw him noticing the cardboard over the broken window. She still didn't know how that had gotten there. The break, yes; the cardboard, no. Had James covered it up this morning before he'd left?

She hadn't said goodbye to him. Hadn't kissed her husband, or told him to have a good day. She hadn't even seen him. In fact, she had spent the bulk of the day wishing she never had to see him again. And now, she never would. Emma wondered what Officer Kim would think if he could look inside her brain. Would he be shocked? Would he arrest her on the spot?

The officer met her eyes as he handed her the water. His dark gaze was full of pity. What must he think of her? Of her family? Of this household? She cracked open the water and took a long, deep drink.

"Ma'am, I'm sorry to have to ask, but was your husband a habitual drinker?" Officer Kim poised his stylus above the iPad. It made him look childish somehow, like a kindergartner playacting at cops and robbers. "Did he often drink and drive?"

Hunter snorted.

"Yes," Emma said, her voice firm. "Yes, to both. This is not his first . . . accident. But I'm sure you know that already. I'm sure you've run his name through the system."

It was somehow important to her that this young man—this child, really—not think she was oblivious. That he understood she was aware of the problem.

Just last night, in fact, she had come so close to calling the police on James—to breaking that sacred household rule. Would this Officer Kim have been one of the people to respond? Probably. The Oakmont Police Department was a small outfit—not much ever happened in this one-Starbucks town with its strict noise ordinances and even stricter overnight parking rules. But her husband, well, she'd never seen him the way he was last night. The rage. The almost magenta color of his face— the lines of his neck standing out stark white as the tendons stretched and strained. What had he said to her daughter exactly? That she was spoiled? Entitled? *A thief*, he'd said. *A liar*. None of it had made any sense. And then the screaming. So much screaming. She worried, now, that she'd never get the screaming out of her head. No wonder Kelsey had wanted to sleep elsewhere tonight. There had been other fights. Bad ones, even. But never as bad as that. Honestly, she wouldn't have blamed Kelsey if she'd asked to move out.

Emma took a breath and looked at Officer Kim. "Was there anything else . . . Officer?"

He started to speak, but at that moment, her daughter flew into her arms.

"Mom," Kelsey said into her neck. "Mom, Mom, Mom, Mom, Mom."

Emma pulled her daughter back, hands on either side of her face, and looked into her eyes even as her own blurred and stung.

"It's okay," Emma said firmly, hoping her daughter would hear her. "Everything's going to be okay."

Kelsey nodded, suddenly mute, and Emma could see her daughter choking on the words. Her hoodie was up over her hair, tied close to her chin, making her look like a baby doll.

Willow came in next, and went right to Hunter, who hugged her so hard it was almost vicious. Then Lizzie, clutching her rattan bag in front of her, the curls of her red hair sticking out in all directions. "Emma?"

A sob escaped her throat as she stood up and fell into her best friend's arms. They cried for five or ten or a hundred minutes, Lizzie whispering that she was so sorry. So very sorry.

"We'll call if we have any follow-up questions," Officer Kim said quietly, and Emma pulled it together long enough to nod. When she released Lizzie, Kelsey instantly took Lizzie's place again. Emma's friend walked over to the garage door and cracked it open. She stood there, arms crossed tightly over her baggy sweater, shoulders shaking as the coroner's team loaded the stretcher into the back of the ambulance.

GRAY

Gray Garrison had been expecting this call. Well, maybe not this call, exactly. A car through a wall, and Emma the one to find him. Why hadn't he careened off the hairpin turn on Cornice Way? Or into the woods on Blueberry Lane? She'd always known the man was going to die in a drunk driving accident, but this seemed so unnecessarily messy.

Emma was crying on the other end of the line, and Gray said all the right things. She knew what her role was, as the best friend, as the wife of the business partner. But she couldn't bring herself to feel sadness, or regret, or even anger. All she could feel, upon hearing that James Walsh was dead, was relief.

"You should have seen Hunter's face, Gray. I don't think he's ever going to recover."

Bile rose in Gray's throat. She couldn't imagine her own boys going through this. It shouldn't have been this way. But maybe James should have thought about that. He should have made a change in his life long ago— for himself, his wife, his family, Darnell. He'd just never had the guts.

"I'm so sorry. It will be all right. You're all about to go through a lot, but you will get through it. We all will," Gray told her friend. "Do you want me to come over?"

"It's okay," Emma said. "Lizzie's here."

Gray's jaw tightened. "I'll come."

A flash of headlights blinded her as a car pulled into her driveway. Gray's eyes darted to the clock, and only then did her blood run cold.

"Actually," Gray said, steeling her voice. "Emma, just hang in there. I'm going to have to call you back."

HUNTER

The glass was everywhere. Hunter couldn't understand how there could be so much of it. The hole in the window was relatively small—about the size of a baseball—but the blast zone seemed to cover the entire kitchen. Carefully, he swept up tiny shards and particles into the dustpan, then took a wet paper towel and went over the floor tiles square by square, snagging up the teeniest bits in the folds. This was not the first time he'd cleaned up broken glass.

Once he was certain the floor was safe for bare feet, he checked the clock. It was almost three in the morning. School in five hours. That was going to be brutal. He tossed the paper towel and used masking tape and the flap from a cardboard box he'd found in the hall closet to cover the hole. Then he got to work on the countertop.

At least his mom was a clean freak. If this had happened at his friend Marc's house, he never would have found all the glass. Marc's mom ran an online gluten-free bakery out of her kitchen and their counters were always covered in test recipes, cookbooks, chopped fruit and vegetables, and half-unpacked grocery bags. This task would have taken Marc hours. But then, Hunter couldn't imagine Marc's crunchy, Toms-wearing, ukulele-playing father launching a coffee mug through a window.

You're the only person who can be you, so be the best you you can be, Marc's dad had once said to Hunter.

Standing now in the middle of the darkened kitchen, Hunter tried to remember whether his own father had ever said anything like that to him. He was sure that he had—a memory hovered at the very edge of his mind—a Little League field, the orange dirt on his cleats—but he couldn't make himself remember the words.

Hunter was wiping off the last countertop when he heard a footfall on the basement stairs. His father's footsteps were unmistakable. When he was sober, they were heavy. When he was drunk, it sounded like a giant was rumbling up the stairs.

Fi . . . fie . . . fo . . . fum . . .

His father had been downstairs in his museum—his sanctuary—for the last three hours. So long that Hunter had assumed he'd passed out down there. The museum was full of every piece of sports memorabilia his father had ever collected—everything from framed, signed jerseys to commemorative bobbleheads to books full of ripped tickets from back when tickets were still printed and ripped. It was his father's favorite room in the house, everything professionally displayed with custom shelves and lighting, and he and his sister weren't allowed to enter without him there. A rule that Hunter had broken many times.

Something glinted in the corner of Hunter's vision. Ignoring the nervous jackhammering of his heart at his father's slow approach, he crouched to sweep it up. He was still on the floor when the basement door shuddered open—a product of it being pushed and kicked at the same time. Hunter held his breath. Silence. His father could move down the hall toward the living room and stairs, or he could come toward the kitchen—toward the light.

He chose the light.

Hunter's strong legs shook as he rose to his full height and his father entered the room. His dad looked surprised to see him there. There was a baseball bat in his hands. Hunter's teeth clenched. He held the dustpan so tightly that the ridges in the rubber handle cut into his palm. The two men stared at each other. Hunter had to remind himself that this was what he was now. Eighteen years old. A man.

He hadn't felt like a man earlier when he'd chased his father across the front driveway as his father chased his little sister—hair streaming, guttural screaming. He'd felt like a confused, desperate little boy trying to stop a charging bull. He saw his hand come down on his father's shoulder. Saw the wildness in his dad's eyes as he turned on Hunter and shoved him, full strength, into the holly bushes. Hunter could still feel the blow of his father's hands on his chest. There were scrapes up and down his arms and on one side of his face from the sharp holly leaves.

His dad had never pushed him before. Had never touched him in anger—not once.

This all went through his mind as he stared his father down now, terrified, livid, and sort of hoping for a fight. He was very aware of the bat, but he refused to look away first. He would hold this man's gaze all night if he had to.

Just say you're sorry, Hunter thought. *Say it won't happen again. Beg for my forgiveness. Do. It.*

But then, something shifted in his father's face. He looked away, shook his head, and shuffled off toward the stairs. Hunter heard him stop on the first step, brace his unsteady weight, and then start the climb. A second later, he heard a clatter. The sound of a wooden bat, bouncing across a wooden floor.

His chest filled with pride as he turned back toward his task and then, the suspense broken, he started to cry. One of these days, his father was going to kill someone. Of this he was suddenly sure.

LIZZIE

There was no way she was ever going to make it through this day. Why, in the name of all deities everywhere, had she ever decided to open a retail store? As a teenager and college student, Saturday had been a sacred day to Lizzie. Saturday meant sleeping until noon, eating sugar cereal with too much milk in front of bad TV, lazing under the closest tree with a book of poetry or philosophy or an Archie comic or playing Frisbee with her brothers and their dog. Then lazy dinners, long drives, and parties and oblivion.

Oh, how she missed those days.

Now, Saturdays meant work. And the worst work of the week. Because Saturday was when the browsers came. They came with their sticky-fingered children and their cell phones, picking things up and putting them down, looking around almost as if they didn't understand how they came to be there. Then they'd shoot Lizzie all sorts of smiles—apologetic ones, pitying ones, commiserating ones, promising ones—as they pushed their strollers out the door. A browser was a browser, and they never bought a thing.

It wasn't that she didn't like people. She actually loved people. She liked to chat them up and hear their stories, listen to their proud-mama boasts or commiserate after a long day at work. People were endlessly fascinating to Lizzie. People who bought things? They were, currently, her favorite kind of people. Especially now that her situation had changed.

With the holidays coming, the decorating side of her business would slow, as people began to concentrate on entertaining and not overhauling. Yes, the retail side would pick up with gift shopping and holiday swaps, but never enough to compensate for the big commissions that reappointing some Wall Street mogul's great room would bring in. Or renovating the kitchen of another bored housewife.

Lizzie paused beneath the skylight in her entryway and tilted her chin up. It looked like a perfect blue-sky autumn day outside, all pumpkin spiced lattes and crunchy leaves underfoot. There would be a ton of traffic on River Street. She should do a flash sale this afternoon. Twenty percent off all ceramics from noon to four? Was it gauche to run a sale the day after your best friend's husband died?

No. Emma wouldn't care. In fact, she would never even know. Lizzie needed to make a living. She'd put out the chalkboard as soon as she opened the doors. Maybe she'd do a special on Emma's photography prints, too. It would be nice to be able to tell her friend that she'd sold a piece or two. Hearing of a sale always brought a smile to Emma's face—imagining her work hanging forever in the living room of some young family. Not that Lizzie thought it would change anything, but it could give Emma a spot of joy on what was sure to be a horrible day.

Horrible days. Lizzie knew from mourning, having lost her beloved dad just five years earlier. This was going to be months of horrible days. She was going to have to make more time for Emma. Be there for her. Help her with whatever she needed—funeral plans, hanging out with the kids, bringing food. She saw lots of spa treatments she couldn't afford in her future.

With a huge yawn, Lizzie dragged her tired ass into the kitchen. She hadn't slept more than three hours, tops, and the skin under her eyes felt dry and heavy. Her nose remained clogged no matter how many times she blew it, the back of her throat was coated in gravel, and even though her whole body was moving at a snail's pace, her mind raced.

James Walsh is dead. Emma is a widow. Everything is going to change.

When he woke up yesterday morning, had he known? No. How could he? He had probably figured that day was going to be just like any other day, and he'd be waking up this morning for breakfast with his family, taking Hunter out to shag balls at the batting cages, or popping by the gourmet deli to order cold cuts and salads, or doing work in the yard. Did James Walsh even do yard work? Probably not. People with that kind of money had landscapers.

Lizzie couldn't get the ambulance—the lumpy form of James Walsh's body under the white sheet—out of her mind. The police had cleared out soon after Lizzie brought Kelsey home and when Lizzie tried to ask Emma what had happened, all Emma would say was, "It was an accident. They're not sure . . . " Her friend had been so exhausted and distraught, Lizzie hadn't wanted to press further.

James's inner life—if he had one—was a mystery to Lizzie. She had barely even spoken to the man in the last ten years. Back in the day, when the kids were in grade school and Emma used to throw barbecues or parties for their birthdays or on the last day of school, he was often away on some business trip or other. If he was in attendance, he'd spend the whole party in the back corner of the yard, smoking cigars with his buddies and laughing his booming laugh. He'd ignored Lizzie's existence, basically, not that she could blame him. In retrospect, she realized he'd ignored most—if not all—of Emma's friends. That was the kind of guy he was.

But he'd always seemed so healthy. So robust. She couldn't make sense of it.

"Coffee?"

Willow, standing near the window next to the Keurig, startled Lizzie half out of her skin. Her daughter, tall, square-shouldered, a presence. She clearly hadn't slept either, or bothered to remove her heavy eye makeup. She looked like she'd just come home from a KISS concert.

KISS. Had Willow ever even heard of KISS?

"Of course coffee. Do you even need to ask?"

Lizzie took out a box of organic granola—no more sugar cereal for her—and sat down at the table, dragging over a bowl that may or may not have been used yesterday. Willow popped a pod into the Keurig and then handed her the soy milk. Lizzie ate on autopilot. Willow fixed her coffee for her and put it down next to Lizzie's bowl, and Lizzie, for a moment, considered diving headfirst into it.

She'd call Emma when she got to the shop. Or maybe she should wait. What if she was sleeping? Lizzie didn't want to do the wrong thing, but the only thing she knew for sure was wrong was not calling. So, she'd call, but later. When would Emma start cleaning out her husband's things? Lizzie couldn't even imagine.

"I still can't believe it," Willow said, and sat across from her, dropping a box of Entenmann's donuts on the table, next to the deck of cards that was always nearby, like a favored accessory. The chair scraping against the linoleum was oddly electrifying, and Lizzie felt almost awake, suddenly. She and her daughter stared at each other through the steam coming off of their mugs. Lizzie's pulse thrummed a frantic beat in her wrists. For half a second, she thought she knew what her daughter was thinking, but then, Willow looked away.

"Poor Hunter," Willow said.

"How *is* Hunter?"

Willow slurped her coffee, then shoved half a powdered donut into her mouth. She lifted one shoulder and spoke with her mouth full.

"I don't know. He barely said anything the entire time we were there. He just . . . cried. I've never seen a guy cry like that."

There was a cold, hard rock wedged into the spot between Lizzie's heart and her stomach. Willow reached for the deck of cards and her hands became a familiar blur, cutting and recutting, spinning and flipping.

"Him and his dad, they were really close, you know?" Willow continued. "Like with the baseball and everything? They just . . . got each other."

Lizzie's eyes filled with tears. She swiped at one before it could fall. Hunter Walsh was a baseball phenom—the perfect son for a man like

James Walsh, who made a living off of crafting the personas of professional athletes the world over. Hunter was being scouted as early as eighth grade, but was applying early decision to Duke. The recruiters would come in the spring, no doubt, but Hunter had already decided to wait until he had a degree, to play for the college team. James must have been so proud of him. And now, he'd never see his son take the field in a professional game, never play catch with him in the backyard again.

The injustice was so acute that, for a second, Lizzie could barely breathe. Sometimes the world did that to her—nearly flattened her with its take, take, take. And then, in the next moment, she would see something beautiful—like a sunset or a bright green caterpillar or a baby laughing—and it would be the give, give, give that overwhelmed her.

She looked at her daughter and cleared her throat. Part of her didn't want to ask this, but she knew she should. "How are you doing with all this?" Willow put the cards down.

"Me? It's just weird. I mean, I *just* saw him." Willow reached for her coffee cup. Her dark purple nail polish glittered in the sun. "But I'm fine."

"You're sure?"

"Yeah, I mean . . . I barely knew the guy." Willow gave her mother that favored look of teenagers everywhere—the one that said *duh, Mom. Why are you asking me such a stupid question?* She supposed turnabout was fair play. She'd certainly given her own parents that look plenty of times.

"Okay. Fair enough," Lizzie said.

Willow shifted in her seat and considered the second half of the donut, but left it in the box. "So . . . what're we supposed to do now?" she asked.

"We're going to do everything we can to support Emma and her family. We're going to be there for our friends."

Lizzie hoped she sounded far more certain and more mature and more solid than she felt. Because what she really felt that morning, as she looked into her daughter's beautiful, dark eyes, was fear.

KELSEY

Your dad mustve been on hella drugs. Was it because he couldn't
stand looking at you?
Maybe he killed himself to get away from you.
Your such a freak walsh. Youre hole family is freaks.

By Wednesday morning, Kelsey had shut off her phone. It wasn't that
there weren't any nice messages. They were just so few and far between
they weren't worth it. She texted Alexa to call her on the landline if she
needed her, held her finger down on the *off* button, and shoved the dead
phone under her mattress.

But now she couldn't sit still.

Kelsey's room was too small. That was the problem. Or maybe it was
just too messy. She needed to throw stuff out. Purge. Clean it from top to
bottom. Maybe even move stuff around. No. Of course move stuff around.
Her furniture had been in roughly the same configuration since she could
remember—her double bed positioned in the same exact spot her baby crib
had been. If Kelsey had learned one thing from watching HGTV with her
mother, it was that a room refresh could fix everything. It could change
your perspective. Your outlook on life. It could change your life altogether.

It was the Wednesday morning of her forced week off from school—both her mother and her guidance counselor had mandated it—when Kelsey got to work. She took all her books and snow globes and little frames and old My Little Ponies—she couldn't bring herself to throw them out no matter how many times she tried—down from her shelves and dusted. She cleaned out her desk drawers, polished the wooden surface, and took out the pink-and-gold desk set her grandmother had sent her from France for her birthday, positioning everything around her computer just so. She tore apart her closet, making a donate pile and a keep pile and then hanging everything in the keep pile neatly on hangers, organizing everything by color.

By noon, she had amassed four garbage bags in the hallway and had only been bothered once, by her nana—the grandmother who lived in the States—who asked her if she wanted a snack.

Kelsey didn't want a snack. She wanted a new life. For the first time ever, she felt like maybe she could have one.

With everything off her shelves and all the throw pillows off her bed, Kelsey went to Hunter's room and knocked on the always-closed door.

"Yeah?"

"Can you help me with something?" she asked, rising up on her toes.

She heard him groan and then the door opened loudly. How did he manage to *open* a door loudly? He must have slammed his hand down on the lever handle with a hundred pounds of force. The room behind him was dark, only a sliver of sunlight shining from beneath the blinds on each of his three windows. The bed was mussed, and crusty plates and dirty laundry littered the floor.

"What is it now?" he asked. Though not entirely unkindly. Hunter towered above her, almost a foot taller and definitely a foot wider. He looked like crap. Well, for him. His skin was pasty and he'd sprouted a zit on his chin, and his hair flopped the wrong way from his part, creating a sort of wing on one side of his head. Plus he smelled rank—like the locker room after a wrestling match. Even so, her friends probably still would have fallen all over themselves at the sight of him.

"I'm moving my furniture and I need a big, strong man to help me." She pitched her voice higher and put on a southern accent for the second half of the sentence. "Would you help me, kind sir?"

Hunter rolled his eyes, but laughed shortly and followed her back down the hall, doing that wide-legged walk that made him look like he was in a western film and had just dismounted a horse.

"Whoa," he said, when he saw the state her room was in.

"I know, right?"

He stepped inside and picked up her old, pink piggy bank off the floor. The coins inside crashed around. "What made you do all this?"

"I just needed a project, you know?"

He looked at her like he was trying to decipher a particularly complex calculus problem. Then he put the bank back down.

"Okay. What do you need me for?"

"I want the dresser over there and the desk across from it and the bed under the window."

Hunter glanced around, assessing the situation, then clapped his hands together. "Let's do it."

They got the desk out of the way and moved the dresser first. Even without the drawers in, it was ridiculously heavy, and Kelsey had to stop five times as they shimmied it across the room. She could feel her father hovering over her shoulder, telling her to just let Hunter do it, that she was weak, that she was good for nothing, and on the last push she let out a half-groan, half-scream that startled Hunter.

"All right there, killer?" he said.

She stared him down. It was a sarcastic nickname he'd had for her ever since she murdered five goldfish in a row in second grade. She'd always hated it. She'd mourned those goldfish. It wasn't like she'd *meant* to kill them.

Hunter averted his eyes. "Sorry. My bad."

He picked up the desk himself, as if it was a bag of popcorn, and plopped it down where she wanted it, then lifted her laptop from the window seat onto the desk. It was open to the website for The Daltry School.

"Wait. Are you applying?" he asked.

Kelsey was shoving a drawer full of socks back into her dresser. "Yeah, well, nothing's stopping me now."

"That's cold."

Kelsey blushed. "Sorry."

It was her father who hadn't wanted her to go. Her dear old dad who had said that no child of his was ever going to attend *art school* as if the words burned holes into his tongue. He'd refused to pay the tuition. He'd refused to pay the *application fee*. But she knew her mother would give her the money, and she knew she would get in. She already had her audition pieces all picked out and perfected. When she got the acceptance letter, her dad would roll over in his grave.

Except, well, he didn't have a grave. Which was kind of a shame. She would have liked to have gone there and read him the letter herself. Maybe she could read it to his urn. Kelsey had yet to cry over her father's death. There were moments in which she wondered if there was something wrong with her, but then she'd feel a phantom throbbing in her throat and remember all the awful, hurtful things he'd said and done to her, and think maybe not.

Hunter went to lift one end of the bed. "By the window? You're sure?"

"By the window," she said.

She grabbed the headboard and they shoved and dragged and dragged and shoved until the bed was right where she wanted it. Kelsey jumped on the mattress, making the springs creak, and looked out at her new view of the backyard.

She hung over the side and lifted the comforter, scanning the floor underneath. When she popped up again, a head-rush blurred her vision. She saw her brother's hand coming toward her and she yelped, shrinking back.

Hunter raised his palms. "Sorry, I was just . . . you looked like you were going to faint or something."

Her hand was on her heart. "Oh. No. I'm fine."

"You're sure?" His expression was wary. "We good, Kels?"

"We're good," she said.

But her hands were still shaking. Hunter looked at them and she tucked them behind her back.

"You'd tell me if you weren't okay, right?" he said.

"Of course I would." Kelsey held on to her own hands for dear life. "I swear."

EMMA

Emma stood at the kitchen threshold, unable to make herself break the plane. There was a time when the kitchen had been the place where Emma lived. She made herself morning smoothies there when she was feeling health-conscious, full-fat cappuccinos when she wasn't. She fixed breakfast for the kids every morning, then sat at the island for hours, going through her most recent photographs and deciding which ones to frame for Lizzie's shop, searching the internet for decorating ideas, or mentions of her old art school friends, and posting projects and inspirations to Instagram. Around one o'clock she'd make herself lunch—a salad from the leftovers or a grilled cheese sandwich or a bagel and fruit. Then, after errands or the gym or whatever else she had to do, she'd be back, cooking dinner, cleaning up after dinner, watching TV while she sipped wine and tried not to look at the clock. The kitchen had been her home— her favorite room in the house.

Was that only days ago? Time really had lost all meaning. But it seemed impossible. Now, all she could do was stare at the garage door and not breathe.

James dead. James *dead*.

It had gotten to the point that her children were regularly bringing her food in her bedroom—reheated casseroles from Gray or Lizzie or from their friends' parents, takeout from the burger place in town, and then, last night, semi-burnt frozen waffles and water.

The leftovers, clearly, were starting to dwindle, and Emma was going to have to start feeding her kids again before they got to thinking that boxed cereal and Trader Joe's pizza were actual nourishment. Which was why, today, after a twenty-minute pep talk under the covers that involved promising herself an afternoon of binge-watching *The Great British Baking Show* guilt-free, Emma finally made it down for breakfast.

The sun shone brightly on the chrome and marble and Italian tile as Emma forced herself to walk toward the garage door. This was the Everest she needed to scale. It was just a door. A broken building behind it. The car was gone. The body, her husband, was gone. All the yellow police tape had been balled up and shoved in the garbage. Someday, some way, she was going to have to open the damned door.

Her hand landed on the gold handle, her palm slick with sweat. How drunk did you have to be to drive through the back of your own garage? He'd been sober enough to hit the button to open the scrolling door. What the hell had happened between that and him pressing his foot to the gas? Had he even been awake? Had he known what was happening?

At some point a cop or a coroner or that sad-looking social worker had said something about his blood alcohol level, but she hadn't registered the number. A certain reading would have gotten him arrested, maybe even sent to rehab, but the reading didn't matter this time.

"Mom!" Emma flinched as her daughter walked into the kitchen, wearing a black turtleneck and jeans. More sophisticated than her usual clothes. "You're up!"

"Yeah. Yes!" Emma's voice was a croak. She cleared her throat and released the door. "I thought I'd make you guys French toast." Provided there was any bread in the house. Or eggs. She really hadn't thought this through.

"Oh." Kelsey flitted over to the refrigerator, executing an elegant twirl before she reached for the door, blond ponytail flying. "I already ate."

Emma's expression must have changed, because her daughter quickly added, "But I could go for French toast."

"No. That's okay. If you already ate, you already ate." Emma went to the sink and rinsed out Kelsey's bowl. At least it looked like she'd cut up a banana into whatever cereal she'd consumed. Her head felt weightless, like it could float off at any moment from lack of substance, but her body felt impossibly heavy, pinning her down.

"No, really. French toast sounds great!"

"No time for French toast." Hunter walked in, grabbed a few protein bars from the pantry, and shoved them in his battered backpack. "We gotta head."

Emma hated that expression. *Just finish your sentence.* She turned off the water. "Head where?"

He looked at her like she was dense. He'd been a teenager for so long now that she was almost immune to the shock of being looked at like that. Almost. "To school," he said.

"School?" Emma *felt* dense. "What day is it?"

"Monday?" Kelsey shook a small bottle of juice.

Clearly, someone had dropped off groceries. Gray, most likely. Emma had to call and thank her. Gray would be pleased to hear that she was finally out of bed.

"I told you to take the week off."

Her kids exchanged a look that Emma didn't appreciate. Her substance-less brain was having a hard time keeping up. "We did. We were off all last week. Nana was here . . . remember?"

There was an awful tickle at the back of Emma's throat. Her eyes flicked to the digital screen on the fridge. There it was, plain as day. 7:23 a.m. October 1. Apparently, it was going to be sunny and 62 degrees. "Of course I remember."

Another Monday? A whole week had gone by? She couldn't remember seeing her mother off, but she must have done it. She did remember the woman tucking her in and smoothing her hair back and thinking, *Did you ever do this when I was little?* And having the distinct feeling she hadn't.

"Okay, well, we should go." Kelsey lifted her backpack onto her shoulder.

"What about your lacrosse bag? Tryouts are this week, right?" Emma asked, feeling proud that she'd remembered as she followed her kids to the front door. Their house, large as it was, had a circular drive and parking area out front, separate from the three-car garage off the kitchen. No one had left through the garage since the accident. The game room was filled to near bursting with condolence gifts—flower arrangements, fruit baskets, boxes of nonperishable artisan food from overpriced delis around the country. Gray had gone through it all the other day and thrown out what was rotting, but still, the gifts kept coming.

"I decided not to try out," Kelsey said, and took a sip of her juice.

Emma blinked. Kelsey had spent the last three weeks doing nothing but work out and practice with the other freshman hopefuls. She'd been carbo-loading and going to bed early. She'd been borderline obsessed. "You're not? Why?"

Kelsey's eyes flashed, and the resemblance to her father in her expression was so stark it momentarily took Emma's breath away. This was not new, this spark of temper in Kelsey, but Emma had never told her daughter how much she reminded her of James in these moments. Kelsey would have never forgiven her for it. Seeing it now made Emma want to reach through time and space and strangle her husband. The very idea that her sweet, lovely, talented daughter had inherited that ugliness, of all things—it made her loathe him.

The Walsh temper was what he'd called it, pinning his viciousness on generations of angry Irishmen. And he'd always shrugged as if to say, *What're you gonna do?*

"I'm just not that into it." Emma could see her daughter measuring her words—trying not to snap. "I'm going to try out for the fall musical instead."

Hunter made a dismissive noise, blowing air through his lips. "Good luck with that. Freshmen *never* make the fall musical."

Kelsey hauled off and punched him in the arm.

"Hey! We don't hit!" Emma said, appalled.

"What is this, kindergarten? It's fine, Mom." Hunter rolled his eyes as if it hadn't hurt, even though it must have stung at least a little.

"Sorry," Kelsey muttered.

"Whatever," Hunter said. "Just don't come running to me when you get cast as Farm Girl Number Three." Then he opened the door to the bright, bright day. The sound of chain saws buzzed in the near distance, a wood-chipper screeching as it chewed through branches. This had been the constant soundtrack of their lives since the storm—that and the hum of generators, which had died down day by day as power returned to one neighborhood after another.

"'Bye, Ma." Hunter gave her a sort of pitying look, then kissed her cheek, which was new. "It's good to see you . . . you know . . . up."

She forced a smile. "Have a good day, hon."

Emma closed the door behind them. She waited for the beep of the alarm system, the pop of two car doors, the engine revving, then moving, then fading away.

And then she was alone. She was always alone when the kids were at school, but suddenly the aloneness felt like a living, breathing thing.

James was never coming home. How many times in the last five years had she wished he would never come home? Idly thought, *What if today's the day he stumbles in front of a cab?* Or *What if tonight's the night he swerves off the road?* How many times had she daydreamed about how that would feel? Having the agency taken away from her? The pressure. The fear. The guilt. The anger. The uncertainty. If he drank himself to death, then she would be free. She would no longer have to constantly obsess about whether to divorce him. About what that would look like. About how she'd survive. It would no longer be her fault that they lived the way they did because they wouldn't be living that way anymore. His death would be the end of her life sentence. Hers and her kids'.

Yes, in her darker moments, she'd daydreamed about it, but she'd never really meant it. The other dream, the more socially acceptable dream, the one where he checked himself into rehab, did two months as an inpatient, and then came home a new man—that was the dream she'd really wanted to come true. But if she was being honest, really and truly honest with herself, it was the dark dream she'd conjured most often.

When had she become this horrible morbid person—a person who could dream her husband dead? At the doorway to the game room, her eyes trailed slowly over the cellophane and cardboard, the silky ribbons and wilting petals. What if she had willed this to happen? James had been an asshole. He'd been a drunk and a bastard and an angry, raging fiend. She'd wanted him gone.

But he'd also, at one point, been her James. The love of her life. The boy she'd fallen for on a rain-streaked boardwalk in October of her junior year in high school, and who had proposed seven years later the second he'd gotten together enough money for a ring. They'd been only twenty-three. Just babies. And so full of the future that they could taste it on the back of their tongues.

She could still remember vividly the look of total awe and pride and hope on his face when he'd gotten down on one knee inside the capsule on the London Eye. The way he'd looked at her, it had made her feel like she was perfect. Maybe not perfectly gorgeous or perfectly smart or perfectly talented in a way that women around the world would measure themselves against, but perfect for him.

And maybe he could have still been that person who adored her— who lived every moment of every day for her. Maybe if she'd done something differently or spoken up more often or taken a stand. Or maybe if she'd left him. Taken the kids and moved in with her mom and actually served up a consequence. Maybe he would have hit that mythic rock bottom addicts were always going on about. Maybe something would have changed. Maybe James—her James—would have come back to her. If only she had ever lived for him the way he had once lived for her.

Maybe this was all her fault.

Emma was back in the kitchen now, unable to recall making the decision to move. She shook herself, trying to regain some sort of consciousness. Her eyes were dry from staring. There was a layer of film on the kitchen counters, and crumbs everywhere. There were dishes in the sink and most likely mold was spawning on casseroles in the fridge. On her phone were dozens of messages from Zoe. She had to call the girl back. And she had to call Gray and Lizzie and the contractor for the cottage. When had they said they'd walk the house and make plans? They'd picked a date, but she couldn't even remember.

She had also missed a couple of photo shoots Lizzie had set up for the two of them—Lizzie occasionally hired Emma to shoot before-and-after pictorials of her bigger decorating projects—but she couldn't deal with that right now. And she knew that Lizzie, God bless her, wouldn't want her to, but still it niggled at her. Things undone always niggled at her.

The doorbell rang. The sound reverberated through the house and startled Emma so badly, she nearly hit the deck. Part of her wanted to crouch down into a corner and wait out whoever it was. She couldn't deal with more well-meaning friends right now.

"Mrs. Walsh?"

It was the raspy voice of Nick Baer, their landscaper. Emma looked at the calendar again. No. Not Friday. Monday. This wasn't his day to be here. Yet she could hear the industrial lawn mowers growling, the weed-whackers whacking. She went to the door.

Nick tugged off his well-worn and sweat-stained baseball cap. He already had large pit stains on his T-shirt and his graying hair was plastered to his forehead. His blue eyes were kind and sorrowful, the creases around them deepening at the sight of her.

"Hello, Mrs. Walsh," he said formally. "I'm . . . I'm so sorry about Mr. Walsh. I don't even know what to say."

"Thank you," Emma replied. There was a long and awkward pause. "Did you need something? It's not your normal day, right?"

She felt uncertain about pretty much everything at that moment.

"No, it's not at that. I came on Friday, but your mother came out and asked us to go . . . She didn't tell you?"

Emma shook her head.

"She said you were sleeping and she didn't want the noise to wake you," he told her. "I would've let it go till next Friday, but you got so many leaves and I didn't want to let 'em sit on the grass for too long, so I figured we'd come do a quick cleanup today and then get back to our regular schedule."

"Oh. Okay. That's great. Thanks for doing that."

She started to close the door.

"Oh! Mrs. Walsh?"

"Yes?"

"Here. We found this in the bushes by the driveway. That's why I rang the bell."

He thrust his fist forward. Hanging from it was a necktie. A light blue necktie with little red dots. One of James's favorites.

Emma was numb as she took the slippery fabric from his dirt-streaked hand.

"Not sure what it was doing there, but I figured—"

"Which driveway?" she asked, her voice high and reedy and not like her own at all.

"The one . . ." He gestured in the direction of the garage, too uncomfortable to finish the sentence.

"Okay, thanks," she said, and closed the door.

She clutched at the tie, her fingers suddenly sweaty. It didn't make any sense. Why would one of James's ties be in the bushes? How long had it been there? It couldn't have been long, or the landscapers would have found it before now. They came every Friday morning like clockwork. They'd come *that* Friday morning. They would have been here at 10 a.m. when James was probably downing his second espresso at his desk on Madison Avenue. His last second espresso at his desk on Madison Avenue, as it turned out. Emma took a few steps into the foyer and leaned against the wall, feeling weak. Was this the tie James had been wearing the night he'd died?

The cops had told Emma that James had most likely made it to the top of the driveway, then passed out, his foot falling on the gas. The car had then accelerated down their steep driveway, caught some air on the lip between the garage and the drive, and crashed into the back wall.

But if that theory were true, then how the hell had his tie gotten into the bushes? Had he gotten out of the car and pulled it off? He often loosened his tie or removed it when he felt agitated or was in the midst of an argument. Had someone been with him? Had he actually gotten out of the car, taken off his tie, tossed it into the bushes, then gotten back in the car and passed out? It didn't make any sense.

She tried to remember what he had been wearing when they'd found him, but couldn't seem to recall a single detail other than the red polo horse and player embroidered into his blue sock. He always wore a tie to work. Every single day. But she hadn't seen him that morning. Had pointedly ignored him like she always did on the morning after a big fight. She had no clue what he'd left the house in.

Then, she remembered the bag. When the people from the funeral home had delivered James's urn, they had also delivered a large, plastic Ziploc bag with his clothing and shoes neatly stashed inside. The bag had been sitting on the mudroom bench for days. Emma hadn't been able to look at it, but she went to it now, the tie clutched in one hand as she picked up the bag and turned it over. Bloody shirt. Torn pants. Folded socks. Shiny shoes. His wedding band. His heavy Gucci watch.

No tie.

GRAY

It was 7:45 a.m., and Gray Garrison had already had a full day. She had gotten out of bed at 4:30, run three miles in the dark, dodging fallen leaves, cracked sidewalks, and shredded power lines, then made a green smoothie and answered emails while she stopped sweating. She always reserved the hour from 5:00 to 6:00 a.m. for personal and family emails, which this morning included the preliminary Thanksgiving email, canvassing her four brothers and their wives and partners to find out how many of them were planning on making the trip this year, and writing back to her son Derek, who was concerned about his father's stress level. Nothing from his twin brother, Dante, of course, who had his head so far up his butt he could see past his molars, but one out of two kids having empathy wasn't bad. She then reviewed the agenda for tonight's town council meeting, put in her order at Whole Foods, paid a few bills, and ordered Italian to be delivered to Emma's this evening for dinner. Who knew what those kids would be eating otherwise?

At six, she took a shower, and she was in full hair and makeup by seven, sitting in the kitchen with Darnell's scrambled eggs, turkey bacon, and coffee ready. Gray wasn't generally a breakfast person, which meant

Darnell usually ordered in once he got to the office, but she wanted to show her support and Darnell was pleasantly surprised.

"I thought I smelled bacon," he said, smiling as he strode into the kitchen. Score one for Gray—she hadn't seen him smile in well over a week. He leaned in for a kiss, his musky aftershave enveloping her, then grabbed the orange juice out of the fridge and sat down. "To what do I owe the surprise?"

Gray sipped her coffee and refolded the *Wall Street Journal*. "I thought you could use a little something positive heading into this week."

"Tell me about it." He dashed pepper onto his eggs, his broad shoulder muscles flexing beneath his crisp, white shirt. She'd always loved the way he looked in a white oxford. It contrasted with his dark skin and brought out the bright white of the teeth they'd paid through the nose for after the two front ones were knocked out during his last season in the NFL. "It's gonna take a while to clean up after last week's shit storm." He took a bite and shook his head. "Fucking James. He couldn't have just died like a normal person with a heart attack or something?"

Leave it to James Walsh to trash the reputation of his own PR company by creating a mess of bad PR, and then not even being there to deal with the fallout.

"It was an accident, hon. He didn't do it on purpose."

He gave her a loaded look. They both knew that this was a gray area. After all, he did have to get himself wasted enough to drive his own car through a wall.

"Well, today you can start turning over a new leaf," she said, standing to rinse out her drained coffee mug. "All you have to do is talk to your people, make sure everyone's on the same page going forward, and everything will be just—"

Darnell slammed his mug down on the kitchen island so hard Gray flinched. When she turned away from the sink, she half expected to see him keeling over of his own heart attack. But no. He simply sat there, posture straight, glaring at her.

"Do you have to be such a goddamned cheerleader all the time?" he snapped. "I mean turn off the relentless positivity for one fucking second, Gray, and actually listen!"

Gray gripped the edge of the countertop behind her. She felt as if she had suddenly been thrust into the room with a stranger. A raging, six-foot-six, three-hundred-pound stranger.

"Darnell?" she said quietly, because she could think of nothing else to do.

Like a switch had flipped, the ire drained out of his eyes and his face slackened. He looked down at the splatter of coffee on the marble and released the mug as if it were on fire. Clearly embarrassed, possibly confused, he averted his eyes and grabbed a few napkins from the center of the island to clean up his mess.

"Sorry. I'm sorry," he mumbled. "I don't know what's wrong with me lately."

Gray released her death grip on the counter. "It's okay," she said, her heart still hammering. "It's a stressful time."

Darnell slid past her to dump the wet napkins in the garbage, then reached for her. She allowed him to pull her into his arms, where, for the last half of her life, she had felt safer and more secure than anywhere else on the planet. He kissed the top of her head and she let out a breath. It was just a blip. He was just on edge. All thanks to James Walsh. A pain in the ass in life and a pain in the ass in death.

"Everything's going to be fine," she said, leaning back to look up at him, but keeping her arms clasped around his waist. "Just get through this week. You'll see."

"I'm sure you're right," he said, then ventured a smile. "You always are."

He kissed her firmly on the lips, then stepped from her grasp and grabbed his suit jacket off the stool where he'd tossed it. "I'd better go. Love you."

"Love you, too!" she called after him.

As soon as the door closed, Gray dropped onto the nearest stool, her legs no longer willing to hold her upright. What the hell was that?

Darnell didn't snap at her. He didn't lose his temper. Even back in his days in the NFL, he was known as the Gentle Giant—never one to showboat or get in anyone's face. He tackled every damn running back he could tackle, sacked every quarterback he could sack, then walked off the field, showered, and came home. To her. It was one of the reasons why he was so trusted in the sports PR business. Never had an off word been said about him in his four years at USC or his six years in the pros before he blew out his knee and was forced to retire.

It was James who had the temper. And Gray, God forgive her, had always been secretly proud of the fact that she had Darnell. That she had the better man. James and Emma may have looked perfect from the outside, but she and Darnell had the solid marriage, the stronger foundation, the mutual respect, and the deeper love. She never would have lorded it over Emma, but she did enjoy it privately.

But now . . .

Yes, James had died, and yes, he'd done it in spectacular fashion for all the papers to write about. But she'd never expected Darnell would react like this. He was a fighter. He was a person who bounced back, who came out the other side of any challenge stronger and ready to take on the next.

But this past week, he'd been different—short tempered and distracted. It could all be chalked up to stress, but she didn't like this version of him. It made her nervous. Because she didn't know what this version of her husband was capable of.

LIZZIE

Lizzie stared at the number on the calculator in front of her.

Ten schools.

$950.

Nine hundred and fifty dollars just to *apply*. She checked the balance on her checking account. That last payment had cleared, thank God, so it wasn't that she didn't have the money, but it was supposed to be going toward the credit card bill she and Willow had racked up during their back-to-school shopping spree at River Hills Mall. Lizzie had known she shouldn't be paying full price for any of the clothes Willow picked out—she knew that they would be going on sale in just a few weeks—but they'd been having so much fun. Willow had been in a rare loquacious mood and filled her mother in on things she otherwise never would have heard about, like her overnight to Ocean City with her friends and the boy she'd kissed by the Tilt-A-Whirl.

She cleared the calculator and eyed the stack of unopened bills. It was bad. She'd let things get out of control. But she'd only done it because she'd had that big job over the summer and thought the final payment would cover it. But then the water heater had gone. And there was Willow's trip to the emergency room when she'd gotten food poisoning working that six-year-old's birthday party. And that out-of-control cell phone bill the week after the storm, calling and texting everyone she knew to make sure they were okay and did they have power and did they need anything. When it rained, as the saying went, it poured.

Lizzie gulped her coffee. Upstairs, Willow pounded around, getting ready for school, late as always. Her music was so loud, the glassware in the kitchen cabinets shivered with every downbeat. Lizzie pushed her hands into her hair. What she needed to do was call Emma. Emma was literally the only person on earth who could help her. Lizzie needed to tell Emma the truth. But the very thought of that made her insides go slack. There was no way she could burden her friend with her situation. Not now. It was a situation of her own, idiotic making, and she was going to have to deal with it. Alone. Like she dealt with most things.

She chewed on the inside of her cheek, her foot bouncing beneath her chair. The house went suddenly quiet and Lizzie grabbed her phone. Emma picked up so fast she must have been holding her cell.

"Lizzie?"

She sounded odd. Distracted. But of course she was distracted. Her husband just died. This was an awful idea.

"Emma, hi! How are you? How's it going?" Lizzie asked. She was sweating. Actual beads of sweat had formed on her lip. Upstairs, the bathroom door slammed.

"Oh. It's going. I don't know."

"Is this a bad time?" Lizzie asked.

"No. Not at all," Emma said. "What's up?"

"Nothing, I just had a quick question." Lizzie stared at the bills, the calculator, the balance on her laptop. Her foot was so manic it was shaking her chair. She closed her eyes. *No.* "I was wondering if you could text me your Realtor's info."

There was a pause. She could imagine the baffled look on her best friend's face.

"The woman I used for the cottage? Why?"

Lizzie stood up and went to the Keurig. She popped in a new pod and shoved her cup under the spout. Would she spend less money on coffee if she bought a regular coffeepot? Why had she splurged on this thing in the first place? It sucked for the environment and she was supposed to be socially conscious.

"I'm thinking about putting the house on the market," she said, whacking the lever on the Keurig down like it had wronged her personally.

"What?" Emma half-shrieked. "You're not moving."

Shit. Lizzie was an idiot. A total blithering idiot. Of course this news would blindside Emma. She'd just lost her husband and now Lizzie was telling her that her best friend was leaving.

"No! No, not moving out of town. Just . . . downsizing," she improvised. "With Willow going to school next year it just seems like the right time. I don't know why I bought this big old house in the first place anyway."

But she did know. It was because she loved it. It was because she was drawn to it as if it had actually called to her. She adored its rickety porch and its stained-glass front windows, the curved banister and the hardwood floors. There were built-in bookcases and intricate moldings, a turret room in the attic and a claw-foot tub in the upstairs bath. Yes, it was too big for just her and Willow, but when she bought it, she had dreamt of filling it with a husband and more kids and maybe a couple of dogs. But she'd never found the right man. And Willow had proven to be allergic to pet dander. So now, here they both were. Two bedrooms too many.

"Oh, Lizzie, really? You've done so much with the place." Emma sounded like she was on the verge of tears.

Idiot. Idiot, idiot, idiot.

"I'd stay in town," she said, feeling a tad teary now herself. "Maybe a Cape Cod or a condo? Or one of those new apartments downtown?"

"Well, if you're sure . . . Margot is great," Emma said. "I'll text you the number. Tell her I recommended you. Maybe she'll give you priority."

The toilet flushed, running water through the old pipes, and Willow came clomping down the stairs in heavy boots and a delicate ankle-length skirt—all sparkles and lace. The girl had a style all her own. She grabbed Lizzie's wallet as Hunter honked his Jeep's horn outside.

"Willow? What're you doing?" Lizzie hissed, holding the phone away from her.

"You said I could go to the magic shop after school, remember?"

The magic shop. It was one of the things Lizzie had always found endearing about this town. That it could have a Williams Sonoma and a Coach and a Lilly Pulitzer, but also a magic shop and a used record store, five different art galleries, and a huge antiques shop with a full NASA space suit on a mannequin out front. Yes, the populace was rich, but they were also quirky. Lizzie related to the latter and aspired to the former.

"Lizzie? Are you still there?" Emma's voice called.

Willow saluted her mother and walked out the door. Lizzie sighed into the phone. "Sorry, I'm here."

"Oh. Good. Listen, can you come over?" Emma asked. "Something weird happened."

Lizzie's heart did a stutter step. "Weird? What do you mean?"

"It's probably nothing, but . . . I don't know."

Lizzie checked her wallet. Willow had swiped fifty bucks. She went to the door, but Hunter was already peeling out. That would have to be dealt with later. Right now, Emma needed her. But for what? Hadn't they all hit their threshold for weird when James drove his ridiculously expensive car through a wall? A cold sense of foreboding skated down her spine.

"I have to go open the shop," she told Emma. "Let's meet over there."

KELSEY

"Kels, you're bleeding."

It wasn't until Hunter said it that she tasted the coppery tang on her tongue and pulled her hand away from her mouth. Her fingernails were a ragged, bloody mess. She placed her hands in her lap and made fists to hide the massacre as Hunter pulled the car into a vacant space. He killed the engine. At the far end of the parking lot, a wood-chipper screeched. It made the tiny hairs on her neck go rigid. When the hell was this town going to be done cleaning up after the hurricane already?

"You okay?"

"I'm fine," she said. "I just don't want to talk about Dad anymore, okay? I want everything to go back to normal."

Just a couple of weeks ago on one of these drives to school, she and Willow had sat in the backseat together and Willow had painted Kelsey's nails the same purple as her own while Hunter turned up that awful new rap song he loved and rapped along with it at the top of his lungs, just to make them groan. It was so weird to think that her father had been alive then, and she'd been laughing and chatting, excited that Willow had asked her to go shopping that afternoon—alone, without Hunter—because they were becoming real friends. Now her father was dead and there was no joy in this car.

Part of her felt like the fact that her father was dead should have made the mood lighter, rather than the other way around. Which she knew made her a horrible person.

Hunter looked in the rearview mirror, locking eyes with Willow, who was sitting alone in the back today. What were they thinking about her? What were they silently communicating right now?

She didn't want to know. She shoved open the door and got out, slamming it behind her so Hunter would have to let Willow out his side. At first, she speed-walked ahead of them, but then she started to notice something. People stopped in their tracks as she approached. They stared and hesitated, like they didn't want to get too close. It was as if the flesh was melting from her face. Kelsey hesitated at the split in the walk where Hunter and Willow usually peeled off toward the junior/senior entrance, and waited for them to catch up.

The cream brick walls of the turreted building rose in front of her. Set on top of a small hill, the main building of Oakmont Day had been built in the late 1700s as part of a wealthy sawmill owner's estate. It was later converted into a school and had been through countless renovations, but it still had that moneyed colonial appeal. The place was hallowed ground for upper-class, Ivy-League-bound North Jerseyans, and Kelsey knew that hundreds of kids who applied every year didn't get in. Her father always told her she should be grateful he paid to send her here, and she knew she should be. But it was the school *he* wanted for her. The school *he'd* forced her to attend. And she wanted out.

"Want me to come with you?" her brother said.

"She's fine," Willow told him. She was rolling a quarter expertly back and forth over the tops of her fingers like it was nothing. Then, with a flick of her wrist, it entirely disappeared. "Right, Kelsey? You're fine."

"Actually . . ." Kelsey said to her brother. "Can you?"

Hunter slid his mirrored sunglasses on. "I'll catch up with you later," he said to Willow, who looked temporarily stung at being dismissed. But Kelsey couldn't care at the moment. She was too grateful to have her brother by her side.

The stares of her classmates on the quad were pitying, curious, and oddly superior—as if having a living father was one more thing they could now lord over her. For a girl who had spent most of her life as the invisible sibling to her athlete-god brother, the attention was disconcerting. But this was her punishment for having a parent who died in such a spectacularly buzzworthy way, with a totaled garage and a flattened hundred-thousand-dollar car. One last parting gift from dear old dad.

Kelsey upped her pace to match Hunter's long strides. She just wanted to get inside and get to Mrs. Tisch's room. Alexa had texted that she was waiting at her locker with a welcome-back surprise, which almost definitely meant her mom's homemade peanut butter cups. This actually might turn out to be an okay morning, if everyone would just stop staring.

She hoped Hunter was wrong about the musical. Performing on stage, attending rehearsals, being part of that community—she needed it like a plant needed water. Was it weird that this was what she was thinking about right now? Maybe she should be thinking about life and death and whether her father was burning in hell.

From the corner of her eye, Kelsey saw Jason Katz, the geek who had taken her as his queen back in the sixth grade, begin his approach. Kelsey started to smile. Jason was awkward, but he could be okay, and she wouldn't have minded a distraction right about then. But then Jason registered the presence of Hunter and nearly tripped himself stopping short. She was still marveling, not for the first time, at the scope of her brother's power, when she heard the words *dad* and *garage* and *total massacre* rise up from somewhere to her left. How much would she have to pay her brother to stick with her through classes, like a bodyguard?

How did it even happen? someone said. *Driving through your own garage? It's so fucked up.*

An odd hollow suddenly opened up inside her stomach, as if some roided-up superhero had just punched a hole right through her. For a second she couldn't breathe.

Dad.

He was actually gone. Actually never coming back. Was this grief she was feeling? Here? Now? Maybe she wasn't dead inside after all.

"What's up?" Hunter said.

"Nothing." They'd reached the door and she ducked inside, breathing a sigh of relief at the cool silence of the hallway. Technically, they weren't supposed to be inside yet, but Kelsey had a feeling no one was going to try to admonish the Walsh kids right now. "Thanks for coming with me."

"Look, it's gonna be weird today," he said, taking his sunglasses off again and looking her in the eye. "Probably all week. Just power through, okay? And text me if you need me."

"Thanks, Hunt."

"Whatever. Don't get all sappy on me now." He gave her a grin, which seemed to take some effort, then strolled off toward the senior hallway. Kelsey hooked a right and beelined it for the arts wing. Someone was in the band room practicing Vivaldi on their clarinet and butchering the crap out of it. Still, the sound was oddly comforting. Normal. Back to normal.

She expected the musical tryout list to be posted on the bulletin board outside the classroom. Mrs. Tisch liked to do things the old-fashioned way, rather then use Sign Me UP!, the app the rest of the school used. But the board was bare. Kelsey glanced into the open class-room. Mrs. Tisch was sitting at her desk, looking at something on her computer and taking notes in a notebook. She was so pretty—slim and blond—the youngest teacher at Oakmont Day. Today she wore her hair in loose tendrils down her back and a formfitting black shirt tucked into a houndstooth check pencil skirt. Kelsey thought that if she was ever going to have a crush on a woman, it would be Mrs. Tisch.

She knocked lightly.

"Kelsey!" Mrs. Tisch stood up and tossed her pencil down. "It's so good to see you. I'm so sorry about your father."

Kelsey lifted her hand. "It's fine."

Mrs. Tisch blinked.

"I mean, I'm sorry. It's not fine. I just never know what to say when someone says that. Do you say *It's okay* or *I'm sorry, too* or *Thanks?* It's not a sentence that has a good response." She gave an awkward laugh.

"Makes sense," Mrs. Tisch said. "So, I bet you're looking for the *Wizard of Oz* sign-ups? I was just about to put them out." She lifted a sheet of paper, then put it back down on her desk. "Unless . . . I mean . . . I'm sure this is a bad time."

Kelsey walked over, grabbed Mrs. Tisch's pencil, and wrote her name in clear, stark print at the top of the list.

"Great!" Mrs. Tisch said. She looked up at Kelsey, who felt suddenly conspicuous. She had always been bad at asking adults for things. Especially cool adults. She simply lost all confidence. "Was there something else?"

"Remember when I told you I was thinking about applying to Daltry and you said you thought it was a great idea and that you would write me a letter of recommendation?" she said in a rush.

Mrs. Tisch's face fell. She placed the sign-up list on a clipboard. "I remember."

Kelsey felt stalled by the unenthusiastic reaction. "Well, could you?"

"Kelsey, I don't know," Mrs. Tisch said. "Mr. Fletcher and I were talking about this a bit last week and . . . I thought you'd decided not to apply."

"No. I mean, yes. But I—"

"It just seems like maybe this isn't the best time to make a big change," Mrs. Tisch said.

Kelsey was now on the verge of tears. She lifted her fingertips to her lips, saw the blood, then tucked them behind her. Her neck felt hot under the stupid turtleneck. Unbelievable. Her father was going to ruin this for her anyway and he wasn't even here. "Oh . . . okay."

"Oh, honey. I'm sorry. Let me talk to Mr. Fletcher. Maybe we can all sit down for a chat with your mom and figure out what's best."

Why did she keep mentioning her guidance counselor? Why was Mr. Fletcher suddenly in charge of Kelsey's life? She didn't have her dad telling her what to do, so, of course, some other male person who had no business ordering her around had decided to step in. This was bullshit. It was *her* life. Hers. Why didn't anyone want her to be happy? Kelsey's throat closed over. She had to get out of there before she burst.

"You can't stop me from applying," she said shakily.

Mrs. Tisch looked Kelsey in the eye. "I know that. I would never try to do that."

"Good," she said. "Because I'm not staying at this school one second longer than I have to."

The way Mrs. Tisch was looking at her made Kelsey want to flee, so that's what she did. She turned around and walked right into Willow.

"Oh my God. You scared the crap out of me." Heat radiated from Kelsey's pores. What had Willow overheard? The older girl raised her hands in response.

"Sorry. I was just going to sign up for stage crew." She put her arms down again and eyed Kelsey. "Hey . . . are you okay?"

"I wish everyone would stop asking me that," Kelsey muttered.

"Sorry. I just figured maybe you'd want to talk, like, without Hunter."

Kelsey's throat was tight. "No. I'm good."

There was the world's most awkward pause. Down the hall, someone screeched and someone else laughed. Lockers slammed. "You still coming over after school?" Willow said.

Kelsey didn't want to. What she wanted to do was back out. She wanted the whole thing with Willow to stop. But she didn't have it in her to say it right now. So instead, she said, "Sure."

Willow actually smiled. "Cool. See you later."

"Yeah." Kelsey burned with internal humiliation. She wished, just once, she could stand up for herself. "See ya."

EMMA

Her two best friends had never agreed on anything for as long as Emma had known them, but as she sat across the table from them at On a Lark, Lizzie's upscale gift shop and interior design studio, she was pretty sure they agreed that she was crazy. Normally one of her favorite places, On a Lark was all huge windows and whitewashed walls with light oak accents, shelves bursting with colorful ceramics, huge photographic books, and fragrant displays of handmade candles. Some of Emma's own architecture photography, set in raw wood frames, was displayed on the back wall, which made her feel proud every time she walked through the doors. Now Emma wondered if she'd henceforth think of this shop as the place her friends decided to have her committed.

"You found his tie," Gray stated, her green eyes narrowing. Subtext: *And I'm missing a client meeting for this?*

"I think she said the landscaper found his tie," Lizzie corrected. Subtext: *I'm a better listener.*

"Insignificant detail."

"I thought there *were* no insignificant details," Lizzie countered. "What's that story you're always telling about the million-dollar settlement you won because of a misplaced comma?"

"It was ten million."

Gray sniffed and took a sip of water from the glass bottle she'd produced out of her bag. Lizzie grabbed a coaster and quickly slid it beneath the bottle before Gray could place it on the reclaimed oak table. The tension in the unopened shop was palpable. Emma chose to ignore it. This was how it was whenever the three of them were alone together, and it was not about her friends right now.

"Yes, but that's not the only thing," she said. "Once I started thinking about the tie, and trying to figure out under what scenario he ever would have taken it off and thrown it in the bushes, I started to realize some other things were . . . off that night."

"Like what?" Lizzie, always one for a good story, leaned in.

"Like he had the top down, and he never drove with the top down unless the weather was perfect. And *never* at night," Emma said. "Also, when Hunter and I found him, the car door was *open*. His foot was . . . sticking out."

Lizzie rolled her eyes closed and shuddered slightly.

"I know," Emma said. "Sorry. But why would the door have been open? If it happened like the police said, and he got to the driveway, passed out, and hit the gas unconscious . . . when did he open the door?"

"Is that what they think happened?" Lizzie asked.

"Well, he was wasted, right?" Gray said. "Maybe he put the top down and didn't even realize it. Maybe he was half out of it, started to get out of the car, and passed out."

"He was *wasted*?" Lizzie asked.

"Why else do you think he drove through the back of his own garage? To test his superhero invincibility?" Gray snapped. "Emma just said he was passed out."

"I know, but—" She looked at Emma. "You didn't tell me he was driving drunk. I thought maybe he fainted or—"

"He always drove drunk. He was like a pro at it," Gray said, oozing judgment. "How he survived as long as he did is a mystery in and of itself if you ask—"

"All right, all right, that's enough," Emma interjected. She sounded like she had back when the kids were in middle school, when they'd gone through their constant-bickering phase. Which she supposed she should be grateful for today because it made Hunter and Kelsey's current friendship that much sweeter. Now, facing down her friends, her cheeks were pink. She didn't appreciate Gray's tone, like she knew everything there was to know about James, like she had the right to spew crap about her husband—even if it was true crap. Also, Lizzie didn't know anything about James's drinking. Unless Hunter had said something to Willow and Willow had passed it along. It wasn't something Emma chose to share with Lizzie. She liked having a friendship that was untouched by the quagmire of her marriage. Lizzie never asked, in a quiet, concerned voice, how things were at home—or whether she was okay, or if she needed anything. Their relationship was, for that reason, easy. Maybe slightly shallower than her relationship with Gray, but no less meaningful to her. She needed Lizzie, just for entirely different reasons than those she had for needing Gray.

Gray checked her watch and Emma shifted in her seat. She knew Gray had to get to the office, and Lizzie needed to open up shop soon.

"Okay, so you've got the tie, the car roof, the door," Gray said. "What're you thinking?"

Gray studied her face as if she were on the witness stand. Emma ran her fingernail along a groove in the oak table. She had no idea how her friends were going to react to this, but she had to say it. She had to talk it through with someone. "What if someone was with him?"

Lizzie looked up. She'd been staring at the floor with a look of extreme concentration, as if trying to solve a sudoku puzzle in her head. "Like who?"

"I don't know, but what other reason would he have for getting out of the car? For taking off his tie?" Emma said, warming to her subject. "What if someone was with him and they . . . did something to him?"

Her two best friends stilled. Out on the street, a child laughed and a chain saw buzzed and a breeze rustled the autumn trees, but inside the shop, dead silence.

"Emma—"

"No! Just hear me out. What if it wasn't an accident?" Emma said. "What if someone was there, and they set it up to *look* like an accident?"

"How would someone even do that?" Lizzie asked.

"I have no idea," Emma said. "But something weird is going on. I can feel it in my gut."

She tried to think back to that evening, wondering whether she'd had a sixth sense that something was off. But no, she couldn't fool herself into believing that. In the few hours before the accident she'd been too livid to feel anything else. She'd said things, done things, texted things she wished she could take back. But it was too late now.

Gray and Lizzie locked eyes and in that moment, there was a hitch in Emma's stomach. Because for half a second, she thought that maybe they knew something. That maybe they didn't think she was crazy, that maybe they *knew* she was right. But then they turned to her and she was disappointed. They had the look of two people who were going in to talk down a hostage-taker. They didn't know James like she did. He was a creature of habit. There were things he simply did not do. Something wasn't adding up. And if she had to figure out the equation on her own, that was what she would do. Though she had hoped that her best friends, or at least one of them, would believe in her enough to get on board.

"Forget it. It's silly," Emma said. "Forget I said anything."

LIZZIE

Right when she thought that maybe he wasn't coming, Ben Thackery appeared at the door of the shop. Lizzie, having spent the entire day inside her head thinking about Emma and James and how it had turned out that she didn't know squat about Emma and James, brightened at the sight of him. He used his shoulder to push the door open, loaded down as he always was with two coffees and a pink pastry bag.

"What have you got for me today?" she asked. Her taste buds were already tingling.

"Apple spice coffee and cranberry scones," he said, his smile excited. She shoved aside her laptop to make room on the counter.

"It smells heavenly!"

Ben beamed. "The apple spice is a new recipe. I added more nutmeg. But the cranberry scones are my grandmother's. I've been eating those since I was in kindergarten."

As always, he watched her as she took a bite. The first few times he'd done this, it had disconcerted Lizzie, but now she found that she no longer minded. In fact, she sort of liked the attention. Ben was not her usual type. He was chubby and average height and a little bit balding on top, but he had kind blue eyes and strong-looking hands, and over the past few weeks she'd come to look forward to making him smile. Plus she adored his positive outlook on life. So few people had that these days. Ben had moved to Oakmont a little over a month ago, bought the old Greek bakery down the street, and turned it into a modern café selling trendy tarts and popovers and the most delicious array of muffins. He'd started bringing free samples to all the business owners on River Street his first week in business, but Lizzie was pretty sure he saved these special Monday evening visits for her. The café was closed on Mondays, and he spent the whole day working on new recipes behind locked doors, only coming out to serve her this closing-time snack like her very own Willy Wonka.

"What do you think?" he asked her now, blowing on his coffee.

"It's ridiculously good," Lizzie told him. "My compliments to your grandma."

"May she rest." Ben bowed his head for a moment, then came back up with that smile on, his dimples showing. "So, I can't stay long today. I have to go to the town council meeting. It's New Business Monday."

"Ugh, town council meetings." They'd made her attend a half dozen of those when she'd first moved to town and put in her proposal for her business. The hoops they'd made her jump through to get her awning approved and ensure her new windows were up to code and on and on. You'd think she'd rolled into town on Spring Fest weekend and announced to all the little kids at the egg hunt that she was opening a sex den.

"It's fine." He shrugged. "Small-town bureaucracy. But how are you? What's new? How was your day?"

Lizzie thought of her computer, the balance in her checking account. But no. She refused to obsess. Especially not when she had started to form a plan. "It was fine," she said and licked a crumb from her lip. "A little weird."

"How so?"

"It's a long story," she said. "And if you have to go—"

"No! It's okay. The council can wait." He laughed. "What's up?"

"Remember my friend I told you about? Emma?"

"Oh! Everyone's talking about her husband," he said, his expression serious for the first time. "So tragic."

"Yes, well . . ." Lizzie hesitated. Should she tell him Emma's theory? Or would that be a betrayal? "I don't know. I'm just worried about her. I don't think she's taking it very well."

"That's understandable, though," Ben said. He picked up the discarded sleeve from his coffee cup and tapped it on the countertop. "It must have been a big shock. Do you know some people are saying it was a suicide?"

Lizzie almost dropped her coffee. "What? No, it wasn't. It was an accident."

"Well, obviously I don't know anything about anything, but that's what some people were saying at the café over the weekend. It was a big topic of conversation."

"I see," Lizzie said, and felt offended on Emma's behalf. But then, now that she thought about it, she wasn't surprised. A few customers had tried to talk to her about it last week as well, but she'd always shut them down—politely, of course, but still. It was all still too raw. She didn't like the way they were using Emma's tragedy as gossip fodder—acting like they were commiserating when really they were scandalized, curious, always hoping someone would feed them a new tidbit of information they could pass on to their friends.

But could James have killed himself? Would that explain all the oddities Emma was talking about? Maybe she should call her. But how do you suggest to your best friend that her husband, her partner in life, the person who was supposed to love, honor, and cherish her, had decided he'd had enough of that and checked out? Lizzie's throat closed at the very thought.

Ten minutes later the scones were eaten and the coffee drained and Lizzie was seeing Ben out, promising to stop by the café later in the week. The sun had gone down while they were chatting—those ever-shorter fall days—and Lizzie was just opening the door for him when Gray suddenly barreled through, her stylish dove-gray trench coat swishing.

"Gray?"

"Hello, Mrs. Garrison!" Ben greeted her.

She looked him up and down, then eyed Lizzie, as if surprised that she had company. "Oh. Hello, Ben. How's your sister?"

"You two know each other?" Lizzie asked. He'd told Gray about his sister's cancer treatments? Just like that, Lizzie felt significantly less special.

"Of course. I know everyone in this town," Gray said.

Right. Of course. She'd forgotten for half a second that Gray Garrison was the all-knowing queen of Oakmont. Gray tugged off a pair of leather driving gloves, finger by finger. The woman had endless pairs of leather driving gloves, in all colors of the rainbow. These were basic black and worked well with the gray of her coat. The gloves were such a silly affectation. No one used freaking driving gloves anymore outside of NASCAR.

Be the change, Lizzie told herself, taking deep breaths. *Be the change.*

"My sister's feeling much better. Thanks for asking," Ben said, his smile as genuine as ever. "I was just heading over to the council meeting to make that statement you all asked for. Did you need a ride?"

"No. Thank you," Gray said. "I'll be right behind you. I just have a bit of business with Lizzie here."

"I already closed out the register," Lizzie told Gray.

Gray gave a short laugh and glanced dismissively around the shop. "I'm not here to *buy* anything." She said it like Lizzie's stock of lovely handmade bowls, Egyptian cotton towels, and original artwork was made out of animal feces.

"I'll just leave you to it," Ben said, edging out the door. "Good night, Lizzie. Gray." And he was gone.

Lizzie sighed. "So why *are* you here?"

"Because." Gray said the word imperiously, leaving Lizzie wondering how anyone could say that word imperiously. "Emma is obviously spiraling. We're her closest friends. We have to convince her to drop this whole *not an accident* thing before she gets obsessed. It's not healthy."

Lizzie was surprised that Gray had put the two of them on the same level as Emma's closest friends. If pressed, Lizzie would never have said the same. *She* was Emma's best friend. She was the one who listened, who gave her a job when she was so bored at home she wanted to pull her own hair out, who was there whenever Emma called. Gray seemed to think of Emma as a puppet to be molded and controlled. Although after this morning's conversation it seemed pretty clear that there was a lot about Emma that Lizzie didn't know—a lot about Emma's *marriage* that she didn't know—information that Gray was privy to. She wondered if Gray had been walking around all day preening over that fact. Add a point to the Gray column.

Lizzie hated the idea of keeping score—even metaphorically. It was so childish. But she was certain Gray was doing it, too.

For once, though, the two of them were in agreement on something. Going off on some wild-goose chase was not going to help Emma grieve properly. And what if James *had* committed suicide? What if that was what Emma discovered in the end? That he wished he'd chosen a different path. Or a different woman? That he had been unhappy in his marriage all these years. So unhappy he'd taken the most drastic way out.

Lizzie was about to ask Gray what she was thinking when she noticed that Gray had made no move to remove her coat, or to sit at the design table. She stood in the middle of the store, her black hair shining under the pot lights, and hanging perfectly straight in a blunt cut to her shoulders. She must have had it trimmed every week to keep it looking that perfect. She must have spent a fortune. Gray regarded her, chin held high, her briefcase clutched in front of her along with those incredibly lush-looking gloves. Lizzie felt the oddest tingling of fear. Gloves were good for keeping fingerprints off of things. Like cars. Like door handles.

"Do you . . . know something?" she asked.

Gray laughed derisively. "Of course, you *would* go there."

"It's a simple question, Gray," Lizzie said, moving behind the counter just to put its heft between herself and this woman. This enemy. "You come in here all jittery and tell me we have to distract Emma, so of course I have to wonder—"

"I've never been *jittery* a day in my life." Gray put her briefcase on the counter and slapped the gloves down next to it, rolling her neck a bit, as if talking to Lizzie was just so trying. "Of course you'd have some half-cocked conspiracy theory, but no. I'm just worried about my friend. Emma, you may not know, has anxiety—she has a tendency to fall down the rabbit hole when the going gets tough."

Lizzie's skin burned at the implication that she didn't know Emma as well as the great Gray Garrison did. Maybe she'd been in the dark about certain things, but she *knew* her best friend. "I've never seen her fall down the rabbit hole," she said. "I'm sure this will pass. She just has to get back into her normal routine. Maybe we should take her out for a hike or something. Some fresh air could do her good."

Another snort from Gray. "Right. Sure. Take her camping. What-ever. Go crazy. But we're in agreement here? This whole murder theory is asinine?"

"I'm not ready to call it asinine," Lizzie said, mostly to piss Gray off.

It worked. Gray's catlike eyes flashed. "Fine. If you want to play this game . . . where were *you* the night James died?"

A chunk of scone rose up Lizzie's throat. She stood up straighter and swallowed hard. "I was home. With Willow and Kelsey. I'm sure Emma told you that I brought Kelsey back that night after the police called." She closed her computer and shoved it into her bag. "Besides, I barely even knew James. Why would I kill him?"

Gray said nothing as Lizzie gathered up some papers and her phone. She should be home by now. She should be making dinner with Willow. She'd been in a semi-peaceful state of mind while Ben was here. Why the hell did this woman have to sweep in and get her all riled up? And what was with all the silence?

Lizzie grit her teeth and zipped up her bag. "You've always had it out for me."

Gray lifted one shoulder, an elegant gesture. "It's not my fault you're unnaturally obsessed with Emma."

"Me? You treat her like she's your child, always telling her what to do and how to do it. And I know for a fact you didn't like James. Where the hell were *you* on the night he died? Where was Darnell, for that matter?"

"Don't you talk about my husband," Gray spat.

"Oh, hit a nerve, did I?" Lizzie wished she wasn't trembling, but she couldn't seem to stop herself. The caffeine from the apple spice coffee wasn't helping.

Be the change . . . be the change . . . bethechange!

"Maybe that's why you're here trying to get me to talk Emma out of looking into what happened. Maybe Darnell had something to do with it. The cops always look at the people closest to the victim, right? Well, we know Emma didn't do it, so who else did James spend every single day with? Do you even *know* where he was?"

Gray whipped her briefcase and gloves off the countertop and tugged at her coat, pulling it taut. "I didn't come here to fight with you. Emma is my oldest and dearest friend, and if you don't have her back, then I will."

Lizzie followed her to the door and locked it behind her, slamming one flat hand against the frame. Her phone buzzed in her pocket and she fumbled it out. A text from Willow.

Are you bringing home dinner or should I start pasta?

Lizzie texted back.

Start pasta. Will be there soon.

She was about to shove the phone back in her pocket when she noticed Gray's Louboutins had paused at the corner. She toggled back to her thread with Willow, which hadn't been cleared in at least a month, and deleted the whole thing.

GRAY

Gray had planned on making chicken piccata for dinner—one of Darnell's favorites. The town council meeting had run over, partially because she'd been late. Gray Garrison. Late. It was unheard of. But the visit with Lizzie had been a last-minute addition to her day's schedule and after that, she was all thrown off. She hadn't even remembered it was New Business Monday until she'd seen Ben standing there with Lizzie, clearly smitten, which had given her pause. What the hell did those two have in common? What had they been talking about? She sincerely hoped Lizzie wasn't gossiping about Emma and James and the accident with other Chamber of Commerce members.

Now it was after eight o'clock and starting to drizzle. She'd have to stop at Whole Foods on the way home and pick up something prepared, which would throw off her whole dinner plan for the week. Unless Darnell was running late as well, which was a definite possibility, all things considered.

She got behind the wheel of her Mercedes sedan and took a breath. Her hands were shaking. Even now, over an hour later. Lizzie had this effect on her on a good day—her Zen, yoga-lady demeanor and long, dreamy pauses burrowing right under Gray's normally thick skin. That and the fact that she seemed to never want to let Gray have the last word. And Gray always got the last word. She'd just spent the entire council meeting having the last word.

There was something about that woman. She was just off. Not to mention her odd daughter. Gray hadn't been around Willow much, but when she was, she always felt as if she were being studied for some invasive experiment, like a grasshopper pinned to a tray and set under a microscope. Gray didn't know how Emma could stand to be around the two of them so much, let alone count Lizzie as a close friend.

When Gray asked Lizzie where she'd been that night—which she'd done offhand and really just to mess with her—Lizzie had almost fainted. Although Gray knew that Lizzie hadn't had anything to do with James's death. Not only did she not have the brains to pull off a murder, but she would never have had the guts—nor the fortitude to keep a secret like that in perpetuity. She was probably one of those weaklings who passed out at the sight of blood. But there had been something in the woman's expression that made Gray ponder. Was Lizzie so obsessed with Emma that she'd thought about getting rid of James? Getting the competition for Emma's time and attention out of the way? Gray knew that Lizzie used Emma as almost a surrogate spouse, after all, weighing decisions with her, consulting her about everything from parenting to diet to refinancing her mortgage. Maybe, in her darker moments, Lizzie had fantasized about having Emma all to herself.

If Lizzie was going to start throwing around Darnell's name as a suspect in Emma's ludicrous murder theory, maybe Gray would start throwing around Lizzie's.

Gray started the car and shook off the last couple of hours. At the council meeting, Ben had made his statement and handed in his paperwork proving the work had been completed on the security cameras at the café, and then Clarissa Kay from the apothecary had asked for another police officer to patrol River Street during prime shopping hours because of the recent spate of shoplifting incidents. Disturbing that theft had become a problem in Oakmont, but she was sure it was just kids being kids. Nothing out of the ordinary. And she refused to let Lizzie ruin her whole night.

She checked her phone. No message. This was not normal. Darnell always called or texted when he was leaving the office, or—if it got too late—let her know what time to expect him.

Lizzie's questions scrolled unbidden through her mind: *Where was Darnell, for that matter? Do you even know where he was?* She should have told that little bitch to mind her own business. Of course, she was the one who'd confronted Lizzie at her place of work. But then, where else was she supposed to do it? Lizzie practically lived inside that shop.

The truth was, no, Gray didn't know where her husband had been the night of the accident. Not exactly. But she'd never admit that to the likes of Lizzie Larkin.

"Call Darnell mobile," she told her car as she pulled out onto the street.

There were a few straggling shoppers jogging across crosswalks, and a gaggle of soccer players shoving each other around on the corner in front of the ice cream shop. The streetlights had come on just as Gray had arrived downtown earlier, and now it was dark enough that they were necessary.

The phone rang, filling the car with its noise. Three times. Four. Voicemail.

Gray jabbed her thumb down on the *end call* button on her steering wheel, frustrated, then looked up and saw the stop sign. She slammed on her brakes half a second before blowing through it and mowing down a couple of girls on skateboards. Across the street, parked in the alleyway between two shops, sat a cop car.

Shit. SHIT.

Gray lifted all her fingers from the wheel to loosen them, then curled them down again. She looked both ways, saw the coast was clear, and kept driving—slowly, responsibly—and prayed the cop didn't pull out after her.

Which he didn't. Once outside the business district, Gray blew out a breath. Lizzie had riled her, and she couldn't let that happen again. She knew herself well enough to know that when she was riled she made mistakes—in the courtroom, in her relationships. She couldn't let that Lilith Fair loser unravel everything.

There was another call she had to make. For half a second, she thought about getting it over with now, but then no. This was not the time. She would go home, pour herself a glass of wine, and make a nice dinner for herself and her husband. Something simple. Easy. It was just going to take time, but soon enough they would get back into their regular rhythm. And then, everything would be fine. No, it would be better.

KELSEY

"Has anyone ever told you your room is a disaster?"

Willow didn't look up from the roll of bubble wrap she was spooling out, unable to flatten it on the floor because of the piles of clothes, cards, books, and magic paraphernalia all around her.

"This is not news to me," she said.

Kelsey sighed and pushed a pair of mud-stained cargo pants farther away from her thigh, wondering how Willow had managed to get them so dirty. She looked down into the box in front of her. It seemed properly packed, like nothing could get jostled or damaged; still, her chest felt tight. There was no air in here. She wished she could open a window, but just getting to the one behind Willow's drafting table would take a certain adventurous spirit and lack of fear for one's safety that Kelsey didn't possess.

"You never brought over that last box of stuff," Willow said.

"You were supposed to come over and pick it up."

"No, I wasn't."

"Yes! You were," Kelsey snapped, startling Willow. "You said you would come over around six and then you didn't show. I still have the text, if you're interested."

"Fine! Whatever. What is this, *Law & Order*? So are you going to bring it over or what?"

"Are you kidding me? No way."

Willow didn't get it. If she'd come over that day like she was supposed to and gotten that damn box out of her house . . . Kelsey couldn't even complete the thought. She shoved the package she was working on away from her in a huff.

"I don't think we should do this anymore," she said.

There. Finally. She'd gotten the words out.

Now Willow looked up. She was wearing wing-tipped green eyeliner today that made her look like a creature from another world. A dark fairy one.

"Why not?"

"Doesn't it feel wrong to you?" Kelsey sat back on her butt, leaning on her hands, but her fingers sunk into something sticky and she sat up again, trying not to grimace. "And it's not like I need the money at this point."

Her mother was going to pay for Daltry—the application fee, the tuition—all of it. Or she would, once Kelsey got around to telling her she was definitely applying. There was no reason for her to be here right now, in this cave of a room with its garbage-dump styling. When Willow turned to the side, Kelsey grabbed the muddy cargo pants and wiped her fingers off on the relatively clean cuff.

"Oh, yeah? So does that mean you don't want this?" Willow tossed an envelope to Kelsey. Carefully, she opened it. Inside was a thick stack of twenty-dollar bills. "Because I'll gladly add it to my tally. Personally, I can use all the cash I can get right now."

She said it bitingly, reminding Kelsey of all the things she had that Willow didn't, then cut off a strip of bubble wrap and shoved it into a box. Kelsey sighed. The problem with having friends who were older was that they were always in charge. There was also the fact that part of her felt like she owed Willow this—that she would always owe Willow something. But she was keeping the cash. Willow had no clue what she'd sacrificed for this little project of theirs. She shoved the money in her bag, closed the flaps on the box, and reached for the roll of packing tape.

"Can I ask you a question?" Willow said.

"Is it about my dad?" Kelsey asked, rankled now.

"How did you know?"

"Because it's all anyone wants to talk about anymore," Kelsey said, zipping the tape across the top of the box. It made an awful, squealing noise that had begun to haunt her dreams. "And no, I don't want to talk about it."

"But, the night of the accident . . . do you think if you'd come over here earlier—"

"I *don't* want to talk about it," Kelsey said again, and she added another loud, hair-raising strip of tape to punctuate her point.

EMMA

It wasn't until Emma started looking for James's briefcase that she realized she hadn't seen it since the accident. Had one of the cops or their techs or whoever actually stolen it out of the car? It was a nice briefcase, given to James by the senior partner at the PR firm he'd worked for after college, when he'd left to start his own business with Darnell. But it was also monogrammed. It wasn't like any random person could walk around sporting it without inviting questions.

There existed the possibility that it had been left in the car, which had long since been towed away and probably torn apart for scrap. Emma wondered how reputable the tow service was that Gray had hired to deal with it. As if Gray would ever hire someone who wasn't reputable. Would they have called her if they found it? Probably.

So, Emma spent all day Tuesday searching the house and cleaning things up as she went. She started with Hunter's room, thinking he might have grabbed the briefcase if and when it had come back from the police station, wanting it as a keepsake he could use himself one day. Of course, that had taken up over an hour as she compiled two baskets full of laundry and an armload of dishes, plus piles of random pens, notebook, papers, Post-its, and coins. For a responsible straight-A student, he'd always been kind of an organizational nightmare. Her little absentminded professor/home-run hitter.

When Emma pushed open the door of Kelsey's room she banged her toe on the dresser and cursed under her breath. Everything was in the wrong place. Neat as a pin, but totally wrong.

"When the hell did this happen?" Emma muttered to herself. Clearly, she had been checked out lately—something she promised herself she would remedy posthaste. She wasn't about to become one of those moms who let her kids go off the rails after a tragedy. Not that moving furniture around was a sign of imminent breakdown, but really—the layout was entirely illogical.

By the afternoon, she was starting to get tired and disgruntled and was beginning to daydream about her bed and her DVR, but when she walked past the game room she smelled something off and knew it was time to deal with the gift baskets. She went to the kitchen for a box of garbage bags and got to work throwing out semi-rotted citrus fruit and fully rotted peaches. She stacked boxes of chocolates and nuts on the pool table and struggled to fit the hard, Styrofoam bottoms of the larger baskets into the Hefty bags. After balling up all manner of cellophane and ribbon and snapping quite a few rubber bands, she noticed that the sky outside was starting to turn pink and she was a sweaty, bedraggled mess.

Had she even showered today? She couldn't recall.

Emma lifted the final basket off the floor—a behemoth filled with sweet and savory snacks that had been sent by last year's NBA MVP—and behind it was the briefcase.

Emma's heart gave a lurch. "How the hell?"

She grabbed it off the floor—it felt light—and sat down in the nearest comfy chair, her back facing the window, which afforded the room's only light—already dwindling at that. The bag smelled like James, like leather and bourbon and a hint of his aftershave. The scent brought angry, regretful tears to her eyes and she ran her fingers over the stamp of his initials: JTW.

"Okay," she said, breathing out. "Let's do this."

She opened the briefcase and realized why it weighed next to nothing—his laptop wasn't there. There were a few folders inside. Random pens. Three opened rolls of mints—of course. She dug through the side pockets and found business cards, a bottle of Advil, and then a prescription bottle. She hadn't known James was taking anything. She tugged out the bottle and read the label. Lipitor. Cholesterol medication. When had he started taking that?

Quickly, Emma searched the rest of the bag, hoping to find his cell phone, but there was nothing else of interest. Just a packet of tissues and some other people's cards. A couple with notes scrawled on the back: *solid guy* or *annoying but useful.*

That's my man, Emma thought ruefully.

Where had he left his computer? Where was his phone? She thought to check the bag of clothes again—maybe the phone was in his suit pocket. Then, she noticed the tab on one of the folders. It was labeled *Emma.*

Her heart all but stopped. She tugged the folder out. It was new—crisp—unlike the few others that were creased and worn. Placing the briefcase at her feet, she laid the folder flat on her lap. Her pulse beat an erratic rhythm inside her wrists. She held her breath and opened it:

COMPLAINT FOR DIVORCE

SHE HAD THOUGHT the shower would calm her. It didn't. Emma stood in front of the foggy mirror in her bathroom, hands braced against the vanity, bent forward and feeling like she was going to throw up or scream or break something or some combination thereof.

Every detail of that night came rushing back at her as if she were living through it all over again. There was supposed to be a party for Garrison & Walsh, or G&W as it was referred to in the industry, at some new venue downtown. They were forever throwing themselves parties to pat themselves on the back for various accomplishments—Emma had lost track of what it was for this time. But she'd told James a month prior that she would go, knowing even then that she was going to divorce him.

That *she* was going to divorce *him*.

She had found herself a lawyer—not Gray, even though divorce was Gray's specialty, because if there was a line in friendship that had to be it—and gotten started on the process, right around the time she'd finally decided to buy the cottage on the far side of town. It had always been a dream of hers to flip a house on her own, and she'd been making excuses for years—not enough money, the market was down, her kids needed braces—not that they didn't have the money for braces, God knew. But it wasn't *her* money, and she'd struggled to imagine how she would explain her dream to her husband. Could never quite picture him reacting with anything other than a scoff, or worse, a sneer. But then her father had passed and left her a nice chunk of change, and six months later, when one of the cottages became available, it was like a sign. That three-block stretch of homes was her favorite in all of Oakmont, and one of few areas in dire need of revitalization. When she'd looked at the place, she'd known instantly, like love at first sight. She'd also known that if she was going to be brave enough to do this, she wanted to do it on her own terms. She needed to get the hell out of her loveless, volatile, long dead marriage.

She'd gotten the papers that Monday, and hadn't told a soul about any of it. She'd decided to just get through the weekend. Let James have this last party, play the good wife one last time, then sit him down for a talk on Sunday night. But then, he'd come home that Thursday in rare form, practically foaming at the mouth, slamming around his man cave in the basement like an animal. She had been trying to herd the kids out of the house when he'd come back upstairs and gone after Kelsey, spouting nonsense, getting right in Kelsey's face. Emma had screamed at him to stop, but he hadn't stopped. And then Kelsey had run, and James had lunged at their daughter. He'd chased her outside, Hunter on his heels, Emma screaming and reaching for the phone.

Emma closed her eyes, shaking now, not wanting to remember the rest. It had been over so quickly. Hunter had caught up to James, and James had shoved Hunter—shoved their little boy—to the ground. It was the look on Hunter's face that had broken her heart. So shocked and hurt and betrayed. James must have seen it, too, because he'd gone back inside and locked himself in the basement for the rest of the night. Emma had retrieved her shaking daughter from the front yard and coaxed her into a shower and into her bed. Hunter had gotten in his Jeep and peeled out.

Hunter's face, though. The scratches on his arms. Her imagination spooling out for her what would have happened if James had caught up with Kelsey. That was what had done it. That was when she'd known she couldn't wait another day. He'd asked her to meet him for a quick bite in the city before the party, and she'd said yes and tucked the papers into her bag. It had all been perfect timing, after all. She'd closed on the cottage that very morning, and that night, she was going to close out her marriage.

But James had never shown. She'd sat at that restaurant, full of righteous adrenaline and sick with anticipation, for over an hour, checking her phone, texting him, calling him, and nothing. He'd stood her up. Probably forgotten he'd even asked her to meet him and gone to the party with his work buddies. The humiliation was all-encompassing. Part of her wanted to go to his celebrity-filled work party and throw the papers in his face. But Emma had never been one for a scene.

She had driven out of the city, cursing him the whole way, breaking the speed limit so wantonly it was a miracle she hadn't been pulled over. When she'd gotten home she'd popped an Ambien and gone to bed, only to find him dead in the garage a few hours later.

And now, this. *He* was going to divorce *her*? Why? He had seemed so content—perfectly happy to live his life as it was, making everyone in the household miserable while pretending to the world that they were this enviable, pristine, healthy family. The man had everything he'd ever wanted. *She* was the one who had been shit upon for the past ten, twelve, twenty years. She was the one who had hung on for far, *far* too long. So what had pushed him to this? Did Darnell know? Did *Gray* know?

The depth of her hurt floored her. She hadn't done anything wrong. *She'd* always been the perfect wife to him. She had taken So. Much. Shit. It was too unfair.

"Mom? Where are you?"

Emma stood up straight and clutched her towel.

"In the bathroom!" she shouted back. "I'll be out in a second!"

She threw on her robe and ran a comb through her hair, glad she'd stashed the briefcase and its contents inside James's closet before getting in the shower so that her kids wouldn't stumble upon it. She took three deep breaths, looking herself in the eyes and exerting as much control as she could over her emotions. Hunter and Kelsey could not be allowed to see her rage—her heartbreak.

Finally, her pulse returned to normal, Emma walked out to find all her bedroom lights ablaze and both her kids standing near the door, looking confused.

"You showered," Kelsey said.

Emma lifted her chin. "Go put your stuff away and go back downstairs," she told them. "We're going out to dinner."

EMMA

11:15 a.m.

14 hours before the accident

Emma felt as if her head was screwed on wrong. She rushed around the house looking for things—her reading glasses, her lipstick, her camera—then finding them in places she'd already looked. Gray was going to be here soon to pick her up and take her to the walk-through at the cottage. If everything went well, she'd be signing the papers right then and there. Closing on the house. Closing on her new beginning. She was so nervous, she felt like she was about to stand up in front of five hundred people to give a talk on a topic about which she knew nothing.

On her fifth run through the living room trying to straighten up and get everything in order, she banged the toe of her shoe on a baseball bat. It was half sticking out from under the couch and she crouched to wrest it free.

"Hunter," she admonished under her breath. He was forever leaving random sports equipment around the house. He must have come home from one of his batting cage workouts with his coach and gone straight to the TV instead of the garage. Someone could have tripped and really gotten hurt. She twirled the bat once, muscle memory kicking in from her brief baton-twirling phase, then held it like a baseball player and stepped into a batting stance. Feeling slightly silly, she swung the bat as hard as she could, and was surprised by the whipping sound the air made around it. She felt powerful, like she could do anything. A giggle burbled up in her throat. She really was giddy. She took the bat downstairs and leaned it by the doorway to the garage so that she—or preferably Hunter—would remember to put it away later.

Her phone buzzed. A text from Gray.

ON MY WAY! And a smiley emoji. Gray never used emojis. This really was a big day.

Emma ran upstairs to grab her bag. The paperwork for her meet-up with James later stuck out the top, and the very sight of it flooded her stomach with acid. This was going to be a big day in more ways than one. She tucked the papers deeper into her bag and went downstairs to wait for her friend.

LIZZIE

Lizzie stood at the kitchen sink, pulling kale leaves from their stems. The sound system she'd had installed a few years back played her favorite chill playlist, which started with Sara Bareilles, moved on to Norah Jones, and ended with James Taylor. The speakers, wired throughout the first floor, had cost her five thousand dollars. What she wouldn't give to have that money back now.

It was moments like these, when she was alone and it was dull outside and dead leaves whipped past the window, that Lizzie wondered if she'd made a huge mistake moving here. It had been almost ten years since she'd made the decision to leave the rural, upstate New York town she'd grown up in and come here. Oakmont had seemed like a dream world with its hippie-meets-preppy downtown vibe and huge parks, its massive Gothic library and tony private school. The public school was fantastic in this village with its ridiculously high taxes, but when Lizzie saw the grounds of Oakmont Day and imagined her daughter running around on the lacrosse fields or singing in the hallowed chapel, she had to have it for Willow. Luckily, her daughter, even in second grade, had a math brain that impressed the most skeptical of headmasters, and she'd been awarded a scholarship. Otherwise, Lizzie might never have met Emma. And

Willow might never have formed her surprising, seemingly unbreakable friendship with Hunter.

Were those relationships enough? Did they balance out the financial strain of keeping up with the millionaires that populated this town? (Even the hippies drove Teslas.) Lizzie hadn't been raised to value material things, and she'd always prided herself on her ability to put together funky outfits from secondhand clothes and old jewelry that had belonged to her mom. But living here had changed her. She hadn't noticed it at first, but over time it crept up on her in small ways. Coveting those sandals everyone had that were insanely expensive for something one wore two months out of the year. Replacing her everyday Target dishes with a set from Bloomingdale's. Upgrading from her Subaru to a Buick. Which wasn't a luxury car, but still. The Subaru had gotten her from point A to point B. What the hell did she need heated seats and satellite radio for?

Lizzie finished with the kale, picked up her paring knife, and was reaching for the onion, thinking it might be nice to have a valid excuse to cry, when a police car pulled up outside the house.

Her grip tightened around the knife's handle. *No.*

Officer Dyondra Miller got out of the car, her black hair pulled into a neat bun, and opened the back door.

No, Willow. Not again.

Lizzie stabbed the knife into the cutting board. Her daughter got out of the backseat, head down, hair covering her face, shoulders hunched. Officer Miller held out a hand and Willow trudged ahead of her up the steps and to the door, where Lizzie met them, shaking.

"What happened?" she asked. It was probably a sign of bad maternal skills that she was actually hoping Willow had been hurt, but the alternative—

"Ms. Larkin." Officer Miller nodded. "I'm sorry to say we had to pick up Willow again after another shoplifting complaint."

Lizzie deflated. "Willow—"

Her daughter shoved past her and made for the stairs, but Officer Miller whistled, loud and sharp. Willow turned, but barely looked up through the veil of her hair. Impressive. Lizzie wondered if she could learn to whistle like that.

"I want you to listen to me and listen good," Miller said. "This is your third infraction. The only reason I haven't booked you yet is because we're friends, and you're talented, and I don't want to see you waste your life. But I can't cover for you anymore." She looked at Lizzie. "The shop owners in town are starting to compare notes. There's talk of banning her from the shopping district. There are at least five other complaints we can't confirm, but people are saying it was your daughter."

"They weren't *all* me," Willow began. "I can't—"

Miller silenced her with a look, her dark eyes cutting. But after a long moment, they softened, and so did Miller's stance.

"Willow, you did a great job at Mary Kate's party. We were so grateful to have a young woman there performing for them. You were like a breath of fresh air compared to all the dirty old men magicians we've seen over the years. But let me be perfectly clear. If you've got a record, no family in this town or anywhere else is going to invite you into their house to perform magic tricks for their kids. And you can forget about college. Is that what you want?"

Lizzie's pulse thrummed in her ears. She stared at Willow.

"No, ma'am," her daughter said.

"Good. No offense, but I'd rather not see the inside of this house again."

The officer bid Lizzie good night, then strolled out onto the porch. Lizzie closed the door and leaned back against it, drained of all energy. She stared at the floor, barely holding back tears of frustration.

"What was it this time?" she asked.

Willow pulled something out of her pocket and tossed it on the floor at Lizzie's feet. It was a pair of earrings—tiny, dangling silver doves, their wires threaded through a small, cardboard square. They were beautiful and delicate and stolen. Lizzie bent and picked them up. The price tag on the back was handwritten: $22.

"They didn't make you give them back?" Lizzie asked.

"When they caught me, I paid for them," Willow said. "I got them for you."

"What?"

"You've been so tense lately. And I know you're sad and whatever. I wanted to get you something. To cheer you up." Willow shoved her hands under her arms.

"Oh, Willow."

Lizzie made a move to hug her daughter, but Willow angled away and she stopped in her tracks.

"Can I go to my room now?"

"Just tell me one thing," Lizzie said. "Why do you do it? Is it the rush? Do you gift *all* the things you steal? Sell them? What?"

"I just . . . I don't know, okay?" Willow straightened her arms and shook her hands, flexing and extending her fingers over and over again. "I don't want to talk about it. Can I just go?"

Her daughter was on the verge of tears, and Lizzie was exhausted. "Yes," she said. "Go. I'll call you when dinner's ready."

Willow stomped up the stairs, slammed the door to her room, and cranked her music so loud it drowned out the James Taylor on the surround sound. Lizzie went back to the kitchen and carefully placed the earrings in a drawer.

She had always given her daughter a long leash, both out of necessity, since she had to work long hours, and out of guilt, because she hadn't given Willow a father or a stable family situation. Asking a lot of questions never went over well and usually resulted in exactly this—moodiness, Willow sequestering herself, the silent treatment. If Lizzie had it to do all over again, she would have been a bit stricter, would have started asking questions from the beginning. But there was no going back now. Especially not after Willow's eighteenth birthday and everything that happened surrounding that particular milestone—all the drama for which Lizzie had felt partially, if not entirely, responsible.

But she couldn't let her daughter become a felon. She had to find a way to put a stop to this before it got out of control. When Willow first expressed an interest in magic back in third grade, Lizzie had thought it was a passing phase. Every kid had that moment when they were fascinated by card tricks and those magic kits that offered up false-bottomed hats and disappearing coins. But for Willow, it hadn't been a phase. The books she'd taken out of the library were never returned. She'd started watching YouTube videos obsessively and asking Lizzie to take her to shows in the city. Every summer in middle school, Willow had attended magic camp at the local community college, and by the time she was fifteen, she was so deft of hand that the camp was begging her to come back as a counselor. Lizzie knew that a lot of people thought her daughter was strange, but she thought it was sort of cool that her beautiful, math-genius girl had such an outside-the-box interest. Willow was unapologetically Willow, and Lizzie loved that about her.

But this shoplifting thing was out of left field. It couldn't be a plea for her attention—Willow never lacked for motherly love. So what was it? A plea for someone else's? If so, whose? Maybe it was an extension of the magic thing. She'd gone as far as she could with that, so now she was using her special sleight-of-hand talents on another playing field. But her daughter was not stupid. She had to know the risks she was taking.

Lizzie wished she had someone to talk to. A husband, a partner, anyone. Usually she would have called Emma to hash it out, but she hadn't let her friend in on this particular facet of her and Willow's lives because she'd felt—well—like a loser. Like a bad mom. Emma's perfect children would never do something like this. Now it felt like it was too late to talk to her about it. Emma would wonder why she hadn't told her the first time it happened, and she didn't have the energy for a long, drawn-out explanation.

Lizzie was just going to have to handle this one on her own, like she did most things. She picked up a knife and cutting board, now more ready than ever to massacre that onion.

EMMA

The waiter placed a steaming pizza down on their table and a huge bowl of salad in front of Emma. Hunter immediately grabbed a slice, pulling half the cheese off with it, and shoved it in his mouth, third-degree burns be damned.

Your father was going to divorce me.

Kelsey pushed her pasta around in her bowl, then reached for the Parmesan cheese.

He was going to leave us. But then he died.

The words were on the tip of her tongue, itching to be said; possibly screamed. Hunter reached for his soda and took a long gulp, eyeing her over his glass.

"You're not hungry?" he asked.

"No. I'm fine." She pushed a forkful of salad past her lips to prove how very fine she was. Over at the corner booth, a family with smaller children was crowded in, the mother leaning toward the father to whisper, but glancing over at Emma.

That's them, she imagined the woman saying. *That family with the father who drove through his own garage.* For the first time it occurred to her that it might seem odd to other people, her and her children going out to dinner less than two weeks after James died. What was the proper mourning period for a husband who was almost never around and a father who terrorized his children? Should she have checked Emily Post? Martha Stewart? In Victorian times they'd all still be wearing black. At the moment, Emma felt like wearing a placard that read BACK THE FUCK OFF.

James should have just left her. At least that sort of thing happened every day. Unlike seemingly unprovoked car accidents on one's own property. She wondered if he'd told anyone he was going to leave her. Darnell? His assistant? A friend? Did James even have friends anymore?

"Mom?" Kelsey said.

"What, honey?"

Kelsey was looking at Emma's fork. Which she realized now she'd been tapping maniacally against the table. She put it down, embarrassed, and folded her hands in her lap.

"How was your day, Kelsey?" Emma asked.

"Oh, just fabulous," Kelsey said sarcastically.

"I'm guessing not fabulous, then?" Emma tried for a light tone.

"Everyone's talking about us," Hunter said, taking another slice. "But I told Kels it'll blow over. We just need a new scandal for people to glom on to."

"At least I'm not invisible anymore," Kelsey said, and took her first, small bite of food.

"Honey. You were never invisible," Emma said.

Kelsey rolled her eyes. Emma sighed. "When are the musical auditions?"

"First round is on Thursday and call-backs are early next week." Kelsey perked up ever so slightly.

"Great. I know you'll do great," Emma said. "What about you, Hunter? How was your day?"

"Fine. Oh, I gotta get the application in to Duke before the end of the month," he told her. "Can you write me a check?"

"Sure, honey." Emma had almost forgotten about Duke. About college. About Hunter leaving. It was going to be so strange next year, just her and Kelsey in that huge house. Maybe Lizzie had the right idea, downsizing. It was James who had wanted the sprawling, modern house in the valley, after all. It had never totally felt like home to her.

There was an odd flutter around Emma's heart. She had never imagined a future outside that house. James never would have sold. But now . . .

"Can you write me a check, too?" Kelsey asked.

"For what, honey?" Emma sipped her water.

"The application for Daltry is due soon."

Her glass clattered against her salad bowl as she placed it back on the table. People at the table in the corner stared.

"I thought we decided you weren't going to transfer."

Kelsey's cheeks flamed red so quickly, Emma thought for half a second that she might be having an allergic reaction. But then she saw the tears and realized her daughter was clenching her teeth.

"What? I'm sorry. Didn't your father—"

"Mom . . ." Hunter said.

"But you said I could go!" Kelsey snapped loudly. "Dad was the one who said no. *You* said you thought it would be good for me! *You* said you thought I'd get in! Why would you—"

"Kelsey, calm down." Emma put her hand on her daughter's leg under the table. Now more than just the corner booth was staring. "Let's talk about this. I'm sorry. I didn't think."

"No! It's fine! If you don't want me to go, I won't go!" Kelsey stood up and balled her napkin. "God, why doesn't anybody want me to be happy?"

"Kelsey, please," Emma said through her teeth, reaching for her daughter but unable to reach her past her chair, which had been knocked askew. "I didn't say that I don't want you to go. I was blindsided by the question, that's all. We haven't talked about it in weeks."

Tears streamed down Kelsey's face and she covered her eyes with her hands. She dropped back into her chair.

"Miss? Is everything all right?" a hovering waiter asked.

"It's fine. We're *fine*." Emma was at a loss. She didn't know what she'd done wrong. Suddenly she was back in her early thirties and Kelsey was a toddler throwing a hissy fit in the supermarket because she couldn't have the cookies *right now*. This was not Kelsey. She'd never been one of those overly emotional, dramatic teenagers. This was too much for her. This whole day was too much. Judgmental Lady in the corner was right—this family was not ready for public dining. She looked helplessly at Hunter.

"I think that Kelsey thought that you were okay with her transferring to Daltry and it was only Dad putting his foot down or whatever that made you say no," he explained. "So now that Dad's"—he paused to swallow—"not here . . ."

"Oh. Oh!" Emma pushed her chair back quietly and put her arm around Kelsey, who leaned into her, sobbing. "I see. I understand."

It *had* been James who had put his foot down. Kelsey was right. Emma had been ready and willing to let Kelsey apply. Acting and singing were her passions and she was incredibly talented. Plus she'd never quite fit in at Oakmont Day, for all the positive talk Emma had tried to throw at her daughter. Emma could imagine Kelsey being so much happier at Daltry, among other talented, eccentric, artsy kids—kids who valued things other than their GPA and their trust funds. But James had said *no kid of mine is going to art school* and *if Oakmont Day is good enough for Hunter, it's good enough for Kelsey* and *I don't know why she thinks she's so goddamned special.*

God, she wished she'd had a chance to divorce him. Why hadn't she done it right then? Why hadn't she walked out *right then*?

"What about the play, honey? *Wizard of Oz*?"

Kelsey rolled her eyes. "We're staging it in December, Mom. I wouldn't be able to transfer until January."

"Right. Well then, of course, Kelsey. Of course you should apply," Emma said, and kissed the top of her daughter's head, just wanting her to be okay. Just wanting them all to be okay. "If that's what you really want to do, we'll make it happen."

KELSEY

School was like another planet. The next couple of days passed by in a whirlwind as people—even upperclassmen—stepped out of Kelsey's way in the hall, asked her if she needed anything, asked her if she was okay. Her teachers excused her from all homework, and apparently, even the random support staff were aware of her tragedy, because Red Hairnet gave her an extra helping of tater tots on Wednesday and Ricky the security dude didn't hit her with his patented side-eye when she went to refill her frozen yogurt.

Kelsey felt famous, but famous for a really awful reason. Like Katniss or a Kardashian. She honestly wasn't sure what was worse—her mostly ignored, sometimes picked-on existence before her dad died or this odd sort of wary deference she was getting now.

Today she sat down at the end of her usual table and hoped that every-one would act normal. Since her return on Monday, her crew had been overly enthusiastic about everything, as if pointing out how amazing the mundane details of life were was going to make the fact that her dad was dead magically be okay.

"Can you believe how sunny it is today?! It's like it's still summer!"

"What a gorgeous skirt, Kelsey! Really flattering!"

"We were so lucky to have Mrs. Tisch for freshman chorus this year, right!?"

"Is that a rainbow!? Look, Kelsey! A rainbow!"

It was all getting a bit grating, if she were being perfectly honest.

And then, Jason Katz decided to mix things up. He put down his Snapple bottle and looked along the table at Kelsey.

"You know, Kel"—she hated when he called her Kel and he knew it—"I've been thinking about your situation and I think it's going to be good for you."

"What?" Alexa Osaka—or Lexi to Jason—was just sitting down as he finished his declaration. She had worn her black hair in two braids today and was sporting a high-waisted denim-and-crop-top look. "Are you freaking kidding me right now?"

Kelsey, though her stomach had twisted into a giant pretzel, decided to play along. "No, I'm curious. How is my dad's car smashing through the back of our garage going to be good for me, Jason?"

He lifted a shoulder like *it ain't no thang.* "The struggle. It'll make your performances deeper." He paused to take a slurp of iced tea. "Truer."

Part of Kelsey wanted to reach across the table, grab Jason Katz by the frizzy hair at the top of his head, and smash his face into his mac and cheese. She could see it so clearly. The blood gushing over everyone's food, his glasses shattered.

Who the fuck do you think you are? You think you can talk to me that way, you little cunt? I'll fucking snap your neck. I'll fucking end you!

Her father's voice was so clear, he could have been hovering over her. She could see the white flecks of spittle at the corners of his mouth. Feel the air move as his meaty fingers swiped at her.

When the vision cleared, Willow was walking past her table, munching on an apple and eyeing Kelsey with a smirk. Kelsey turned away from her—let her go find her table of black-clad, wannabe New Yorker friends—and saw that Alexa was also watching her curiously, almost as if she could tell what Kelsey had been thinking. Alexa picked up a fry, dunked it in ketchup, and threw it at Jason's head. It hit the side of his face, then plopped onto his shoulder, leaving a red smear.

"Hey!" he shouted.

"Keep your stupid-ass opinions to yourself," Alexa said, while the rest of the table laughed. Christine Flagg, who had caught some of the ketchup trail, just wiped it off her shirt and said nothing.

Who knew? Maybe Jason was right. Kelsey did feel pretty confident about the monologue she'd performed at auditions yesterday. And when her voice had cracked on "She Used to Be Mine" it had been out of emotion, not an inability to hit the notes. She hoped Mrs. Tisch had caught that.

"Are you okay?" Alexa asked Kelsey under her breath. "Do you want to get out of here?"

But before Kelsey could answer, Felicity Wells—*the* Felicity Wells— appeared at the end of their table, all glorious red hair, spicy perfume, and glistening lips. God, Kelsey truly hated the cafeteria. This place was a personality minefield.

"Kelsey! There you are!" Kelsey's friends stared at their trays. All except for Jason, who gaped at the girl like she was his very first sunset.

"Yes, here I am. Right where I always sit," Kelsey said. Being treated like a freak/celebrity all week had made her a bit punchy. But then Felicity's eyes flashed and she wished she could take it back. It occurred to her that if people saw Felicity deigning to speak to her in the cafeteria while Kelsey was sitting at a table with all her "drama geek loser" friends, then her stock might actually rise. Not that she cared. Except that she kind of did. Sometimes. It was complicated.

"What's up?" she asked Felicity, putting on a smile.

"Well, my mom wanted me to tell you that you and your mom are totally welcome to come over to our house anytime for free facials." Felicity's mother was a cosmetics salesperson, always hosting makeover parties that Kelsey's mom never attended. Her father made legit millions in international real estate or something, and was always traveling. Kelsey had once overheard Gray telling her mom that Felicity's mom had a master's in education and the cosmetics thing was just to keep her from tearing her hair out from boredom. If she had a master's in education, Kelsey wanted to know, then why wasn't she out there educating people in something other than facials? "It really helps to unwind when you're stressed."

Alexa snorted and Felicity scowled at her. Kelsey could see this conversation going very wrong very quickly. "Thanks. That sounds great."

"Cool. So, listen, I have to ask." She leaned in slightly, still holding her tray full of salad. "Were you there? You know, when it happened?"

Kelsey stiffened.

"Why are you even here?" Alexa snapped. "Go sit with your little posse and snapchat your caloric intake for the day. Go on." She flicked her fingers.

"You don't have to be a bitch, Osaka," Felicity said. "I'm just talking to her."

"No you're not. You're exploiting her for gossip," Alexa said, lifting another fry full of ketchup.

"Alexa, don't," Kelsey said.

"Don't what?" Felicity asked, clueless.

Alexa pulled the fry back and—

"Is there a problem here?"

It was Mrs. Tisch. Alexa shoved the French fry in her mouth.

"No problem," Jason said, going red at the sight of a teacher. "Felicity was just leaving."

Felicity made a huffing noise and strolled away, nose in the air, like she was on a catwalk. Everyone at the table, including Mrs. Tisch, followed her with their eyes until she was seated on the other side of the room. Sometimes, Kelsey thought if she could just learn to walk like that, all her earthly problems would be solved.

"Kelsey, can I see you in the hallway?" Mrs. Tisch asked.

Kelsey's core body temperature was roughly one million degrees Kelvin. Between Willow being all up in her business, the encounter with Felicity, and recalling the last conversation she'd had with Mrs. Tisch, she felt like she could seriously punch something. She shoved her chair back and speed-walked outside to the patio, realizing that Mrs. Tisch probably meant the hallway or her office and not caring. She sucked in fresh air and blew it out slowly, wondering why in the name of Taylor Swift she was on the verge of tears.

Through the wall of windows, she could see Willow watching her. What did she want from Kelsey? To move into her room? To wear her skin? What?

"Hey, hey. Are you all right?" Mrs. Tisch laid a comforting hand on Kelsey's back.

"I'm fine." Kelsey forced herself to look the teacher in the eye. Would people ever stop looking at her like that? Like she was a pathetic loser on the verge of a nervous breakdown? "What did you want to talk to me about?"

Maybe she was going to warn Kelsey that she wasn't getting a part. Or give her a definitive no on the recommendation letter. Where was Mr. Fletcher? Didn't he have the balls to come tell her himself that he was taking away her one shot at happiness? They just didn't understand. She had to get out of this school that was her father's dream for her. She needed to be around people who didn't know who her dad was or care. If Daltry accepted her application for a midyear transfer, she might be able to convince her teachers to let her do the rest of this semester's course work from home. It was all right there within her grasp. Things would be better at home without her dad. Things would be better at school if she were at Daltry. Everything would just be better.

"I read your essay for Daltry and it's great," Mrs. Tisch said. "Thanks for sending it to me. It reminded me of why I thought you'd be such a perfect candidate in the first place. So, I just wanted to give you this." She held out a sealed envelope, writing scrawled across the flap.

Kelsey's eyes widened. "Is that—"

Mrs. Tisch nodded, smiling. "They make you sign the envelope after you seal it so they know it's confidential, but I emailed you a copy. I thought you'd want to read how exceptional I think you are."

"Oh my God, Mrs. Tisch!" Kelsey blushed and her eyes burned all over again. "Thank you," she said. "Thank you so much."

"It's my pleasure, Kelsey. Though we really will miss you," the teacher said, clutching her own hands. "And don't tell anyone I told you this, but you're going to want to check the call-back list first thing after school today. I was really impressed, Kelsey. Really impressed."

"Thank you!" Kelsey beamed, trying not to crush the precious envelope in her sweaty palm, or focus on the fact that her teacher had just intimated that she had a shot at a real part. Screw Felicity. Screw her dad. Screw this whole damn school. Everything was turning around. "I'll be there."

GRAY

"You're here late."

Gray looked up from the character reference she was vetting for one of her nastier divorce cases—she was repping the kind-but-gullible husband of a woman who had won a small lottery prize and disappeared on her husband and kids for four straight years before coming back and trying to claim their house—and saw her administrative assistant, Tameeka Phillips, hovering in her doorway.

"Yes, this was just so engrossing I lost track of time," Gray replied. This was a lie. She hadn't lost track of time—she simply hadn't wanted to go home and stare at the clock waiting to see if Darnell would text or call. Better to be here where she could keep busy—and rack up billable hours. "Did you need something?"

"No," Tameeka said. "Just wanted to check *you* didn't need anything."

"Oh, I'm fine. Don't hang around because of me," Gray said. "Just lock up on your way out."

"Thanks, Ms. Garrison," Tameeka said, and practically bolted for the door. Most likely she had plans with her fairly gorgeous boyfriend and thought she was going to have to order in sushi for Gray and hunker down with her for the night. Was it sad that Gray almost wished it was one of those nights? She enjoyed the camaraderie of digging through financials and timelines with Tameeka and the paralegals. It made her feel young. Because, well, that was what she'd done with her time when she was young.

Okay, yes, that *was* sad.

With a sigh, Gray checked her phone. It was after six. Nothing from Darnell. Did that mean he was almost home, or had he uncharacteristically spaced on contacting her again? It wasn't that she was one of those women who needed to know where her man was at all hours of the day, it was that he—of his own volition—had always kept her informed. Now that he didn't, it was as if she'd been set adrift, and it was all his fault. He'd basically trained her to expect his updates, and then taken them away.

Where was Darnell, for that matter?

Gray shook her head, to clear it of Lizzie's voice. The question had been scrolling through her mind unbidden for the past few days. Lizzie had sounded so smug when she'd said it. Did Lizzie know something Gray didn't?

She sat with the question for a moment, then laughed. No, no, no. If there was one certainty in this world, it was that Elizabeth Larkin did not know more about any one subject than did Gray Garrison. Especially not about this.

When she looked back down at the brief, Gray's eyes literally crossed. She reached for the pile of mail in her in-box instead and grabbed her letter opener. The envelope on top was from the scrapyard, a check made out to Emma Walsh care of Gray Garrison. Gray placed the check into her briefcase, feeling self-satisfied. It was amazing, really, that Lizzie considered herself to be such a great friend to Emma. Look at all Gray had done for Emma since James died—dealing with the funeral home, the tow service, the junkyard. Making sure her kids were fed. She was even starting to help Zoe at the firm with arrangements for a memorial. What had Lizzie done? According to Emma, she'd called and asked for a referral to a Realtor. *She* was asking *Emma* for favors and advice when she should be doing everything in her power to be there for Emma and her family. Ridiculous.

Gray picked up her cell and dialed Emma.

Voicemail. Did no one answer their phones anymore? She waited for the beep.

"Emma, I've been thinking, we should get back to our weekly runs this weekend. I think it would be good for you to get out of the house and get some exercise. Call me back."

The second she ended the call, her phone rang. Darnell. Her chest swelled with relief. He must be home and wondering where she was. She picked up.

"Hi, hon," she said smoothly, shoving the letter opener into the next envelope.

"Gray," he said, his voice a low rumble. "Don't get mad."

GRAY FUMBLED WITH her briefcase and keys while simultaneously trying to scroll through contacts on her phone as she walked to her car. Three feet from the door she dropped the keys, then the phone, and almost screamed in frustration.

The police station. Pulled over. Erratic driving. Shouting at cops. Issued a warning.

You've gotta come get me, Gray. They're impounding my car.

It had turned out it was his third speeding infraction in two weeks. His license was being suspended pending a hearing. He hadn't told her. Gray and Darnell never kept secrets from one another, and now this.

What the fuck was wrong with her husband? She had seen him angry before. It wasn't as if he'd never been upset in his life. That awful day when the boys were in Little League and the opposing team's coach had grabbed Derek's arm when he'd talked back. The morning that Dante had put a baseball through the three-thousand-dollar French window three days after it was installed. There had been marital tiffs and spats, the occasional night spent on the couch, but ever since the day his best friend died, things had changed. She'd never forget the way he looked at James when he found out what the man had been doing behind his back. It was like a switch had flipped. Doctor Jekyll, meet Mr. Hyde.

Gray crouched to the ground and said a quick prayer before she picked up her phone. Shattered. Of course. She was literally the only person she knew who had never broken a cell phone. Until today. Cursing under her breath, she grabbed her keys and unlocked her car. Once inside its hermetically sealed cabin, she gripped the steering wheel and screamed, shaking her head so hard her hair flew and stuck to her lipstick.

After about five seconds of this, she was done, and she felt idiotic, even though she knew not a soul could have seen her. She took a deep breath, smoothed her hair down, and checked her face in the visor mirror. With a fingertip, she pressed a dot of spittle off her chin. Then she pushed the button to start her call and said, very calmly, "Call Mo Tornambe."

Mo ran the desk at the Oakmont Police Department. She was the one who decided what news went out and what news stayed in. This news—former Super Bowl–winning NFL linebacker and partner in the PR firm Garrison & Walsh cited for erratic driving and disorderly conduct a week and a half after the salacious death of his business partner—most definitely could not go out. Especially not if Lizzie started running her mouth, saying she suspected Darnell had something to do with James's death. She could so easily see this snowballing, and that was not about to happen on her watch.

"Oakmont PD, this is Mo," the woman said.

"Mo!" Gray trilled as she popped her car into gear. "I hear you haven't been to see a Giants game all season. What do you say to four seats in the Delta Sky Box for the next four games?"

EMMA

Emma waited until the kids were happily ensconced in their rooms on Sunday night, doors closed, Hunter's hip-hop music warring with Kelsey's show tunes, then went straight to her bedroom, where the very sight of her bed disgusted her. The sheets hadn't been changed in weeks. There were torn and snotty tissue balls everywhere, and crumbs upon crumbs upon crumbs. Before she knew what she was doing, she had torn the whole thing apart—removed every pillow from its gray pillowcase and the comforter from the striped duvet. She'd ripped off the sheets and piled them on the floor, then added throw pillow after throw pillow. When she was done, she went to the windows and shoved them open, the cool autumn breeze billowing the curtains.

In the very back of the linen closet, under various sets of 800-count Egyptian cotton in various tones of grays and whites and blues, Emma found the Ralph Lauren sheet set she'd splurged on at T.J. Maxx when she and James were first married. The bottom sheet was white with purple flowers, the top sheet white with purple stripes, the pillowcases a mix of both. Shabby chic was what the look had been called at the time, and it was all the rage, but James had hated them, and somewhere between Hoboken and Oakmont they'd been retired to this dark place, never to be seen again. Emma carried them to her bedroom and made her bed as if it were an Olympic sport, moving quickly and efficiently, grunting and sweating and blowing her bangs out of her eyes. When she was done, she snapped the white comforter—duvet-free—over the top of the bed. As a final touch, she dug out a bottle of lavender sheet spray someone had given her as a gift once and spritzed it all over the pillows.

It looked and smelled like a dream. Emma took out her phone and crawled to the center of the bed. *Her* bed. There, she did the thing she'd been dreading doing since the night James died. She opened her messenger app.

The texts to James started innocently enough.

Parking the car. Will be at the restaurant in 10.

Then:

At a corner table in back. Ordered merlot.

Then:

Are you on your way?

I thought we said 7:15

I ordered appetizers. Is all ok?

Just scrolling through, Emma's underarms began to prickle. She could remember so vividly how she'd felt sitting at that table by herself as the booths and two-tops around her had started to fill up. People ate alone in Manhattan all the time, she was sure, but she wasn't used to it, and she felt conspicuous, with her tiny purse and her brown envelope with the divorce papers tucked beneath it on the table. It was obvious to the world that she was meeting someone—someone important enough for a brown envelope—and yet that someone was standing her up.

What the fuck, James? Where are you???!

I'm not going to sit here all night.

If you think I'm coming to this party after sitting here by myself all night you're insane.

Fuck this. Hope you have fun tonight.

And then, the pièce de resistance.

I hope you drink yourself into oblivion, asshole. I hope you drive
off a cliff. I hope you die.

Emma's throat closed over and she tossed the phone aside, disgusted
with herself and holding back angry, embarrassed, guilty tears. The truly
scary thing was that if he'd come home that night, if he were still alive,
those texts could have been texts she'd sent on any other night. That was
how unhealthy their relationship had been—how twisted their marriage.
They seemed prescient and awful and damning now, but if not for the accident, she would have deleted them the next day with a shrug.

Had James read any of those texts? Had he laughed them off? Rolled
his eyes and ignored them? Where had he been when she was sending
them, exactly? At the office? At a bar? Getting the party started early
downtown? He'd never replied to a single one.

She had to find James's phone.

Emma jumped up and grabbed the briefcase out of the closet, uncer-
emoniously dumping its contents onto her freshly made bed this time.
Definitely not there. She dug through the interior compartments just in
case and came up with nothing but lint under her fingernails. Jogging on
her toes, she raced downstairs and grabbed the plastic bag full of his
clothes, scattering them across the marble floor. No phone.

Had it been in the car? Was it flattened for scrap like the rest of the
contents? Or did the police have it? If they'd had it, wouldn't they have
returned it to her by now?

Emma balled up the clothes and took them back upstairs with her,
not wanting the kids to find a pile of their father's bloodied garments
when they got up for school in the morning. She tossed them onto the
floor of James's closet and turned back to the bed. She was out of breath.

Well. There was always one way to locate a cell phone. Whenever she
misplaced her own—which was more often than she cared to admit—she
had one of the kids call it so they could locate it by ring. She picked up
her own cell, clicked James's name, and held down the call button. If it
was somewhere in the house, she would hear it. James never turned off
his notifications. He was just too important for that.

It wasn't until the line had rung three times that it occurred to Emma that James's cell would have run out of charge days ago. Wow, she needed some actual sleep. Rolling her eyes at herself, Emma was about to hang up, when the call clicked over to voicemail.

This is James Walsh. The sound of his voice stole her breath right out of her. *Sorry to have missed your call.*

As the beep sounded, Emma's heart slammed. She hung up the phone, but then instantly wanted to hear him again. She redialed and gritted her teeth.

The phone rang once, then, a click.

"Hello?"

It was a woman on the other end.

EMMA PACED HER room, her cell phone slick with sweat from her palms. She'd hung up instantly, on instinct. But why? That was *her* husband's phone. Who was that woman? Why the hell did she have James's phone?

She braced herself and called back. This time, it didn't even ring.

This is James Walsh. Sorry to have missed your call . . .

"Shit," Emma whispered into the darkness. She shoved a hand into her hair.

Was James having an affair? Before she could even complete the thought, she knew the answer. Of course he was. Why else would some random woman have his phone? She flipped her own phone over and checked her text history again. The last time James had texted her that day was at 4:30 p.m., sending her the name and address of the restaurant. She'd texted him at least twenty times after that missive and not one message had been answered. So at some point after 4:30 p.m. and before he died, some woman had gained possession of his phone.

She must have been with him that night while Emma was sitting alone in the restaurant. They must have been together when she was sending those angry texts. Had he read them in front of this woman?

Had they laughed at her? Felt sorry for her? Humiliation burned inside Emma's chest.

Abruptly, she stopped pacing. If this woman was with James that evening, she could have also been with him that night. This could explain everything. The mystery woman could have been the person James was talking to in the driveway. The person who had wanted the top down. The one he'd taken off his tie for, gotten out of the car for. Maybe they had both gotten out to chat or argue or come into the house. Maybe he was going to introduce his wife to his mistress and see what happened. Maybe he intended to give Emma the divorce papers and tell her he was running off with Phone Girl. Or, perhaps, they had simply parked and started making out in the driveway and James's tie had come off and been tossed in the bushes . . .

Bile rose in Emma's throat and she dove for the bathroom, bending over the toilet, but nothing came all the way up. She guzzled water and dragged the back of her hand across her lips, staring at her wide, wild eyes in the mirror.

He was having an affair. The rat bastard was cheating on me. No wonder he wanted a divorce.

Maybe he and his girlfriend *had* argued. Maybe they'd gotten out of the car to have it out and this woman had *murdered* her husband somehow, then staged the accident to cover it up. Stranger things had happened—on TV at least. But no. That was ridiculous. People didn't do that sort of thing off the cuff. It took planning to cover up a murder. It took brains. Emma could tell just from the woman's *hello* that she wasn't an astrophysicist.

But something had happened that night. Emma could feel it. Just like she knew she was never going to rest easy again until she found out what it was. And she had a feeling that this other woman was the key.

GRAY

The morning was dreary, the sky scattering cold spittle on the windshield. Gray drove in silence, Darnell, in the passenger seat, seeming to fill the car with his bulk. Her brain kept veering from its morning ritual of listing all the things she had to accomplish before lunch, distracted by the overwhelming scent of his aftershave, only slightly less potent than the tension between them.

She bypassed the turnoff to the parkway and headed through downtown Oakmont toward the New Jersey Transit station at the top of the hill. She had suggested a car service, even a Lyft, but Darnell had been fixated on taking the train, as if it was his cross to bear for what he'd done.

"I'm sorry," Darnell said, breaking the silence so suddenly Gray flinched.

"Darnell, you spent the entire weekend apologizing," Gray reminded him. "It's okay. I'm certain it'll all blow over. Charles will make sure it does."

She'd called the firm's lead attorney the night before, and he was confident he'd have Darnell's car and license back within a couple of days and the charges thrown out. No harm, no foul.

"He'd better. The last thing the firm needs right now is more bad PR," he said, running his large hands over his thighs, the expensive fabric of his suit swishing.

Fucking James, Gray thought, and wondered if Darnell was thinking it, too. Though she did also notice that he wasn't entirely taking responsibility for the possibility of bad PR, as if this was somehow Charles's problem to handle. Didn't he realize that if he hadn't lost his temper and acted like a certifiable maniac, there wouldn't be anything *to* handle?

"I've been in touch with Zoe a few times," Gray said, attempting to change the subject. "We started talking about details for the memorial."

Darnell blew out a breath. "Do we really have to jump through that particular hoop?"

"You know we do. How is it going to look to the rest of the industry—to your clients—if you just ignore it?"

Darnell muttered something under his breath. The only word Gray could make out was *Judas*.

She turned into the parking lot. Up on the platform, a couple dozen commuters scrolled on their phones beneath the meager shelter of a tin roof. One man stood stalwartly in the rain, staring up the tracks, as if his concentration could make the train come faster. Gray sighed at the dreariness of it all. Thank God she'd taken the leap and moved her offices out of the city before the boys were in middle school. She had detested commuting in all its forms.

"Fine," he said. "But if we're going to do it, we may as well do it right. Spare no expense. Let's give that asshole the send-off he doesn't remotely deserve."

"We're definitely on the same page." She glanced over at him and found herself unable to hold his gaze. This was new, and she wasn't having it. She forced herself to meet his eyes and stay there. "Are you okay?" she asked. "Is there anything you want to talk to me about? You know you can tell me anything, right?"

Darnell clicked the button on his seat belt and turned away from her. "I'm just under a lot of pressure right now, you know that," he said tersely.

"Let's just get through this sham of a memorial. After that, things'll get back to normal." He gave her a perfunctory kiss on the cheek, his lips barely touching her skin, got out of the car, and walked off without another word.

Gray stared after her husband. Never had he blown her off like that. Not once in their whole marriage. Didn't he see she was trying here? Darnell had always had the utmost respect for her feelings, no matter what. She didn't like the way he was shutting her out. It made her feel like he was hiding something.

What if he hadn't gone to the party that night like he said he did? What if he'd driven back to Jersey, too?

Gray gripped her steering wheel as the train horn sounded in the near distance. Darnell was on the platform now, a hulking form, nearly twice the size of any of the other passengers. His trench coat could have acted as a pup tent for the woman standing closest to him. Gray had a sudden flash—Darnell reaching over and shoving the petite woman in front of the oncoming train. The squeal of the brakes. The screams of the crowd. But then the train had stopped and the people were boarding and there was no blood, no carnage. It was just her heart pumping as if there was.

She picked up her phone and called Derek.

"Hey, Mom. What's up?"

She loved that he didn't point out the early hour. If she'd called Dante she would have had to try three times before she woke him up, but Derek, she knew, was either out for a run or on his treadmill. He was a morning person, like her.

"Hey, baby. How are you this fine morning?" she asked.

"I'm on mile nine." She could hear the slight hitch in his voice from the exertion. "What about you?"

"On my way to work." The bells on the train clanged as it slowly began to roll out of the station. "How's the training going? Are you getting enough protein? Enough sleep? Did you read that article I sent you from *Men's Health*?"

Derek was running his first marathon in the spring, a goal he'd set for himself over the summer. That boy decided to do something and did it. Just like his mother.

"Yes, Mom," he said. "I'm working with the firm's nutritionist, remember? I'm doing it right."

"That's my boy. Listen, baby, can you do me a favor and keep an eye on your dad today?"

"Keep an eye on him? What does that even mean?"

"Just . . . let me know if he does anything out of the ordinary," she said, already regretting making this call. Derek was the more sensitive of her two boys, and she realized now that this was only going to worry him. Maybe it should have been Dante she enlisted. All she would have had to do was promise him a meatloaf dinner next weekend and he'd be in.

Gray heard a few beeps on Derek's end and knew he was turning off the treadmill. She could hear the whir of the belts now as it slowed down.

"Is everything okay?" he asked.

"Yes, honey. He just hasn't been sleeping very well since James died," she told him, which was a lie. She was the one with insomnia. Darnell had been sleeping the sleep of the dead. "It would just make me feel better if you had his back this week. Even more so than usual," she added.

"Sure. Cool. I'm on it."

"Great. Thanks, baby," she said.

There. She'd done something. She'd taken action. Her pulse stopped thrumming and her shoulders relaxed a bit. There was nothing more she could do short of holding her husband's hand all day like a preschool teacher. Darnell was a grown-ass man, and she had to get to work. Maybe if she acted as if everything was normal, that would make it so. But as Gray turned her car onto the parkway, she thought of Emma and wondered . . . what must it feel like to know she'd never see her husband again?

EMMA

Emma was brushing her teeth—and trying to recall when the last time was that she'd brushed her teeth—when her cell lit up with Zoe's 113th call.

She spit into the sink and hit the green button. Progress. But progress she instantly regretted.

"Emma! Oh my God! You picked up?! Oh my God!"

Emma closed her eyes. Was that the voice? The one she'd heard when she called James's cell? It was always the assistant, wasn't it? But no. Zoe's voice was sweeter, more upspeaking, more nasal. Thank God. She wasn't sure she could handle it if she found out James had been screwing sweet little Zoe.

She had told her husband not to hire the girl straight out of college because kids today needed a couple of years to learn how to be professional before they started representing one of the partners. She'd known Zoe would undoubtedly show her age—probably at a vital moment like when the president of Major League Baseball called, or some reporter with a scandalous scoop on one of James's clients decided to try the grill-the-assistant approach—and here Zoe was, showing her age. Not that James had ever listened to Emma. At least not recently.

"Yes, Zoe, I'm here."

"Oh, Emma, I'm so . . . How are you? Are you okay? I'm so sorry for your loss."

This poor girl was calling to comfort her and all Emma was doing was mentally dressing her down. Emma blinked at her reflection in the huge mirror that ran the span of both her and James's sinks. His toothbrush was still in its holder; a washcloth he'd left on the edge of the porcelain had hardened as it dried.

"I'm sorry for your loss as well."

"Thanks." Zoe sniffed. "I mean, you don't have to say that? But . . . thanks."

Emma wondered if James had been a good boss. He used to be, she thought. Back when they discussed things. He always made sure people felt appreciated, stressed out over giving fair reviews, advocated for more time off and work-from-home days. Had Zoe liked working for him? Was she going to miss him? She found herself hungry for information about the husband she only sort of knew, but she couldn't find a way to ask.

"Is everything okay? Is there anything I can do?" Zoe asked. "How're the kids?"

"The kids are fine. I mean, not fine, but, you know."

"Yeah. I mean, no. I mean, I can imagine?" Zoe said, then gave a short laugh or sob—it was difficult to tell. "I'm sorry. I sound like an idiot."

Emma pulled the phone away from her ear to check the time. She was supposed to be meeting Lizzie at the cottage at ten and it was almost nine thirty. It was her first day actually doing something that mattered to her and she didn't want to be late.

"Zoe, was there something you needed, or—"

"Yes!"

Emma blinked. "Okay . . ."

"I'm sorry. I just . . . I've been trying you for days and I have to talk to you about the memorial."

Thunk went Emma's heart.

"The memorial?"

"Yes, James's memorial. The phone's been ringing off the hook with people who want to know when they can pay their respects." There was a long pause as Emma closed her eyes against the reeling of the room and the spinning of her brain. They seemed to be going in opposite directions. "Do you . . . have something planned?"

Emma and James had never once discussed this. They were still so young—not even forty-five. They'd never talked about whether they would be buried together or interred together or whatever the word was. She'd had no idea whether he wanted to be cremated or buried or torched on a frickin' raft out at sea. It was Gray who had suggested cremation. Due to the *condition of the remains* was how she'd put it, laying a hand gently on Emma's arm, which was all Emma had needed to hear. If there was one thing she was sure about when it came to her dead husband, it was that he wouldn't want anyone to see him looking less than coiffed.

Emma felt a stress laugh burbling up in her throat and bit down hard on her tongue. One of the things she hated most about herself was her tendency to crack up laughing in stressful or sad situations. Also, she cried when she was angry. And smiled when people told her bad news. When her parents had dropped the bombshell that her dad had stage-four liver cancer, she'd grinned. There was something seriously wrong with her face.

"No. I don't have anything planned. Honestly, Zoe, I don't think I have it in me."

"But, Emma, James was beloved around here."

Beloved, Emma thought. *Is that even possible?*

"And all his clients have been calling . . ."

Emma closed her eyes and braced her free hand against the vanity. She couldn't do this. She couldn't plan some huge party honoring her husband right now. Maybe not ever. He'd been cheating on her. Preparing to divorce her. He'd screamed in Kelsey's face the night before he died and shoved Hunter to the ground. What if they asked her to do a eulogy? What was she supposed to say?

She thought of Lizzie and tried to hear her friend's calming voice inside her head. Then, just like that, she knew what Lizzie would tell her to do. She would say that Emma didn't have to do everything. That it was okay to let other people help her. Especially with the things she felt incapable of doing.

"Can you take care of it?" she asked, holding her breath.

"Yes! Yes, we can definitely take care of it." Zoe sounded relieved. "As long as you're okay with that."

"Absolutely," Emma replied. "Just tell me where to be and when and I'll come. I just really am not up to planning an event right now. You understand."

"Of *course* I do," Zoe said. "In fact, I was on the phone with Gray just yesterday and she said you might feel that way, so we're already looking into venues. MSG offered us the Delta Sky Club."

That was just like Gray, anticipating what Emma needed before she even knew she needed it. What would Emma do without her?

"That sounds perfect," Emma said. "James would love that." *The rat bastard.*

"We figured we'd do it on a weekday to minimize the turnout as much as possible."

"The turnout?" How many people were they expecting?

"He had a lot of friends, Emma. But you know that. A lot of friends and colleagues who want to pay their respects."

Aside from Darnell, Emma knew of no friends. Over the last eight years or so, James had gradually stopped talking to everyone they used to socialize with. His frat brothers from college, the guys from his first job, even the friends he'd made coaching Little League in town when Hunter was little. They didn't go to cocktail parties or brunches anymore. Didn't attend his high school friends' annual Super Bowl/reunion party—James was always working anyway. She assumed he still saw some of the dads at Hunter's baseball games in the spring, but the rest of the year, all he did was work. Work and travel for work and drink and stumble home and get up at the ass crack of dawn to do it all over again.

"I was so glad Gray reached out to me about it," Zoe said, starting to sound more like herself, more comfortable in the conversation. "I was a little worried that things might be tense between you all after everything that happened the night of the accident."

Emma stood up straight. She realized the water was still running and turned it off, bringing silence down around her like a cocoon.

"I'm sorry. What?" she said.

There was a long pause. Someone was talking to Zoe on her end. She covered the receiver and everything was muffled for a moment and then, suddenly, she was back.

"Emma, I'm so sorry. Darnell just got here and I've got to go," Zoe said quickly. "I'll email you with the details and if you could just maybe send me a list of people you'd like to invite? That'd be great."

"Wait, Zoe—"

"Bye!"

She hung up. Emma stared at the phone. What tension? What "everything that happened"? Was it really Darnell who had interrupted her or was that an excuse? Emma normally would have just let it go, but she wasn't feeling entirely like herself this morning—the person who usually ignored and avoided and acted like everything was fine. She was feeling more like someone who wanted answers. Her thumb came down on the call-back button and Zoe, whose single most important directive was to answer every call, didn't pick up the phone.

LIZZIE

"I can't tell you how much I love this place." Lizzie ran her hand along the chair rail in the dining room of Emma's cottage as dust danced around her in a shaft of sunlight. She had to raise her voice to be heard over the wood-chipper running just outside at the neighbors'—they'd lost a lovely old oak in the storm. The tree guys had shown up five minutes after Emma pulled wildly into the driveway—Lizzie had been waiting on the porch, and had thought for a second that her friend was trying to recreate her husband's accident. When Emma got out of the car, she'd seemed distracted, but now that they were inside the house, Lizzie wondered if she'd just imagined it. "What're you going to do first?"

"Knock down that wall and that wall to open up the kitchen," Emma told her, lifting her long-lens camera to her eye and snapping a photo. "And I want to do sliders to the deck out back, which will, of course, be rebuilt."

"And upstairs?" Lizzie asked.

"I figured I'd knock out the dormers to make room for a true master suite," she said. "And I'll convert that laundry utility room behind the kitchen into an office, and build a mudroom next to it with the washer-dryer and some cute lockers."

"You've really thought of everything," Lizzie sighed and popped open the beveled glass door of one of the built-in corner china cabinets. It let out a pleasant, spicy scent. "I hope you'll keep these. They give the room such character."

"Of course," Emma said. "But they'll need to be—"

"Stripped, sanded, and stained," they said together. Then laughed.

Emma took a couple more pictures and gazed around the room. The chipper let out a loud peal and Lizzie went to the window. The men were feeding a huge chunk of the tree trunk into the mouth of the machine. Its monstrous teeth ground it to shreds in ten seconds.

"What's your reno budget?" Lizzie asked, then blushed. "I'm sorry. Is that gauche?"

"No. What's a little money talk between friends?" Emma said. "Besides, you're going to be lending your expertise, right? I hope? You should know the numbers."

It made Lizzie's chest swell a bit, knowing Emma had that kind of confidence in her, but when she heard the number, she had to concentrate to keep her jaw from dropping. It must be nice to have that kind of cash to throw around. She should just ask Emma to lend her some money. She should just tell her why she needed it. For half a second she had the wild notion that she would actually do it, but when she turned around and opened her mouth, she chickened out.

"Well. It'll be gorgeous when you're done," Lizzie said instead. "There's a good aura in this place."

"Yeah?" Emma gripped her own elbows beneath the camera hanging from its strap around her neck, as if trying to hold herself together through brute force. "I just can't believe I closed on this place the very same day James died. It makes me feel as if his spirit is lurking around here somewhere, waiting to see me fail."

"Why would he want to see you fail?" Lizzie looked at Emma. There was something off about her. Shaken. Like she'd just been using a jackhammer before she got here.

"Emma," Lizzie ventured when her friend didn't answer, "you don't have to talk about this if you don't want to, but the other day Gray sort of implied that James . . . had a drinking problem?"

Emma snorted a laugh.

"Is that a funny question?" Lizzie asked with genuine curiosity.

"No. I'm sorry. It's just . . . you're one of my best friends, and there's this huge part of my life that you know nothing about. That's on me, of course. I know that," Emma said, looking Lizzie in the eyes, her expression entirely open and honest. "So, here goes. Yes. He had a drinking problem. He has *always* had a drinking problem. In fact, it didn't at all surprise me that he managed to get drunk enough to drive himself through our garage."

"Oh, Emma."

Lizzie could hardly believe it. She'd had no clue. Not one single inkling. To her, Emma and James's marriage had looked perfect. It was the thing that she and every other single woman on the planet aspired to. He was rich, handsome, doting. He had this amazing, glamorous job that took him all over the world, yet he always seemed to be there for the big events, always on and always charming. He'd chosen Emma and she'd chosen him and they were going to be together forever.

But apparently, it was all just a smoke screen, and one so carefully created that even Lizzie—who thought she knew everything there was to know about Emma—hadn't suspected a thing.

"He came home three, sometimes four nights a week, so blitzed out of his mind he was barely coherent." Emma's gaze trailed away from Lizzie's and came to rest on the dusty wood floor. "No. That's not true. Sometimes, he was just drunk enough to be mushy. *Overly* attentive. Too touchy-feely and annoying. That was a normal Tuesday. It would get worse as the week went on. Wednesday he'd either be truculent or quick tempered. Thursday it was usually all-out war. Sometimes, on Fridays, like if Hunter had a game, he'd be close to sober, but if Hunter didn't have a game . . . well . . . your safest bet was to be asleep by the time he got home."

Lizzie's heart felt sick. She touched a hand to her chest. "My God, Emma."

"I know. Shocking, right?" Emma's eyes welled and she gave a short laugh. "Apparently the whole town thought we were this perfect family. And why not? The man was all about appearances. Nothing worse than bad PR. Sometimes I wonder if he chose the most remote and private house in town just so he could hide it. But guess what, James? Driving your car through your own house is no way to fly under the radar!"

She looked at the ceiling as she said this, as if James really was haunting the place.

"Emma, I'm so sorry. I really didn't know." In that moment Lizzie felt so bad for her friend and so guilty for not being there for her. But there was also just the slightest touch of irritation. How *could* she be there for her if Emma never told her?

"Of course you didn't," Emma said, lifting a palm and then letting her hand slap down. She sniffled and removed her camera, placing it back in its bag on the floor. Then she dug in her purse for a Kleenex. Lizzie produced one first. Emma took it and blew her nose. "I'm sorry I never said anything."

"It's okay." Lizzie reached for her hand, took it, and squeezed. "I know now. He didn't . . . did he . . . hurt you? Or the kids? I mean, physically?"

"No. But he came close, so many times. He'd break . . . things. Glasses, doorknobs, windows. Once he hit a refrigerator so hard the details of his fist were embedded in the door for days. You should have seen the face on the deliveryman when he brought the new one and hauled the old one away. I cried for an hour afterward." She turned toward the window, gaze unfocused. "Every time he came home and picked another fight I wondered, is this the night? Is this the time he goes too far? Will he hit me? Will he hit Kelsey? What if Hunter gets in the way? And then I'd wish I'd done something. Left him. Confronted him. Called the police. But it was always too late. And then it wouldn't happen and we'd move on and I'd think it won't be that bad again. It can't. That had to be the last straw. And then he'd be normal for a few days. Sober. Sweet. Attentive. To me. To the kids. And I'd really start to believe that was the last time. That everything was going to change. But it never did."

"Oh, Em."

Emma turned into Lizzie's shoulder and cried. Lizzie wrapped her arms around her as best she could and held on tight. All she could think was that the cliché was true—you never knew what went on inside someone else's marriage; you never knew what happened behind closed doors. Maybe she'd dodged a bullet, here. Maybe all this time, she'd been better off alone.

"I'm sorry," Emma said finally, wiping at her face with her hands. "What you must think of me."

"I think you were in a shitty marriage and your husband took advantage of your goodness," Lizzie said, handing her another tissue. "And I think you're lucky you all came out of this alive."

"Not all of us," Emma said grimly.

"Well." Lizzie sighed.

For a few minutes Emma blew her nose and they listened to the scream of the wood-chipper.

"I just wish you had told me," Lizzie said finally.

"The thing is, Lizzie," Emma stared at the mottled tissue in her hands, "it turns out I'm really good at keeping secrets."

EMMA

"You didn't have to do all this," Lizzie told Emma, surveying the spread on the kitchen island.

Emma smiled. She was feeling pretty proud of herself, actually. This morning she'd whipped out all her favorite recipes—bacon and Gruyère quiche, arugula salad, Greek bruschetta, and pumpkin muffins. It was as if not cooking for the last few weeks had caused some kind of culinary buildup inside her brain, and once she started, she'd been like a whirling dervish. Totally focused, nonstop action. It had taken her mind off things for a few hours, anyway, and she'd felt more like herself than she had in weeks.

"Please. You guys have done so much for me since . . . well, I owed you both."

Gray turned away from the window as if noticing the food for the first time. "You really should get someone out here to demo the garage," she said, tugging out one of the island stools. "It can't be good for you—or the kids—to come home to that every day."

"We haven't used that door or the back driveway since it happened." Emma ignored the twist in her gut and poured her friends tall glasses of iced tea, the cubes of ice clicking as the cups were filled. "It's sort of out of sight, out of mind. But I'll deal with it soon."

"I know a guy, if you want his number," Gray said and sipped her tea.

"Sure. Text it to me," Emma replied.

Gray reached for the salad, eyeing the green folder Emma had placed next to her own empty plate. "So . . . are you going to keep us in suspense, or do you want to tell us what's in there?"

Emma hesitated. All morning she'd been feeling more and more uncomfortable about the idea of sharing this with her friends—Gray especially. She could be so judgmental. For as long as they'd been friends, and as many times as Gray had been there for her, the advice she gave was always tinged with the slightest bit of condescension. As if she was thinking *I would never have tolerated this* or *Darnell would never do that to me.* Emma had called her on it once or twice, but Gray always denied it and for the most part, she valued Gray's opinions and guidance. This, though—this was huge.

Emma decided to just rip off the Band-Aid. She opened the folder and handed it to Gray, who put the salad tongs down.

Her eyes widened. "What the hell is this?"

"He was going to divorce me," Emma said as Gray started flipping pages. Lizzie put her tea glass down with a clatter and got up to look over Gray's shoulder. "And I'm pretty sure he was having an affair."

"What?" Gray said.

Lizzie's hand flew up to cover her mouth.

Emma relayed the story of the phone call and the woman's voice on the other end.

"Did you ask her who she was?" Gray said.

Emma shook her head. "I just hung up. I think I panicked."

Gray went through the papers again, more slowly this time. "Well, he wasn't fucking around. This is one of the top family law firms in the state. Not as highly rated as mine, of course, but—"

"God, Gray, are you really finding a way to make this about you?" Lizzie snapped.

Gray set her jaw. "I was merely stating a fact. You don't have to jump down my throat."

"Ladies, please," Emma said.

They both blinked, remembering, apparently, that she was there. Lizzie reached for Emma's hand across the island. "Do you think he was going to leave you for this other woman?"

Gray clucked her tongue. "That's an awful thing to say."

Emma sighed. "Maybe. I have no clue."

"But you can't be that surprised by this," Gray said, gesturing at the papers. "Your marriage was unhappy for a long time."

There it was—the condescension. But Lizzie spoke before Emma could.

"*That* was an awful thing to say."

"Can you two please back off each other?" Emma said. "I invited you over here to talk this through, not to bicker."

Gray glared at Lizzie and Lizzie glared back until finally, Gray took a long, deep breath and refocused on Emma. She tapped her perfectly shaped fingernail on the folder. "You really have no idea who this woman was? Have you tried calling back?"

"Yes, but it goes straight to voicemail now. She must have turned the phone off." Emma served herself a sliver of quiche and reached for her fork. "I also checked his personal email—the man never changed his password—but it was nothing but junk mail, and I haven't been able to hack into his work account—yet. Gray, do you think Darnell could get me in?"

"Maybe. He's a little slammed right now, but I'll talk to him."

"What if this woman was with him that night? What if she knows what happened out there?"

Or caused the accident somehow? she added silently, not wanting to endure the look Gray was sure to give her if she voiced her suspicion aloud. Instead, interestingly, Gray and Lizzie eyed one another. There was that odd inkling again, that they knew something she didn't. If they did, why didn't they just tell her?

"What?" Emma said.

Lizzie took a bite of muffin and Gray closed the folder.

"Nothing. We're just worried about you."

Emma sighed and chose to ignore Gray's comment, as well as the fact that the two of them were suddenly referring to themselves as a "we" when two minutes ago they were about to rip each other's heads off. "What would you do if I were just another suspicious client, Gray? What would you advise?"

"Usually if we think someone is cheating, we just hire a PI," Gray said, placing some salad on her plate. "It obviously helps our case if we can get hard evidence."

"That sounds so seedy."

"Seedy but effective."

"Maybe you should just let it go," Lizzie suggested, picking at the top of her muffin. "I mean, does it really matter who she was now that he's . . . gone?"

Emma didn't respond. It did matter to her. Lizzie wouldn't understand. She'd never been married. Never even been in a long-term relationship since Emma had known her. But this was her husband. The man who had chosen her and only her. Supposedly. She wanted to know what sort of woman James would have risked their marriage over.

And she was certain, at this point, that this woman had been with James the day he died. If not actually here, physically, at her house when the accident occurred, then at the very least with him in the city while Emma was waiting in the restaurant like an idiot for him to show. When else would she have gotten her hands on his phone? She wanted to meet this woman. She wanted to look her in the eye and ask her what she knew about her husband—what the hell was going on with him that day.

"I mean, unless you think he left her something in the will," Lizzie said.

Emma's head snapped up. "The will?"

"Shit. I didn't even think about that," Gray said. "You should call your estate lawyer. Who did you guys use? Cantor Feldman?"

Emma's heart was doing an odd flutter-step thing that made her put her fork down. "We had our wills drawn up at the same time. Everything just goes to me and the kids."

"Unless he had it revised and didn't tell you. It happens all the time," Gray said. "Seriously. Call your lawyer. I'll do it if you want me to. I can—"

"No. It's fine. I'll take care of it," Emma said.

The last thing she needed was Gray hearing the details of James's will before she did. Suddenly she wanted her friends gone. She wanted to go upstairs and scream into a pillow until her vocal cords snapped. He wouldn't. He couldn't. If she found out he had done this, if he had undermined their wills and left something—*anything*—to some random nameless, faceless female and shortchanged her or the kids . . . she would find a way to travel back in time and kill him herself.

GRAY

Back at her office, Gray couldn't sit still. The mistress thing was an angle she hadn't even considered. James Walsh was a jackass, yes, but he was also a hard worker. He'd lived for the work, for the schmoozing, for the travel, for the deal-making. She paced the rug in her large, corner office. Did a man who worked that hard and spent any free moment he had getting half in the bag have time for a mistress on top of a family? Something about it felt off.

Gray paused as a notification came through on her computer, and she checked her email. One hundred fifty-three unread messages. She was really falling down on the job. She sat and clicked open the first message— a rant from one of her former clients about spousal support. She forwarded it to the paralegal team.

Maybe she should help Emma figure out who this mistress was. There was no way her friend was going to give up until she found the home-wrecker, no matter what Lizzie said. She'd seen it in enough spurned women's eyes over the years—Emma needed to know, and she wasn't going to stop until she got hard evidence. Gray couldn't have pristine, naïve Emma running out and trying to hire a private investigator.

She couldn't even believe she'd said that out loud. What had she been thinking? It had to be the fact that she'd been caught off guard. Divorce papers. That was not something she had seen coming.

Call the contractor. That was what she needed to do. If she simply texted the number to Emma as she asked, there was a chance it would never get done; and if she accomplished one task, she'd feel more on solid ground and able to tackle the next thing. She picked up her phone and saw a string of missed calls and two voicemails from Derek.

Shit.

She'd turned her cell notifications off at Emma's so she could focus and had forgotten to turn them back on. Gray shoved herself out of her chair again and called him back without listening to the messages.

"Mom?"

"Derek? What's going on?"

"No one's seen Dad all day."

Gray reached out and crushed the leafy frond on a window plant one of the assistants had put in her office without permission.

"What? I put him on the train myself this morning."

"Carlos said Dad told him to clear his day, and then never showed." Derek sounded beyond tense. "And Mom? Felix Woodson just tweeted that he was dumped by his PR firm. Except he used a lot of expletives. The phone's ringing off the hook. Apparently he's not the only one."

"Dumped? I don't understand."

"He was one of James's biggest clients," Derek said. "And Selena Fitzgerald's agent just called, freaking out. He said she was dumped, too."

Gray was starting to sweat. She couldn't wrap her head around this—couldn't keep up—and she hated that feeling. It happened to her so infrequently she didn't know how to process it.

"She said Dad told her personally."

Gray turned around and sat on the windowsill, the corner digging into her ass through the fine wool fabric of her skirt. "Derek, I don't understand. Are you telling me your father is dumping James's clients?"

"It sounds that way. But if he is, he's not doing it from the office. No one knows where he is."

Damn it, Gray, she chastised herself.

She should have known he would do something like this. Darnell was all about loyalty. All about trust. And after what James had tried to do to him, well, this did seem like the right move. But he could have done it discreetly. How could he go off the cuff and start cutting people? He'd given Gray no warning that something like this was going to happen— that he was planning anything out of the ordinary. Had he even talked to the firm's lawyers? Had he looked at these athletes' contracts or consulted the board? He had to know that a sweeping gesture like this would have consequences, and a rant on Twitter would be just the beginning. For a man who couldn't shut up about the firm not needing any more bad PR, this felt like a rash move.

"Mom," Derek said, lowering his voice. She could picture him ducking in his chair, trying to get some kind of privacy in that damn open floor plan. "It's all the people who James was going to—"

"I know," Gray said. "I figured that out myself."

"Maybe I shouldn't have told Dad," Derek said. "Maybe I should have just kept the whole thing to myself."

"Derek, no. You had to tell the truth and I'm glad you did."

"But if I hadn't—"

"Baby, listen to me. You did what you had to do. You were a good son *and* a good employee. Every single thing that has happened as a result of this is on James Walsh, may he rot in hell. Do you understand me?"

"Yes, ma'am."

"Good. Now call back Selena's agent and see if you can find out where your father is," she instructed her son. "He must be meeting with at least some of them in person somewhere—that's why he cleared his day. Find out where and then call the lawyers. These people can't be tweeting slander. We need to shut them down."

"Okay. Okay. I'm on it," Derek said, sounding better now that there was a plan. Gray, meanwhile, was busy throwing things into her bag and slamming her laptop closed, totally unclear on what she was doing or where she thought she was going. Was she going to drive into New York City and check every restaurant and café for her husband? "Mom, I'm worried."

"I know, baby," she said, trying to sound far more confident than she felt. "But everything's going to be fine. I've got this."

KELSEY

"It's so annoying that they picked *The Wizard of Oz*. There's like three female roles."

"And one of them you've got to paint yourself green and wear a snaggle tooth."

"Please. We'll be lucky to get cast as munchkins."

"Or flying monkeys."

Everyone around Kelsey laughed as Jason hunched his back and pretended to flit around, flapping his hands like wings. The other freshmen kept looking over at Kelsey. They all knew she was the only ninth grader to get a call-back, and they probably thought she was an egomaniacal bitch for not participating in their self-deprecating chatter. But they didn't get it. They were nervous, yeah, but it was different for them. This was just their freshman play. What were they risking, really? An ego blow? Having a program as a keepsake? For Kelsey, this was everything. Her whole life hinged on the next five minutes.

Kelsey turned away from her peers. Her stomach was roiling in a way that was making her sweat and she felt like if the cast list didn't go up soon, she might literally turn inside out. She kept checking over her shoulder for Hunter, who was supposed to meet her outside the school theater to drive her home, but there was no sign of him.

Willow was here, though. Of course Willow was here. She was standing with a few other members of the stage crew against the wall next to the case where Tisch would post the list. The four of them were just watching the hopeful actors, occasionally whispering to each other and rolling their eyes, as if hoping for something was just so juvenile.

Kelsey didn't care. She wanted a part. Something that would look good on her Daltry application. She wanted to hit *send* already.

"This is intense," Alexa whispered to Kelsey. "Makes me glad I have my spot in jazz band on lock."

Kelsey attempted a smile. It almost made her puke. "Thanks for being here."

Alexa gripped her hand. "Solidarity, girl."

"Shit, there she is."

Someone squealed and even the seniors began to twitter as Mrs. Tisch strode across the paver patio and over to the bulletin board outside the theater doors. People jostled each other out of the way, then angled for a glance at the cast list she held expertly away from them. Overhead, the gray skies rumbled.

"All right, you heathens, back up!" she said with a laugh.

Somehow, she unlocked the glass door protecting the board, posted the list, closed the door and locked it again, then got out of there without getting trampled or even the tiniest bit stepped on. On her way back to the main building, the wind whipping her hair across her face, she didn't look a single soul in the eye. The woman was a pro.

The crowd surged forward, but Kelsey hung back. It was pointless to try to elbow her way to the front anyway; especially humiliating to do so and then find out that she was, in fact, Munchkin #12.

"I'll go," Alexa said, noting her hesitation.

Kelsey only nodded. There was a part of her, of course, that dreamed of being cast as Dorothy, just so she could shove it in everyone else's face, but she knew that wasn't even a remote possibility. She simply wanted to be on stage. No. She wanted something with lines. That was the only thing that would do for her Daltry application. They would know how competitive the arts were at Oakmont. And a speaking part for a freshman—even a small one—would—

"No. Freaking. Way."

Felicity Wells was standing right in front of her, looking like she wanted to shave Kelsey's eyebrows off. Kelsey's heart fluttered.

"What?"

"Congratulations," Felicity said. "You're the Wicked Witch."

"What?!" Kelsey blurted. "Shut up. You're just messing with me."

Then Alexa was there, her face beaming with pride. "No. She's totally not. Come see!"

Alexa grabbed Kelsey's arm and somehow, using centrifugal force, flung her to the front of the crowd. Kelsey ran her finger down the cast list, and there she was—fifth on the list after Dorothy, Scarecrow, Tin Man, and Lion.

WICKED WITCH OF THE WEST . . . . Kelsey Walsh

"Oh my God!" she blurted.

"Kels?"

She turned around and ran right into Hunter.

"What is it?" he asked, concerned.

"I'm the Wicked Witch!" she cried, and flung herself into his arms. "I got a real part!"

"Holy shit! That's awesome!" Hunter crowed. "Congratulations."

And then she and Alexa started screaming and clutching each other and jumping up and down.

"It's obviously a pity part," someone behind her said.

Kelsey stopped screaming. She hadn't recognized the voice, but a few prissy sophomore girls were pointedly trying *not* to look at her.

Suddenly, Willow was there. "What did you just say?" she demanded, angling herself between Kelsey and the other girls.

Kelsey's jaw clenched. She didn't need Willow to defend her. But the look of terror on the sophomores' faces almost made it worth it. After the briefest hesitation, the obvious leader of the group stepped up. "Just that Mrs. Tisch loves a good sob story. Of course the girl with the dead dad got cast."

"Hey. Back off. My sister earned that part," Hunter snapped.

The ringleader blushed hard, turned around, and strode off, her friends scurrying after her. Kelsey wanted to put her fist through the brick wall. Why did people have to be such assholes? Why did they have to ruin the one good thing that had happened to her in the last three miserable weeks?

"They're just jealous," Alexa said.

"Alexa's right. Don't pay any attention to them." Hunter put his strong, heavy hands on her shoulders. "You're the best actress I know. You beat out seniors for that part. You should be proud of yourself."

"You totally should, Kelsey," Willow put in, and glanced at Hunter as if for approval.

"I am," Kelsey said, forcing a smile. She pulled out her phone. "I'm calling Mom."

"I'll text you later." Alexa grabbed her and hugged her. "Congratulations!"

"Thanks, Al."

Her friend jogged off toward the school and her soccer practice, while Hunter asked Willow if she needed a ride.

"I'll go get my stuff," Willow said, jogging over to the nearby stairs.

"What are you doing?" Kelsey hissed.

"What?" he said defensively. "I'm giving her a ride home."

Kelsey blew out a sigh as Willow strolled over to them, slinging her backpack on. "Do you guys want to grab some food, or—"

"Do you always have to be all over us?" Kelsey blurted.

"Kelsey!" Hunter admonished.

"What? I'm just sick of it. She's, like, obsessed with us. Every day she's at our house or you're out with her. I can't even have one moment—*this* moment—without her hovering around like some creature out of a Wes Craven movie."

"Hey! Not cool," Hunter said. "Willow just defended you back there."

But it didn't matter. Willow had already turned around without a word, but she did hold up her middle finger as she strolled off.

"What's the matter with you?" Hunter asked.

"You want to go after her?" Kelsey challenged. "I'm sure I can get a ride from someone else."

Hunter shook his head and started toward his car, speed-walking away from her. Kelsey told herself it didn't matter—that by the time they got home he would forgive her. She turned away from the parking lot and called her mother. The phone rang only once before her mom picked up.

"Kelsey? Well? What happened?" her mother said.

"I got the Wicked Witch!" Kelsey said. "I'm the only freshman with a speaking role!"

Her mother crowed. "Oh, sweetie! That's amazing! I'm *so* happy for you!"

"Thanks, me too!"

"Come home so we can all celebrate."

"We're on our way."

Up ahead, Hunter was already revving the Jeep's engine. Kelsey hung up the phone and tipped her head toward the cloudy sky. She was going to kill this part. She was going to get into Daltry and leave this place and its resident assholes behind. And her father, wherever he was, could kiss her little ass.

When she opened her eyes again, the smile fell right off her face. Willow was up at the top of the hill, standing beneath the gathering clouds, glaring down at her. Nothing was ever enough for that girl. Nothing would ever be enough.

LIZZIE

"You've done such a lovely job with the place," Margot Crandle said, running her hand along the polished oak banister on the main stairs. "The pride of ownership really shines through."

Lizzie's heart swelled. She'd worked her fingers to the bone restoring the stairs the woman was now climbing in her stockinged feet, having taken her shoes off just inside the door. Lizzie tried to see her home through the Realtor's eyes. It wasn't often that she got the chance to really look around her house and take stock of everything that she had done to return it to its former glory. When she'd bought the place, the elderly widower moving out had allowed things to fall into ruin after the death of his wife ten years prior. Most of the doors hadn't closed properly, having been warped by the nonstop running of ancient window air conditioners. The radiators in several rooms had seized up with rust. There were windows off their tracks letting the cold in all winter and the heat in all summer, and various critters had made their homes in the darker corners of the second floor.

But today, you would never know it. As Lizzie trailed Margot up to the second-floor hallway, she half wanted to drop-kick the woman out the door. She couldn't leave this place. She couldn't trust that whoever bought it wouldn't destroy everything she'd done to make it a home—her home. Willow's home.

It was when she really looked around the house that she felt like she was worth something.

Of course, she'd felt a similar swell of pride earlier when Gray latched on to her comment about James Walsh's will. It was basically the first time the woman had acknowledged Lizzie had something to contribute to one of their conversations. So pathetic, she thought now. One affirmation from Gray Garrison had made her morning.

But it wasn't just that. Something was off with Gray. She wasn't holding herself with the same haughty tilt of her head that Lizzie was used to. Did it have something to do with Darnell? Lizzie couldn't get it out of her head, the way Gray had looked at him as he stood at the train station yesterday morning. She hadn't meant to spy—not really. But she'd been coming out of the café, all bolstered by a morning flirt with Ben, and the station was right across the way. Spotting Gray's car there had made her do a double take, and then there was the way Gray's eyes were locked on her husband. She'd looked almost . . . scared.

"And what's in here?" Margot asked, reaching for the closed door to Willow's room as if she was about to open a present.

"Oh, please forgive the mess," Lizzie began to say, preemptively embarrassed. "My daughter—"

But the words died in her throat. Willow's room was spotless. When Lizzie had asked her to straighten up the night before, she hadn't expected Willow to do anything other than *maybe* throw some clothes in the hamper, but this? One could actually walk the hardwood floors, see the antique moldings. The built-in bookshelves around her bed had been . . . dusted? And the bed was made. The room even smelled fresh, like dryer sheets had been left out all night. Maybe that talking-to Officer Miller had given Willow had really struck a chord with her. She had been fairly quiet and noncombative the last few days.

"Another lovely room," Margot said, turning in a circle and looking up at the crystal chandelier Lizzie had installed when Willow went through her brief glam phase in fourth grade. She made a note of something on her iPad, then looked up at Lizzie, curiosity lining her pretty, middle-aged face. "So, why are you selling?"

"Oh." Lizzie felt flustered by the question and touched the curls near her ear. "I've just had some unforeseen financial challenges crop up," she said, then laced her fingers together. "And I'm trying to do the responsible thing."

"Well, I'm happy to work with you. I can get an appraiser up here early next week and we can go from there." The woman handed Lizzie her card. "When you do decide to put it on the market, make sure you have someplace to go, because it'll get snapped up quickly."

"Thank you," Lizzie said, and pushed the card deep into her pocket. There was still one thing that could save her. It was a long shot, but all she had to do was hang in a little longer and maybe it would come through. Maybe she wouldn't have to sell her home. But if it did come through, she'd hardly have a reason to stay, a thought that made her feel hollow. Life. It just kept getting more and more complicated. "I'll walk you out."

GRAY

Gray strode through the offices of Garrison & Walsh, chin up, looking no one in the eye. The place was abuzz, phones ringing, people gathered at each other's desks, gossiping—surely talking about the boss and whether everything was going to hell. Some of them fell silent as she passed, but she kept her eyes on her husband's closed office door.

"Mrs. Garrison," Carlos said, standing up from his glass desk. Darnell's assistant was normally one of Gray's favorite people, but she didn't have time for chitchat right now. His tie was slightly loosened and he looked like he could use a nap. "He's not here."

"I know," Gray said smoothly, though she'd been hoping he would be back by now. It was almost 4 p.m. Certainly he had to be done fucking up his entire life's work at this hour. "I'm just going to wait for him in here."

She shoved open the door and paused at the threshold. Darnell's office was a disaster area. There were papers everywhere, workout clothes balled on the leather couch. He'd taken most of the framed jerseys off the walls and they sat piled beneath the flat-screen TV, their nails sticking out and a few holes visible. Shaking, she had just started to close the door behind her when Dante and Derek appeared as if from nowhere.

"Mom?" Dante said and engulfed her in a cigarette-smoke-scented hug. "What's going on? Have you talked to Dad?"

"I haven't yet, but that's why I'm here," she said, looking each of her boys steadily in the eye. Normally she would lecture Dante about the smoking, but she couldn't focus on that battle right now. "You two just get back to your desks and go about business as usual. I'm sure everyone here is taking their cues from you right now."

The twins exchanged a dubious look but did as they were told. Gray closed the office door and walked over to Darnell's workspace. Next to his computer was a pile of random paperwork, and it had been dropped atop a coffee spill that had long since dried.

Gray sat down hard—the seat of her husband's desk chair much lower than she was used to—and rolled forward.

Where was Darnell? What was he thinking?

Something peeked out from beneath the piles of paper. She pushed them aside and one of the bottom sheets stuck, adhered to the desk surface by the coffee stain. When it tore free it revealed a series of jagged white scars in the top of the dark wood desk. Heart pounding, Gray touched the violent slashes with her fingertip. There were at least three dozen of them, all roughly the same size, all evenly spaced. Darnell had made them deliberately.

What the hell?

Gray dug out her phone. She tried Darnell for the hundredth time. Voicemail. She closed her eyes, took a deep breath, and opened Darnell's calendar on his computer, using the password he always used: #52751119515#, His college jersey number, his pro jersey number, the boys' birthday, and their anniversary.

His calendar for the day was clear, just as she expected it to be. She looked through the files on his desktop and found one labeled JTW. James Thomas Walsh. Her pulse thrummed in her ears as she opened it, and then everything seemed to go still. Daily reports from William Brady, a PI Gray herself had used. Reports dating back six months. When James left the house, when he arrived at the office. Whom he'd met with, where he'd gone to lunch and with whom. There were photos and printouts of phone records and emails.

Darnell had been following James's every move, well before he'd learned the truth about what James had been up to. He'd suspected something, and he'd never told Gray.

The evidence was stacking up. If she were a detective, this would be enough for her to call the man in for questioning. Glancing at the closed door, Gray dug a thumb drive out of her bag, copied the folder to it, and deleted it from his desktop, then expunged his trash. Once the task was complete, she sat back in the chair and sighed, wishing like hell she knew where the man was, what he was doing, and whom he was doing it to.

GRAY

11:45 a.m.

13½ hours before the accident

"Ready to close on a house?" Gray stood in the foyer at Emma's, butterflies beating around her own heart. It was a big day, in so many ways.

For years, Gray had urged Emma to do something for herself. To join a club, or take a class, or sell cosmetics out of her house, for God's sake. Something to make her realize she was a real person with real talents and wants and needs. Someone who didn't have to sit at home every day to wait for the human hurricane to arrive and then pick up the pieces in the aftermath. When Lizzie had started displaying Emma's work and paying her to help take photos and update On a Lark's website, it had been a relief for Gray—though she had been perturbed that it was Lizzie who had managed to pull Emma out of her shell and not her.

But whenever Emma went out on a job for Lizzie, or sold a photo, it was as if the young, vibrant woman Gray had once known came peeking out from behind the curtain. When Gray first met Emma, she'd been so different—so full of color and life and joy and ideas. Yet over the years, it was as if that color and life had seeped away, leaving behind a withered, gray husk. The work with Lizzie was great, but it wasn't enough. And Gray had started to feel as if the whole idea of reclaiming vibrant Emma was a bust.

But then it had happened. She and Emma and Lizzie had been out for brunch for Emma's birthday. Lizzie had pulled out a new *Elle Decor* and Emma had started critiquing it. Pointing out where a kitchen color scheme didn't quite work, or where a skylight would have made all the difference, and Gray had pounced.

"You should flip a house," she'd said.

And Emma, of course, had laughed. But Lizzie had latched on to the idea—one of the rare moments in the past ten years that she and Gray had been on the same page.

"Yes! You'd be amazing at that, Emma!" she'd said. "Every time we go to a home to photograph it, you notice when a wall has been taken down or point out where wainscoting or a tray ceiling could improve the feel of a room. Why didn't I think of this?"

"You guys are crazy," Emma said, shaking her head and sipping her coffee. "Where would I even get the money?"

"I'm sure James would invest," said Lizzie, who clearly didn't know anything about James. Which, admittedly, made Gray feel as if she had one up on Lizzie—as if Emma considered her the better of the two friends.

"Or you could use the money your dad left you," said Gray, who knew every intimate detail of Emma's life.

And that was when she'd seen it. A true spark of life—of defiance—in Emma's eyes. She *could* use her dad's money. She could do this—do something for herself—and not involve James *at all*.

"I don't know," she'd said. "Maybe."

That had been the first hurdle, but it had actually taken months to convince her—to wear her down with carefully placed comments and questions. *I noticed there's an open house on Cavalier Street this weekend. Maybe we should check it out . . . Did you see what they did to the old Figueria place? Horrible. You would have done a* much *better job . . . Oh, your mom's coming up this weekend? Maybe now's a good time to ask her about the money?*

But all it had really taken was for one of the cottages to go up for sale. For some reason that Gray had never been able to fathom, Emma had always loved those cottages on the west side of town. They were some of the oldest, least charming houses in the entire village, but Emma saw something in them. And now that Gray had been inside one, she could almost sort of understand. Emma could make that place beautiful—a sweet bungalow for a small family or a single mom or an artsy millennial couple. And if she did a good job, she'd inspire the homeowner next door to renovate—or sell to someone else who would. One house at a time, Emma's inspiration could improve the entire neighborhood. Maybe she could even flip more than one.

"Yes! I can't believe I'm finally doing this," Emma said now, and looked around. "What did I do with my purse?"

"Check the kitchen," Gray suggested. "And do you have an umbrella I can borrow? It's getting overcast and I didn't bring one."

"Gray Garrison, unprepared? Will wonders never cease?" Emma smiled. "In the mudroom."

Emma ran back into the kitchen and Gray walked into the spacious mudroom. There were sneakers and shoes on the floor, and she lined them up by pair, then tucked them under the bench, where they belonged. On the wall hung a few jackets and an old dog leash, still there even though Emma's golden retriever had died three years ago. Gray clucked her tongue. Sometimes she worried about Emma's inability to move on—to get over things.

Gray found what she was looking for and shoved it in her bag just as Emma came around the corner.

"Found it!" Emma announced. "Oh, I wanted to tell you, I'm meeting up with James before the big party tonight, so I won't be riding in with you. I hope that's okay."

"Of course. Don't worry about it," Gray said. "I'll survive."

She always did.

EMMA

A pot of stew bubbled on the stovetop while Emma sat at the kitchen island surrounded by cell phone bills, her laptop open to Google number search. Emma couldn't believe she'd considered the possibility of hiring a private investigator, even for a second—although she had sort of enjoyed the image of knocking on the door of some square-jawed, hard-nosed, stubble-covered rogue who would *give it to her straight*. How hard could it be to uncover the truth about her own husband? It wasn't as if they'd kept separate finances or she didn't know where he went every day. After leaving a message for their estate lawyer, Evan Cantor, Emma had dug into their accounts. It had taken her half an hour to pull up and print out the last two years' worth of phone bills, and now she had a record in black and white of every single person James had called. If there were any mysterious strangers on this list, she would find them.

She had started with the day he died and worked backward from there. So far all she'd found were calls to agents and sports venues, media outlets and reporters. A handful of numbers were registered private, which meant they were probably direct lines to the famous athletes James dealt with on a daily basis. She supposed James could have been having an affair with a world-class tennis player or an Olympic soccer star, but she put the chances at low that a woman that successful would go for a guy like him—which she supposed didn't say much for her own self-esteem. But she could cross the pro-athlete bridge if she came up with nothing elsewhere.

She'd called a few of the numbers, then hung up if she got a man on the other end. She'd stricken a line through those, then highlighted all the women. She hadn't spoken to any of them. There were far more strike-throughs than highlights, sports and sports journalism apparently not having made the same strides as other industries in the whole equal-workforce movement. She was just hanging up with some guy at Nike when her kids walked in.

Kelsey tossed her bag on the floor and slumped into the nearest chair. Hunter went right for the stew.

"Hi, guys." Emma closed her laptop and tugged the papers into a pile. "How was your day?"

"Annoying. People suck," Kelsey said, not lifting her head. "I can't wait to get out of that place." She lifted her phone and opened her email, then sighed and closed it.

"Honey, you sent the Daltry application last night. They probably haven't even opened it yet."

"I know," Kelsey said.

Hunter filled a bowl with stew and opened a drawer in search of a spoon. "What're you doing?" he asked.

He shoveled some food into his face—it had to burn, but he didn't react—then used his free hand to paw through the pile of bills.

"What's all this?"

"Nothing," Emma said, then decided she didn't feel like lying to her kids. "I was just trying to figure out who some of the people were that your dad was calling and texting."

Kelsey sat up straight. "Why?"

"Yeah. Why?" Hunter asked around a mouthful of potatoes and meat.

A hot flush crept up Emma's neck and into her face. She lifted her shoulders, then got up and retrieved a bowl for herself and another for

Kelsey, giving herself half a second to figure out how to answer that question.

"Do you think he was having an affair?" Kelsey asked, sounding intrigued—almost excited.

Hunter froze, then put his spoon back into his bowl. "Dad wasn't having an affair."

"Why not? Why else would Mom be stalking his phone records?"

"Mom?" Hunter said.

Emma put the empty bowls down on the counter. She turned to face them, clutching the edge of the countertop behind her on either side. Their whole lives, Emma had tried to be truthful with her kids, as much as she could without hurting them. This didn't seem like the time to give that up, however humiliating the truth was. But when she looked into Hunter's eyes, so vulnerable and defiant all at once, she lost her nerve.

"I don't know, you guys," she said. "It's just something I'm looking into."

"Can I help?" Kelsey stood up, suddenly full of energy.

"Kelsey, I—"

"I'll totally cold-call them," Kelsey said, walking around the island to open the laptop.

"And say what?" Hunter asked. "Hey. This is Kelsey Walsh. Were you having an affair with my dead dad?"

"Hunter—"

"Dad was *not* having an affair!" Hunter shouted. He dropped his bowl into the sink with a clatter that startled both Emma and Kelsey, then grabbed the pile of bills, crumpling them in both hands.

"Hunter!" Emma cried, making a grab for the pages. All that work.

"This is so fucked up!" he shouted, angling away from her. He turned and shoved the whole wad into the garbage, covering it up with the goopy, dirty detritus of carrot and potato peels, eggshells and coffee grounds. "You guys want to make him out like he was evil, but he *wasn't evil.*"

Emma's heart was in her throat. "Oh, Hun—"

"I don't want to hear it, Mom." Hunter snatched his duffel bag up off the floor. "I'm going upstairs."

Emma locked eyes with Kelsey until they heard Hunter's bedroom door slam. Then she turned and leaned into the counter, just breathing. Hunter never lost his temper. Ever. It was like watching a dormant volcano randomly explode. How could she have thought that the truth, in this case, was in any way appropriate? He'd just lost his father. They all knew the man had been flawed. She didn't need to taint her son's memories of James even deeper. Emma felt like the worst mother imaginable.

"He probably texted her," Kelsey said in a small voice. "Everybody texts. Or snapchats."

"I can't imagine your father on Snapchat," Emma said, before she could stop herself. "And I don't have his phone."

"What about his computer? If he synched his messaging app to his computer, it would have a record of his conversations," Kelsey said. "Unless he deleted them."

The room temporarily tilted. How had she not considered that? But then, the laptop was missing, too. It was almost as if someone was trying to hide something. But James couldn't have known he was going to die that night, and he was the only person with a motive to keep this information a secret. Other than—possibly—the mistress herself.

"Let's just leave it." Emma reached for the ladle Hunter had left lolling in the stew and dished up dinner for herself and her daughter. She handed Kelsey a bowl, then ran her hand over her long hair. "You know what we should work on instead? Deciding which monologue you should use for your audition for Daltry. Let's concentrate on the future for tonight."

LIZZIE

The only drawback of Ben's café was that it shared a parking lot with The Tap Room, one of only two bars in the town of Oakmont. The other, Varka Lounge, was more on the outskirts and attracted a younger, trendier crowd—twentysomethings who still lived with their parents while commuting into the city or working from home on their start-up whatevers. The Tap Room was the place where people Lizzie's age went after work or after the kids were in bed or when they couldn't take their spouses anymore. Thanks to local ordinances, it closed at eleven during the week and midnight on Fridays and Saturdays, but sometimes, when Lizzie was walking into Ben's at seven o'clock on a weekday morning, she could still smell stale beer and vomit in the air. *Who drinks themselves sick on a Monday night?* she thought, moving to an outdoor table slightly farther from the lot, then wondered if James Walsh had ever done just that.

The idea made her heart hurt. What must it have been like to live with that man? Part of her wondered whether Emma and the kids weren't better off with him gone, now that she knew the truth. *May he rest*, her brain automatically added to the shameful thought.

Lizzie lifted her café au lait—on the house, no matter how much she argued with Ben—to her lips and slowly trailed her gaze toward the train station, telling herself she was not sitting there with the express purpose of spying on Gray and Darnell. It was simply a beautiful morning. The kind of morning that begged to be enjoyed outdoors, preferably not downwind from a puddle of puke.

"You alright out here?" Ben asked, popping outside even as the line at the counter began to snake toward the door.

"I'm fine!" she replied with a smile. "Get back to work!"

"Not before giving you this." He produced a beautifully plated chocolate croissant from behind his back, a little rose made out of white chocolate resting next to it.

"Ben, that looks amazing. But I could never eat something like that for breakfast. I'll gain ten pounds!"

"You have to eat the whole thing to get to what's underneath."

Ben grinned and ducked back inside. Lizzie, blushing, lifted the croissant and saw that there was a paper doily on the plate, and she could tell something had been written on the underside of the circle at the center. Her heart flipped over and she put the croissant down again, ripping a tiny bit off the top. She couldn't stop smiling. Secret messages on croissant doilies? She felt like the romantic heroine in a French film. But she wasn't going to look like a desperate housewife and read it right now. She didn't want to do it while Ben was most definitely watching her.

Instead, she opened the local newspaper she'd grabbed and told her heart to quit its teenaged antics. *We're not in high school anymore*, she admonished herself silently, and scanned the real estate section, trying to concentrate on the condo prices. Lizzie hadn't officially listed the house yet, still hoping for that miracle reprieve. And when she saw what the places by the reservoir were listing for, it made the lait from her café curdle in her belly. It wasn't like they were a steal. Even if she got top price for the house, she wouldn't be banking much more than she'd need for Willow's first year at college. Was she really going to have to downgrade to an apartment rental?

She whipped the newspaper closed, deflated, and tore off a larger piece of the croissant. That was when she saw Gray's Mercedes pull into the parking lot across the way. This time, however, Gray eased into a space and killed the engine. The other morning she'd simply idled in the center of the lot until Darnell was on the train. Lizzie picked up the paper again and slouched slightly behind it, eyeing the couple over the top of the page. They both got out. They didn't speak. Darnell simply ducked his head to look at his phone and walked away.

This was new. What had happened to Gray and Darnell, the perfect lovey-dovey pair? And why was he no longer driving to work? It was possible his car was on the fritz, but didn't people with that kind of money have backup vehicles? Or get loaners from the dealership? Or rent something?

Lizzie was so involved with her theorizing, she almost missed the fact that Gray was now walking toward her. Lizzie snapped the paper all the way open and held it up to hide, just waiting for Gray to accuse her of stalking. But Gray breezed right by the outdoor tables and into the café, eyes on her phone. Lizzie couldn't help watching her through the window. She bypassed the line and walked right over to Ben, who startled at the sight of her. He came out from behind the counter and the two of them disappeared down the hall to the bathrooms at the back.

That was odd. She began to rise out of her chair when suddenly Gray reappeared—no Ben—and strode through the shop and out again. This time, it was too late for Lizzie to hide without calling even more attention to herself, so she grabbed the door pretending to be coming through. Gray just about tripped over Lizzie's foot.

"Watch it!" Gray said, before looking up and recognizing Lizzie.

"You're the one with your eyes glued to your phone," Lizzie replied. She glanced down to see what had Gray so riveted and spotted a tiny pulsating circle on a map. It was moving steadily south along what appeared to be train tracks.

A tracking app? Was Gray tracking her husband?

Lizzie averted her eyes, pretending she hadn't seen. "It's a beautiful day, Gray. Maybe you'd be less tense if you tried to enjoy it."

Gray's nostrils flared, but she walked away without getting in the last word. Score one for Lizzie. She went back to her table and pulled the doily out from underneath her croissant.

Go on a date with me?

Lizzie grinned and looked into the shop just as Ben was coming out from the hallway. She expected him to look up at her and make eye contact—to see if she'd read the note—and was ready to mouth a happy *yes*, but that wasn't to be. As if he'd entirely forgotten she was there, he trudged back to the counter, head down, pushing an envelope into his back pocket.

EMMA

Nine. Nine half-empty bottles of alcohol. Emma had lined them up on the kitchen counter, where they glinted prettily in the sun streaming through the unbroken side of the window. She had searched only half the house. If she kept this up, she was going to be able to play her very own game of "Ninety-nine Bottles of Beer on the Wall," except with bourbon and scotch and vodka, and one oddly shaped bottle of vermouth.

It had been going on all day, this Easter egg hunt of hers. This morning, when she got out of bed, she'd been infused with an odd sort of manic energy, and instead of going back to the computer, she had waited until her children left the house, the sound of the Jeep engine faded to nothing, to launch her search. She hadn't been sure, at first, what she was looking for, but she'd found the first bottle in the back of a drawer full of carefully bagged and preserved hockey pucks in the basement. From there, it had only gotten more interesting. The bottles had been stashed in such highly creative places, she almost wished James were here so she could congratulate him. There was one inside the old DVD cabinet she'd been meaning to clean out forever but he always teased her she never would. Another was found in the ignored spare powder room, inside the heating grate, where nothing but a tepid whistle of warm air ever came through. But it was when she found a baggie of cocaine, shoved up inside the pool-table ball return, that she'd almost lost it.

Drugs? James had been doing *drugs*? Since when? How? Did he have a dealer? Emma wasn't naïve. She knew that those in positions of power, like her husband, had access to all kinds of shady people and illicit substances, but she had thought that alcohol was James's preferred demon. Now, she had no clue what to think anymore.

Hunter played pool with his friends in the game room all the time. How would James have felt if his children had found his drugs? If they'd used them? She could just as easily imagine him patting Hunter on the back as he snorted his first line of cocaine as she could imagine him getting enraged at the very idea of Hunter touching drugs. And the realization had left her sitting on the floor of the game room for half an hour, her back against the wall, clutching the baggie and knocking her head against the plaster lightly, over and over again. If Gray or the kids had walked in on her at that moment, they would have called an ambulance.

Maybe she did need to be committed. What kind of person was she? What kind of mother? That she let this happen under her own nose. *Under her own nose.* It was when her own unintentional pun registered in her addled brain that she got up and, recalling every random cop movie she'd ever seen, went to the bathroom, and flushed the baggie down the toilet. Then flushed again for good measure.

Now Emma systematically opened the bottles of alcohol and, one by one by one, dumped the contents down the kitchen sink. She took out a new garbage bag and shoved the bottles inside, then tied up the bag and brought it to the front porch, where they'd been keeping the garbage cans lined up since James's accident, none of them wanting to venture into the garage. She shoved the bag into the bottom of one of the cans and moved another bag on top of it, reminded of the way Hunter had made a similar move with the phone bills. James was three weeks dead and they were still cleaning up after him. Still protecting each another from his deepest, darkest secrets.

It was 2 p.m. She still had time. Back inside, Emma jogged up the stairs. By the time she got to her room, her entire rib cage seemed to be pounding, rather than her heart. She strode over to James's closet and yanked open the double doors. The scent overtook her. Dry-cleaning with an undertone of cologne overlaced with just the faintest hint of bourbon. That smell was always there, whether pungent on his breath or simply clinging like an afterthought to his clothes. For the rest of her life, whenever she caught a whiff of Maker's Mark, she'd feel her husband there with her.

Emma stepped inside. She reached out and ran her hand down the slick lengths of the leather belts before moving on to the suits. They were arranged by season, and then by color within the season. They were rotated on a quarterly basis, so that right now the fall collection was at the front, the linen summer suits placed at the back. Nothing was ever stored away. James wanted his whole collection to be in one place so that he could admire it whenever he liked. He'd never told her this, but every now and again she'd catch him in there, looking around with a satisfied expression on his face. Each hanger was oak with a gold hook, and each one was situated exactly two inches from the next. His marriage, his home life, his head might have been total fucking mayhem, but his closet was as orderly as a ruler.

Emma put her hands, back to back, between two suits and, feeling a little thrill of rebellion, shoved them aside in opposite directions. The hangers made a satisfying screech as they parted and a random giggle bubbled forth from her throat. Damn, it was satisfying to mess up his shit. She pushed a few more suits aside, then felt something in one of the pockets. Her heart caught as she fished around in the silken pouch. It was a one-thousand-dollar chip from the Luxor in Vegas. She tossed it over her shoulder and, with renewed determination, got to work.

She searched every suit pocket and every pair of pants, coming up with a couple of business cards and a receipt from a restaurant in the city for more than five hundred dollars. For lunch. Moving on to the shirts was fruitless. Apparently he didn't use those pockets for anything, but then she came to the sweaters. At first she simply lifted them, peeking between folded cashmere. There didn't seem to be anything there, but on the third shelf she moved a deep purple V-neck and heard something hard hit the back wall of the closet. Too short to see what it was, she ripped all the sweaters down and uncovered a half-empty bottle of Absolut.

"Mother fucker," Emma whispered to herself. *Make that ten.*

She walked to the bathroom and poured the vodka down the drain.

Now she was shaking with rage. She went back to the closet and yanked the rest of the sweaters from their shelves. Two more bottles rained down around her. Scotch. Bourbon. Emma dumped these as well, then moved on to the shoes.

There had to be something else in here. Something that would reveal him to her. Something that would make her connect the man she had married to the woman she'd heard on the other end of that phone call. She yanked out loafers and oxfords and boots and dozens of pairs of pristine free sneakers—gifts from reps at Nike and Adidas and Under Armour. At the very back of the closet she found an ancient pair of New Balance she was pretty sure he'd worn when the kids were little. They were red suede—very faded—with big white N's emblazoned in leather. The sight of them made her pause, her breath caught in her chest. They'd been young and happy once.

Slowly, Emma reached for the shoes. One felt slightly heavier than the other. She tipped it and three more chips fell into her hand. But these were different. They were AA chips. Two months. She remembered that. She'd actually attended the ceremony, feeling proud and hopeful until three nights later when he'd come home and thrown up in the potted plant next to the front door.

The other two were one-month chips. Was this for real? He'd been one month sober two other times? Emma sat back on her ass on the plush carpet, the chips heavy in her hands, and thought back. Hunter's freshman soccer season. James had come home early a lot during November and gone to watch Hunter practice. It wasn't Hunter's favorite sport, but he was still a star at it, though he'd given it up after that year to focus exclusively on baseball. James had taken them all out to dinner to celebrate the win against Valley. He hadn't had a drink that night, but that wasn't so unusual—he almost never drank in front of the family. Had he been sober that whole month? She vividly remembered him calling her on Thanksgiving—he often missed the holiday because he had to be at one of the NFL games—and being utterly incoherent. Was that the night he'd given up? Fallen off the wagon, as the saying went?

But if he was trying, why wouldn't he tell her? If she'd known, she could have supported him—been there for him. Had he just gotten in the habit of not telling her anything? Maybe he hadn't wanted to get her hopes up—had suspected he would fail and didn't want to see her disappointment. Or maybe keeping secrets was all he knew how to do anymore.

Emma turned the third chip over in her fingers. When could he have possibly earned this? Maybe he hadn't. Maybe he'd just gone to the meeting and claimed he'd been sober for a month. She wouldn't put it past him. Emma stacked the chips carefully on a low shelf, then pulled herself up. She'd really made a mess of the closet. There were tangled sweaters everywhere, peppered with shoes and sneakers, and several silky ties had slid off their hanging rack to the floor. She felt heavy, suddenly. Like she'd run out of steam.

Then her eyes fell on the drawers. There were only three of them. They were where James had kept his watches and cuff links and a couple of bottles of cologne. Lazily, warily, Emma pulled the top one open. *May as well finish the job.* The watches were all in their boxes and she lifted each one out and carefully replaced it, finding nothing underneath. She wondered, absently, if Hunter would want any of them. Did kids his age even wear watches anymore? Maybe he'd use them when he was older. When she finally got around to actually cleaning this closet out, she'd save them for him. In the second drawer were the cuff links, and there was nothing interesting there either.

In the bottom drawer, along with the bottles of cologne, were dozens of medals still on their lanyards from the 10K races and half-marathons James used to run. She had no idea he'd saved them. The sight of the bright ribbons brought on another pang of nostalgia. A longing sigh for what might have been. What if he'd chosen his health over his habit? His family over the bottle? Where might she be right now? Where might he be? It was an abyss she refused to dip her toe into, for fear of getting sucked in for all eternity.

She lifted the ribbons in the bottom drawer, half-curious, half-terrified as to what else she might find, and uncovered another cuff link box. Black, with gold lettering: GC JEWELRY. She slowly picked up the box, her pulse doing an awful warning dance that she ignored, and pried the top open. Inside, nestled against black silk, were a pair of cuff links shaped like footballs with tiny diamonds as the lines. Revolting. There was a small card wedged into the top of the box, written in red pen.

For my Valentine . . . xo, JM

"Mom?"

Emma shoved the cuff links back in the drawer and slammed it. Half a second later, Hunter and Willow were standing there, looking down at her.

"What are you doing?" Hunter asked stiffly.

"I just . . . figured I'd start packing up some of your dad's stuff. To donate," she improvised.

Willow glanced at Hunter, then strolled off across the room—not out, as Emma expected her to do. She paused near Emma's dresser and began casually opening Emma's jewelry boxes, as if it were a totally normal activity. Emma shoved herself to her feet.

"Are you kidding?" Hunter demanded. "Already? He *just* died. We haven't even had his memorial yet."

"I don't know, Hunter. It was just something to do," Emma said. "I don't have to. I was just—"

"Whatever," Hunter said. "Come on, Willow."

Willow looked up as Hunter stormed out of the room but made no move to follow him. She lifted Emma's grandmother's pearls out of her large jewelry box and held them up against her neck, turning sideways to admire herself in the mirror above Emma's dresser.

"You've got some dope stuff, Mrs. Walsh," she said.

Was the girl mocking her? As long as Emma had known her, Willow had never called her Mrs. Walsh. It was always Emma or, as a joke, Auntie Em.

"Thank you?" Emma said sarcastically. She felt like she was being somehow violated and wanted Willow out of her room. Badly.

"Don't worry about Hunter," Willow told Emma, as if she were an older, wiser sister. "He's just in the anger stage of grief."

Then she placed the pearls back in the jewelry box, slammed the top down, and walked out.

LIZZIE

Lizzie sat at the kitchen table, going over the planned promotions for the shop leading up to Christmas. If they had good weather for the next few weeks and foot traffic maintained, she could project a profit for the season—but not much of one. All the stars would have to align, and people would need to be in a spending mood. But she chose to remain optimistic. Tonight, anyway. Maybe things weren't as dire as she thought they were. Maybe Willow could get a scholarship and they wouldn't have to sell the house.

She sipped her wine and did a few yoga breaths, knowing she was deluding herself, but telling herself it was okay to do that every once in a while. It was, in fact, necessary for her sanity. Besides, things really were looking up in one facet of her life—she had a date. A real, Saturday-night date the following weekend with a guy she liked—a guy with potential. A guy who knew how to bake.

The front door opened and Lizzie heard Willow twirling her keys.

"Hello?" her daughter called.

"In the kitchen!"

Willow appeared, backpack on, gum popping.

"It's late. Did you eat?"

"Emma ordered Thai." Willow went to the refrigerator and retrieved a bottle of water, which she guzzled.

"You were at Hunter's again?" Lizzie asked.

"Yeah. Why?"

Her daughter capped the half-empty bottle and returned it to the fridge.

"Nothing." Lizzie entered a few numbers into Excel, then deleted them, then corrected them. "You've been spending a lot of time over there lately."

"So? Why shouldn't I be?" Willow asked, fiddling with the basil plant in the front window.

"It's just . . . I feel like Emma and her kids could use some time to themselves," Lizzie said carefully. "It's a weird time for them right now."

Willow dropped her hands heavily at her sides. "Yes, Mom. I'm aware of that."

"I'm just saying—"

"I know what you're saying," Willow said, striding past her. "I'm going to go finish my homework."

Once her daughter was gone, Lizzie let out a deep sigh and sipped her wine again. There should be a special reward in heaven for parenting a teenaged girl. Or some sort of awards ceremony. *Best Handling of an Awkward Situation Without a Meltdown, and the nominees are . . .*

The phone rang. It was Emma. Immediately, Lizzie thought of her odd encounter with Gray outside the café. Should she tell Emma about it? Was Gray actually *tracking* her husband? Without his knowledge? And the woman thought Lizzie had an obsessive relationship with Emma. Such a hypocrite. And to top it off, Gray acted toward Emma as if Darnell was the perfect husband, like she was so appalled by James's supposed cheating behavior. So why the hell was she following her own husband around? Because she trusted him implicitly? What a joke.

She wondered what Gray had pulled Ben aside to talk about. She'd thought about asking him when she'd gone back inside the café to accept his invitation, but she'd felt like a stalker and decided it best not to come off that way before they'd had a chance to go out. He'd been so excited when she accepted the date. Every time she thought about the broad smile on his face, she felt a tiny thrill.

"Hi, Emma," Lizzie said into the phone. "How's it going?"

"You're never going to believe what I found in James's closet," Emma hoarse-whispered. "Cuff links. A Valentine's gift. From someone with the initials JM."

Lizzie's heart sank. She grabbed her wineglass and drained it. "Oh my God, Emma. I can't believe it."

"Me neither." Emma sounded stunned, but also, somehow, excited. "It's true, Lizzie. It's all true."

WILLOW

2:15 p.m.
11 hours before the accident

"You sure about this?" Hunter asked as Willow got into the Jeep.

"Sure I'm sure!" She clicked her seat belt, pushed her hair out of her face, and smiled at him. She was manic with nerves, but she wasn't about to back out. Backing out was not an option.

"You're being weird. And, like, smiley."

"And this is worth commenting on because . . . ?"

"Willow. I'm serious. He's not gonna like this."

"I think that's been firmly established," Willow said. "Now drive."

Hunter shook his head and pulled away from the curb. She'd met him around the corner from school, each of them having snuck out half an hour before last bell from different classes on opposite ends of the building.

"It's just . . . there's a lot of stuff you don't know about."

"So tell me," Willow said.

Hunter's nostrils flared and she saw his jaw muscles working as he kept his eyes on the road. His forearms flexed when he adjusted his grip on the steering wheel, and she noticed a smattering of angry, red scratches on his tanned skin. "I just want you to be okay," he told her.

"I appreciate that," Willow said matter-of-factly, though deep down, she was touched. "And we never tell a soul." She held up a fist. "Code of silence, right?"

Hunter rolled his eyes. Code of silence was something they'd come up with in third grade when they'd used his mother's favorite casserole dish to serve microwave popcorn to their friends and dropped it on the kitchen floor, shattering it into a dozen jagged pieces. They'd covered it up with newspapers in the garbage can and sworn each other to a "code of silence," which didn't even make any sense, but they'd been using it both sincerely and jokingly ever since. Willow knew that if any of her hipster friends or any of Hunter's preppy crew ever heard them say it, they would have been summarily disowned. Neither group understood the bond between Willow and Hunter—hell, sometimes she barely understood it—and they definitely wouldn't get code of silence.

Hunter, however, knocked his fist into hers. "Code of silence," he intoned. They shared a smile and drove on.

EMMA

The kids were in bed; the house was silent. Emma sat in the living room, her laptop closed on her lap, eyes focusing and unfocusing, trying not to imagine her husband with some random woman. Trying not to think about what she looked like. How they'd met. Whether they did things together like go on dates, or whether it had just been about the sex. What had they talked about? Had James shared details about Emma with his mistress?

Emma and James themselves had rarely talked to each other. She wasn't sure she could remember the last time they'd had a conversation longer than "The dryer died" or "The landscaper ran over a sprinkler head again" or "We need bananas."

It was almost absurd, how far back she had to go, but after a great deal of mind-wracking, she landed on her birthday, this past April. To her great shock, James had come home from work on time and taken her out to dinner. She had already prepared her own favorite meal—chicken Milanese and mashed potatoes—and baked herself a cake. The kids had seemed delighted by the turn of events, and not just because they were getting the house to themselves for a night, but because it had been a night without drama, and their parents had looked, if not happy, at least calm. Emma remembered sitting in the car on the way to the restaurant and feeling nervous. What were they going to talk about all night? What was he thinking? But it had turned out okay. Not romantic, but nice. He'd told her about his recent trip to Mexico to sign some big soccer star. She'd asked a lot of questions to keep him talking because she was still so flabbergasted, she couldn't think of what else to do.

On the way home, they'd driven by the old cottages on the edge of town. One had been for sale and, on impulse, she'd told him to pull over so she could grab one of the sell sheets. James had actually obliged without impatience or argument, and she'd sighed looking at the photos of the interiors—so quaint and everything original. Shabby, but fixable.

"I've always thought it would be fun to renovate one of these," she'd said.

"You're so funny," he'd replied, glancing in his side-view mirror.

And she hadn't asked what he'd meant, because she didn't want to know.

Emma clicked over to realtor.com and looked at the cottage. Not the one from that night, but hers. The one she'd just bought, the day James died. The listing was still up, but marked UNDER CONTRACT. What would he think of the fact that she now owned a house all her own? That she'd negotiated a fair price and had started drawing up plans? Would he laugh at her? Would he be surprised? Impressed? She had no idea.

She opened her computer, willing her brain not to go where it wanted to and continue that conversation to its inevitable end.

"You're so funny." She could hear his voice so clearly—the exact inflection that made it land somewhere just shy of an insult, just left of a challenge. So funny for seeing the beauty in something past its prime? So funny for thinking she could do something worthwhile? So funny because she thought that bringing a historical home like that back to life *was* worthwhile?

Emma shut her eyes and saw him looking at her in the half light from a streetlamp, and wondered: had he liked even one teeny, tiny thing about her?

She opened his Facebook page. It was the first time she'd gone on the site since he died, not wanting to endure all the flat condolences of people she knew well enough to friend on social media, but not well enough that they might actually call in tragic circumstances. She wasn't interested in that false bullshit. What she was interested in were James's connections.

The first post she saw was from the verified account of an international baseball star.

RIP BRUTHA. THE DERBY WON'T BE THE SAME WITHOUT YOU.

God, she hated social media. Did these people actually think it meant something, posting a message on the page of a person who'd died, as if he was ever going to see it? She gritted her teeth and began to scroll. Each time she came to a post from an unfamiliar female, she paused, trying to read between the lines to see if there was anything there.

WE'LL MISS YOU, JAMES.

TAKEN TOO SOON.

HEAVEN HAS A NEW ANGEL.

Vomit.

She kept scrolling. The messages went on and on and on. Just when her vision was starting to get bleary and she was thinking this was a pointless endeavor, she found her. Jennifer Mahone. Verified account. A tiny round photo of a gorgeous woman with glowing brown skin, a flawless smile, and a birthmark on her chin.

THE WORLD WON'T BE THE SAME WITH OUT YOU, JIMMY.

"Jimmy?" Emma muttered aloud. James couldn't stand to be called Jimmy.

She clicked on the woman's image, even as part of her screamed to leave it alone. Jennifer was a reporter at ESPN. Married. Two adorable, chubby-cheeked kids. So maybe she wasn't the JM Emma was looking for. But then again, who knew? If one person in the relationship was cheating, why not both?

Was Jennifer the woman who had answered the phone? Maybe she would call ESPN tomorrow and track her down. She wondered if she'd recognize the voice if she heard it again. How had she even got hold of his phone? Why would she answer it over a week after his death? If she got hold of Jennifer, maybe the woman could explain.

Emma made a note of the name, then went back to James's page. After a few more minutes, she found another JM. This one older, a vice president at an advertising firm. In a relationship, her status said. Janet McElroy. She was blond. Fit. Fake tan. Botoxed. She wore too much makeup and the hair was clearly a dye job.

Was this woman there when James died? Did she know what had happened?

Bile rising in her throat, Emma quickly noted the woman's name, then closed out Safari, unable to endure any more. She had an awful feeling that her dreams were going to be filled with Jennifers and Janets tonight, one or both of them doing things with or to her husband. Things that Emma hadn't done with him or to him in years. Maybe this was why women hired PIs to do the investigating in these situations. To avoid making themselves sick.

GRAY

Gray was one of those drivers she couldn't stand. She was doing five miles an hour on Madison Avenue, even though the midday traffic was mercifully light. Cars and cabs kept flying up behind her, slamming on their brakes, then making a big show out of zooming around her. On a normal day, if she came up behind a Mercedes braking every two seconds, she would have leaned on her horn and cursed the driver out.

Where was Darnell? The app put him half a block ahead of her. But it was lunchtime, and all the ad agencies had belched out their suit-clad worker bees who were intent on tracking down their kale superfood salads. Usually, Darnell was easy to spot among a crowd, but not when half the men were tall and coiffed and athletic.

He'd explained away the letting go of all James's disloyal clients as a necessary purging to reset the culture at Garrison & Walsh. The boys had come out for dinner on Tuesday and they'd all gone to their favorite sushi restaurant and had a lovely time catching up and not talking about James at all. On Wednesday, Darnell had taken the day off and played golf with some friends. She hadn't decided, yet, what to do with the information she'd stolen from his computer and Darnell hadn't mentioned it, so she was content to forget she'd ever seen it. For a little while there, Gray had even allowed herself to imagine that everything would be okay.

But she still broke into Darnell's phone and installed the tracking app—the one her favorite private investigator had recommended because it was "virtually impossible" for the trackee to find on their device. And while yesterday Darnell had gone straight to work and home again, today, he'd gotten off the train and started wandering around South Street Seaport. When Dante called to say his father hadn't shown up at work and he was worried, she hadn't been surprised—she'd known exactly where Darnell was—but she had been spurred into action. She'd typed up a sick-day message to her assistant and gotten right on Route 4.

Now, an hour later, she was doing a very bad tail job and pissing off everyone on the road. Her cell phone rang and the light right in front of her car turned red. She slammed on her brakes.

"Call from Emma Walsh," her car informed her in its soothing voice.

Gray couldn't ignore a call from Emma. She hit the connect button on her steering wheel, scanning the crowd that had gathered on the corner.

"Hi, Emma. Thanks for calling me back. I wanted to let you know I hired the crew to come demo the garage."

"Gray—"

"They're coming on Thursday. I'll send you the contractor's number."

"Gray!"

"His name is Zack and he's—"

"Gray! Stop talking! I have something to tell you."

Gray's mouth snapped shut. The light turned green. And at that moment, she spotted Darnell. He was walking purposefully down the street, with his back to her. Unlike her, he looked like he knew where he was going. Thank God. She was starting to think that taking a sick day was going to end up being a total waste.

"It's all true," Emma informed her. "I found a Valentine's gift from his mistress."

"What?" Gray slammed on her brakes. The truck behind her stopped about half an inch from her back bumper. In the rearview mirror, Gray could see the sweaty man behind the wheel screaming at her. She glimpsed a spot up ahead and pulled in, even though it was right in front of a fire hydrant. "Emma, no. Are you serious?"

Up ahead, Darnell shoved open the glass door to a gray, granite high-rise. Gray killed the engine, said a quick prayer to the parking gods, and switched the call from her car to her phone. She climbed out and rushed over to the sidewalk.

"Yes. It's a pair of expensive cuff links and the note says it's from someone with the initials JM. I found them last night."

"Who the hell is JM?" Gray asked, wracking her brain even as she rushed to catch up to her husband. She got to the glass-fronted building and brought herself up short. Darnell stood six feet away in front of a bank of elevators. If he turned even slightly to the left, he would see her. Gray stepped sideways, almost tripping over a dog leash held by an elderly woman, and stayed as hidden as she could behind a pillar, while keeping an eye on Darnell.

"I have no idea. I mean, I found some women on his Facebook page, but who knows if it's them or not? He has over five thousand friends on there," Emma said. "But at least now I have something to go on. I have to find this woman, Gray. I have to find out what she knows."

Gray took a deep breath. Her pulse pounded in her temples. She had a decision to make here. Shut down Emma's curiosity and put an end to this nonsense, or dive in. The thing was, she was starting to feel a bit curious herself. *Did* this JM person know something? Had she been close enough to James before he died to have intimate knowledge of his plans? And if Emma was right, and she'd actually been there that night . . . Gray couldn't even go there.

"Send me a picture of the note," she told Emma.

"What? Really? Why?"

Inside the building, Darnell stepped sideways to let a few people out of the elevator, then slid into the car. Gray waited five seconds, then strode into the lobby.

"I want to see if I recognize the handwriting. You never know." She knew she'd never recognize some random woman's handwriting—she just wanted to get off the phone. Later she could come up with an actionable plan.

"Okay. I will. Thanks, Gray. You have no idea—"

"I'm so sorry, Emma. I have to go," Gray said. "But I'll call you back as soon as I can and we'll figure this out."

She hung up on her friend. She had to concentrate. One glance around the lobby gave her nothing. It was just another building with marble floors, potted plants, and piped-in jazz music. Gray stepped over to the elevators and her eyes scanned the directory. Doctors' offices. Dozens of them. She waited for Darnell's elevator to stop, which it did on the twelfth floor. Then it turned around and started its descent. *Bingo.* Gray found the twelfth floor on the directory. Doctors Mira Patel and Helena Wellhammer.

Gray had never heard of either one of them, but if their offices took up the entire twelfth floor of a building this size, they must have been doing well for themselves. She took the elevator up to twelve and exited into a smaller lobby with a double, smoked-glass door dead ahead. The names PATEL & WELLHAMMER were etched into the glass in gold. The door opened and Gray stepped to the side, worried it might be Darnell or that he'd be standing just inside and see her. A short, thin gentleman with a mustache and beard stepped out. He smiled and made to hold the door, but she shook her head and followed him back to the elevator.

"Excuse me," she said, as they waited. "What sort of medicine do doctors Patel and Wellhammer practice?"

"Neuropsychology," he said, his brow knitting over the odd question. What was she doing on their floor if she didn't know?

The elevator arrived and they stepped in, but Gray was now on autopilot. This couldn't mean what she thought it meant. It just couldn't. On the bottom floor, the man got out and looked back at her. "Are you all right, miss?"

"Fine!" She forced a smile. "Just fine."

She walked back outside, no longer caring if she had a ticket or if the car had been towed. Darnell was consulting the doctors for a client. That had to be it. That was what she would tell herself to get her ass home safely and to make herself act normal for the rest of the day. Her car was, in fact, still there, and she got behind the wheel. She'd call Emma once she got over the bridge. Let her friend's marital problems distract her from her own. Alive or dead, the men in their lives were causing nothing but stress.

EMMA

"Hi, Zoe. It's Emma Walsh."

"Emma! Hi!" Zoe trilled. "I just got your email."

"Oh, good. Let me know if you have any questions once you've had a chance to go over it."

Emma had finally compiled a list of friends and acquaintances for Zoe to invite to James's memorial. This had been accomplished through more stalking of his Facebook page, as she'd jotted down the various former Little League coaches and parents of Hunter's friends who'd left condolences. It had, at least, justified her spending more time on there, but she'd yet to uncover any more women with the initials JM. She *had* discovered a few men with those initials, but she wasn't even allowing her brain to go there.

"Great. Will do," Zoe said.

There was an awkward pause and Emma knew it was her turn to speak—her turn to ask the question she'd called to ask. She closed her eyes and sat down at the kitchen island.

"Zoe, would you happen to know whether James had any important contacts with the initials JM?"

"I'm sorry?"

Emma could hear typing in the background. Clearly, Zoe was attempting to multitask. She thought about simply hanging up. Putting herself out of her misery before it really ramped up. Zoe might be a tad silly, but she wasn't stupid. She was going to see right through this line of questioning. Emma had to ask herself how important this really was to her. Was it worth her pride? Worth not being able to look Zoe in the eye at James's memorial?

Answer? Yes.

"The initials JM," Emma repeated, pressing the pads of her fingers into the marble countertop. "Maybe he used it as shorthand on his schedule? It would have been someone he met up with regularly. For lunch or dinner or . . . drinks."

Sex. Someone he met up with for sex.

"Ummmm . . . not that I know of," Zoe said. She stopped typing. "I'd have to check his emails and his calendar. Is this important? Because I'm pretty busy just now. I could maybe take a look and call you back?"

Emma had the distinct feeling that Zoe was rambling—trying to buy herself time. She knew something. She had to know. The assistant always knew. But why bother protecting James at this point? Emma wanted to ask, but she felt a momentary pang of pity for Zoe. She didn't need to be put in the middle of her former boss's marital drama.

"That would be great," Emma said. "Just let me know when you have a chance."

It wasn't until she hung up that she thought it odd that Zoe didn't ask why she was asking. Yes. She definitely knew something. At this very moment, Zoe could be calling JM and warning her that the wife was suspicious. *Shit.* That call had been a complete tactical error. She shouldn't have needed Zoe to check his calendar because she should have been able to check it herself. But she still had no idea where his computer was. That was what she should have asked Zoe about—whether his laptop was still on his desk at the office. Such an innocent question. So easy to answer. And getting hold of his computer would help tremendously.

Emma felt like an amateur. Maybe she did need a PI. She picked up the phone, ready to call Zoe back and beg, but it rang in her hand, nearly startling her out of her chair. The call was from Cantor Feldman. Emma hit *talk*.

"Hello?"

"Emma? It's Evan Cantor."

"Evan!" Her voice broke. Emma stood up and began to pace. "Good to hear from you."

"Yes, well, I wish it were under other circumstances," he said, his gravelly voice low. "I'm so sorry for your loss."

"Thank you," she said. "I—"

"So listen, I'm out of the country at the moment, but I'd like to schedule a formal reading of Mr. Walsh's will when I get back. Say the Friday after the memorial?"

Emma paused in front of the butcher-block counter she used for slicing bread and pulled out one of the bigger knives from the knife block, the *zing* running right down her spine.

"A formal reading?" She turned the blade this way and that, watching it catch the light. It distracted her from the fact that her pulse was doing insane things. "I've read his will. I'm aware of what's in it."

"He didn't tell you?"

"Didn't tell me what?" Her grip on the knife handle tightened.

Evan Cantor let out a world-weary sigh. "Mr. Walsh made some recent changes to his will."

Emma's skull felt suddenly weightless, as if someone had pumped it full of helium. She couldn't believe it. Gray was right. Again. "What kinds of changes?"

"Don't worry, Mrs. Walsh—all joint holdings still go to you," Cantor said. "Mr. Walsh just made a few additional, specific bequests."

"What does that mean? How recent was this?"

"We'll discuss it on the day. If you have any problems with my proposed meeting date and time, please contact my office."

The line went dead. Emma turned the knife around and, before she even realized what she was doing, stabbed it so hard into the butcher-block countertop it made a crack that splintered outward like a lightning bolt.

Unbelievable. How was Gray *always* right? She called Gray's number and it rang a few times, then went to voicemail. She tried again. Same result. Emma groaned in frustration, grateful that the kids were out so she could be as loud as she wanted. She could call Lizzie, but Lizzie wasn't who she wanted to talk to right now. Gray would know what happened next—whether she could contest the will, if she had any rights.

This was when living in the same town as her best friend/lawyer came in handy. Emma grabbed her bag and headed for her car.

GRAY

Darnell seemed perfectly normal. He had come home early and was helping her make dinner. He was making conversation. Talia Lennox was
getting promoted to senior vice president and would move into James's
old office. Zoe Wang would take over as her assistant. Dante had joined
the business book club, much to everyone's surprise. Darnell said nothing
about doctors Wellhammer and Patel.

Gray pulled the lasagna out of the oven and placed it on a cooling
rack. Darnell reached for it, but she slapped his hand away.

"It needs to rest for fifteen minutes," she said.

"And we'll still be eating two hours earlier than usual," he said, turning off the water in the sink and leaning back against the kitchen counter.
"Wonder what we'll do with all that free time tonight."

Gray would normally have been intrigued by this invitation, but tonight she had to force a smile. Never in her life had she felt scared to talk
to her husband, and she refused to feel that way now. She flat out refused.
She opened the refrigerator and pulled out arugula, carrots, and tomatoes
to get started on the salad like it was any other day.

"So, which doctor are you seeing? Wellhammer or Patel?"

Darnell, who had gone back to washing pots and pans, froze. The water continued to rush over his hands.

"Where did you hear those names?" he asked.

"What kind of doctors are they, anyway?" she asked, wanting to see what he'd say.

Darnell brought his fist down on the water spigot and turned around. "Gray, where did you hear those names?"

She stepped away from the counter and crossed her arms over her chest. "I followed you."

"You *what?*"

"Darnell, earlier this week you went around causing a stir, cutting ties with James's clients without consulting me or anyone at work. Then, today, I get a panicked call from Dante telling me you didn't show up at the office," she said—which was the truth, if not all of the truth. "Excuse me if I'm worried."

"So instead of calling me to see where I was, you *followed* me? How did you even find me in the first place?" he demanded. "What the fuck, Gray?"

The doorbell rang.

"Don't talk to me that way."

"I'll talk to you however the fuck I want to talk to you!" Darnell roared.

He picked up the burning-hot casserole dish, full of steaming lasagna, and hurtled it across the room with both hands. Gray screamed as it shattered against the wall, taking down a one-of-a-kind painting with it and splattering sauce and noodles up and down the walls. The crash was magnificent.

"Darnell!" Gray shouted.

"Gray?" Emma's voice, coming from the front hall. "What's going on?"

It was as if Darnell didn't hear her. He advanced on Gray like an angry bull, nostrils flared, eyes wild, one hand outstretched as if he meant to choke her. This was not her husband. This was someone she didn't recognize.

James. James Walsh behaved this way. Not her Darnell.

"Darnell!" It was Emma who screamed his name. Gray saw her enter the room behind her husband. "What are you doing?"

He didn't even seem to register that Emma was there.

"Darnell! Stop!" Gray cried, hoping to wake him up, hoping to snap him out of it. Before he could back her into the corner, she ducked and spun, sweeping his legs out from under him in one swift tae-kwon-do move she didn't even know she remembered from college. He crashed to the floor, all three hundred–plus pounds of him going down in a flailing mass, his head banging against the thick edge of the counter as he went.

"Gray!" Emma breathed, rushing over to her.

"Oh my God!" Gray's hands covered her mouth. What had she done?

Darnell rolled over onto his knees and curled into a ball, head down between his elbows. It was a grotesque version of child's pose, all bulging shoulders and thick thighs straining against the fabric of his thousand-dollar wool pants. He rocked there, forward and back, forward and back, as if revving up to launch himself through the wall ahead of him.

"Gray?" Emma's voice was shaking. "Should I call an ambulance?"

"No. No." Gray clutched Emma's hand.

"Darnell?" she whispered, tears streaming down her face. She half expected him to turn on her, teeth bared, snarling. Her fingers trembled as she released Emma and reached out to touch his arm, kneeling next to her husband. "Darnell? Are you all right?"

He looked up at her then, but he wasn't growling. His eyes were full of sorrow and fear. Tears coursed down his cheeks; his forehead furrowed with deep, wavy creases. There were welts on the palms of his hands, burns from grabbing the casserole dish.

"Darnell?" she wept. "What's going on with you? What's happening?"

He didn't answer. He simply curled into her, head on her knee, turned on his side, and sobbed. Gray looked up at Emma, who was white as a sheet, and knew it was going to be a long night.

EMMA

When Gray invited Emma over for a run that Sunday morning, she'd thought they were actually going to talk. Preferably over one of Gray's fantastic yogurt parfaits. But no. When Gray said run, she meant run, and now Emma was a sweaty, jellified mess trying to keep up with the much fitter Gray as she crested the third of three hills.

"Okay. I'm done now," Emma said, half doubled over and panting as she hobbled toward her friend. Gray was jogging in place, waiting for her to catch up. "The widow needs a break."

Gray quirked an eyebrow. "Really? You're playing the widow card?"

"Oh, look! A park!" Emma pretended to have just noticed the small playground and benches across the street. "How nice to see our taxpayer dollars at work."

She made her way to the nearest bench and sat. Gray came over and put her foot up on the back to stretch out her quads.

"You really should stretch."

"You really should sit down already and tell me what's going on."

Emma could feel Gray tense up behind her. After the episode at Gray and Darnell's house on Friday night, Darnell had gone upstairs to shower and Gray had told her that the stress of James's death had Darnell up nights. That he wasn't eating or sleeping and his temper had been short. Emma had pointed out that these factors didn't explain away the fact that he'd been about to physically attack Gray and she'd had to whip out some sort of hidden ninja skill to get him to the floor, but Gray had waved her off and said it was fine. Knowing it was not fine, Emma had allowed Gray to usher her to the door because she knew that arguing with the woman was pointless, but she'd fretted all day Saturday until she'd gotten the text inviting her here, and Emma had promised herself she wasn't leaving without answers—without knowing her friend was okay.

Gray did a few more stretches before finally joining Emma on the bench. "It looks like Darnell has CTE. Chronic traumatic encephalopathy. It's something a lot of football and hockey and soccer players suffer from."

"Oh my God, Gray. Of course, I know what it is." Emma had lived with a man who lived for sports, and was raising a son who was an athlete. This particular disease didn't affect baseball players the way it did people in contact sports, but Emma knew everything about it there was to know.

"Well, he's had a few episodes lately, like the one you witnessed on Friday." Gray looked down at her manicured hands. "We're meeting with his doctors later this week so they can explain to me how bad it is. How . . . progressed it is. I'm sorry I didn't tell you about it then, but to be honest, Darnell and I hadn't even talked about it yet and I wanted to know for sure before I told you what was going on."

"Oh, Gray, I'm so sorry." Emma put her arm around her friend. Gray didn't lean toward her or throw her arms around her or anything—she wasn't that sort of person. But she did relax slightly, which Emma took as a good sign. "Is there anything I can do?"

"Please, Emma. No. You're dealing with your own stuff right now. We'll be fine." Gray brushed a nonexistent something off the sleeve of her hoodie. "Just please don't tell Lizzie."

Emma blinked. "Why not?" she said, even as she wondered why she ever would.

"I just don't want her to know my personal stuff," she said. "You know

I'm not friends with her the way you are and I'm not ready for this to be public."

"Okay," Emma said, though she did feel offended on some level. Did she think Emma would be close friends with someone who would run around spouting Gray's business?

"Thanks for telling me," Emma said. "And I know that what happened the other night wasn't technically Darnell's fault, but Gray . . . if you're in danger—"

"I'm not in danger," Gray said automatically.

"I love Darnell. You know I do. But if he has no control over—"

"Emma." Gray said her name like a warning. "You saw how I took him down. I can take care of myself."

KELSEY

"We've been studying DNA for a few weeks now, and predicting eye color, hair color, and other factors based on recessive and dominant genes, but it's not only our physical traits that are determined by our heredity."

Kelsey sat with her laptop open, ready to take notes. She tried not to stare at the odd pattern of adult acne on Mr. Wooster's chin. It looked a bit like Italy. She wondered if that was something he'd inherited from his parents. Or if teaching loudmouthed, overprivileged, prescription-drug-popping teenagers all day had something to do with it.

What would science classes be like at Daltry? She knew she'd still have to meet a basic requirement, but she sure as hell wasn't going to be taking any more of this AP crap. Even if she utterly failed as an actress, biology was not a field she was going to be exploring. It had fucked things up for her enough already. Kelsey itched to check her phone for a notification from the school, but Wooster had no tolerance for cell phones in class and collected them in a butterfly net on the wall at the beginning of each session.

"You can also carry with you various mental illnesses like depression, bipolar disorder, schizophrenia, as well as the propensity toward alcoholism and drug addiction," the professor continued. "Environmental factors also play a role in pushing a person toward these behaviors, but certain combinations of genes have been shown to be a factor."

Kelsey's mouth was dry. Wooster turned to draw a complex gene configuration on the whiteboard. Behind Kelsey, Cory Dean sneezed *"Doomed"* into her ear.

It was the new theory of the day. That Kelsey's father must have been a closet addict. Heroin, most likely. That he'd been shooting up in the driveway and slipped off into the blissful abyss and driven himself through the garage. She glanced across the room at Alexa, but her friend was doodling intently in her notebook.

"Of course, if you have a history of mental illness in addition to a history of addiction, your chances of becoming an addict yourself rise exponentially."

Wooster delivered this news as if it was a fascinating tidbit of information. Rather than a life sentence.

"Poor Kelsey," someone sang in the back of the room. "May as well sign her up for rehab now."

Why did everyone hate her so much? There was no way people were saying these things to Hunter. They wouldn't dare. And Hunter was so much more like her dad than she was. They had no clue. No freaking clue what life had been like in her house.

Kelsey began to shake. Her hands were first, trembling, so slight no one would have noticed. Then her heart joined the party. It felt twenty-five times too small for her body and nitro-charged, like a tiny hornet pinging its way around the empty vessel of her chest. Suddenly all the colors were too bright, and everything blurred at the edges. In a snap, she couldn't breathe.

She had to get out of here. The door? The window? Under the desk? She couldn't be around all these people. But Wooster would never stop talking. The heat was coming on now. Pulsating from underneath her skin, and she knew what was next. She wanted to cry out—get someone's attention—but her windpipe had closed completely.

It doesn't matter it doesn't matter it doesn't matter

Who the fuck do you think you are?

He doesn't matter he doesn't know me he doesn't matter

You think you can talk to me that way? I will fucking end you!

I can't I can't I can't can't can't can't—

They're right, you know. You're doomed. You're a freak. A loser. I'll never let you go.

"Mr. Wooster?" Alexa. Alexa was talking.

"Yes, Miss Osaka?"

"Kelsey needs to go to the nurse."

Her eyes rolled wildly to Alexa, who gripped her forearm firmly, but tightly, and pulled her out of her chair.

"Then why doesn't Kelsey tell me her—"

Wooster stopped talking as Alexa dragged Kelsey past the desk. The door slammed. Their shoes squeaked down the hall. *Too far. Too far. Too far.* And then a shove, a blast, and air.

"Breathe! Holy shit, Kelsey, breathe!"

Kelsey doubled over and sucked in the coldness that surrounded her. Purple spots burst across her vision. There was a gum wrapper in the grass. The scent of burning leaves in the air. Paper pumpkin decorations hung in one of the lower building's windows.

"Are you okay?" Alexa's hand was on her back and her face tipped into view.

Kelsey managed to nod, then cough, spittle flying from her lips.

"That was a bad one, huh?" Alexa asked as Kelsey tentatively stood up. She turned into her friend and they found themselves in an awkward hug, Kelsey gripping the back of Alexa's sweater for all she was worth. "You scared the shit outta me."

"I hate him, Alexa. I hate him so much."

"I know," Alexa replied. "It's okay. It's okay." She pulled back and looked Kelsey in the eye. "Hey. Kels. Look at me. He's gone. He can't fuck with you anymore, all right? He's gone."

Kelsey nodded—though she wasn't so sure about that—then sat down on the grass, but then, suddenly, she was crying. Huge, fat sobs that just came and came and came. Alexa put her arm around her as Kelsey tried and failed to get ahold of herself. She was so goddamned sick of crying. Why did he do this to her? Why had he made her this way? Then, all the way across the quad, another door opened and out strolled Willow. Kelsey sucked in a breath at the sight of the older girl. Willow had driven to school that morning. Willow could get her out of here. It didn't matter that they'd barely spoken lately. They were practically family.

Willow moseyed toward them, all combat boots and blue eyeliner. It was only third period. There was no way she was supposed to be out here. But then, neither were they. Willow paused in front of them and kicked Kelsey's sneaker with her toe. Not lightly.

"What the fuck are you crying about?" Willow demanded. She was obviously still pissed about what happened after the cast list went up.

"Her dad just died, asshole," Alexa replied, fabricating an excuse on the spot, as the best of best friends do.

Willow laughed. "Please. You hated the guy. That's not why you're crying."

"I didn't hate him," Kelsey said thickly. "*He* hated *me*."

Willow rolled her eyes. "Oh, boo freaking hoo. Some of us never even had a father to hate."

Kelsey glared at Willow for a suspended moment, daring her to say another word. If she did, she was going to launch herself off the ground and tear her fucking throat out. She could do it, too. In her current state, she could do anything.

Then, her eyes fell on Willow's hand. Her thumb was crooked into her pocket, and on her finger was a gold filigree ring.

"Is that my *mom's*?"

Willow shoved both hands fully into her pockets.

"What? No."

"Why do you have my mom's ring?" Kelsey demanded, standing up.

"Whatever." Willow yanked the ring off and threw it at Kelsey. It bounced off her chest and way too close to a grate in the walkway. Alexa dove for it and stood up to hand it to Kelsey. "I was going to give it back anyway," Willow added.

Kelsey fumbled with the ring and shoved it on her own finger. "What the hell is the matter with you? You haven't taken enough from my family?"

"Shut up," Willow said. "And you'd better not tell your mother or Hunter about this."

"Are you kidding me? They should know there's a thief walking around our house," Kelsey shot back.

Willow's eyes flashed with fear, but then she relaxed. "You're not gonna tell."

"Watch me."

"If you tell them, I'll tell everyone what I know about you," Willow said. "You wanna risk that?"

Kelsey glared at her.

"What's she talking about, Kelsey?" Alexa asked.

Kelsey licked her lips and looked sideways at her friend. "Nothing."

Willow laughed. "Yeah. That's what I thought."

"Stay out of my mother's room," Kelsey said through her teeth.

"Maybe I will, maybe I won't," Willow replied. Then she turned and walked away.

"What the hell was that?" Alexa said. "I thought you guys were friends."

"Please." Kelsey sniffled, looking down at the delicate ring on her pink-from-the-cold finger. "She doesn't even know what that word means."

LIZZIE

Emma placed Lizzie's vegetarian baked ziti in the preheated oven, then popped open a bottle of white wine. Willow had gone straight upstairs to Hunter's room, where they were now playing some ridiculous online game that involved guns and dance-offs. Lizzie did not understand how her intelligent, creative daughter could spend time numbing her brain out like that, but it wasn't a habitual thing, so she let it go. When she and Hunter had first met in grade school, it had been Minecraft they bonded over, and she sometimes wondered whether the two of them had anything in common outside a love of all things pixelated.

"So, I talked to the estate lawyer yesterday," Emma said, pouring out a generous helping of wine for herself and another for Lizzie. "For about five seconds."

Lizzie took a long sip of her wine and then placed her glass down carefully on the counter. She started to pull out plates from the cabinets, while Emma went for the napkins and cutlery.

"Only four," Emma told her. "Kelsey is going over to a friend's after rehearsal."

Lizzie distributed the plates around the kitchen island, wondering if Emma and her family ever used the huge, sunken dining room at the back of the house. The furniture in there was all Lexington antiques. The table alone was probably worth a fortune. Yet she'd never seen the family gathered in there, or even seen a picture of a special event put on in the dining room. Even for birthdays, they all gathered around a cake or a pie on the kitchen island or outside on the patio by the pool.

"What did he say?" Lizzie asked.

"Actually, he said James made some *recent changes* to his will," Emma told her, widening her eyes like *can you believe it?* "He made *additional specific bequests*, was the way he put it. He scheduled a formal reading for after the memorial."

"Wow." Lizzie had no idea what to say to that. Her mind raced, looking for the appropriate response to land on. But what? Why would James have done that? How recent was recent? It was almost as if, somehow, he'd known he was going to die. Then, a thought hit her so fast it tumbled right through her brain and out her mouth. "What if he named names?"

"What do you mean?" Emma asked.

"Sorry." Lizzie shook her head, blushing. "I mean, what if he named the mistress—JM—in the will? What if he left her something specifically? Then you'd know who she is."

Emma crumpled a napkin in her palm. "Why would he do that? He'd have to know I'd be the first person to be made aware. He'd be caught."

"Yes, but he'd also be dead."

Emma made an odd laughing/choking sort of sound.

"Sorry. Sorry. God, I'm bad at this." Lizzie sucked down some more wine and let out a breath. "What I mean is, maybe he figured that if you were looking at the will, that would mean he was gone, so what does he care if he's caught?"

Emma frowned, mulling this over, and sat heavily on a stool across from Lizzie. "Shit. What if he *did* name her? Oh my God, I'm never going to make it. I'm going to die of curiosity first."

"When is this happening, exactly?" Lizzie asked.

"Next Friday," Emma replied.

"Do you think he'll call her?"

"Who?" Emma said.

"The lawyer. Do you think he'll call JM? I mean, if she's named. She'd have to be there, right? Isn't that how it works? Whoever's named in the will is there for the reading?"

Emma doubled over in her chair and Lizzie jumped up, afraid her friend was going to pass out. What was the matter with her? Why couldn't she keep her inane and highly inappropriate thoughts to herself?

"Are you okay?" Lizzie placed her hand on Emma's back.

"I'm fine. Just the thought of that." Emma covered her mouth with one hand and stood up. "I was going to bring the kids. Maybe I shouldn't. They can't handle having some random woman thrown in their faces."

She leaned back against the refrigerator as if it were a life raft and the only thing standing between her and the abyss. "Is that really how it works?" she said, her eyes desperate as she looked at Lizzie.

"I don't know. It's how it works in the movies." Lizzie went to the sink, wet a towel with cool water, and handed it to Emma, who immediately placed it on her forehead. "But who knows if that's how it happens in real life?" She hugged herself for half a second and then the timer went off, indicating the ziti was ready. Upstairs, the kids cheered and hollered over some moment well-played.

"You should call Gray," Lizzie told Emma, as much as it pained her to say it. "If anyone has the answers, Gray does."

GRAY

Gray hadn't sat on a bench in Central Park since she was in her twenties. Once they'd moved out of the city, they'd never come back to the park for leisure activities. It was just a place to cut through, an obstacle when traveling from Darnell's office to the ballet at Lincoln Center or to the West Side Highway and the quickest route home. But on that Thursday, after meeting with Dr. Patel, Gray and Darnell simply sat, hand in hand, staring at the leaves as they drifted down from the trees. A little girl in a bumblebee costume was having professional Halloween pictures taken, posing on a nearby rock.

"We'll get a second opinion. A third," Gray said. "And I'll do research myself."

Darnell took a breath. She thought, for one dreadful beat of her heart, that he was going to disagree with her. But his chest deflated and he said, "Okay."

"I just wish you'd told me sooner. We could have gotten ahead of this. We could have—"

"There's no getting ahead of it. Not really. You heard what the doctor said. CTE is progressive. There's no cure."

Yes, Gray had heard what the doctor said. She'd heard that the headaches Darnell had been getting for the past year weren't caused by stress, but by traumatic brain injury. She'd heard that, yes, these sorts of concussion-based injuries were slightly more common in running backs and receivers—people who got tackled and not the people who did the tackling—but that it wasn't so far out of the ordinary as to be a shock. She'd heard that Darnell would go through periods where he was completely normal—the kind, patient Darnell she and her boys had always known and loved. But that there would also be random lashing out, like thrown casserole dishes, and impulsive decisions, like letting half their clientele go. Short-term memory loss was common. And depression. And suicidal thoughts.

"We may have found the one thing you can't fix, my love."

Darnell said it as a joke, but it caused a gag reflex so strong inside of Gray that she was barely able to keep herself from vomiting on his shoes. Gray's grip on her husband's hand tightened. It didn't matter what he said, or what the doctor believed, or what the research claimed. She *would* fix this. She would gather him up in their marriage and be his tether to the world.

"Maybe I should retire," Darnell said, and shook his head. "Sonofabitch. If only James hadn't—"

"It's fine," Gray interrupted. She refused to let him go down that road. He was better off without James Walsh. Emma was better off without James Walsh. If that man were here, he would still be another problem to solve, not part of the solution. "We don't need James. I'll handle this. *We'll* handle this."

Gray was in control. Gray was always in control.

EMMA

One thing Emma had always loved about living all the way down at the end of the cul-de-sac, at the bottom of the valley, was the trees in the fall. There was always one week when they seemed to suddenly burst into their natural splendor, the reds and oranges so vibrant it was like driving through a tunnel of fire. As she drove home from Whole Foods that Thursday morning, the trees were having their moment. She slowed to a crawl and stared through the windows, owning her sense of awe.

She could still enjoy these things. Even with what she'd been through, going through what she was going through. There was still beauty in the world, James and his divorce papers and JM be damned. Part of her did wonder, though, whether JM had ever seen James's sprawling home. Whether she'd coveted it. Was James really divorcing her to be with this other woman? If so, she was out there somewhere, too, in mourning, all her dreams for the future dashed.

Emma didn't want to think about that. She wanted to see JM as a villain. That was about all she could handle.

As she slowly coasted past the top of the driveway that led downhill to the garage, a flash of light caught her eye. She hit the brakes and they squealed. There was a van down there. And some sort of construction vehicle—bright yellow and pristine looking, like it had just rolled off the lot. But something else was off. With a gasp, she realized what it was. The garage was completely gone.

Emma executed a sharp turn and bumped over the top of the driveway. Her throat closed over as she took the steep hill. Never would she understand why the builders didn't find a way to grade this damn driveway better. If they had, there was a good chance her husband would still be alive, and she wouldn't even know about JM. She'd still be miserable, yes, but blissfully, ignorantly miserable.

Emma pulled her SUV up behind the—back-hoe, was it?—and killed the engine. Three men were tossing boards and siding into a dumpster that already sat on a flatbed. They were almost done cleaning up. All that was left of the garage was the flat, concrete surface of the floor. In its place was a POD, white and red and shimmering in the sunlight.

"Um . . . who's in charge here?"

"That would be me."

A tall, gangly man with a white mustache and shaggy hair sticking out from under a panama hat walked over to her, tugging off his leather gloves. "You the owner?" He checked his phone. "Emma Walsh?"

"Yes. And you are?"

"Zack," he said. "Gray told me you'd be out."

"I was out. For all of two hours. How did you do all this in less than two hours?"

"I promise my guys a steak dinner and they get after it," he said, and two of the men by the dumpster hooted.

"Anyway, we're all set here. All your stuff's in the POD over there." He tilted his head. "We'll haul the rest of this junk away by the end of the night."

"Okay." Emma blinked in the sun, confused. "I don't . . . What do I owe you?"

Zack was already climbing behind the wheel of the van. "Gray took care of it," he said, and slammed the door before she could ask anything more. He reached out and handed her a card. "Gimme a call when you're ready to rebuild."

Within seconds, all the men were gone, leaving her with a dumpster, a POD, and a—front loader? She had no idea. She was about to call Gray and tell her she'd pay for her own damn demolition, when her phone vibrated in her pocket. Oakmont Day School.

Her heart skipped a beat, as it had whenever one of the kids' schools called midday. What was it? Fever? Throw-up? Bullying? School shooting?

"Hello?"

"Mrs. Walsh, it's Mr. Fletcher at Oakmont Day."

Mr. Fletcher. Kelsey's guidance counselor.

"Yes?"

"Everything's fine, but Kelsey's had another panic attack. We think you should come pick her up."

ANOTHER PANIC ATTACK. That was what he had said. *Another.* As if this had been one of many. As if the school was at its wits' end with her daughter. If this was *another* panic attack, shouldn't Emma have been informed of them before now? When had this started? After James's death? Before?

She speed-walked into the school, groceries still jammed into the trunk of her car, ice cream undoubtedly melting, meat going bad, and signed in at the office. Kelsey was sitting on one of the cots in the nurse's office, one arm gripped over her stomach, looking wan.

Had she thrown up? Maybe the counselor had been mistaken.

"Honey! Are you okay?" Emma put the back of her hand to Kelsey's forehead. Cold. Clammy.

"I'm fine, Mom. Can we just go?"

Kelsey slid from the cot, pulling her backpack with her, and headed for the door. Emma was torn between wanting to do whatever her daughter needed and getting some answers. Mr. Fletcher was nowhere to be seen, but the nurse, Ms. Fraimen, was at her desk. Emma let the door swing closed behind Kelsey and leaned in over the computer.

"Oh, you can sign her out at the front office," the woman said with a kind smile.

"No, I know, it's . . . Can you tell me . . . has this happened before?" Emma asked.

Ms. Fraimen offered a patient smile. "Second time this week. Earlier this week it was Biology. Today it was History."

"So, twice?"

"I think three or four times now, total. Since the beginning of the year." The nurse tapped some keys on her computer. "Yes, twice in September." She turned the screen toward Emma so she could read the notes. "The first couple weren't too bad, and we see these sorts of things a lot when eighth graders transition over to the high school. She seemed to level out, but then this week . . . well, they were doozies."

Doozies. Is that the medical term? Emma thought, but did not say.

"Thank you." She walked out after her daughter, vowing to call Mr. Fletcher later and read him the riot act. Four panic attacks. Four. And this was the first she was hearing of it? This was unacceptable. She hoped to God Kelsey got accepted at Daltry, because she wasn't staying here, that was for damn sure.

Kelsey was already in the car, head back, eyes closed. Emma slammed her door.

"Can we talk about this later?" Kelsey asked before Emma could even open her mouth to speak. "I just want to take a nap."

"Have you not been sleeping?" Emma asked, practically peeling out of the parking lot. She knew that lack of sleep could lead to anxiety attacks. She'd been there herself. Maybe this was why Kelsey had seemed to be so moody lately, so quick to cry. Aside from the loss of her father, if she wasn't sleeping, she'd be emotionally on edge.

Kelsey lifted her shoulders and let them fall heavily. "Not really. Every time I close my eyes, I just see Dad. Like, lying there. Dead."

Emma's heart split in two. How could she not know this? Why hadn't Kelsey told her?

"So I've mostly just been binge-watching things on Netflix. You're right, by the way. *Gilmore Girls* is really good."

Her daughter had been watching *Gilmore Girls* without her?

Emma pulled the car up to a stoplight and breathed in and out. She could smell the produce in the back of the car and hoped it wasn't all going bad right under her nose. Clearly, she should have gone shopping earlier. Or emptied the groceries before coming to school. She couldn't do anything right. Not one, little, thing.

She had promised herself she would be there for her kids. That they would talk about things. That this disaster wouldn't break them apart, but make them stronger. The depths of her failure on all counts astounded her.

"Well, the next time you want to watch *Gilmore Girls*, call me," she told Kelsey. "Because once you get to the Logan years, we're going to need to discuss."

Kelsey smirked. "Sounds like a plan, Mom."

She was asleep before Emma pulled into the front driveway.

KELSEY

Kelsey grabbed the cardboard box out of the back of her closet, the items inside rattling around. She used her foot to kick the door closed and everything in the box shifted to one side and began to tip. With a yelp, she righted it again and took a deep breath. There was no reason to be this nervous. No one was home. And besides, if her dad walked in right now, she'd just throw the whole thing at him and tell him he was right. *Good for you, Dad! I'm an asshole and it's all because of you!*

Not that her father had ever come home in the middle of a weekday. Hell would have to freeze over first. Or every professional athlete would have to up and die of some rare overachiever disease.

She snorted at her own lame joke and went downstairs. Willow had told her she'd be by around six to pick up the box, but she just wanted to get it over with so she wouldn't forget. Plus, Laura Cartwright's mom was picking her up in ten minutes to go play a practice lacrosse game at Gateway Park. She had to keep her skills up if she was going to make JV and have any shot of her father caring that she existed.

At the kitchen door to the garage, Kelsey shifted the box to her hip to reach for the door handle and saw a bat leaning in the corner next to the doorjamb. There was a signature scrawled down the shaft. *Derek Jeter #2,*

1998. It was barely legible, but she had been indoctrinated enough in Yankees lore to know who #2 belonged to. Her heart thunked. What the hell? This was her father's prized possession. What was it doing out of the basement?

Her first instinct was to return it to its case. If her dad found it out of place, he'd definitely blame her. He blamed her for everything. But then a dark, evil little thought wormed its way to the front of her mind.

His most prized possession. If someone had presented this scenario to her dad, he would have 100 percent told them she didn't have the guts.

She picked up the bat, shoved it into one corner of the box, and stuffed the whole thing under the shelving on the far side of the garage.

LIZZIE

"I'm not wearing clothes from Ann Taylor," Willow said sulkily. "Do not even *think* about stepping foot inside that store."

Lizzie raised her palms. Truth be told, *she* didn't even wear clothes from Ann Taylor. Most of what she had in her closet was from the secondhand store in downtown Oakmont or things she picked up down the shore or ordered from the Sundance Catalog when she felt like splurging. Shoved into the very back of her closet under a plastic bag was her one black suit from Banana Republic, which she busted out for funerals only. She'd bought it when her father passed on and, luckily, it still fit.

"Fine. Then where would you like to go?" Lizzie asked.

Willow looked around, hands in the pockets of her long cardigan sweater. She splayed them out at her sides, like wings, bringing to mind a vampire bat. "Um, home? Why are we even at the mall?"

"I told you. You need something to wear to James Walsh's memorial." Lizzie kept walking, only now realizing that half the stores in the mall had turned over since the last time she was here. Yankee Candle Company was not going to help her. Nor was Teva. Or the Christmas Shoppe. Where were all the clothing stores?

"I have plenty of black clothes, in case you hadn't noticed," Willow said, trudging along next to her mother. A couple of girls walking by looked Willow up and down and she actually snarled at them. "Besides, I thought we *weren't spending money right now*," she said, adding air quotes for maximum sarcasm.

Lizzie paused in front of a shop that appeared to sell only wind chimes and dream catchers. Her nerves were frayed and she had the same sense of impending doom she'd carried with her back when she was commuting into the city and that random sniper was on the loose, causing terror up and down the eastern seaboard. She vividly remembered standing at the bus stop near her parents' home and fully believing that if the number 108 didn't come around the corner in the next five minutes, she was going to be shot in the head.

Everything could implode at any moment. That was her ultimate takeaway from James Walsh's death. What if she lost Willow? What if she lost Emma? What if she lost their house? The closer they got to the memorial, the more she felt as if they were all sitting on a runaway train and she was the only one who realized it, and she didn't have the power to pull the emergency brake. There was nothing she could do to stop the inevitable devastation. The only choice was to wait it out and hope for an epiphany that would save them all.

Lizzie took a deep breath. *Be the change. Be the change. Be the change.* Someone touched a wind chime and it made a beautiful trilling melody. It felt like a sign. She needed to calm the hell down. Before long, she would have her answers. One way or another, she'd be able to move forward.

"Mom?"

Lizzie looked her daughter in the eye. "Some things are worth spending money on. And yes, I know you have plenty of black clothes, but you can't wear ripped jeans and an over-washed sweatshirt to a memorial service. You need to show some respect."

Willow tipped her head back and groaned toward the skylights two stories above her head. "I could have just come here myself, you know."

Lizzie gave her daughter a pointed look.

"Oh, what? Now you don't trust me around stores?" Willow demanded.

"Go three months straight without being delivered to my home by a police officer, and we'll talk trust."

"Fine," Willow snapped. "Let's go to Forever Twenty-One."

"Thank you." Lizzie kissed her daughter on the forehead and said a prayer for inner peace.

EMMA

Emma sat down gently on the edge of her daughter's bed. The teacup on the table was empty, and the white noise machine she'd dug out of the closet was set to ocean sounds. It was the same machine Kelsey had in her room as a baby, and Emma could still predict down to the millisecond when the seagulls would caw. It had been the soundtrack of her long, sleepless nights, breastfeeding and soothing and crying and yawning. She didn't miss that level of exhaustion, but part of her wished she could reset the clock and do just about everything differently.

"How're you feeling?" Emma asked.

"Oh, like I'm about two years old." Kelsey pulled the blankets up under her chin. "You sure you don't want to dig out the farm animal mobile? I know you've got it somewhere."

"That seems like overkill," Emma joked. She glanced around, still orienting herself in the new furniture configuration. The curtains on the bay window, now right behind Kelsey's bed, were flimsy at best. "Are you sure you want the bed here? The sunlight must hit you first thing in the morning. That can't be helping with this whole sleep situation."

"I'm not moving it back," Kelsey said.

Emma raised an eyebrow.

"What? The room has better feng shui this way."

Wrong. The girl was completely wrong. But Emma wasn't about to correct her. Not when her eyelids were already getting droopy.

"We'll talk about it in the morning." She leaned in to give her daughter a kiss on the cheek.

"I'm not moving it," Kelsey repeated.

"Fine, fine." Emma waved her off as she stepped to the door and shut the light. "Sleep well, honey. No phone, and I'm taking the computer."

"Okay."

Emma grabbed the laptop off the desk. It came to life when she touched it, opening directly to eBay. She slapped it closed and tucked it under her arm. She'd check on Kelsey again in fifteen minutes. Hopefully the chamomile and lavender would have done the trick by then.

Downstairs, Emma placed the computer on the kitchen counter and walked over to what had formerly been the garage door. Now it opened on to a big slab of nothing and a POD storage system. It was so surreal, standing there at the top of the step down to the open world. It was almost as if the garage had never existed. As if James had never been there.

The doorbell rang, startling her half to death. Emma hurried over to keep whoever it was from ringing again and swung open the door.

"Gray! Is everything okay?"

Gray gave her an irked sort of look. "Well. It's like we've swapped places."

Emma bit her lip.

"Everything's fine!" Gray said. "Did you forget?"

Gray whipped out a stack of papers—a list of names. Emma's eyes went wide. "Is that the list for the memorial?"

"Confirmed RSVPs," Gray said, striding inside. "And there are four female JMs on here."

Emma was about to close the door when headlights flashed, and a car pulled into the front circle behind Gray's. It was Lizzie. Emma couldn't believe it, but she *had* forgotten. Between coming home to find her garage obliterated and getting the call from the school, she'd entirely spaced that she'd made this date with Gray to go over the list, and invited Lizzie to join them. Maybe she was growing? Maybe it was a sign that she should just drop it like Lizzie had suggested so many times?

She waited for Lizzie to get out of her car and gave her an air kiss at the door.

"How's it going?" Lizzie asked, toying with the silver rings on her fingers.

"Fine. Gray's already inside."

"Great." She didn't even sound sarcastic when she said it, and she seemed oddly distracted as she breezed past Emma into the kitchen.

"Oh, hello," Gray said coolly.

"Don't be so happy to see me, Gray," Lizzie replied. "It's embarrassing."

Emma rolled her eyes. Sometimes she thought her friends were going to actually duel over her. She closed the door and joined them.

Gray had the eight pages, typed, single-spaced, laid out on the counter-top. Emma saw that the names were already highlighted, but that was not where her focus fell.

"All these people are coming to the memorial?" Her voice was stran-gled.

"James was pretty popular," Lizzie stated.

"It's gonna be a scene," Gray confirmed. "Pretty much everyone Darnell and James ever did business with is going to be there."

"How's Darnell doing with all this?" Emma asked, watching her friend carefully.

"Fine. He's fine," Gray replied. She looked past Emma at the wine fridge. "Do you have any rosé?"

Emma knew she was skating on thin ice even coming close to the Darnell subject with Lizzie around, so she resolved to keep herself in check.

"I do," Emma said. "And truffles. I bought them this afternoon."

Once the wine was poured and the chocolate distributed, Emma and her friends gathered around her laptop and brought up James's Facebook page. Jennifer Mahone was on the confirmed RSVP list, and Lizzie actually whistled when she saw her profile picture.

"Oh, Darnell *loves* her," Gray supplied, taking a sip of her wine. "If she's on ESPN, I'm not allowed to change the channel."

Emma squirmed in her seat. She had this awful sense that James was leaning over her shoulder. His derisive laughter was clear as a bell in her ear.

"But I'm sure it's not her," Lizzie said, patting her knee in a comforting way. "She's clearly not James's type."

"What? Young? Hot? Successful?" Emma asked.

Lizzie took a slug of wine and pulled her rings on and off.

"What about Jelena Martinez? Look her up," Gray directed.

Emma typed the name in the search bar. "There are a few, but this one's in New York." She clicked on her profile. "Doesn't look like they're connected on here, but . . . yeah, she's a board member at The Willis Foundation. James was on that board for a while, too."

"Must be her. But she's ancient," Lizzie said, reaching over to click on a picture of Jelena with her adult children and grandkids. "I think you can cross that one off the list."

"Unless he had some kind of fetish," Gray said.

Emma laughed, and only then did Lizzie laugh, too.

"What about Janet McElroy?" Emma said. "Did she RSVP?"

"Yep. She's on here," Gray said, and chucked her chin at the computer. "Let's see her."

Emma brought up her profile. Her friends tilted their heads in opposite directions and Emma had to take a bite of chocolate to keep from giggling. Why was this fun? They were trying to pinpoint which of these women her husband was sleeping with, and she felt giddy.

"Maaayyybeee," Lizzie considered.

"She does look a little like you," Gray conceded.

"Is that what it is?" Lizzie asked. "I was going to say she looked familiar."

And that's when Emma understood. She was giddy because her

friends were getting along. She'd finally found the thing that bonded them: mutual distaste for her husband.

"I don't know. She looks a bit stick-up-her-butt to me," Emma said. "What's the last name on your list?"

"Jasmine Missoni."

Emma gulped. She did not like the sound of that.

Lizzie stopped chewing on a white chocolate truffle. "Isn't she a model?"

Fingers trembling, Emma typed in the name. Instantly, half-naked pictures of a woman with shimmering South Asian skin, perfectly thick eyebrows, and an intricate tattoo across her back filled her screen.

"Oh, God, I really hope it's not her," Emma said.

And then she and her friends doubled over laughing.

GRAY

Dr. Patel was a small woman. In her sixties at least, she wore huge red-framed glasses and had her hair mid-parted and pulled back in a sleek bun, like an Indian Ruth Bader Ginsburg. But her handshake was admirably firm, and when she welcomed Gray into her office, she did not go over to her desk and sit, but stood dead center in the room and clasped her hands in front of her.

"Thank you for seeing me," Gray said, tugging off her caramel-colored driving gloves. "I realize you have a packed schedule." Considering the fact that she hadn't been able to squeeze her in for five minutes all week long.

"Mrs. Garrison, as I'm sure you're aware, I cannot speak to you about your husband's condition without him present. Doctor–patient confidentiality."

"No, no, of course," Gray said. Oddly, a nervous laugh escaped her. It seemed there really was a first time for everything. She straightened her shoulders, her Birkin bag dangling from her forearm, and reminded herself of who she was. Gray Garrison. Best of New Jersey Attorneys list ten years running. Town Council president. Food Bank of New Jersey board member. Never intimidated. Never thrown off her game. "I was just in the city for meetings today, and I was hoping you could clarify something for me."

"You've been using the internet," Dr. Patel said with a kind smile.

Gray felt a flash of irritation. How dare this woman assume she was just like every idiot off the street? But yes, of course, she'd been *using the internet*. Who could resist the siren song of Google and WebMD when her husband had basically been issued a death sentence?

She cleared her throat, clinging to a vestige of control over the conversation. Part of her wanted to turn tail and run for the street, maybe pop over to Fifth Avenue and do some damage on her AMEX Black. But she reminded herself she wanted these answers. Ignorance was never bliss. She took a deep breath.

"You've obviously studied Darnell's brain scans at length and you discussed the quote-unquote *possible side effects* of his condition."

"Yes . . ."

"Knowing what you know about the current state of his brain," Gray said, steeling herself, "could he be violent? Could he . . . actually hurt someone even though he's normally a gentle person?"

"Yes," Dr. Patel confirmed, completely placid.

"And could he black out? Could he . . . forget something he'd done?"

"Yes," Dr. Patel repeated.

Gray swallowed and pressed her palms together, doing everything she could to keep herself steady. "Is it possible, in your opinion, that he could black out an entire night?"

"Yes," Dr. Patel said. "At this stage, that is very possible."

LIZZIE

It wasn't that Lizzie hadn't had a date since Willow was born. She had, in fact, had a couple of semi-serious relationships. But the last one of those had ended three years ago, and the dates since then had been spotty at best. There was something about going out with Ben—not just hanging out at the café or in her shop—that was making her almost sick with nerves. That was how she knew she really liked him.

When he came to pick her up, Willow answered the door before she could get there and gave him the third degree, as if Lizzie were her daughter and Ben, her prom date.

"Have you ever been married?"

"Once, for two years. Turned out she didn't want to be married to a man."

"How old are you?"

"Forty-three."

"Any kids?"

"None."

"You sure about that?"

That was when Lizzie had interrupted. She'd placed the lovely wild-flowers Ben had brought her into her daughter's hands, asked her to make sure to put them in water, and walked out to Ben's car with him right in step with her, though her ankles were irritatingly wobbly.

Now they were sitting across the table from each other at Armando's, her favorite Italian restaurant in Oakmont, and the conversation was flowing so well she wondered why she'd ever felt nervous. She knew how to talk to Ben. Of course she did. They'd been talking with each other almost nonstop since they'd met, and he'd yet to say anything that stumped her or made her feel uncomfortable or shocked her in the slightest.

"You know, you never did tell me what you did before opening the café," Lizzie said, as the waiter cleared their dinner plates.

"No?" Ben averted his eyes. "I could have sworn I did."

"Nope. When I asked you, you said it was too boring to talk about." Lizzie drained the last of her wine. "Were you an accountant or something?" she joked.

He laughed. "Worse. A hedge fund manager."

Lizzie stared. "No."

"Yes. I worked up in Greenwich, Connecticut. Lived there, too. It was quite the scene."

Lizzie couldn't believe it. When she thought of hedge fund managers she thought of young men with slick hair and expensive suits, donning aviator sunglasses as they slipped behind the wheel of their Ferraris or Bentleys or whatever other cars were worth more than her house. Was Ben . . . rich? No. She could hardly picture him without jam on his sleeve or flour in his hair, let alone wearing Armani.

"I only stayed in it long enough to open the café and have a little to fall back on," he said. "It was definitely too stressful for me."

"A little something to fall back on. Sounds like a dream come true," Lizzie mused as the waitress placed dessert menus in front of them.

Ben tilted his head. "If you ever need advice on anything in that arena, I'm happy to help," he told her. "I do have a way with the numbers, even if it's not what I want to do for a living."

Lizzie smiled at him. "That's really nice of you. I may take you up on it."

"Do you want to get dessert?" Ben asked.

"I don't know," she said, and his smile faltered a bit. "Oh, I don't mean I'm not having a good time, but I'm so full and also, I think you've spoiled me for other people's desserts."

Ben laughed, pleased, and wiped his mouth with his napkin. "Well, luckily I stashed some leftover tarts in the fridge before I left earlier. We can always sneak back there and have a private dessert."

It wasn't exactly an invitation back to his house, but it felt close, and Lizzie blushed. She almost begged off, not knowing where, exactly, it might lead. But then she remembered that feeling she'd had earlier this week—how fragile everything felt. Why not seize the moment?

"Okay," she said. "Sure."

Ben signaled for the check and Lizzie was about to go to the bathroom to freshen up, when Gray and Darnell walked in. Gray wore a perfectly fitted black coat and red gloves, her shiny hair up in a high ponytail and her eyes adorned with shimmery makeup that could have been ripped off Cleopatra's face. It was a small restaurant, and Gray spotted them almost immediately. To Lizzie's surprise, she whispered something to Darnell and came right over.

"Hello, Gray," Lizzie said.

"Look at you two!" Gray said, her enthusiasm completely fake. "Are you on a date?"

Lizzie's face burned with embarrassment. What were they, in high school?

"Yes, in fact, we are," Ben said, and Lizzie felt flattered by how proud he looked.

"That's so nice. Darnell and I are as well."

They all looked over at Darnell, who lifted a hand in greeting. For an awful moment, Lizzie was certain Gray was going to suggest that she and Darnell join them, but then she smiled broadly.

"Well, I just wanted to say hello. You two kids have fun!" Then she swept back over to her husband, greeting people at almost every other table as she went. Sometimes it seemed to Lizzie that Gray didn't talk to people because she wanted to or because she was interested in them, but because she needed to look important. Now, everyone in the room knew that Gray was popular, connected, the belle of every ball. Lizzie, suddenly, surprisingly, felt almost sorry for her.

"She's a character," Ben said.

"Right?" Lizzie replied at a whisper. "But I thought you two were friends."

"I wouldn't say friends. She just helped me figure out how to deal with the town council and their whole security ordinance."

The waitress placed the check on their table and thanked them before whirling away to her next customers.

"Security ordinance?"

Lizzie made a move for her wallet, but Ben waved her off, thank God, and took out a credit card. "Yes, you probably didn't have to deal with this, but I had town-installed security cameras on my building when I moved in and apparently the guy who owned the place before me never had them brought up to code. He was fighting the town on who should pay for them. Which makes sense because they're ridiculously expensive. But Gray knew a guy and helped me get a deal."

"That was nice of her," Lizzie said, but she wasn't surprised. Gray always knew a guy. Lizzie supposed this explained the encounter she'd witnessed at the café the other day. Gray was probably giving him the name of the person to call or helping him with paperwork. She really was involved when it came to the town and the business district, especially. A good citizen all around. Except when it came to Lizzie.

Ben handed the check and card back to the waitress and Lizzie excused herself to head to the bathroom. Gray and Darnell were still waiting at the hostess stand, and Darnell smiled at her approach.

"Lizzie! You look lovely." Ever the gentleman, he leaned in to give Lizzie a quick kiss on the cheek.

"Thank you!" Lizzie said. Was it just her, or were his eyes slightly unfocused? She tried for a better look, but he turned slightly, and she decided to drop it. This was her night, and she wasn't going to start obsessing about Gray and Darnell. "Well, you two enjoy your dinner. I'm just off to the ladies' and then we'll be going."

"Have a good night," Darnell said.

"It was good to see you," Lizzie told him. She quite purposefully said nothing else to Gray.

EMMA

Emma felt conspicuous walking into Oakmont Day in the middle of a sunlit morning, her rubber-soled riding boots squeaking on the shiny wood floors. Everything was hushed, the only noise the sound of the breeze rustling the leaves and the far-off cooing of the chorus rehearsing scales. Kelsey was one of those voices, and the sweet harmony of the song nearly broke her heart. Were her children ever innocent, growing up with the father they had?

Mr. Fletcher gave her a grim smile when she knocked on the wall of his cubicle in the guidance office. It was a crime that at a school this exclusive and expensive, the guidance counselors sat in an open floor plan. Weren't they the only ones who had conversations that other people shouldn't overhear?

"Mrs. Walsh. How are you doing?" he asked, gesturing at the chair next to his desk. He had a small, ceramic jack-o'-lantern full of sugar-free lollipops next to his computer.

"Fine. I'm fine." She placed her bag on the floor and tucked it under the chair, then sat, shoulders tense. "But I'm worried about Kelsey."

He retook his seat and leaned too far back—so far Emma was concerned he might tip over and end up on his spine with his legs and arms in the air like a stranded beetle. The idea of trying to disentangle him from his office furniture did not appeal. The man had a bushy beard, uneven yellow teeth, and breath she could smell from three feet away. Definitely a garlic bagel situation.

"That's understandable," he said after a long pause.

"Four panic attacks since the beginning of the year? Why wasn't I notified?" she asked.

"Well, to be honest, Mrs. Walsh, if we called in the parents every time one of our students had some sort of dramatic episode, you all would have to rent bunk space here."

He gave a short laugh. Emma's face burned.

"I don't find this funny. I'm worried my daughter isn't coping well with her father's death."

"No. Of course." He put his feet flat on the floor and leaned into his desk. "I've already provided your daughter with this reading material, but I'll give it to you as well." He passed her a trifold pamphlet titled DEALING WITH THE DEATH OF A PARENT. "We also have a list of family and pediatric therapists we recommend. If you'd like me to email that to you, I will."

"Yes, please," Emma said.

She detested the idea of sending Kelsey to a therapist, though. Emma's father had been a therapist, and living with him and his platitudes her entire life had made her highly suspicious of the whole practice. Ever since Willow had said that thing about the anger stage of grief, Emma had been hearing her father's voice in her mind—a voice she hadn't heard in real life in over a year. Him patiently explaining to her the five stages of grief after her grandmother died. Explaining her mother's mood swings away with a list out of one of his psychology textbooks. She was only twelve, but she'd still wanted to tell him to stuff it. She'd always hated how whenever anyone in the house had an emotion, he'd nod and smirk like he'd seen it coming. As if his psychology degree somehow made him prescient. It was one of the reasons she avoided therapy herself, even though she knew on some level that she could have used it. The very idea made her bristle. As far as she was concerned, therapists existed to make other people feel stupid.

"If you peruse that document right there, I think you'll see that Kelsey's current behavior is perfectly normal for a girl her age dealing with grief. It's perfectly normal, in fact, for anyone dealing with the sudden, violent loss of a loved one."

Emma opened the pamphlet. In the third section was a list of possible behaviors, including a short temper, rapid mood swings, panic attacks, insomnia, loss of appetite, and isolation.

"I overheard some of Hunter's friends discussing an upcoming memorial?" he asked.

"Yes. It's on Wednesday," Emma told him. "The day after tomorrow."

"Well, I think that will be good for Kelsey. Often kids see the funeral or the memorial as a moment of closure. They need that sense of ritual to help them move on. I'll bet you see things start to turn around after that."

"You think?" Emma said, irritated at herself for wanting to believe in everything this quack was saying.

He nodded, his mouth set in a wise line. "Of course, grief is a process. It's not predictable. But time heals all wounds, as they say. The best thing you can do is be patient and listen if Kelsey wants to talk. Just let me know how it goes."

Feeling dismissed, and really not wanting to prolong this meeting, Emma gathered her bag and shoved the pamphlet inside. "I will. But I would also appreciate it if you would notify me the moment she has another one of these attacks."

"Understood."

"Thank you, Mr. Fletcher."

Emma headed for the outer door of the office, feeling like at least she now had a plan. Get through the memorial, and if Kelsey didn't start to improve, she could call one of these therapists the school worked with. In the meantime, she was going to make sure Kelsey ate right, got the rest she needed, did her homework—all the things she'd always done until her husband up and died. Kelsey clearly needed routine, so it was time to stop indulging her own grief and anger and concentrate on her daughter. Emma was almost out the door when the sound of quiet sobbing distracted her.

"There are other scholarships you can apply for," a woman said in hushed tones. "I promise this is not the end of the world."

"Like you even care."

Emma froze. Was that Willow? Instinctively, she glanced around the corner. Willow sat, slumped in a chair next to her counselor's desk, one hand covering her eyes.

"Willow, honey? Are you all right?"

The girl sat up, startled. Black and purple eye makeup had melted down her face, giving her the look of a maudlin clown. In the space of five seconds, several different emotions flashed through the girl's eyes. Shame, anger, guilt . . . fear? Then back to anger again.

"Excuse me. This is a private session," the counselor said.

Emma ignored her. "Willow, what's wrong? Do you want me to call your mom?"

Willow stood up and shoved past Emma, but not before she very distinctly said through her teeth, "Fuck. Off."

LIZZIE

James Walsh had lived a big life. Much bigger than Lizzie had ever real-ized. She'd known he had an important job—that he'd hobnobbed with famous people and flown all over the world and attended big sporting events. But until she saw the illustrious crowd packed into the owner's suite at Madison Square Garden, the basketball court lit up on the floor down below, she didn't truly understand.

There was something about the whole scene that made her feel nervous—conspicuous somehow. She didn't belong here in her Banana Republic suit and Nine West heels. The women in this room could have bought and sold her business in a blink. That woman over by the bar talking to LeBron James? She could have bought it with the ring on her finger.

Lizzie usually prided herself on not giving a crap about fashion or what she could and couldn't afford. She overhauled bedrooms and living rooms and dens and libraries for people with money to burn, and never gave a second thought to what opinions they might have about her peas-ant skirts or her frizzy hair or the secondhand scarves that made her feel exotic and cozy all at once. But this crowd was intimidating, and even she with her great sense of self couldn't help but feel small.

Ben had offered to come with her, but Lizzie had politely declined, thinking it would be gauche to bring a date to a funeral. Now she was wishing she'd let him come along. Their date had ended with delicious desserts and coffee, and some almost chaste making out in one of the booths at the back of his café. It had been basically perfect—exactly the amount of physical contact Lizzie was ready for at that moment. It was only after she got home that she'd started wishing she'd ripped his sensible oxford shirt off.

"She's over there."

Emma grabbed her arm and Lizzie almost spilled her wine. Most of the night, Emma had been stationed at the top of the room in front of a huge poster of James shaking hands with President Obama, greeting the long line of guests like the princess of some small European nation. Lizzie didn't know how she'd gotten all the way to the far side of the crowd without being waylaid, but here she was.

"Which one?" Lizzie asked. Emma had obviously spotted a JM, and Lizzie scanned the room trying to pick her out of the crowd.

"Janet McElroy. Will you go talk to her? Gray has Jelena Martinez cornered and I'm going to go see if I can find that model. I'm not sure if she showed."

Emma's eyes were like two sparklers on the Fourth of July. There was an excitement in her voice that Lizzie had never heard before. Her friend was taking some odd, sadistic pleasure in this little detective game of hers. Although Lizzie herself was curious, she couldn't understand why Emma was so hell-bent on finding this person. Did she really think JM had something to do with James's death? Or was she just trying to prove that James couldn't play her the fool? It seemed a bit late for that.

"What am I supposed to say?"

She wasn't Gray Garrison, attorney at law. She had no idea how to interrogate a person.

Emma grabbed a flute of champagne off the tray of a passing waiter and handed it to Lizzie.

"Lizzie, you're amazing with people. You make everyone you meet feel comfortable in seconds. Just talk to her, get her chatting about the men in her life. You can do that with your eyes closed."

Lizzie was flattered. She had no idea Emma had noticed this about her, or that anyone would view it as a useful talent.

"Okay then. I'm on it."

"Thanks." Emma kissed her cheek and was gone.

Lizzie gulped the champagne, then placed the empty flute on the bar. She approached Janet McElroy, who was typing something on her phone, alone in a room full of people. Perhaps they had something in common.

"Hello," Lizzie said. "I'm sorry for your loss."

The woman looked up. She had pale, acne-scarred cheeks and her short blond hair was almost white. Her blue eyes locked on Lizzie and there was a sudden spark of recognition. Startled, Lizzie took half a step back, and then her stomach filled with ice water.

"It's Elizabeth, isn't it?" The woman sniffed. "I'm surprised to see you here."

"JJ?"

Lizzie was shocked that the woman remembered her after all this time. She certainly hadn't placed her when she saw her photo on Facebook, though she'd never known JJ's last name, so that might have acted as a particular memory barrier. But seeing her in person was a whole different story. She still held her head at the same, imperious angle. Still had a way of looking down her nose that made Lizzie feel judged. Just being in her presence brought back a rush of memories that Lizzie had kept at bay for what felt like a lifetime.

"I haven't gone by that name in years. Nicknames are a tad childish once you're out of your twenties, no?" The woman tucked her phone into her black clutch purse and reached past Lizzie to pluck a glass of white wine from the bar. "Were you and James still in touch?" She seemed incredulous at the very thought.

"Yes, well, our families are friends." For the first time in her life, Lizzie understood what it meant to feel hot around the collar. Even though she wasn't wearing a collar. And instead of anger making her body temperature rise, it was fear. Pure, white-hot fear.

JJ's—Janet's—eyebrows rose. "That's interesting."

"You're not still with Garrison and Walsh."

Lizzie glanced around the room and saw that Emma was with Gray now, over by the windows, the two of them chatting up Jennifer Mahone. The model must have been a no-show.

"No, no, no. I left ages ago. I have my own advertising firm now. Thank God. That company was a toxic place for women. I'm surprised anyone survived." She looked Lizzie up and down, then sipped her wine. Lizzie cast about for something to say to end this conversation, but she couldn't seem to remember any useful words. Then JJ noticed someone over Lizzie's shoulder. "If you'll excuse me. My girlfriend just arrived."

She turned sideways to slide past Lizzie, but paused a few feet away. "I hope you got everything you wanted, Elizabeth. Some way or another."

EMMA

Emma had finally found Jasmine Missoni. The woman didn't speak a word of English. And while she wouldn't necessarily put it past James to sleep with her anyway, the model had been on the arm of the single hottest male Emma had ever seen in real life—a soccer star from Italy who had almost made her knees buckle telling her that his heart was with her at this terrible time. If Jasmine Missoni could get a man like that, she wasn't looking twice at James Walsh.

Where was Gray? She hadn't seen her since she'd spoken to Jelena. Darnell was in the corner holding court with some of the NFL players in attendance. It was possible Gray was with him and just dwarfed by their bulk. She started across the room, when she felt a hand on her shoulder.

"She's here. Jenny Mahone."

It was Gray, having just walked back in from the hall. She lifted her chin discreetly and Emma saw the woman, wearing a tasteful black fit-and-flare dress, shaking hands with Hunter near James's urn. A tall man with dark skin stood with his hand on the small of her back, his hair salt-and-pepper, a diamond earring winking on his left earlobe.

"Who's that with her?"

"Husband, apparently. He's some bigwig at Under Armour."

Emma surveyed the seemingly perfect couple. Jenny Mahone looked over, as if she could feel the heat of Emma's stare. The second they locked eyes, Jenny looked away.

"Oh, God. Did you see that?" Emma said. "It's her. It has to be."

"Stay here," Gray told her.

It took Gray less than five minutes to separate Jenny from her husband and drag her over to Emma, who was just parting ways with the commissioner of the NHL. It really was amazing how many important people had carved out time to be here. Somewhere, James was feeling mighty full of himself. The thought made Emma want to take his urn and throw it through one of the huge windows over the basketball court. Especially when she saw Jenny up close. Her glowing brown skin, her high cheekbones, her flawless eye makeup.

"Jenny Mahone, this is Emma Walsh."

With all the poise of a woman whose life was lived on television, Jenny held out a hand. "Mrs. Walsh. I'm so sorry for your loss. I wish we could have met under different circumstances."

"Were you sleeping with my husband?"

"Oh, okay. We're just going there," Gray said as Emma glanced from Jenny's outstretched fingers to her face.

The answer was written clear as day. The woman was an ESPN reporter, not an actress. She glanced over her shoulder, and her hair let out a lovely rose-based scent as it moved. Once certain her husband was out of earshot, she leaned in toward Emma.

"Did he tell you that?" she whispered.

"No, I found the cuff links you gave him for Valentine's Day."

Jenny blinked. "That was six years ago."

Tiny blue and purple spots peppered Emma's vision. "You've been together for six years?"

"What? No! Not . . ." She took Emma's arm and tried to tug her toward the wall but Emma wouldn't—couldn't—move. She was worried if she took a step, she might just keel over. Jenny huffed an impatient sigh that made Emma want to slap her.

"Oh, I'm sorry. Are we inconveniencing you?" Gray demanded. "You're the one who slept with her husband."

"Yes, I know. But *my* husband is right over there." Jenny lifted a hand at her side. "We weren't married when James and I were . . . a thing, but we were dating. And we have two kids now and a good marriage. I'm sorry, I know I have no right to ask this, but I just don't want him to know."

"So it's been over for how long?" Emma asked, trying to keep up.

"Over five years. It only even lasted a couple of months," Jenny said quietly. "I was only twenty-two. Just a kid. I know that's not an excuse, but to say I had no clue what I was doing is an understatement. I was interning at G and W at the time and I was . . ." She took a deep breath and straightened up. "Well, I was an asshole. I'm sorry if I caused you any pain. But, for what it's worth, that's not the person I am now."

Emma glanced at Gray. She felt for the girl. Was that ridiculous? She seemed genuine. And six years ago? James would have been almost forty, and her boss. The predatory nature of the situation made her intestines twist.

"Look, I know you don't know me, but I hope you can forgive me," Jenny said. "And I really am sorry for your family's loss."

Without another word, she turned and walked back to her husband at the bar, lacing her fingers through his. Lizzie appeared seconds later, looking pale and a bit unsteady.

"Well, Janet McElroy is out. Not that she can't be bisexual, but she's over there with her girlfriend and I got a very anti-patriarchy vibe."

Emma reached for Lizzie's hand and squeezed it. "It was Jenny Mahone."

She wouldn't have thought it possible for Lizzie to lose any more color, but she went almost translucent. "No. Really?"

"Yes, but it happened six years ago when she was single and practically a baby herself." Gray's expression was grim. "She's married with kids now."

Lizzie covered her mouth with one hand. "So it's a pattern. It's more than one."

"Sorry. I don't follow," Gray said. "We found JM. Done deal."

"No. Not a done deal," Emma said, wondering how she was supposed to make it through the rest of the night. "If they ended it six years ago, then it wasn't Jenny who had James's phone. It was someone else."

KELSEY

A fork clanged against a champagne glass. Another someone wanted to make a speech about her father. At weddings, clinking a champagne glass with your fork meant the couple had to kiss. At this particular event it meant that someone Kelsey didn't know was going to make another speech about what an amazing person her father was. How he was so funny and big-hearted and charming. How thoughtful he could be. How kind. Remember that time he lost five golf balls during one round with Tiger Woods and laughed it off? So laid back. Or when he called my daughter once a week for three months after she had her appendix out, just to check if she was okay? The compassion. The empathy.

Kelsey had her appendix out when she was twelve. Her father hadn't even come to the hospital.

"You want to burn this place to the ground, don't you?" Willow asked, sidling up next to Kelsey with a glass of champagne. She had a way of doing that—silently appearing with no warning. She was wearing a sparkly bracelet that Kelsey was sure didn't belong to her. One of these fancy women was going to go to remove her jewelry later tonight and discover it missing. Kelsey would have bet money on it.

"You're drinking?"

"What're you, a nun?" Willow slurped from the glass. "Want me to get you one?"

"Um, no thanks." Kelsey was feeling punchy. In fact, she did sort of want to burn the place to the ground, but she'd never admit to Willow that she was right.

"What the hell did I do to piss you off so much?" Willow asked under her breath. "The whole eBay thing was *your* idea, remember? Forgive me if I don't want to give it up now that we're making bank."

Kelsey grit her teeth. This was *so* not the time. So not the place. And also, Willow was right. It *was* her idea. But she'd changed her mind. She wished things could just go back to the way they'd been before her dad died. But she wished they could go back to the way they'd been and still have him be gone. Why couldn't he just have left them, like other asshole fathers did? Why couldn't he and her mom have just gotten a divorce?

"And I was going to give the ring back. I swear I was."

Kelsey's head was beginning to pound. "Will you please just leave me alone?" she blurted, loudly enough that a few people around them turned to stare. Willow's pale face flushed with heat. She looked, suddenly, murderous. Kelsey turned her back on her. Returned her attention to the speeches.

It simply made no sense. The gushing, effusive, borderline manic things these strangers had to say about James Walsh. Everyone really did love this person. To these people he was a fine specimen of a human being. Vaunted. Revered. Beloved. It seemed he saved the raving psycho side of himself for his family. Home was the place you could be who you really were, after all.

As this new speech began, Kelsey zoned out. Her mother was no longer at her station in front of the ridiculously large Obama poster, which was good, because most of the night she'd looked like a marble statue of herself—her expression grim and focused, blue veins showing through her skin under the unflattering light. Maybe her mother had bailed. Kelsey would be pissed about being deserted, but she'd totally understand.

There was a polite smattering of applause when this last speaker was through, and then Darnell stepped up to the microphone.

"Thank you, Stacey, for sharing that lovely memory," he said, his voice low and lulling through the speakers. "Now, Hunter Walsh, James's son, would like to say a few words on behalf of the family."

People around the room whispered and murmured, anticipating her superstar brother, the apple of his father's eye, taking the microphone. There wouldn't be a dry eye in the house once this was over. Everyone glanced around, over their shoulders, on their toes, but Hunter didn't materialize. Kelsey looked at the corner of the room where he'd been hanging out with his friends all night, sneaking drinks and laughing inappropriately.

"Where's your brother?" Alexa asked, shoving through the crowd to join her and Willow.

"I have no idea."

"Hunter?" Darnell prompted, looking across the room. He was taller than half the people here, so he had a good perspective. But Hunter didn't show.

Then, something hard pressed the small of Kelsey's back and she tripped forward. A few people gasped and someone spilled their wine, but when Darnell's eyes fell on her, they lit up.

"Kelsey!" he said, relieved. "Everyone, this is James's daughter, Kelsey Walsh. Did you want to say a few words, honey?"

Kelsey turned around and saw Willow smirking at her from behind her champagne glass. *Fuck you very much*, she said with her eyes. But Willow simply laughed. Alexa's mouth hung open in shock. *What are you doing?* she mouthed. Clearly, she'd somehow missed the fact that Willow had shoved her out here. There was no way she was going to do this. What the hell could she possibly say to all these James Walsh disciples?

My father was an asshole who berated me every chance he got and threatened to kill me the night before he died, all because he was convinced I did something for which he had no proof.

That would go over well.

But then, she remembered what her mom had said about her meeting with Mr. Fletcher. That the memorial might give her closure. She'd said it with such underlying hope, like she thought the doors of Madison Square Garden might be the magical portal through which they'd all have to step in order to return to normal. More than anything, Kelsey wanted her mother to stop worrying about her.

She stepped forward and took the microphone from Darnell.

"Hi, everyone," she said, and adopted an appropriately sad face. "I guess I'll say a few words about my dad, since my brother's a dirty no-show."

There was some light laughter and Kelsey felt buoyed. Though she was definitely going to atomic-wedgie her brother later. If she physically could. She was momentarily distracted by a woman in the front of the crowd, almost as tall as Darnell in strappy heels, wearing a slinky black dress that could have been ripped from the red carpet at the Oscars. Were these really her father's people?

"My dad did everything a good dad was supposed to do," she began. "He provided for his family. He gave us a big house out in New Jersey. A private school education. Got Hunter all the best coaches so he could hone his talent and signed him up for every travel league he could find. But he also supported my dream to be a performer." The lie felt like acid burning through her tongue. "He came to all my recitals when I was little and encouraged me to work on my poise and public speaking. Which is coming in handy right now."

More laughter.

"But my dad was really so much more than that," she continued. "He had so much energy and exuded such strength." *Like the time he put his fist through the wall right next to my face.* "And so much passion." *Which he displayed through boundless fits of anger.* "He worked a lot, don't get me wrong, but when he was home, we really felt his presence." *Raging through the house breaking windows and plates and mugs and picture frames, telling us all how worthless we were, how ungrateful.* "Everyone loved my father." *At least all of you did, clearly.* "And it makes my heart feel full to know that he's touched so many lives." *Bullshit.*

Her eyes brimmed with tears as she looked out at the sea of strange faces, all attention riveted on her. She wished she'd had the father she'd just described. She wished she'd known the man these people had worshipped. She wished it with all her broken, blackened heart.

"So on behalf of my brother and my mother and my whole family, thank you all for coming," she said. "I know I, for one, will never forget this night."

EMMA

After Kelsey's surprise eulogy, Emma needed a break. She went to the bathroom and locked herself in a stall for five minutes, where she just let herself bawl. Several people came and went while she snotted all over herself, blowing into toilet paper and coughing so hard she actually thought she might throw up, but no one bothered her. They must have figured that, this being a memorial service, crying was to be expected, and Emma was grateful to be left alone.

She didn't understand anything. That much was clear to her. Because if Kelsey's speech had been sincere, then she knew absolutely nothing about her daughter. If Kelsey's speech had been an act, however, then she was at turns extremely concerned and beyond impressed. Her daughter was some actress. But to be able to get up in front of a group of such world-renowned luminaries and improvise a speech like that seemed borderline pathological.

Tomorrow she would call the therapists on the list Mr. Fletcher had provided. Clearly, growing up in their household had damaged Kelsey in ways Emma couldn't even begin to understand.

Decision made, she felt much better. She smoothed the front of her skirt, cleared her throat, and prayed her waterproof makeup had survived her breakdown.

When she opened the door, Zoe was standing at the sinks. She looked away guiltily.

"Oh, hello, Zoe," Emma said. She smoothed her hair and leaned toward the mirror. Her nose was red, her eyes bloodshot, but at least she didn't look like a raccoon.

"Are you okay?" Zoe asked meekly. She wet a paper towel and handed it to Emma. Her thick, dark hair was piled on top of her head in a sleek bun, and she wore earrings that dangled almost to her shoulders. "Can I get you anything?"

Emma smiled gratefully at her and saw that Zoe, too, had been crying. "No, thank you. I'll be fine."

"Well. Just let me know."

Zoe started to leave, when Emma remembered there had been something niggling at her. She also had this overwhelming feeling that she didn't want to be alone, but she wasn't ready to go back to the crowd yet, either.

"Zoe, wait."

The girl turned slowly, her shoulders slightly hunched, as if she'd been caught at something she wasn't supposed to be doing.

"You wouldn't happen to know where James's laptop is, would you? He never came home at night without it, but it wasn't in his briefcase." Emma touched the cool paper towel to the back of her neck.

Zoe pressed her lips together and averted her eyes. "Um . . . I think it's still at the office?"

"Really? That's so weird. Do you have access to it?" Emma felt emboldened by the chat she'd had with Jenny Mahone. Until that moment, she hadn't known she was capable of such nerve. Maybe she hadn't been, before all this happened. But now, she didn't give a shit anymore.

"Not really? Mr. Garrison confiscated it after the fight."

Emma shook her head. She felt like she had whiplash. "I'm sorry, what? Confiscated it? After what fight?"

Zoe made a sound that brought to mind a mewling kitten, and bounced a bit on her knees. It was pretty clear she wanted out of this conversation, but that was not about to happen.

"Look, I wasn't there for the whole thing, so I don't know the entire story? But they got into a fight."

"Who, Zoe? Who got into a fight?"

"Darnell and James?" Zoe said, and chewed on her lower lip.

"No. They never . . ." But Zoe looked so pained that Emma stopped talking. She swallowed hard, remembering something Zoe had said to her a couple of weeks ago—how she and the Garrisons might have tension between them *after everything*. "What did they fight about?"

"I'm not totally sure? But it had something to do with money and clients, and Darnell said, 'Did you really think you could just leave? Do you really think I'm that stupid?' And then he hit him. James. I mean Darnell hit James."

"What?!"

Emma's hands flew up to cover her mouth. Until last week, Emma would never have been able to imagine Darnell hitting anyone, let alone her husband—his best friend. But after what she'd witnessed at Gray's house, she wasn't so sure. Still, James must have done something horrible to make Darnell react like that—especially in front of someone young and impressionable like Zoe—an employee, no less. It must have been a betrayal of biblical proportions.

"When? When did this happen?"

"The night James died?" Zoe had chewed all the lipstick off her bottom lip. "I mean, that evening, I guess."

"Oh my God." Emma braced both hands on the sink and leaned in. "What did James do?"

"Well, he was furious. All red in the face and bleeding?" She looked at Emma and blanched. "Anyway, he spit in Darnell's face, and then they took his computer and security escorted him from the building. Which was good, because I swear I thought Mrs. Garrison was going to kill him herself. She—"

"Gray was there?"

Emma stood up straight. An odd sort of coldness sluiced down her spine.

"Well, yeah. They were going to that party."

"Gray was there. Gray Garrison. The night James died. And Darnell hit my husband so hard he drew blood."

"Um . . . yes?"

Emma walked past Zoe out the door.

GRAY

Gray kept one eye on her watch and the other on Darnell, who was deep in conversation with a few of the company's board members. She just wanted to get out of there before someone did or said something to make Darnell snap, and now that Emma had half-solved her mystery-woman puzzle, she felt like they could reasonably make their escape. If only Darnell wasn't viewing this memorial as an opportunity to put his employees, clients, and investors at ease.

"I need to talk to you."

Emma's voice was like steel. Gray gave her a quizzical look, but her friend was already stalking through the crowd and out into the hallway. Confused, Gray followed. From the corner of her eye, she saw Lizzie notice them and follow as well. Of course.

"Emma? What's wrong?" Gray asked, as soon as they were free of the room.

Emma kept walking, however, until she was a good few yards down the long hallway. Then she whirled on Gray so fast that Gray stopped short and Lizzie walked right into her from behind.

"Darnell and James had a fight the night James died? About James *leaving?*"

Gray instantly regretted all the sushi she'd grabbed off passed platters this evening.

"Emma—"

"Did you know he was going to divorce me before I showed you the papers?" Emma demanded, shaking. "Did you know he was having an affair?"

"No." Gray splayed her fingers and stepped cautiously toward Emma, as if approaching a raging bull. "That is not what the fight was about."

"Then what was it?" Emma asked.

Lizzie moved past Gray and over to Emma, putting her arm around her to try to steady her. Gray wanted to bite the woman's head off when, to no one's surprise, she looked over at Gray as if she were a piece of dirt.

"I came into the city that night to go to the gala with Darnell," Gray said slowly, in as calm a voice as she could muster while her heart was frantically pinballing around her chest. "When I stepped off the elevator, I heard the shouting."

"They were already fighting when you got there?"

"Yes. I followed the voices to James's office and arrived right when Darnell hauled off and punched James."

"Oh my God!" Lizzie said unhelpfully. "Why? I can't imagine Darnell hitting anyone."

Gray and Emma locked eyes, but Emma said nothing.

"I know. That's what I thought," Gray said, her rib cage tight. "I couldn't believe my own eyes. But James had clearly done something to set him off."

Set him off. She wanted to take the words back the moment she said them. She knew how they sounded, and braced herself as Emma and Lizzie exchanged a look. In that brief moment she tried to discern whether Lizzie knew—whether Emma had broken her promise—but no. She knew Emma would never betray her. In that way, Emma was definitely the better woman.

"Gray, you don't think Darnell was the one who was at my house that night, do you?" Emma said. "That he—"

"No. No way," Gray said, shaking her head. "Darnell couldn't kill someone, let alone his best friend. No matter what he'd done."

"Are you sure about that?" Lizzie asked venomously. The question in Emma's eyes asked the same thing, except it was far more loaded than Lizzie's words, because Emma knew. Emma had seen.

The truth was that Gray had no clue what Darnell had or hadn't done that night. He very well could have been this mysterious person Emma was so keen on finding. But even if Darnell had been there—if he and James had rekindled their argument in the driveway—there was no way he could murder anyone. Darnell had once hit a deer on the side of the road and felt sick about it for a week. If he'd hurt James, Gray would know. Unless, of course, he didn't remember. But that possibility was so slim—and so awful—that she refused to consider it.

Gray shot Lizzie a look that should have stopped her heart cold in her awful little chest, then turned to Emma—focused on her best friend. "Yes. I'm sure," she said in her firmest voice. "Darnell did *not* kill James."

Emma pushed her hands up into her hair and stepped away from Lizzie, pacing toward one wall and then the other.

"So what were they fighting about? What would make Darnell hit him?"

Gray took a deep breath. She looked over her shoulder toward the memorial, which was starting to sound more and more like a party as the alcohol was drained and the voices grew louder. Would it even matter to Darnell if she told the truth now? Or, at least, a version of the truth? It was over. With James gone, there was nothing for him to lose.

"James was poaching clients. Some of the big ones," she said quietly. "He was planning to leave the business and set up his own shop."

"What?" Emma breathed.

"He would have destroyed the business, Emma," Gray continued. "And you know how much it means to Darnell—to my whole family. The boys would have lost their jobs . . . And Dante never got his degree. He'd never get another position in the business if we went under. And all their employees . . . they're like family to Darnell."

"Oh my God," Emma said. "This is insane."

"When Darnell found out, he felt so betrayed," Gray continued. "You know how those two were. When they went into this together all those years ago, it was supposed to be a partnership all the way, so this . . ."

Emma looked as if one stiff breeze would knock her over. "When was this supposed to happen?"

Gray cleared her throat. "Soon. And from what Darnell has heard in the days since James passed, he was apparently setting up shop in Los Angeles."

"Los Angeles?" Emma repeated. She locked one arm around her own waist and pressed the heel of her hand into her forehead. "This is not happening. How did I not know about this?"

"I don't—"

"Shit, Gray. Is there anything else about my life you want to tell me?"

That was when it hit her full in the chest. Darnell didn't have anything to lose anymore from the truth coming out, but Gray did. Emma was looking at her as if she, herself, had been the one sleeping with James. The mysterious, possibly nonexistent person who had been there that night to coax him out of the car, slip his necktie off, throw it in the hedges.

"No," Gray said, looking Emma in the eye. She decided to leave Derek out of it. There really was no reason to share his role in all of this. "That's really all I know."

For a long moment, none of them spoke. A round of loud, male laughter went up inside the owner's suite.

"I would have told you about it. Obviously, I would have," Gray told Emma. "But then James died, and it seemed . . ."

"Moot?" Emma supplied sarcastically.

"Not exactly. I just didn't want to cause you any more pain."

Emma's expression morphed into one of disgust. "I can't believe you, Gray. I'm an adult! I don't need you deciding what I can and can't handle."

"You really do have to control everything, don't you?" Lizzie added.

"Back off, Lizzie. This has nothing to do with you," Gray snapped, glad to finally have an excuse to tell her off.

"Don't talk to her that way," Emma said. "Lizzie has been more of a friend to me than you have. At least she listens to me. At least she doesn't think her way is the only way."

Emma's words were like a gunshot to Gray's heart. Emma was her oldest friend and Gray was Emma's. She would do *anything* for the woman—and had. All Lizzie ever seemed to do was take, take, take in her relationship with Emma. She called for advice, to cadge cookware, to ask Emma to watch Willow, to borrow money. Gray refused to believe that Emma's friendship with Lizzie had anything on her friendship with Gray, and she was not about to let Lizzie take Emma away from her.

"Emma, let's just go somewhere alone and talk about this," Gray began. "You have to let me explain the—"

Emma drew herself up so straight and so proud that Gray stopped talking. "I don't *have* to do anything."

She took Lizzie's hand and stormed off, but paused halfway to the door and looked back. "Oh, and I want my husband's computer back. You see that it happens."

DARNELL

5:30 p.m.

7 hours and 45 minutes before the accident

The office had all but emptied out, everyone going home to change for the party or running out to grab drinks together beforehand, having changed in the restrooms already. Darnell loved these days, when the whole company had an event to attend. The vibe in the air had been festive all day, and when the assistants and associates got all dressed up and cologned and perfumed, it made him feel young again, watching them gather into groups and laugh and talk on their way to the elevators. He loved having his own company, loved having the ability to give these opportunities to kids just starting out. In a way, he felt like all his employees were his kids. He felt responsible for them and their education in adulting, as they called it. When one of them left to pursue another opportunity, he felt proud as well. If you love something, set it free and all that jazz.

He really had to get up from behind this computer and start getting ready himself. Gray would be here any minute, expecting him to take her out for a quick drink and a quiet chat before the mayhem. But he couldn't stop staring at the PI's latest rundown on James. The man was up to something. Darnell could feel it in his bones. There had to be a pattern to these extra meetings he was taking. Something he was missing. Maybe if it weren't for these debilitating headaches, he'd be able to see it. Even now, he felt as if a giant boxer was pounding repeatedly on the inside of his skull, radiating pain from his brow bone across his cranium to the back of his neck.

There was a quick rap on his door. Derek. He had his own way of knocking. "Come in, son."

Derek stepped inside and closed the door behind him. He'd already changed into his tux. He seemed jittery, but then, of his two boys, Derek was the one who was always moving, always fidgeting, always in motion.

"What's up, kiddo?"

"Dad," Derek said. "There's something I have to tell you."

By the time his son was done telling his story, the blood was roaring in Darnell's ears. Here it was. The answer. It all clicked inside Darnell's mind in a rush of white-hot ire.

"How long have you known about this?" Darnell asked.

"A while," Derek answered vaguely. "I'm really sorry, Dad. I just didn't know what to do. And Mom said—"

"You told your mother?"

"Kinda."

"And you got all of this from Zoe?" Darnell said. "She knew about it?"

"No. I mean, she just figured it out. Don't be mad at her, Dad. It's not her fault. And at least she told me everything she overheard, right?" He gulped, and Darnell could see in his face how much this girl meant to him. There would need to be a conversation about fraternizing on the job. But not now. "You're not going to fire her."

"Don't worry about Zoe," Darnell told his son. "I have bigger things to deal with."

He flung open the door to his office but looked back at Derek. "You did the right thing, telling me."

Derek gave a grim nod and then Darnell saw James, red-faced, gunning for his own office at the back of the open area. Sonofabitch looked pissed off already. Well, his day was not about to get better.

LIZZIE

Lizzie couldn't sleep. In her entire life, she had never felt this much rage, and she didn't know what to do with it. Willow's lights were out; the house was silent. It was well after midnight, Lizzie and Willow having spent some time at Emma's house with her and the kids after the memorial, making sure Emma had settled, which she had somehow done. Probably the crash after a five-hour-long adrenaline rush. Meeting all those people, accepting their condolences, interrogating the JMs, and then that fight with Gray.

Really it was no wonder she'd passed out before Lizzie had even closed her bedroom door. But for some reason, Lizzie wasn't coming down the same way.

Who the fuck did Gray think she was? Keeping all those secrets about things that directly affected Emma's life? Not that Lizzie had never kept a secret. She'd even kept one or two from Emma. But this was different. This was life or death. As much as Lizzie liked and respected Darnell, she didn't believe Gray for a second when she asserted that Darnell couldn't have killed James. There had been something in her eyes as she said it—fear? Uncertainty? A combination of the two? Emma might not have picked up on it, but Lizzie had. Darnell was dangerous. Even his wife knew it. Maybe this was why Darnell and Gray seemed to be having issues—why Gray was tracking Darnell's every move. Maybe Gray was covering up for her husband, or afraid he was going to kill again.

After debating the temperature outside for a few minutes, Lizzie threw on her down parka and went out to the garage. In the middle of the space was not a car, but a dining table—an antique piece she'd found at a garage sale and had been restoring for the past couple of weeks. She grabbed a sanding block and tackled the left side. Someone had allowed their children to use it as an art table, and it was going to take hours for Lizzie to remove all the dried paint and glue stains, but it would be worth it. She was still debating whether to sell the finished product or keep it for herself. But there would be no point if she ended up selling the house. She was sure that wherever she was going, she wouldn't have enough room for a table this size. Besides, it should be displayed in some grand dining room somewhere, a conversation piece. She'd be doing the original craftsman a disservice by hauling it off to some boxy apartment building never to be seen by anyone other than Willow and her friends.

The longer Lizzie worked, the more of a rhythm she got into, the more her pulse began to slow. At least Emma had told Gray off. At least it seemed like she was starting to see the woman for the control freak she really was. But Lizzie was still bothered that Emma didn't believe Darnell could be dangerous. Gray had just proven herself to be the worst sort of liar, so why was that the only lie Emma continued to believe? What sort of freakish mind control did Gray have over her?

Emma didn't know about the tracking app Gray had on her phone. But maybe she should. Maybe that would prove to Emma that even Gray didn't totally trust her supposedly perfect husband.

Lizzie had to do something. She had to prove to Emma, especially now, that she was the better friend—that she was the one who was there for Emma no matter what. That, at least, would be a start.

EMMA

That night, she woke up with a start, heart pounding, the desperate tenor of her nightmare still ringing in her ears. James had been falling and she had been grabbing for him, but she couldn't hold his weight even though he begged and begged, and she'd finally had to let him go. She could still hear his scream: guttural, terrified. Catching her breath, Emma whipped off the covers and put her head between her knees.

He was going to leave you. He was going to betray Darnell and every-thing they'd built. He was going to take that woman on the other end of the phone, move to California, abandon his kids and never look back.

Emma let out a wail, then covered her mouth, hoping her kids hadn't heard. There was no chance of her falling asleep again, and she knew, suddenly and with absolute clarity, what she needed to do. She threw on sweats and sneakers, wrote a note to her kids, and left the house.

At first she kept the car quiet, listening to the clicking of the turn signals and the shooshing of the leather steering wheel through her fingers, but as soon as she hit the parkway, she turned on '90s on 9 and cranked up the volume. A few songs she sang along to. A few others made her cry. One made her scream at the top of her lungs, the rage coursing through her hot and unexpected.

"Don't hate me for saying this," Lizzie had whispered on the way home from the memorial, "but I think you need closure."

She was whispering because Kelsey had fallen asleep in the backseat. Willow had gone in Hunter's car, and Emma felt as if she and Lizzie were two parents of a newborn baby, driving around in an attempt to keep the kid asleep.

"Closure," she'd said.

"I know it's going to be hard to get, what with the person you need to hash it out with being gone, but all this anger and resentment you're holding on to . . . it's not good for you, Em. It's going to eat you alive."

"I'm not pissed at Gray because I need closure with James. I'm pissed at Gray because she's controlling and thinks she always knows what's best for me and it's enough already."

"Don't get me wrong. I'm not suggesting you shouldn't be pissed at Gray," Lizzie had said. "But I think it's time to let James go."

"Lizzie, I appreciate the advice, but you don't know what it's like. James and I . . . we used to be happy. We really were in love. I have to at least hold on to that, or my whole life becomes one big mistake. Just because the older he got, the more he became an unmitigated dickhead doesn't mean I'm not handling this in a healthful fucking way."

There was a pause. Kelsey stirred.

"Okay, and maybe I also need closure."

She was there before she knew it, turning off at the exit for Point Pleasant Beach. Record time, James would have said. But of course she'd made record time, it being October and the middle of the night and all.

Emma parked at the closest spot to the boardwalk that wasn't a handicapped spot and checked around to make sure no erstwhile police officers were lurking. She had no idea whether it was illegal to be on the beach at 3 a.m., but she didn't particularly want to explain what she was doing there to anyone—not even a stranger. She held her coat tightly to her chest, bracing herself against the cold ocean wind as she walked the boards. The lights were on, at least, and there was not a soul in sight. For half a second she was gripped by fear, realizing that no one knew exactly where she was, but then the rhythmic crashing of the waves soothed her. Nothing bad was going to happen to her while she was on this particular mission. That would have been so wrong on a karmic level it would have made the earth turn inside out.

Her phone rang for the fifth or sixth time since she left the house. Gray. Again. She finally held down the button to turn it off. For the first time, she wondered if maybe the firm had confiscated James's cell phone, too. But if that was the case, then why would someone have answered it? Regardless, she'd have to ask Gray about that, too. If Gray had known that Darnell's lawyers had had the phone all this time and had let Emma go on this wild mistress goose chase, Emma was never going to speak to her again.

After strolling for a few minutes, Emma found the spot. The very spot where James had skateboarded into her and knocked her swirled ice-cream cone to the ground and said the first words he'd ever said to her—"Oh, shit. Sorry." She was pretty sure she'd fallen in love with him when he flipped his long bangs out of his eyes and smiled at her. They'd visited this spot once a year for ten years until life got in the way. Maybe if they'd kept that tradition up—made their relationship a priority in their lives—things would have ended up differently.

But she wasn't going to think like that anymore.

Emma took the nearest set of steps down to the beach and walked until the toes of her sneakers were kissed by the very edge of a foaming wave. She reached into her pocket and took out her wedding ring. Emma had never been a big one for dramatic gestures, but somehow, she needed one for this. She needed to prove to James and the universe and herself that she was serious. It was time to put him and all the anger and fear and confusion and bullshit behind her. She was going to focus on herself. On her kids. On the future. She couldn't pretend that James had never happened, but she could stop obsessing about him like she had when he was still here.

"James," she said out loud. "I want to say thank you for leaving me with two amazing, beautiful, and good-hearted kids."

She reached back and threw the ring as hard as she could into the waves. It was so dark, and the ring so small, that she didn't see the splash.

"May you rot in hell."

GRAY

Until James Walsh died, Gray Garrison had never called in sick to work on a day that she wasn't deathly ill, but here she was, doing it for the second time in as many weeks. On the morning after the memorial, having slept maybe two or three hours, she left a voicemail for her assistant telling her she wouldn't be in and would be unavailable all day. She saw Darnell off to work, then attempted to go back to sleep, but her racing thoughts prevented it. Around 8 a.m., she hauled herself up and out the front door to retrieve the *New York Times*. Darnell had left it on the doorstep for her, knowing she didn't like to bring the bag it came in inside, in case it was wet from the sprinklers.

My man, she thought with a smile, followed by a pang. He wasn't quite the same man anymore, was he? She was going to have to get used to that.

Gray was bending to pick up the paper when she saw movement out of the corner of her eye. A car was just pulling away from the driveway. A silver crossover of some kind. Gray saw a flash of red hair, and then heard the squeal of brakes as the car stopped down the street.

Her heart skipped a beat. Was that *Lizzie*?

Gray slammed the door and tossed the paper on the hall table. She hustled into the kitchen and grabbed her phone. Was Lizzie stalking her now? Was she going to transfer her obsession from Emma to Gray?

She went to her contacts and hit Lizzie's name with her thumb. Her arm shook as she held it to her ear. It rang four times before voicemail picked up. Gray almost ended the call, but then thought better of it. She took a deep breath—in through the nose, out through the mouth—as Lizzie's irritating voice chirped the outgoing message.

"Don't think I didn't see you, *Elizabeth Larkin*," Gray said, biting out her full name. "Stay away from me and stay away from my family or you will regret it."

She ended the call, then dialed Darnell. He picked up right away.

"How are you feeling, my love?" he asked.

Gray's insides melted slightly.

"I was fine until I went outside to get the paper and saw Lizzie watching our house."

"What do you mean, watching?" he asked, with a calm that irked her.

"She was just sitting out there on the street, her beady eyes on me." Gray went to the front windows and peeked out. "You know I've always thought her interest in Emma was borderline disturbing. What if she's unhinged?"

Gray suddenly remembered bumping into Lizzie at the café last week. Had she been watching Gray then, too? Did she know Gray had gone there to meet with Ben?

"Don't worry about it, Gray," Darnell said in his best no-nonsense voice. "I'll take care of it."

"You don't have to do anything," she said, feeling silly at his taking charge. This was Lizzie. The woman could barely run her own business and clothe her daughter. It wasn't as if she was a threat. "I know you've got a lot on your plate."

"No. It's fine. I've got it," he said. "You get some rest and I'll see you tonight."

Gray said goodbye and hung up the phone. It was odd, how well he'd taken that call, how he seemed like he'd almost expected it. But maybe it was just his not flying off the handle—that he'd seemed more like his old, reasonable self—that was throwing her.

EMMA

The Cantor Feldman offices were in a converted mansion near downtown Oakmont, with a working fountain in the center of the paver driveway and a bell at the front door. A receptionist came and ushered Emma, Kelsey, and Hunter to Evan's office at the rear of the building, which overlooked expansive gardens through a wall of French doors. The hedges were meticulously trimmed, the lawn cut in perfect rows, and orange and yellow mums burst from hundreds of stone pots. Emma wished she could appreciate the beauty of it all, but she was too busy trying to control her nerves.

When she came around the corner into the office, she half expected to see a dozen mistresses sitting in rows of chairs facing Evan's desk waiting for their fair share, but there was no one there other than Charles Lipschultz—Garrison & Walsh's lead attorney—and Evan himself. Emma let out the breath she'd been holding all morning. She knew the possibility still existed that other women—Jenny Mahone included— could be named in the will, but at least she didn't have to look at them. Now she didn't know what to hope for—that James had left something to his current mistress so that she would finally get a name, or that he hadn't.

If the will didn't name names, then Emma was going into the city to get James's computer back herself.

"Emma, it's good to see you." Evan rounded his desk and placed his meaty hands on the sides of Emma's arms, leaning in for a cheek kiss. He was so tan his skin looked like her favorite leather bag and his brown eyes were shot through with tired, red veins. "I'm so sorry for your loss."

"Thank you."

He released her and looked at Hunter and Kelsey. "Kids."

"Hello," Kelsey said meekly.

Hunter was silent.

"Well, have a seat." Evan gestured at the chairs across from his desk. Emma nodded at Charlie, unsure as to why he was here. He looked much older than the last time she'd seen him—the wrinkles in his forehead deeper, the skin under his chin saggier, his blue eyes watery—but his posture was still ramrod straight and his gray suit pressed. He nodded back, then returned to texting on his cell phone. Even with her kids at her sides, Emma felt very alone. Part of her had been certain that Gray would be here, even though they hadn't spoken since the memorial. After twenty-four hours of calling, Gray had apparently given up, and the fact that she hadn't shown for this meant that she'd gotten the message. Emma was still angry at her, but the initial shock and ire had faded enough that she felt stung by Gray's absence.

What if Emma had gone too far? Could she even imagine a future that didn't include Gray?

"Well, let's get right down to it," Evan said. "As I mentioned on the phone, James made some recent changes to his will to deal with the dispersal of certain specific assets in his private collection."

Kelsey sat up straight. "Mom?"

"Sorry, what?" Emma said. "His private collection?"

"His sports memorabilia collection," Evan clarified. "James bequeathed certain game-used baseballs to the National Baseball Hall of Fame in Cooperstown, New York, for example. And he's asked to have various items donated to the Hockey Hall of Fame, the Pro Football Hall of Fame, the World Golf Hall of Fame, et cetera, et cetera. All the interested parties are on speaker phone to hear the reading." Evan gestured at a flat speaker in the middle of his desk, and Emma felt heat rise up her neck. Dozens of people were listening to this?

"Mom? No way. There's no way Dad did that," Hunter protested.

"And then there's the fact that certain assets technically belong to the company," Charles put in, scrolling on his phone. "There are some items James procured during the execution of official company business. Mr. Garrison would like those items returned to the Garrison and Walsh collection."

Hunter slumped back heavily in his chair and looked past Emma at Kelsey, whose mouth hung slightly open in shock. Emma wasn't sure if there was a specific piece of memorabilia that Kelsey had her eye on, or if it was simply the pointed *screw you* that was upsetting her—James's collection had to be worth a ton of money—but she put her hand on her daughter's knee.

"I'm sorry, but James specified many times that his memorabilia was going to be left to his children."

"Apparently he had a change of heart," Evan said, rather coldly, Emma thought. He lifted the document, printed on heavy stock, and handed it across the desk to Emma. "The bulk of the collection still belongs to the family, but this is an itemized list of the things he's bequeathed to others."

"I'd like a copy of that as well so that we can dispute ownership of any assets we believe belong to the company," Charles said, eyeing the list over Emma's shoulder. He smelled of tobacco and cough drops.

"Of course."

"And that's it?" Emma said, as Hunter plucked the list from her hands. "There were no other . . . specific bequests?"

"No." Evan lifted another copy of the list. "But he asked that I read the list aloud so that everyone is clear; and Charles, if there's anything you'd like to contest on the spot, please do let me know." He cleared his throat and began to read. "Lou Gehrig game-used baseball, 1925, to the National Baseball Hall of Fame."

Hunter got up and stormed out of the room, and Kelsey shot out of her chair to follow. Emma gathered her things as Evan continued to read. Clearly, this was for the benefit of Charles Lipschultz and whoever the phantom people were on the phone. She could see no reason why she had to be there for this charade. By the time she rejoined her children in the lobby, they were arguing in harsh whispers.

"Kids! What's going on?" she asked quietly, glancing around at the closed doors to the other offices.

Hunter stopped talking mid-sentence and Kelsey walked off in a huff, heading for the parking lot.

"Is she okay?" Emma asked.

Hunter ran a hand through his hair. His skin was blotchy, and she was reminded of how red he used to get as a kid when he was trying not to cry on the pitcher's mound after a series of bad pitches, or during a particularly sad movie.

"It's just . . . it's bullshit, Mom!"

"Language!"

"I'm sorry, but . . . some of that stuff . . . it's . . . it has sentimental value for us," he said, looking at the floor. "Remember how Dad used to take us to Yankees Photo Day? Or when we were in the Giants Kids Club? A lot of that stuff we got signed together or we were at the games with him when we were little. How could he just give it away?"

Emma pressed a hand to her chest. She could have killed James for doing this to the kids. Why did the one curve ball he'd thrown them in this new will have to affect them and not her? She would have been much happier to deal with a slew of mistresses. At least that would be her cross to bear and not theirs.

"Well, maybe he didn't give *that* stuff away. Maybe it's more the things that are part of history. None of us were around when Lou Gehrig was playing. Why don't we go back in and listen to Evan read the list? Maybe that will make you feel better."

At the far end of the marble-floored lobby, Kelsey shoved open the door and let it slam. The sound seemed to reverberate in the hushed lobby.

"No. It's fine," Hunter said. "I've got the list. I'll look at it later." The page was now a crumpled ball in his palm. "Let's just go home."

———

IT WAS AMAZING how quickly one could get to the East Side in the middle of the day. Within the hour, Emma was tossing her keys to the parking attendant and striding into the mahogany-and-glass offices of Garrison & Walsh. It had been so long since she'd made an appearance, it took her a moment to navigate the open office area to the back, where the partners' suites were. The receptionist just let her through when she heard who she was, but Emma had no such delusions that getting past Zoe would be as easy.

But Zoe wasn't at her desk. It was a sign. It had to be. Emma stepped up to James's door, gave a quick plea to the universe for luck, hoping against hope that they'd left James's computer in his office, and opened it.

The room was untouched. They hadn't cleaned it out yet. It smelled of James, all leather and whiskey and aftershave. But his computer wasn't there. The monitor was, but the wires hung down behind the desk, attached to nothing.

"Here for this?"

Emma turned around. Darnell stood there, holding a small, silver laptop in his massive hand.

"Gray told me you might stop by," he added.

Startled at having been so quickly caught, Emma backed up a step. As guilty as she felt for thinking it, she still wasn't entirely sure that Darnell hadn't come after James that night in the driveway. After what she'd witnessed at Gray's house, it seemed totally possible. From what she'd read about CTE, he could have done something to James and not even known how to stop himself. Covering it up with the accident was another story, though. He would have had to be in his right mind to do that.

"I'm not gonna hurt you, Emma," Darnell said, and held out the computer at arm's length. "And we haven't wiped that yet."

"You're just going to let me look at it?" she asked, taking the laptop and hugging it to her chest.

Darnell lifted his massive shoulders. "I have nothing to hide. Fair warning, though—not sure I can say the same about James." He turned toward the door, then stood in the open doorway for a moment. "I'm sorry about what you saw the other night. For what it's worth, I'm seeing a therapist and a whole slew of doctors to make sure it doesn't happen again. And I really hope that you and Gray are able to fix this rift between you. She really loves you, you know." He gave her a sad smile. "I'll leave you to it."

And he closed the door.

Emma ran to the desk and plugged the laptop into the monitor. She could process that little encounter with Darnell later. For now, she had work to do. The computer awoke instantly.

WELCOME JAMES WALSH

And then:

ENTER PASSWORD.

Emma sat down in the rolling chair. She tried his usual password. Access denied. She tried it again, just in case she'd mistyped. Access denied. She tried a few others she knew he'd used over the years, clueless as to whether the system was set to lock her out completely the more times she tried. Access denied. Access denied. Access denied.

There was a framed photo of her family on the desk, a sheen of dust across the glass. Emma picked it up and used her sleeve to wipe it clean. Bermuda. 2014. She tried her birthdate, then Hunter's, then Kelsey's. Access denied.

Groaning, she slipped the frame into her bag. On a hunch, she began opening desk drawers, looking for scrawled passwords. Instead she found a couple of flasks, a thousand business cards, and an envelope full of cash. She shoved that into her bag, too. That was when Zoe walked in.

"Emma?"

Emma stood up, caught. "Zoe! Hi!"

"Darnell said to check if you need anything." She stood uncertainly by the door. "What are you doing here?"

"Oh, I was just . . ." She looked at the monitor. "You wouldn't happen to know the password."

Zoe opened her mouth to respond, then her expression shut down.

So close, Emma thought.

"I really can't," Zoe said. "That's James's private stuff."

"Zoe, Darnell gave me the laptop. He's fine with me looking at it and James isn't here. All I want is to see who my husband was emailing with the few days before he died. I had no idea what he was up to, and it seems like Darnell and Gray and even you didn't really know either. I just want answers and I can't get them from James. This is my only option."

She said this hoping against hope that Zoe hadn't been planning on pulling a Jerry Maguire and going with him, because if she had, those emails would likely implicate her as well as James. She also said this knowing that Darnell and his lawyers had likely already looked through all of James's emails and logged and saved any information they needed.

Zoe wiped her hands against her hips, clad in a black pencil skirt. "Okay, fine." She crossed over to James's desk and rapid-fire typed on the remote keyboard. The welcome message dissolved and his wallpaper—a shot of Yankee Stadium packed to the gills—appeared.

"What was it?" Emma asked, curious.

"'GiantsYankeesKnicks' all one word," Zoe said, and rolled her eyes.

"Classic," Emma muttered. "Thank you, Zoe."

Emma sat down again and opened James's email. There were dozens of unread messages. She scrolled past them quickly, figuring his mistress would have known not to email him after he was dead, and got to the read emails from the day he died. Zoe stepped back as Emma began to open various missives and skim them.

"I'll just go back to my desk?" she said. "Call me if you need me?"

Emma nodded but didn't look up. The answer was here. It had to be. But after twenty, thirty, forty minutes of searching, it appeared the answer was actually not here. Her husband had written to countless people about countless things, from the mundane:

Coffee next week?

to the ridiculous:

We need three cases of Dom, a platter of Texas ribs and peanut butter and jelly with the crusts cut off. If he sees crusts on his sandwiches, he'll bail. Even if it is a cover story.

But nothing scandalous. No plans to meet up with a woman that night. She checked the sent emails as well, and the most interesting thing in there was his promise to the party planner to donate a signed jersey to the door prizes for the event that night: One Evan Longoria signed jersey.

That was what James and Kelsey had argued about the night before he died. He'd been looking for something to donate as a door prize and accused Kelsey of messing with his stuff. She had thought it was ridiculous at the time—Kelsey was *not* a sports fan—but maybe she'd been wrong, since it seemed her daughter did have an interest in his collection.

Her adrenaline was waning. Feeling sluggish now, Emma opened the trash folder. Zero items. She glanced at the phone, wondering if she could somehow summon Zoe, but decided to get up and walk to the door instead. She peeked out. Zoe looked up from her typing, startled.

"It just occurred to me . . . haven't you been reassigned? Why are you still sitting here?"

"Ms. Lennox is going to take this office eventually, but we still have to have it packed up and cleaned," Zoe said. "I'm just waiting for Darnell to give me the go-ahead."

"He hasn't yet?"

Zoe shook her head. "The assistants think he's avoiding it." She quirked her lips to one side. "Because he's sad?"

"Oh." Emma felt a pang, and wondered if that was, in fact, the reason, or if there was something more practical and legal at play. She felt, suddenly, like she really shouldn't be here—like she shouldn't have bothered Darnell. "Zoe, is there a way to retrieve deleted emails? The trash file on his computer is empty."

"Oh. They get archived?" Zoe said. "I can get one of the techs to retrieve them from the server, but it'll take a while. Maybe a day or two?"

"If you could do that for me, I would so appreciate it," Emma said. She stepped out of the office and closed the door behind her. Zoe still looked a bit skittish, so Emma put a hand on her shoulder. "If anyone questions you about it, just send them to me, and I'll play the crazed, grieving widow card."

"You don't seem crazed to me," Zoe said, narrowing her eyes slightly.

"Believe me," Emma said. "I have my moments."

LIZZIE

"Why are we doing this again?" Willow asked, hands stuffed deep in her pockets as she trailed Lizzie toward Emma's front door. Loaded down with paper bags full of food, Lizzie blew a curl of hair off her forehead. She'd spent half the day waiting for the phone to ring and wasn't sure how to feel about the fact that it never had. Plus, Gray hadn't done a single thing out of the ordinary in the last forty-eight hours—at least not during the odd times Lizzie had been able to catch up with her. Other than skipping work yesterday and catching Lizzie watching the house, it had been business as usual. Now that the adrenaline from the night of the memorial had waned, Lizzie was starting to understand that she had neither the time nor the talent to be a PI.

"Because Emma and the kids probably had an emotional day," she replied, nodding at her daughter to ring the bell. "So, we're helping out by bringing dinner over."

"Yeah, I get that. But why are we *surprising* them?" Willow asked. "And wasn't it you who said they needed time to themselves?"

Lizzie was saved from concocting a logical answer by Emma swinging open the door. She had the phone at her ear and her eyes widened at the sight of them.

"What's all this?"

"Dinner!" Lizzie lifted the heavy bags a fraction of an inch. "We thought you could use a break."

"Oh, wow, Lizzie, you didn't have to do that. Come in. Both of you, come in!" She stepped aside, clicked the phone off, and took one of the bags from Lizzie. "I was just ordering a pizza, but now I don't have to. Thank you."

"Hunter and Kelsey upstairs?" Willow asked.

"Yes! You can head on up," Emma said.

Lizzie followed her friend into the kitchen, where a glass of white wine stood next to her open laptop. There were clippings from home décor magazines spread out all over the countertop and a home remodeling website open in her browser. Everything appeared to be normal. No signs of a nervous breakdown. Emma turned on the oven and started to unpack the food.

"You really didn't have to do this."

Their eyes met for real for the first time and Lizzie exhaled a breath. Emma was acting just like Emma. It hit home suddenly that this was all that really mattered—Emma's friendship. She could survive without her house, but she couldn't survive without her closest friend. Everything was going to be okay.

"I wanted to. Really." She took out one of the big salad bowls and closed the cabinet with her elbow. "How did it go today with the lawyer? Was Gray there?"

Emma sighed. "Nope. She was a no-show."

It took some effort for Lizzie not to smile. It seemed like the rift between Emma and Gray wasn't going anywhere. She knew she shouldn't feel giddy about it, but she did. For the first time in the ten years Lizzie had known Emma, she had her all to herself.

"And there were no surprises?" Lizzie asked, transferring the salad from its tin container into the glass bowl. "No names named?"

Emma shook her head and took a sip of her wine. "Nope," she said, popping the "p." "Honestly, Lizzie, I kept waiting for some glamorous woman in Hollywood sunglasses and a wide-brimmed hat to walk in. Clearly I've seen too many soap operas in my life."

Lizzie laughed, but it took more effort than it should have. Emma started to clean up the clippings, organizing everything into a pile.

"No, the only surprise was that James left a lot of his sports memorabilia to museums and places like that," she said. "It kind of threw the kids for a loop. They thought it was all going to them."

"Oh. Well, that seems fair, though, right? It's almost . . . philanthropic."

"Hadn't thought of it that way," Emma said. "The kids went to school for the rest of the day, but I've been dealing with the emotional upheaval ever since they got back. Can you believe Kelsey asked me if they could contest the will? I mean, does she really need to hold on to a tennis ball signed by Anna Kournikova? Was she even that good?"

"I never followed tennis," Lizzie said.

"Me neither."

Emma put the clippings in a drawer, then went to her computer and closed the renovation site. Behind it on the browser was a garish red and yellow page with the words GARDEN STATE PRIVATE INVESTIGATORS! scrawled across it as if written in spray paint.

"Wait. You're still thinking about hiring someone?" Lizzie asked.

"No. I don't know," Emma said with a wave of her hand. "That woman—the one who answered my dead husband's cell phone—is still out there, and as much as I try to tell myself it doesn't matter and to just move on . . . I don't know if I can."

"You can," Lizzie said definitively. "Come on, Emma. Do you know the size of the can of worms you'll open up if you hire a detective? What if that woman was just the tip of the iceberg? What if James was keeping other secrets from you? Bigger secrets? You already know he was going to screw over Darnell and move to Los Angeles. Do you really want to know what else he was capable of? And we're not just talking about the here and now or the recent past, but there could be years of—"

"Stop!" Emma lifted her hands.

Lizzie's heart dropped. "Sorry, I just—"

"I get it, okay? My husband was an asshole. And I know you said I needed closure, and I tried to get it, but it didn't work. I can't stop thinking about all this shit he was keeping from me, Lizzie. I feel like an idiot. And I get that some people wouldn't want to know, but I guess I'm just not one of those people."

Emma slapped the laptop closed and sat on the nearest stool, placing her head in her hands. Guilt curled like campfire smoke through Lizzie's chest, and she reached over to rub her friend's back.

"I'm sorry. Really. Obviously, whatever you want to do . . . I'll be here for you."

"Thanks," Emma said. She blew out a sigh. "Look, I'm not going to let it take over my life or anything. The kids—especially Kelsey—need me right now and my primary focus is on them. But I feel like I need to know what my husband was up to. I just want to know, and then maybe I can really move on."

"I get it, I do. But you also have to take care of yourself, Emma. Take some time for you." Lizzie froze with her hand on the center of Emma's back. She remembered that first conversation with Gray after Emma had dropped her suspicions about the necktie— how she'd suggested they take Emma out for a hike. Perhaps she'd been on to something there. "What if we got away for a night or two? Had a girls' weekend. You need to take a break from all this . . . thinking."

Emma laughed and tilted her head sideways on her hand. "Ya think?"

"Didn't James give you a gift certificate on your last birthday for that new spa out in Newton? Did you ever use it?"

"I totally forgot about that." Emma sat up straight. "No. I never did."

"Well, we should go! Just you and me," Lizzie said, warming to the idea. "Maybe new surroundings and some meditation will give you a fresh perspective. Not to mention a good hot stone massage."

Emma smiled up at Lizzie. "You know what? I think that's a great idea."

There was a sudden shriek from the second floor and Emma and Lizzie both went running.

"Kelsey?" Emma called.

Hunter and Willow stepped out into the hallway, and Kelsey was already jogging down the stairs, grinning from ear to ear, her face flushed. If this was what emotional upheaval looked like on her, Lizzie was confused.

"I got an audition!"

"You did?" Emma shouted, then ran up and hugged her daughter. "Oh, Kelsey, I'm so proud of you! When is it?"

"Next Saturday," Kelsey said. "If I nail this, Mom, I'm in!"

"That's awesome, Kels. Congrats," Hunter said.

"Kelsey, that's so great," Lizzie added.

She glanced up at her own daughter, expecting her to congratulate Kelsey as well, but Willow simply turned around and walked back into Hunter's room.

EMMA

"So, you're sure we can do this?" Hunter asked, his eyes bright as he looked at Emma. She was busy taking "before" pictures of the living room, complete with the wall they were about to demolish. "The whole house isn't going to come crashing down around us, right?"

"You have no faith in your mother?" she asked, smiling goofily as she put her camera back in its case.

It had been a long time since she'd seen him look this excited about something, and of course it was breaking down a wall. When he was little, he'd been Handy Manny for Halloween one year and had spent two months prior and one month after the holiday not building things, but taking things apart. Also, having long conversations with his tools.

"It's not that. But I know what a load-bearing wall is. I've seen enough of your shows to get the point."

"It's not a load-bearing wall," she said, feeling sort of proud that he'd learned something through all her TV bingeing. "I checked with the contractor."

"All right then." He lifted his sledgehammer. "On the count of three?"

They counted together. "One . . . two . . . three!"

And then they swung. Hunter's hammer made a clean hole. Emma's barely made a dent. Hunter looked at it and laughed, which made Emma laugh, too, but also made her more determined. She took another swing, this time letting out a screech to back it up, then another, and another, until her hole matched his.

"Nice work," Hunter said, leaning in toward her hole as if to inspect it. "But if you're going to keep screaming like that, I think I'm going to have to disown you."

She smiled, and they got back to work. And as hard as it was, and as much as her muscles protested, she found she loved every minute of it. She loved working side-by-side with her son, who miraculously had nothing to do this afternoon and even more miraculously had decided to come here with her rather than sit in his room and play whatever the hell his current game of choice was. She loved the sweat pouring out of her. The dust flying everywhere. She loved how, every once in a while, when she paused to catch her breath, it would dawn on her all over again that this was hers. *Her* house to do with what *she* pleased. Something all her own.

Maybe Lizzie was right after all. Closure. Doing something for herself. Moving on. She just needed to embrace it. Until Zoe got back to her with those deleted emails, anyway.

Finally, they'd gotten the wall down to the studs, and Emma stepped back to admire their work. Now the sight lines were clear from the front door all the way back through the kitchen and dining room to the back sliders. The place was so much brighter, it was like an entirely new house.

"Water break?" Hunter suggested.

"Donut break," Emma replied.

She went to the old, barely functioning fridge and pulled out two bottles of water, two bottled Dunkin' Donuts coffees, and a box of donuts. They ate them over the kitchen counter and drank silently for a few minutes.

"Mom? There's something I want to tell you."

Emma's peaceful frame of mind was shattered by his sudden seriousness. "What's wrong?"

"Nothing. Well, not . . . it's just . . . I overheard you and Gray talking to Jenny Mahone. At the memorial."

Shit.

"That's why I bailed and missed my speech. I needed air, I guess."

"Oh, honey."

Hunter took a swig of coffee, then carefully twisted the cap back on. "So, it's true. He was having an affair."

She could see the disappointment all over his face. The heartbreak. Even as he tried to look unaffected. Her poor baby. Eighteen years old with the body of a man and still, he could so easily look like her baby.

Damn you, James.

"Listen, kiddo. That was a long time ago." She wasn't about to tell him there was a more recent woman. There was simply no point. "But your dad and I . . . things weren't good."

"I know. I did live in our house." He pressed his lips together. "But still, it's a dick move. And I'm sorry." He looked her in the eye and she could see what a great effort it took. "I'm sorry he did that to you, Mom."

His voice broke, and she hugged him so fiercely she was pretty sure she scared him. When she pulled back, she made him look her in the eye again. "You do not have to apologize for your father. Or for anyone, ever. We are not your responsibility. Do you understand me?"

He studied her face for a long moment. "Yeah. Okay. Yeah."

Emma swallowed, and her throat was so tight it hurt. She felt like an idiot—the clueless, jilted wife. What he must think of her. He must be so ashamed. She wished she were smarter, better, cooler, more sophisticated, more self-assured. Gray would have known her husband was cheating, and she would have done something about it. She would have had the pride to know it wasn't a reflection of her, but a statement on how weak her husband was.

Emma, however, couldn't help thinking it *was* a statement on her. Because if he'd loved her enough, he wouldn't have done it. He would have gotten help. He could have gotten better. It was as if James had found every way possible to show her how very little she meant to him.

"Mom? Are you okay?" Hunter asked.

She shook her head. Closure. Moving on. Doing something for herself. She grabbed her hammer and let out a barbaric scream as, with one swing, she took out the closest cabinet.

"I guess we're doing the kitchen now," Hunter said.

———

THAT NIGHT EMMA found herself staring at the TV in the living room, when the phone rang and kicked her brain into actual consciousness. The TV wasn't on, and Emma couldn't for the life of her imagine how long she'd been staring at it. She'd been walking through the room and had the sudden memory of the day she and James had bought the TV, probably one of the last decisions they'd made together. How big should they go? Was seventy inches overkill? The basement theater room had a projection screen. Should they put one in the living room, too? In the end, he'd ignored everything she'd had to say anyway and gone bigger, fancier, 4K, 3D, UH, whatever. She never used it anyway. Emma and her kids had often been confined to the top level of the house while James, the beast, roamed the floors below.

Gray's name flashed on her phone screen. For the first time in days, she picked up.

"Hello, Gray."

"Emma? Wow. I can't believe you answered."

Sarcasm. Perfect. "What do you want?"

"How long are you going to be mad at me?"

"I don't know." Emma straightened the throw pillows on the couch. "My crystal ball is in the shop."

Gray blew out a breath, short and loud. "Fine. I just wanted to let you know that Charles and the estate lawyers want to send someone to your house to catalog all the sports memorabilia and get this whole thing over with."

Emma fumed. "So why didn't Charles call me? How is this any of your business?"

"He *thought* we were friends and it would be better coming from me."

"Fine. But tell them no. The kids and I will do it."

"Emma, I really think you should just let them take care of it," Gray said. "Why create more work for yourself?"

"Well, I really don't care what you think at the moment, Gray. Hunter and Kelsey and I will organize everything and pack up what's meant for other people. We'll be in touch with Charles and *my* estate lawyers then."

She hit *end* and called up to the kids. Hunter came out of his room and roused Kelsey, who was most likely plugged into her headphones.

"What's up?" Hunter asked, leaning on the railing.

"We have to go through all your dad's stuff and sort it out for the lawyers," Emma said.

Her kids exchanged a look. "Mom, seriously? We're really doing that?" Kelsey asked.

"Doing what? Following your father's last wishes? Yes, unfortunately, we have to."

"This is bullshit!" Hunter snapped. "There's no way I'm helping them take what's rightfully mine."

Emma felt suddenly exhausted. "Hunter, what exactly do you want me to do? Take Major League Baseball to court?"

"Maybe!" Kelsey cried. "It's not fair."

"I don't even understand why you care, Kelsey," Emma said. "You never followed any of these teams."

"I know, but . . . but . . . I care because Hunter cares." Kelsey threw up a hand. "And maybe that's why you should care, too."

"I do care. I just—"

"You just don't want to be bothered putting up a fight," Hunter said. "Fine. Whatever."

So much for that bonding they'd done earlier.

"Hunter—"

"Forget it, Mom. You can do this one yourself."

Hunter stalked off to his room and slammed the door. Seconds later,

Kelsey did the same. Well. That had gone perfectly. Emma walked to the couch and collapsed onto it. For half a second she considered calling Gray back and conceding the point. Let her send the cadre of lawyers or whomever they hired to do such things. But no. She wasn't going to admit Gray was right. She couldn't. Not right now. She reached for the phone to call Lizzie.

GRAY

It wasn't like she was checking up on him. She was simply surprising him for lunch. This wasn't completely unprecedented. Sometimes, when she had a light day or meetings in the city, she'd pop in and take him out. Perhaps Dante and Derek would be able to join them and they could make it a family thing. The truth was, Gray needed some time with her family as much as she needed to check that Darnell was okay. Everything felt so fragile at the moment, like her whole life could be blown to the far reaches by a soft breeze.

But she knew she couldn't keep ditching work like this. Sooner or later, she was going to have to get used to the fact that his life had to go on the same way it always had. Until it couldn't anymore.

Gray left her car in the parking garage under the building on Madison Avenue and rode the elevator up to the lobby. She took her time walking around the modern, chrome-and-granite space, enjoying the feeling of opulence and ownership she always felt here. Garrison & Walsh wasn't the only company in the high-rise, but the owners had given each of the public relations and advertising firms housed there a display case in the lobby, to showcase what they were all about. Gray paused in front of the photo of her husband and James Walsh posing with the Stanley Cup. Positioned around it were various PR awards, replicas of Super Bowl rings, and more framed documents—articles covering the bigger PR moments in some of their most illustrious clients' lives.

It had been a good run. For just over twenty years, the two men had made this thing work. She remembered so clearly when Darnell first told her that he was going into business with James Walsh. Even then, she hadn't loved the guy on a personal level. He was fun to be around, good at a party, a talented speaker and storyteller—traits his daughter inherited. But there had always been something about him that felt off—predatory, self-aggrandizing, egotistical. When Gray first met Emma, she'd both fallen in love with her and started wondering what was wrong with her that she could have tied herself to such a man. But he was an amazing businessperson. A natural connector of people. He was the kind of guy other guys wanted to hang out with and women wanted to impress. Perfect for his chosen profession. And she had since learned that there was nothing wrong with Emma aside from her having a bargain-basement level of self-esteem coupled with a huge, naïve heart.

Darnell and James had hung their first shingle in a modest office suite just a little too far south and a little too far east to feel prestigious, and started out with a handful of mid-list clients. And look at their company now. One of the top five firms in the business. They couldn't let it all fall apart.

Gray's eyes pricked. She knew she was partially at fault for the current distressing state of things. James was gone, and who knew how long Darnell would be able to hold it together? But there were things she could do. Advice she could give. Moves Darnell could make to protect his legacy. She refused to believe all was lost.

Shaking her hair back, Gray moved toward the elevator bank and almost tripped over her own two feet. Lizzie Larkin was walking out of one of the elevators, head down, her raucous curls hiding half her face. For half a second, Gray thought she must be seeing things, but no. It was definitely her. There was no mistaking that particular sense of style.

"Lizzie!"

The woman started as Gray grabbed her arm and dragged her toward the U of couches near the window.

"What the hell are you doing here? Are you stalking my husband now? My boys?" Gray could have torn the woman to shreds in her current frame of mind. But then she noticed that Lizzie's face was red and blotchy, her pale skin unable to mask a thing.

"Don't worry about it, Gray. I'm done," she said, her voice thick with tears. "I won't be bothering you again."

Before Gray could even recover from the shock, Lizzie had slipped her garish sunglasses on and disappeared through the revolving doors.

EMMA

Emma was driving to Ben's café for some coffee when the email came through. The second she saw Zoe's name on her phone, she quickly pulled into the parking lot between Ben's place and The Tap Room. She threw the car in park before it stopped rolling and her body was thrown forward against the seat belt, but she didn't notice. Outside, the world was gray, and a stiff wind tossed brown leaves across her windshield.

The email was huge, the attachments totaling hundreds of megabytes. Her phone wouldn't be able to handle it. Luckily, her car had Wi-Fi. James had convinced her to pay for the subscription so that the kids could play games or watch movies on long trips. But really, it had been for him. So he could download files if he were ever stuck in the car with them, which he rarely was. Now, she could have kissed him for suggesting it.

Emma dug her laptop out of her bag and had Zoe's email open within seconds. She'd sent a zip file of all the email chains that had been deleted from James's computer during his last week at work. Emma whooped with glee and made a mental note to send the girl flowers.

Heart pounding, she started to click through. At first, she could hardly absorb what she was seeing, she was clicking so fast. Then she took a breath and told herself to slow down. There were addresses at

ESPN, Sports Illustrated, MLB, USTA, NFL, MLS, a bunch of agencies and advertising firms, and a ton of random Gmails. But then she saw something that was completely out of place. Which was exactly what she was looking for.

WillowpointY242@oakmontdayK12.edu

Willow? What?

The title of the email chain: I NEED TO TALK TO YOU

Emma's vision grayed at the edges. Why would Willow Larkin, daughter of her friend, friend of her son's, be emailing her husband?

Fingers trembling, Emma clicked open the chain.

The first email, the newest in the chain, was from James.

Fine. 4 pm. Coffee shop at 2nd Ave and 54th. If you can't come into the city it's not my problem.

Emma cupped one hand over her mouth and scrolled to the top of the email chain. She took a breath, said a prayer that this was not what she suspected it was, and began to read.

From Willow:

I NEED TO TALK TO YOU

You can't ignore me forever. Do you want me to call your precious Emma?

From James:

RE: I NEED TO TALK TO YOU

Stop calling me. Stop texting me. Stop trying to get in touch with me. There's no relationship here. Do you understand that? There is nothing between us.

From Willow:

RE: RE: I NEED TO TALK TO YOU

Please. I just need to see you. This one time. I need you to explain it to my face. I'll skip out early today. I'll come anywhere.

From James:

Fine. 4 pm. Coffee shop at 2nd Ave and 54th. If you can't come into the city it's not my problem.

4 p.m. the day he died. He'd met Willow Larkin at a coffee shop in

the city at 4 p.m., then stopped texting Emma back. Had he taken the girl somewhere? Was that why he hadn't shown up to meet her before the Garrison & Walsh party? Because he was off somewhere fucking her best friend's daughter?

No.

Emma closed the laptop. She was going to throw up. When she opened the door she almost fell out onto the busted-up, cigarette-strewn asphalt, but she managed to steady herself and stood. She pressed her hands against the side of her car and breathed and breathed and breathed. There was a viscous puddle of something at her feet, oil or brake fluid, a twisted rainbow forming at its slick center.

"Mother *fucker!*" she shouted, and kicked the tire. Which, of course, didn't give. Pain shot through her foot and up her leg and she bit down on her lip while clutching her sneaker in one hand. She turned and leaned back against her SUV, tears welling in her eyes.

Willow? *Willow?* She was a child. Only turned eighteen a couple of months ago. She knew from Jenny Mahone that her husband had liked his mistresses young, but this was over the line. How long had it been going on? She couldn't . . . wouldn't consider it. She pressed her eyes closed in an attempt to keep her imagination from going anywhere near it. Poor Lizzie. She was going to hate Emma.

A baby wailed nearby and Emma's eyes popped open.

Lizzie.

How was she ever going to face Lizzie again?

Emma let her foot go and straightened her leg, her toes still throbbing. Across the street, Debra Klauss, the owner of the independent bookstore, held the door open for a series of happy families, all plaids and suedes and cozy sweaters and expensive strollers, welcoming them for toddler story time. The wind chimes hanging from the colorful awning above her head sang in the breeze.

Emma closed her eyes again. She had to think.

Had it been Willow who answered James's phone? Had she been

there the night James died? Maybe she hadn't gotten into the city. Maybe they'd met up later. Maybe he'd had her in the car when . . .

Bending at the waist, Emma braced her hands on her thighs.

"Emma? Are you okay?" It was Ben. He wore a waist apron and was approaching her with a bottle of cold water. Ben, who Lizzie was dating. Sweet, café owner Ben. Lizzie was just starting a new chapter in her life. Selling her house, dating a new guy, being hopeful. She could never find out about this. Emma could never tell a soul.

"I'm fine. Thanks, Ben. Just felt dizzy for a second there."

"Here. Sip this." He opened the water and handed it to her. She took a gulp and attempted a smile.

"Thanks. I should go."

"You sure you should be driving?" he asked. "You look a little pale."

"I'm fine, really. Thanks for the water."

She saluted him with the bottle and, somehow, managed to drive away.

BEN

He stood outside on the corner while Jackson Regal, the man from the security company, finished installing the new cameras on the side of the building. This whole thing had been a bit of a chore, but now that Ben saw the new equipment, it seemed like it was worth it. These cameras were a lot sleeker and less of an eyesore than the old ones.

"All right, that was the easy part," Jackson said, coming back down the ladder and tugging off his work gloves. "The problem is, you're gonna need all new wiring on the other end. That wasn't on the work order the town council sent, so I didn't bring the kit."

"Really? So what does that mean?" Ben asked.

"Means I gotta come back on Monday."

At that moment, a sleek, black BMW came careening into the parking lot and almost smashed right into Jackson's truck, which was parked across the first two spots. The man driving dropped a few F bombs, audible even though the roof on his convertible was up and the windows were closed, and Ben and Jackson exchanged a look. The car's brakes squealed as he zoomed into another spot, then got out of the car. He was wearing suit pants, no jacket, and a light blue tie slightly loosened, and he wavered on his feet as he walked toward them. One of his eyes was purpled and bruised, half swollen shut.

"This should be good," Jackson said under his breath.

"Is that your fucking truck?" the man spat at Jackson.

"Yes, sir, it is."

"You couldn't park it at the back of the fucking parking lot?" the man demanded. "You could kill someone."

Ben and Jackson looked at one another again. A half dozen retorts ran through Ben's mind. About how this man was clearly drunk and had one good eye and *he* could kill someone driving that way. About how the truck was just sitting there and he was the one who'd been speeding recklessly into a parking lot. About how he was an overprivileged jackass who could keep his opinions to himself.

But although Ben often thought these things, he was not the type of man who would ever say them. He was a peaceful man. A live-and-let-live kind of guy. And this piece of shit wasn't worth fighting with anyway. Jackson seemed to come to the same conclusion.

"Sorry. Won't happen again."

The man threw out a few more epithets, then turned and walked into The Tap Room. Ben was both relieved that the guy wasn't entering his own establishment in that condition and disgusted that he wasn't done drinking.

"Too bad your cameras are down," Jackson said. "That footage might come in handy if he tries to drive home later and kills himself."

KELSEY

Kelsey wished she had a costume. The raggedy black dress, the green skin, the crooked nose. There was something about standing there in the middle of the dusty stage with the house lights on, wearing her Oakmont Day hoodie and PINK sweatpants, that made it more difficult to summon the Wicked Witch of the West's evil laugh. Did that make her a bad actress? Probably. Emma Watson would be able to transform into whatever character was asked of her even if she was standing there in her bathrobe.

Her father's voice: *You're a worthless piece of shit. You'll never amount to anything.*

Her own voice: *Fuck. You.*

She'd done a fantastic job on the eulogy, after all. Several people had come up to her afterward with tears in her eyes. One woman had pressed a hundred-dollar bill into her hand—which Kelsey had given to a homeless woman outside the arena half an hour later. Now, Kelsey pointed at Rachel Falesto with her perfect Dorothy braids—typecasting all the way—and crooked her finger slightly as if she had arthritis, channeling her grandmother. She let out the laugh she'd been practicing in her room at night. It seemed to last forever, and when she was done the silence felt like it had weight. Everyone was staring at her.

Kelsey wondered if Emma Watson had a dickhead for a father.

"Great!" Mrs. Tisch said. "Great job, Kelsey. And then we'll have the purple smoke and Kelsey, you'll exit stage right and the lights will go down for the next setup. Good job! Let's take five, everybody."

Kelsey quickly walked off stage, clutching the hem of her sweatshirt in both her sweaty hands.

"That was awesome," Frankie Potts said, and wiped his nose with his sleeve.

"Thanks." She ducked her head and made for backstage, where her backpack and water bottle were. It was colder back there, somehow, and her teeth began to chatter. Which was weird. Because it definitely wasn't *that* cold. She dove for her backpack and sat on the floor, leaning her back against the wall. Her entire body was shivering now, out of control. She gripped her elbows and tried to stop it. People walked by, but she avoided eye contact. Like a three-year-old she was trying to believe that if she couldn't see them, they couldn't see whatever the hell this was that was happening to her. Not another panic attack. Her mother would put her in therapy.

"Hey."

Willow kicked her foot.

"What?" Kelsey snapped, clenching her jaw.

Willow seemed to notice something was amiss. "You okay? Why are you shaking?"

Kelsey felt a pang. Of guilt. Of nostalgia. Of something she couldn't name. But she shoved it away. "Like you care. Just leave me alone."

"Are you, like, tweaking?" Willow whispered.

"No!" Kelsey shouted. And the shouting stopped the trembling for a moment. Inspired, she stood up and started to bounce like a boxer. Somewhere in the back of her mind, the phrase *shake the sillies out* echoed. Something her father used to say? When had her father ever said anything as whimsical as that? She threw a few air punches, imagining he was in front of her.

"Ooookay." Willow eyed her from behind heavily blackened eyelashes. "So, listen, our moms are apparently going away to a spa on Friday and staying overnight. We should throw a party. At your house."

"Ha!" Kelsey stopped punching and hugged herself. "No way."

"Yes way."

"I have my audition on Saturday."

"So?"

"So I need to get a good night's sleep. And Hunter needs to bring me if my mom doesn't get back in time." Even though her mother had sworn on an actual Bible that she would be back in time. "We can't have a party."

"Um . . . having a party on Friday night is not going to affect your brother's ability to drive you to an audition on Saturday afternoon. It's Halloween this week. People need to party."

"Why can't we do it at *your* house?" Kelsey asked.

"Because your house is bigger, more private, and Hunter has more friends."

These were not points Kelsey could dispute.

"Hunter will never go for it. He doesn't break the rules."

Willow scoffed. "I'll take care of Hunter."

"Why don't you just back off him already? He's *my* brother," Kelsey said. "Get your own fucking family."

Willow glared at her. "Screw you, Walsh."

Kelsey watched her go, trying to remember why she had ever thought they were friends, and trying to wrap her brain around the fact that she was clearly stuck with her for life.

EMMA

"Toss me that tennis ball, would you?" Lizzie held out a hand.

"Lizzie, you've done enough, really," Emma said. "I can finish this up on my own."

My husband was sleeping with your daughter. Willow saw him the day he died. It was her. Your Willow is the girl we've been looking for all along.

Her stomach flooded with bile. She hadn't eaten all day.

"Stop trying to get rid of me already," Lizzie joked, looking over at Emma.

Emma quickly glanced away. She'd barely laid eyes on Lizzie since she arrived to help sort through James's collection just over an hour ago—instead pretending to be engrossed in the task at hand. James had kept a digital catalog of all the memorabilia he'd acquired over the years, and Emma had kept her eyes busy comparing his list to the list from the lawyers and checking things off as they inventoried everything. Along the way, she and Lizzie had discovered that there were several items missing from the basement collection—items that appeared in James's catalog but were not displayed where they should have been. But then, it was possible James had brought some of them to work or donated them or given them away as gifts. Emma just kept hoping that none of them would appear on the list the firm's lawyers had sent over.

Emma had tried to convince Lizzie not to come, but Lizzie insisted that she had nothing else to do anyway and wanted to help Emma in any way she could. There was no dissuading her. So now here she was, working alongside the woman whose daughter her husband had defiled.

She should just tell Lizzie. Just get it out. If she didn't, it was going to eat her alive. Every time she came to this conclusion, though, she'd think of how she'd feel under the same circumstances—if Kelsey and Darnell . . . And she'd be right back where she started, biting her tongue until she tasted blood.

"Are you okay?" Lizzie asked, lowering the clipboard she'd been using to make lists. "You're acting odd."

"Am I?" Emma's voice was reedy. "I think I'm just tired. I haven't been getting much sleep," she improvised.

Sleep. God. She had a horrible feeling she was never going to sleep again.

"Let's just finish this last pile and then I'll make you some lavender tea and you can go to bed early," Lizzie offered, reaching out to touch Emma's crooked knee. Emma flinched and Lizzie sighed.

"What's the matter? Are you mad at me or something?"

"No! Honestly. I'm just out of it." These vague excuses were going to start getting old soon.

You should hate me, Emma thought. *You should want to burn this room to the ground.*

Lizzie bent forward at the waist and stretched past Emma for the one lonely tennis ball that had somehow found its way into the basketball section of the room. She noted the date and signature on her list, then placed it with the other tennis things—mostly balls in small jewel cases, with a few signed programs from major tournaments sprinkled in. Then she glanced around, and Emma took the opportunity to do so as well, glad to focus on anything other than Lizzie.

There was something about taking apart the basement—James's

so-called museum—that was akin to plundering an ancient royal's tomb. All his precious belongings, for years enshrined behind glass and in protective cases, were now strewn about the floor or piled up in corners and labeled. Emma wanted to trash it all, regardless of what the kids wanted or were due, and ignore James's wishes. Her husband had been a lying, cheating, dishonorable drunk, and having anything he'd cared about anywhere near her made her skin crawl.

She tried to envision what this place could be now that James was gone. She'd have to do something with it, once she'd purged it of all his crap. It was prime square footage. But it had always belonged to her husband. Perhaps she should put his ashes down here and have the whole room hermetically sealed. Clearly, he'd cared about these possessions more than he'd cared about his family. Why not let him spend all eternity with them?

"Thanks again for doing this." Emma offered a wan smile.

"It's no problem. Really." Lizzie didn't look up.

She didn't seem entirely herself, either. She couldn't know, could she? What Willow and James had been doing?

"So, did you ever call that PI?" Lizzie asked, eyes still on the clipboard.

"Oh, that. No," Emma said. "Actually, I think you were right. I think I'm just going to drop it."

"Really?" Lizzie was surprised. "You were so adamant."

"I know, but . . ."

But I already know who it was. I don't have to look anymore.

"I've given it a lot of thought and I don't need to do this to myself. James made life miserable enough while he was here. Now that he's gone, I don't have to be miserable anymore unless I choose to be."

Lizzie's face brightened behind her smattering of freckles. "Emma, I'm so proud of you. That's a really healthy choice."

God, this was awful. "Thank you."

To give herself an excuse to look away, Emma reached her arms to the sky and stretched. Her back cracked in three places. This project she'd taken on was far more labor intensive than she ever would have been able to predict. She'd known James had a lot of crap in this basement, but she definitely hadn't realized the extent of it. There were dozens of drawers and every one they opened had revealed a new array of treasures, from championship pins to mini pennants to bobblehead dolls to commemorative plates. There was even a chunk of field grass from the old Yankee Stadium vacuum-sealed inside a Plexiglas cube. Yes, her husband had purchased dirt and hidden it away for safekeeping.

The good stuff—the rare gems and conversation pieces—had been displayed in glass cases with prime lighting, but the random crap was abundant, and concealed behind solid oak doors. The man had been a stealth hoarder.

"Well, I think this is a good time to take a break," Lizzie said. "We got all the baseball, tennis, hockey, and golf items cataloged."

She dropped her checklist and pushed herself into a fairly impressive downward-facing dog. Her back cracked, too, and she was younger than Emma, so the sound of it made Emma feel slightly better.

Emma pushed herself up off the floor and to her feet. Lizzie was right. They'd made a lot of progress. There were neat piles separated by sports. The larger piles were of things they were going to keep, and next to each was a smaller pile of things James had bequeathed to some organization or player. It really wasn't much, but Emma still wasn't sure which items Darnell and Charles and "the company" were going to lay claim to. She hoped it wouldn't be anything Hunter coveted, because she didn't want to get into a long, dragged-out fight over some random hockey stick or a signed mouth guard. (Disgusting.)

"So, what are we missing so far?" Lizzie asked Emma.

Her friend went into an upward-facing dog as Emma grabbed her list. "There are a couple of tennis balls, a golf glove, a few baseballs and pucks, but nothing James left to anyone yet. Except the Derek Jeter bat."

Emma glanced at the case where the bat used to live. It had been James's pride and joy—the centerpiece of his collection. A bat used in the 1998 World Series and signed by Yankees captain Derek Jeter. She could still remember the night James came home with it. His eyes had been so glazed she had assumed he was drunk, but for once he'd been quite sober—simply giddy over the fact that he'd managed to get Jeter to sign something in the midst of all the mayhem and the crush of press. The bat had to be worth thousands of dollars and James, the bastard, had left it to the Baseball Hall of Fame. That one was going to hurt for Hunter. If they could even find it.

"Where the hell could that have gone?" Emma mused.

"You should ask the kids," Lizzie said, standing as well.

"They get pissed at me every time I so much as bring this up." Emma sighed and looked around. "They see this as their father ripping their legacy out from under them."

Lizzie scoffed, and it sounded oddly sarcastic to Emma.

"What?" she asked.

"Nothing," Lizzie replied, tucking a curl behind her ear.

No. Something was up, but Emma wasn't about to ask. If she and Lizzie got into some deep conversation, who knew where it might lead? Standing there, right next to her friend, she felt separated from her by a yawning, dark chasm, and her heart broke a little. It was exactly what she'd been afraid of. She was going to lose Lizzie over this eventually. Somehow, some way. James had been dead for over a month, and he was still ruining her life

LIZZIE

Willow wasn't home when Lizzie got there after helping Emma pack up the last of the things in the basement. The door to her room was closed, but the light was on, and Lizzie went in, telling herself she was just going to flip the switch, conserve energy. She was surprised to find that the space was still relatively clean. Willow's laptop was not on her desk, the cord that attached it to the monitor snaked across the desktop over a pile of playing cards, and there were a few balled-up socks on the floor, but that was about it.

It was the little plastic cases on the hockey pucks that had gotten her thinking. They seemed oddly familiar, and then she'd remembered—she'd found something similar in the kitchen garbage can about a month ago and never got around to asking Willow what it was.

Now, Lizzie acted casual, as if this were any other breaching of her daughter's space for mundane straightening up. She plucked up the socks, flattened them out, and went to the closet to toss them in the hamper. When she opened the door, a jumble of crap came tumbling out—clothes and books and a lacrosse stick and a makeup kit, which exploded and spewed a million half-used products across her feet.

"Well. That explains the cleanliness."

Lizzie blew out a sigh, then laughed. At least her daughter had tried. She knelt and scooped the cosmetics back into the bag, then tossed it on the hastily made bed. After a quick sort through the clothes, trying and failing to figure out what was clean and what wasn't, she decided to dump it all in the hamper. It was as she stood that she saw the boxes from the corner of her eye. There were three of them, brown, cardboard, roughly the same size, stacked just inside the closet. Probably, before she opened the door, they'd been hidden by the pile of clothes. Next to the boxes was a roll of packing tape, a black Sharpie, and a tangle of bubble wrap.

Lizzie experienced a sixth-sense shiver down her neck. She shoved the clothes into the hamper and glanced at the top box, hoping to see the colorful label favored by Willow's favorite internet shop for magic supplies, but she knew that wasn't what this was. Those boxes were usually black and green. This was something else.

The box hadn't been sealed, but there was an address label affixed to the top:

Lionel Miller

43 Violet Lane

Tallman, Kansas

Who the hell was Lionel Miller in Tallman, Kansas? Mouth tacky, Lizzie reached a finger over and lifted the flap on the box.

EMMA

She woke up so early it was still dark out, and when she rolled over she expected to see James sleeping next to her. Then she remembered. Her eyes welled so fast, it was as if someone had turned on a fire hose inside her body and she was on her back, gasping for air.

James is dead. James is dead. James is dead.

Emma was never going to see her husband again. She pressed her hands to her forehead. What was wrong with her? Where was this coming from? Was this going to be her life now? Never knowing when she was going to start hyperventilating? She sat up, forced her breath into a more normal rhythm, grabbed a tissue, and blew her nose.

Okay, stop. Think. Calm down.

It had been just over a month. Where was James now? She looked up at the ceiling, trying to imagine a heaven. Trying to imagine James's heaven. Could he see her right now? No. God. She had to stop thinking like that. Even if heaven *was* real, James wouldn't be spending his time there watching her. He'd be stadium-hopping from Barcelona to Sydney to Los Angeles—there was probably some sort of game happening somewhere in the world at every moment of the day. Getting to see soccer and baseball and cricket and tennis and golf all in one day would be his bliss.

The only way he'd be watching her would be if he was pissed off at her. If he wanted vengeance for something. Or if he wanted to catch her in the act of doing something wrong—something he suspected while alive, but could never prove. Like eating all his granola bars or shrinking his favorite underwear.

Maybe he was watching Willow.

Emma grabbed a pillow and screamed into it. She wished she could talk to him. She wished she could ask him *why?* When? How? *Why?* He was the only one who could tell her what had really happened. How he'd gotten home safely, but been drunk enough to die that way. Whether Willow had been there with him, in the driveway. Or Darnell. Or anyone. Had he met with Willow that afternoon? If so, when had this big fight with Darnell happened—before that meeting or after? She wanted a timeline. She needed answers.

She pulled her knees close to her chest and stared across the hazy room. That last day. What had been different? Answer: nothing. It had been just like any other day after a big blowout. She'd slept late. Felt guilty. Wondered if the kids were okay. Felt the crushing defeat of having failed her children. Again. The only difference in that day was the decision she had made to tell him that she was divorcing him, but he couldn't know about that. She hadn't told anyone. And then he was dead.

Nothing was ever going to be the same again. Holidays, birthdays, family vacations. Those moments when James had been at his best. Thoughtful. Funny. Loving, even. They would never get a chance to see that James again. The kids . . . would they miss that part of their dad?

The kids. Hunter didn't know about Willow, did he? Or Kelsey. Would Willow have told them? No. She was eccentric, but she couldn't be that dense.

Emma glanced at the clock: 5:13. There was no chance of her going back to sleep. She threw the covers aside and got out of bed. She would make a big breakfast. Cooking always distracted her brain from heavier thoughts. And right now, she needed out of her brain in a major way. She was halfway down the stairs when she heard a clatter.

Her heart, that ridiculous thing, completely stopped. *James?* "Hello?" she said.

"Mom?"

Exhale. "Hunter?"

He appeared at the bottom of the stairs, half a protein bar in one hand. He was dressed for running—shorts, sneakers, sweatshirt, earbuds.

"Sorry. Did I wake you up?"

"No. No, of course not."

She patted his shoulder and walked into the kitchen, beelining it for the coffeemaker. "I hope you're going to wear something reflective."

He rolled his eyes. "My sneakers practically glow."

"Hunter, please." She dumped coffee into the filter and went to fill the pot. "I don't need any more tragedy right now. At least put on a white baseball cap."

"I don't have a white baseball cap."

"There are about a hundred of them in the basement. Have your pick." She gestured vaguely in that direction.

Hunter didn't move. Emma finished setting up the coffeemaker, then hit the button. When she turned around, he was chewing slowly, looking off toward the hallway to the basement.

"Hunter, can I ask you a question?" Emma said.

"You just did," he joked, an old standby.

"Hilarious," she said flatly. "Seriously, though, do you have any idea what happened to the Derek Jeter bat?"

"What happened to it? What do you mean?" he asked. He wrapped up the rest of his protein bar and shoved it in his pocket.

"It's not downstairs," she said. "Did you or Kelsey do something with it?"

"What, like hide it?" he snapped.

"What? No! I just thought you guys might have been playing with it—"

"We're not five, Mom."

He was putting in his earbuds, zipping up his sweatshirt.

"Hunter, I know. I didn't mean it like that," she said as he started to turn away. "Hunter, I'm talking to you!"

"What, Mom?" He tipped his face toward the sky briefly, as if fed up. "I have to go for my run before all the cars are out."

"Forget it." She was blushing angrily, and felt embarrassed by his dismissal of her. "Forget I said anything."

Hunter blew out another, audible sigh. "I don't know where the Jeter bat is. Maybe Dad brought it into the office. He kept going on about that door prize thing, remember? He needed something to give away at that stupid party the night he died? Maybe it was that."

"No. He donated a jersey. Evan Longoria," she said, feeling like she was on autopilot.

"Well, maybe he decided to add the bat at the last minute."

"Okay, but why would he have donated something he'd already bequeathed elsewhere?" she asked.

"Hell if I know, Mom." Hunter began backing toward the foyer, palms turned up facetiously. "Why the fuck did Dad do anything?"

KELSEY

One second, it wasn't happening, and then all at once, it was. One second she was walking to history class, and then people were jogging toward her and past her, looking over their shoulders—scattering. Someone whispered Hunter's name and then Kelsey was moving against the current, running toward whatever it was they were fleeing from. She heard shouting. Hunter, shouting. Around the corner, into the senior hallway, just as a girl yelped and a slam sounded, so loud it reverberated through Kelsey's teeth.

"Oh my God, your brother's hulking out."

Two freshman girls hovered nearby, one filming with her phone, the other clutching her books. Up ahead, a crowd. And in the center, there was Hunter, with his fist impossibly imbedded in a locker door, blood dripping on the floor. Willow, of all people, cowered in front of him. His fist was right next to her face. Her posture was cowering, but she gazed at him defiantly.

"What did you do to him?" Kelsey demanded. She grabbed her brother's arm and gingerly tugged on it, detaching flesh from metal. The gashes were deep, the skin peeled back. When he saw it, he went green and staggered sideways a step.

"Oh, that's classic, Kelsey. He tries to punch me in the face and you blame me?" Willow's voice was shrill, not her own, and Kelsey could tell that she was trying not to cry. "Always blame the woman!"

She threw her arms up, performing for the gathered crowd, the poised phones. Then she turned around and jogged out the back door, shoving it open so hard with the heel of her hand that it slammed back against the outer brick wall.

The crowd began to disperse.

"What the hell happened?" she asked her brother, who was now cradling his arm against his chest, blood dripping down under his shirt-sleeve. "Did you really try to punch her?"

"No! I would never do that. I wasn't aiming for her face. I didn't . . . She was just talking all this shit about Dad. Like out of nowhere. And then I didn't even realize what I was doing and I punched the locker." He sucked in air past his teeth. "Shit. Kelsey."

One look in his eyes told her what he was thinking. This was the kind of shit their dad did. Intimidating them. Scaring them. *Almost* hitting them. It was a special kind of terror, never knowing if or when the switch would flip. Not knowing whether today was the day he'd choose to cross that line.

Hunter didn't want to be like him. Neither did Kelsey. But maybe it was too late.

"Come on, I'll take you to the nurse."

She put her arm around him as the bell rang, and together they walked through the empty halls, little sister, for once, taking care of big brother.

GRAY

There were about a million things to do. Arguments to be written. Settlements to file. The budget for the firm's holiday party to be approved. Dante and Derek's birthday was coming up, so there was that trip to plan. There were appointments to be made. Notes to go over for the next council meeting. Emails to answer. Bills to be paid.

A best friend to cajole into forgiving her. Even though she didn't believe that keeping James's actions a secret had been wrong.

But Gray couldn't do any of it. Her concentration was nil. Seeing Lizzie at his office yesterday had raised too many questions. This had gone on long enough and the tipping point had arrived. She had to talk to Darnell. She had to know what he knew. What he'd seen. What he'd done.

He was in bed, a newspaper tilted up in front of him, his reading glasses at the end of his nose. She hated to disturb his moment of peace, but if she didn't, she'd never have any for herself.

"Darnell, where were you the night James died?" she asked.

He looked up at her, standing in the doorway of their bedroom, still wearing her suit from work, her heels dangling from her fingers at her side.

"I was at the office party. You know that."

He went back to reading, as if this wasn't anything more important than a discussion about the carpet cleaners. Gray went to her closet, put her shoes in their appropriate place on their appropriate shelf, and braced her hands against the wall for a moment, giving herself strength. Back in the bedroom, she crawled onto the comforter beside him and took the paper out of his hands, folding it and placing it between them. Darnell looked at her, curious.

"No, later that night. Or the next morning, to be more accurate." When he said nothing, she had to bite back her frustration. "Emma called me to tell me James was dead, and while we were on the phone, your car pulled into the driveway."

Darnell blinked. He turned his head so he was facing forward again, and his brow furrowed. For an awful moment, Gray was sure he was going to tell her he didn't remember, but then, he did.

"I was at Powerhouse," he said. "I was still amped up after the party, so I drove over to the gym. Heavy bag workout." He bit his lip and fisted his hands, doing a comical little jab-jab-cross. "I'd forgotten about that. Still had some adrenaline in me, apparently."

"So you were at the gym." There was a giddy sensation, like champagne bubbles, rising inside Gray's chest. The gym had a half dozen security cameras. It had to, being open twenty-four hours. She could get that footage. If push came to shove, and Lizzie forced her, she could use it. "For how long?"

"An hour. An hour and a half." He shrugged, then really looked at her. "Why are you asking?"

She didn't want to tell him she was worried about Lizzie—worried that the woman was still whispering in Emma's ear about hiring a PI, and doing the job herself in the meantime. She hadn't mentioned the odd encounter with Lizzie to Darnell yesterday because she'd wanted a nice, drama-free lunch with him and the boys, and that was exactly what it had turned out to be—the four of them laughing over salads and burgers, making plans, being themselves again.

But why had Lizzie been crying? Had she actually seen Darnell? Had she witnessed one of his episodes?

The thought terrified Gray. That Lizzie might have seen that side of her husband. That she might have uncovered the ugly truth about Gray's life. Lizzie couldn't know.

"Gray?"

"Did you see Lizzie Larkin in your office yesterday?" she asked.

"How did you—"

"I bumped into her in the lobby." Gray's stomach was suddenly slick with worry. "She seemed . . . upset."

Darnell took in a deep breath, his already broad chest expanding beneath his white T-shirt. He removed his glasses, folded them, and pinched the bridge of his nose.

"There's something I have to tell you," he said, looking her in the eye. "And you're not gonna like it."

LIZZIE

"I restocked the Prandhya stoneware, but I think you're going to need to call and order more," Aurora said. "I don't know what's going on, but her bowls and mugs are suddenly our most popular items."

"That's great!" Lizzie said, but her voice had a quaver in it. She was itching for Aurora to leave. The street outside was dark, the packs of colorful daytime trick-or-treaters having gone home to count their loot. Halloween was normally one of Lizzie's favorite holidays. She usually closed early to run home and be there for as many candy-grubbers as she could. This year, though, she hadn't been able to get into the spirit of the holiday, and there were things she needed to do before she went home to talk to Willow.

"Well, I guess I'll see you tomorrow." Aurora shouldered her leather bag and paused at the door, probably waiting for Lizzie to ask what she was doing tonight. Lizzie pretended to be distracted by a text.

"Yes, see you tomorrow! Happy Halloween!"

Aurora shrugged, and was gone. Lizzie went to the door and locked it, then shut off all the lights. In the back office, she pulled out her laptop and opened it, tapping one finger on the desk as it booted up. Password, internet, bank website.

The screen lit up in blues and greens as she opened her accounts. Her heart did a pitter-patting dance inside her chest as she scrolled down, feeling hot with anticipation.

And there it was. Her new balance. Lizzie sat back in her chair and smiled.

EMMA

Emma had gone back and forth about it all day. Cancel the overnight with Lizzie, or don't cancel? If she wanted to stay friends with her, Emma was going to have to find a way to spend time with her one-on-one. But this seemed like too much, too soon. She was very much on edge, and worried that she might simply blurt out the truth—especially if she got too relaxed or too drunk.

But was it possible to get too relaxed at this point? The knots in her shoulders felt like cannonballs.

Emma stared at the contents of her closet, her overnight bag open at her feet. The truth of the matter was, she needed Lizzie. Especially now that things with Gray were such a mess. Maybe that was selfish of her, but didn't she have the right to be a teeny bit selfish right now? James was the one who'd royally fucked up, not her. She couldn't hold herself responsible for every mistake he'd ever made. She couldn't let his horrible life choices ruin both her closest friendships.

She was just going to have to figure out a way to be normal around Lizzie. To swallow what she knew and try like hell not to choke on it. Moving on. It was what Lizzie wanted her to do, and she was right. Forward was the only way through.

GRAY

Gray had barely slept the past three nights. She couldn't believe Darnell had thought she wouldn't want to hear his news. It was the greatest news of all time. Horrible that he'd kept it a secret from her these many years. Insane that he'd used so much of the firm's money. But the information itself, the things Lizzie Larkin had done . . . it was like music to Gray's ears.

She was finally rid of the woman. Or she would be. If only she hadn't promised Darnell she wouldn't tell.

That was what had really kept her up, and had distracted her all day. Should she be loyal to her husband or to her best friend? Yes, Emma would be hurt. Devastated, potentially. But she would get over it. Wasn't it better to know? Wasn't that, in fact, the rhetoric Emma had been spouting the last few weeks? She wanted the truth—was desperate for it—and Gray had truth to tell.

Besides, the more she thought about it, the more she couldn't really see how telling this news would be a betrayal of Darnell. Yes, she'd be breaking one, small promise, but the revelation of what he'd told her could have no blowback on him. It only re-solidified the fact that he was a good man. That he was the best of men.

Which was why, less than seventy-two hours after swearing to him that she wouldn't tell, she was calling Emma's number. She needed her friend back. Really, she needed her now more than ever, what with Darnell's condition. So yes, this was a selfish act. But it was also a benevolent act. And a vengeful act. And a prideful act. It was so many things, Gray felt dizzy trying to contain them all.

The first try went to voicemail. Gray cursed under her breath as she paced her office and called again. She would keep calling until Emma picked up. And if Emma didn't pick up, she would drive over there. Now that she'd made the decision to tell, she had to get it over with.

Finally, a connection. Some fumbling. The sound of wind whooshing. Then, "Gray?"

"Emma! Thank God. I keep trying you."

"I know, I know, but now's not really a good time," Emma said, distracted. "I'm on my way to Lizzie's. We're going to a spa for the night."

Alarms blared in Gray's head. "What? Emma, no. That's not a good idea. I need to talk to you."

"It's going to have to wait until I get back." Emma's voice was both firm and exasperated. "I'll call you tomorrow or Sunday."

"Emma, I really don't think it's a good idea for you to—"

"Oh, shoot. Gray, I'm getting another call."

"Emma—"

"I have to take this. Talk to you soon."

And she was gone.

EMMA

It was Lizzie who Emma clicked over to speak to, half hoping she was going to cancel and make the decision for her.

"Lizzie?"

"Emma, hi! Just making sure you're still coming." She sounded oddly manic. "We need to hit the road if we're going to make tonight's evening meditation."

"I'm almost there," Emma said.

"Great. Just leave the car on and I'll come out. Do you have the gift card?"

"Yes." Emma's hackles went up out of nowhere. There was something about Lizzie always doing things on the cheap or expecting Emma to pay that got under her skin at the oddest moments. "Yes, I have the gift card."

Emma hung up the phone and tried to shake it off. It wasn't her money they were spending, anyway, it was a gift from James. And didn't James owe Lizzie? Didn't they both?

Suddenly, everything around her—inside and outside the car—went into sharp relief. Emma had heard about people having epiphanies, but she was never sure she'd had one herself. Now she was positive she'd never had one, because this clarity of vision was an entirely new experience.

What was owed to Lizzie.

Was it at all possible that Lizzie *had* known what was going on between James and her daughter?

The light up ahead went from yellow to red, and Emma stepped on the brake, glad to have the excuse to stop. She gripped and released the steering wheel over and over again, trying to make sense of the thoughts swirling around in her mind.

Could this be why Lizzie had tried to focus Emma's attention on Darnell when she'd said she suspected someone had been there the night James died? Why she'd initially dissuaded Emma from looking for a mistress? Or from hiring a private investigator? Because Willow was the mistress and Lizzie knew about it?

Emma put her forehead on the steering wheel as more memories rushed back at her. Lizzie asking about the will. Wondering if there would be names named—whether the beneficiaries in the will would have to attend the reading. It had been a bit much, actually, now that she thought about it. Had Lizzie imagined that James might leave something to Willow?

Her throat closed over and she felt like she was choking. A horn honked and Emma looked up. Green light. She gasped in a breath and floored it. James screwing a child. Her mother, her *friend*, knowing about it. She didn't know whether to be angry at Lizzie or ashamed. Why hadn't she told Emma? Why hadn't she stopped it?

She didn't know what to think, what to do, what to say. She only knew she had to get to Lizzie. She had to find out whether Lizzie had known. But what if she *didn't* know? What if it was all conjecture? Emma could be driving like a bat out of hell over to Lizzie's house to tell her that her husband had taken advantage of Lizzie's daughter.

This brought her foot slightly off the gas, but she kept driving anyway and soon she was there, pulling into the driveway, getting out of the car.

Emma staggered toward the house, eyes bleary, hair whipped sideways by the wind, still with no conceivable plan in mind. Lizzie swept out the front door with her bag, ready for a lovely spa weekend, her wild hair loose around her shoulders, her floral print suitcase bumping down the steps behind her. She took one look at Emma's face and dropped everything.

"Emma? What's wrong?"

"Did you know?" Emma blurted. Tears leaked from the corners of her eyes.

Lizzie paled slightly. "Know what?"

"About Willow. And . . ." She swallowed hard, hand on her stomach. "James?"

Lizzie blinked about a thousand times. She put the suitcase down and raised her hands. "Emma, listen, I—"

"Oh, God. It's true. They were sleeping together. Oh my God." Emma wavered on her feet, but couldn't go forward toward Lizzie or back toward her car. If she took a step, she'd go down. So she simply stood there and rocked back and forth like a boat on a wind-tossed sea.

Lizzie looked stricken. "Wait. What? No. No! Emma, no. Willow and James were not sleeping together!"

"I have emails, Lizzie! Willow was begging him to see her again. On the day he died! Begging. And you knew about it, didn't you? All this time, you knew!"

"Emma, calm down. Just . . . take a breath and listen to me." Lizzie was there. Right there. In front of her. Gathering up her hands.

"Willow was not sleeping with James. She was James's daughter."

KELSEY

Her mother had already left for Lizzie's to pick her up and go to the spa, kissing Kelsey on the cheek, promising again to be back before her four o'clock audition so that she could take her. The woman just blindly trusted that neither of her kids would ever throw a party. Of course she thought that. A month and a half ago, neither of them would have ever considered it. Just imagine James Walsh stumbling home to find his kids doing whippets on the lawn with a bunch of half-in-the-bag minors. She could only imagine what that shit storm would have looked like. Would he have freaked out and told everyone to go home, or would he have grabbed a bottle out of Rico Thomas's hands and pounded it? Hard to tell.

Still, she kind of couldn't believe Hunter had said yes. Maybe he was trying to make it up to Willow after almost punching her in the face. In fact, maybe Willow had goaded him into almost punching her in the face so that Hunter would agree to the party out of guilt. It was a manipulation Kelsey could easily imagine Willow pulling off.

Whenever Kelsey thought about that day, taking Hunter to the nurse, helping him explain, she felt oddly gratified. Or was it vindicated? Because seeing him there, with his fist in the locker next to Willow's huge eyes, she knew for the first time how Hunter felt. Whatever the DNA test said, he didn't think of Willow as his sister. Because he never would have done that to Kelsey. Never in a million years. It made her feel powerful, knowing this. Like Willow couldn't control her. Not anymore.

The other important takeaway from that day was that Willow hadn't reported Hunter. She hadn't told her mother or their mother. She'd kept his secret. Which meant that Willow, who Kelsey had previously believed to be strong and defiant and untouchable, actually had a weakness, and that weakness was Hunter. It was as if her entire worldview had changed in that one moment. If Willow wasn't going to tell on them, then maybe Kelsey could stop being so damn nice.

Downstairs, people were beginning to arrive. Kelsey smoothed her hair and applied a bit of lip gloss, checking herself out in the mirror over her dresser. From this angle, she could see her bed and wondered if she should lock the door. The last thing she wanted was anyone fooling around in here, or going through her things. She dug the key out of her desk drawer and shoved it deep into her pocket, then clicked the lock and walked out. Hunter was just emerging from his own room. Downstairs, bass pounded through the surround-sound speakers and pool balls clacked. Willow greeted a newcomer with a shriek.

Kelsey's pulse was all wrong. She could feel it in parts of herself where she'd never felt it before. In her face, between her toes. She and Hunter regarded each other for a long moment, then he started walking toward her and was about to slip past her down the stairs without a word.

"Are you sure about this? If the cops come, you're the one who's getting arrested and Mom is gonna freak."

Hunter looked up at her, his face half in shadow. "The way I figure it, we're going down anyway. Might as well go down in a blaze of glory."

LIZZIE

"I can't believe this! You're my best friend! I can't believe you've been *lying* to me all this time!" Emma shouted. "How? How did you . . . ? It doesn't even make any sense. The kids were in grade school when you moved here. How did you—?"

Emma went on like this for a few minutes, pacing and ranting, and Lizzie thought it best to just let her. If she tried to explain, if she tried to talk over her in this moment of shock, nothing would register.

But then the rain started to come down—fat, cold drops so vicious they stung—and Lizzie managed to tug her friend into the foyer by the arm, dragging her suitcase back in along with them.

Now they were in the kitchen, and Lizzie had somehow managed to put together two steaming mugs of tea. Emma sat at the table, sideways in a chair, completely drained of energy. Lizzie placed a mug on the table near her friend and sat.

"Are you okay?" she asked Emma.

Emma flinched and said nothing. She'd gone semi-catatonic.

So, here they were. The day Lizzie had been dreading for the last ten years had finally come. She could still remember the first time she'd met Emma, behind the school at second-grade pickup. By then she'd done enough googling of James Walsh to know what her name was, what she looked like, and that she had a daughter as well as the son who had been born just weeks before her own child. Lizzie had come to Oakmont Day prepared to hate Emma Walsh. For all her lovely smiles in the photos she'd found online, she'd assumed Emma would be a spoiled bitch, a woman who knew her vaunted place and lorded it over everyone else. She'd driven by their house, she'd looked up the price of the luxury SUV Emma drove, she knew they'd gone to Turks & Caicos and Disney World and Italy in the last year.

Emma Walsh had a charmed life. She had the life Lizzie should have had. And she hated her for it.

And then, Emma introduced herself. She welcomed Lizzie and asked her all sorts of questions about herself and about Willow. She gasped over the address of the house Lizzie had purchased, saying it was one of her favorites in town and that if she'd had her choice she would have lived in an old Victorian or cottage and not the modern monstrosity her husband had chosen.

Ungrateful, Lizzie had thought. But then in the next second, no. Because Emma was so free of guile. She was so genuine. It was clear she was only a woman who disagreed with her husband's preferred architecture style. A woman whose husband was a cheater and who was clearly, blissfully, ignorant of that fact.

When Emma had invited Willow over for a playdate, Lizzie had accepted. Yes, she wanted to see the inside of that house, but more than that, she wanted to know this woman. Wanted to know what Emma was that she, Lizzie, was not. The friendships that had blossomed that day over animal crackers and apple juice, and coffee and lady fingers, were a surprise. And now, ten years later, she was on the verge of losing it all.

"I guess I should start at the beginning."

Emma looked at her, expression blank.

"I was just out of college, a design assistant at a big firm in New York, commuting in from my parents' house." Lizzie cupped her hands around her mug, but it did nothing to warm her. "Basically, I ran for fabric

swatches and coffee and whatever else anyone needed, but it was an excit-
ing job. We got to decorate the penthouse apartments of some pretty fabulous people, but my boss wanted to get into corporate and was
constantly networking and schmoozing. Then, one day, she came back to
the office with a huge announcement—she'd gotten us our first corporate
gig—the new offices of Garrison and Walsh.

"I met James on my second day there," Lizzie continued. "He was so
handsome and larger than life—"

Emma glanced away and Lizzie's mouth snapped shut. This wasn't a
time to wax poetic. She sipped her tea and it scalded her tongue, but also
gave her the jolt she needed to keep going.

"We flirted some," she said in a more clinical tone. "I was flattered.
He was clearly powerful. And he didn't wear a wedding ring. I thought he
liked me. I thought that maybe . . ."

Outside, the wind whistled and threw a smattering of raindrops
against the windows like a hail of bullets.

"Anyway, we slept together." Lizzie averted her eyes. "A . . . few times.
And then I got pregnant."

She didn't bother telling Emma how it ended. How that awful
woman JJ had walked in on them having sex in his office and threatened
to report James to Darnell and HR. What had ever come of that, Lizzie
had no idea, but she assumed, now, that James had somehow paid JJ off
or fired her and covered up whatever complaints she made. The woman
was clearly bitter about the whole thing. But after that, James had never
called Lizzie again and never responded to her attempts to contact him.

"Hunter is a month older than Willow," Emma said, her voice quiet.
"So when he was sleeping with you, he already knew—" She paused, took
a quick breath. "He already knew I was having a baby."

Lizzie wished she could summon James Walsh back from the dead
and strangle him for doing this to the both of them—for causing Emma
this much pain over and over again. But maybe this would be the end of
it. Maybe, if she could just get this story out, they could deal with the
fallout and Emma could begin to heal. She took a breath for courage.

"I didn't tell him until I was three months along. That was what all the websites and books advised. Don't tell anyone until you're sure the baby's sticking around. I can still remember how nervous I was the day I went to his office to share the news. I was half scared he'd tell me to have an abortion and half hopeful he'd—"

Her throat closed over. It was unbelievable that it could still make her so emotional after all this time. But over the years the emotions had changed. At first it had been humiliation and anger that had made her choke up when she thought of that time in her life. Now she just felt sorry for the girl she'd been. There were so many things she would have done differently if she could.

"Oh my God. You thought he might want to raise the baby with you," Emma said, and faced forward in her chair for the first time. "You thought he might ask you to marry him."

Lizzie gave her friend a rueful look. "It sounds so stupid now." She anxiously turned her tea mug around and around with her fingertips. "Anyway, that's when he told me about you. He told me he was married and that you were pregnant, too. He basically told me to get the hell out of his office and not come back."

Emma's mouth hung open for half a second and then she closed her eyes. Lizzie almost ran for a bucket, because she was certain her friend was going to throw up. But then the moment passed. Emma took her first gulp of tea and winced. She leaned forward and put her head in her hands, elbows propped on the table.

"So what did you do? How the hell did you end up here? In our lives?"

The million-dollar question. "I was still living with my parents up-state, so they helped me through the birth, and right after Willow was born, I sent James a photo of her and a letter, asking for support." She looked up at Emma. "I kept waiting for you to find that letter. You've been looking all over the house . . ." Her stomach twisted and she kneaded her fingers together. "But I guess he must have thrown it out."

"So, he said no?" Emma said.

Lizzie gave a short, sarcastic laugh. "No, actually. He wrote back and said he would help."

"What?" Emma was stunned.

Lizzie nodded. "He started sending me a monthly check, and then later it was direct deposits from Garrison and Walsh, as if I were an employee. And it helped me save enough money to eventually move here and buy this house."

Emma looked flabbergasted. "How long did he . . . ? I mean, was he still sending you this money?" She sat up straight again, her brow furrowed. "Is that why you were so interested in the will? Because without him here—"

"The checks were going to stop coming," Lizzie finished. "Yes. There was part of me that thought . . . I don't know . . . that there would be some lump sum or college fund or something in his will. I don't know."

Emma put her face in her hands again. "I don't know what to say. Why *wouldn't* he put Willow in his will? He obviously cared. If he was sending you money all that time." She let her hands drop.

Lizzie felt horrible as she said, "That's the thing, though. It turns out he wasn't sending me that money all those years."

"I don't understand," Emma said.

And then the doorbell rang.

GRAY

"Where is she?" Gray said the second Lizzie opened the door. She pushed into the house, shoving the hood of her raincoat down off her hair. It wasn't as if she thought Lizzie was going to do Emma physical harm—there was no reason to at this point, and besides, Lizzie didn't have the stones. Still, she needed to get Emma out of here, away from this woman. She needed to regain control of the situation. "Emma?"

"Gray?"

She was sitting at the kitchen table, jacket on, hair wet, a mug of tea in front of her. There was another mug across the table and a packed bag on the floor. A cozy little cup of tea before they embarked on their trip. At least she'd gotten here in time.

"Come on." Gray waved her hand in a *let's go* gesture. "I'm taking you home."

"Why?" For the first time Gray noticed that Emma seemed drained, her skin glossy and wan.

"You can't trust her, Em," Gray said. "She's been lying to you for ten years."

"I know," Emma said.

Gray barely heard her, didn't register the words. "Willow is James's daughter."

"She *knows*," Lizzie said, coming up behind Gray, hugging herself with her hands tucked under her arms. She was wearing some sort of weird afghan poncho thing that was far too garish and far too large.

"You *know*?" Gray breathed, placing her hands on the back of an empty chair. "How?"

"She just told me," Emma said.

"I'm sorry." Gray cupped her skull with her hands. "You have been obsessed for weeks with finding your husband's mistress and now you find out that *she* had an affair with him and you're just sitting here having tea with her? Why are you not furious?"

Emma's eyes looked very tired. "I don't know, Gray. Maybe I'm in shock. How do *you* know about Willow?"

Lizzie calmly went to the cabinet for another mug, her ugly sweater shifting around her. "Did Darnell tell you?"

"Did Darnell tell her what?" Emma demanded.

"That he was the one paying me off," Lizzie said, filling the mug from the teapot. At least her hand was shaking, Gray noticed. Because the calm in this room was all wrong. "Darnell was the one sending me monthly checks all that time."

"He . . . what?" Emma looked at Gray. "*You* knew about this?"

Gray raised her hands. "I only just found out."

No need to mention that *just* meant earlier this week. Emma stood up and started pacing, running her hands through her hair. "This is insane. I don't . . . why would Darnell do that?"

Lizzie handed the steaming mug to Gray. Gray stared into it for half a second before narrowing her eyes at Lizzie.

"Do you have any vodka?"

She didn't want to stay here a moment longer, but clearly Emma wasn't leaving, and now she felt blindsided. Lizzie had told Emma the truth? Why now, after all these years? Her body was still quaking with adrenaline as her mind fought to catch up to what was happening.

"Gray, talk. What did Darnell know? Where did this money come from? Why would he *do* this?"

Gray glanced at Lizzie, who lifted one shoulder, giving her permission to tell the story. As if she needed Lizzie's permission. This was *her* husband's decision—her information to tell. At least Lizzie had fished out an Absolut bottle from somewhere. She poured Gray a couple of fingers and handed over the glass.

"Apparently, just after the *affair*," she said frostily, "Darnell found some letter from Lizzie on James's desk. He asked James what he was going to do about it and James said he wasn't going to do anything. He figured the problem would just go away."

Lizzie blew out a breath, and Gray took a gulp of vodka to keep from shooting the woman an understanding look. Because yes, men could suck the way no one else knew how to suck. Especially James Walsh.

After Gray had complained to her husband about Lizzie's stalking, he'd called Lizzie and set up a meeting. When Lizzie had gone to Darnell's office, he'd told her the truth about who had been subsidizing her all these years, and told her that if she would stop watching his house and making his wife skittish, he'd continue the payments. The truth was, he was going to continue the payments anyway, but Lizzie didn't need to know that.

"Darnell tried to convince him to take responsibility at the time, but when James refused, Darnell stepped in."

Emma's eyes shone. She shook her head, and Gray knew that she was absorbing this latest revelation about James's character. It couldn't feel good. How much could one woman take before she shattered?

"Darnell told me he did it because he was worried I'd go to the press and make a big stink out of it," Lizzie said, handing Gray a mug full of black coffee. "He was worried about potential—"

"Negative PR," all three of them said in unison.

And then Gray and Emma locked eyes and somehow, miraculously, laughed. Lizzie looked at them like they were crazy. But this was just more evidence of the deep connection between Gray and Emma—their long history of shared moments and dumb personal jokes. However petty it was, it gratified Gray that Lizzie didn't get it. However she could illustrate that Lizzie Larkin was on the outside, she would do it. If it helped remind Emma of how long they'd been friends. If it helped win her back. When their laughter finally abated, Lizzie angled herself between Gray and Emma.

"But I think he also did it because he's legitimately a good person," she told Gray. "Now, having spoken with him about it . . . I can see that about him. I'm sorry I ever thought he might have had something to do with James's death."

Gray's eyes darted to Emma, but Emma was just watching Lizzie, her expression almost mystified. Which made sense. Considering the amount of shocking information she'd just had spewed at her, it might take hours—maybe days—for her to sort through it all.

"Anyway, I'm just eternally grateful. If you guys ever need anything . . ." Lizzie continued. "I mean, not that I'm really in a position to help you in any way, but you know."

Gray was stunned by Lizzie's generosity. After all these years of rivalry and snarky remarks and undercutting, it was just so simple for her. Gray's family had supported her family, and all else fell away.

Then Lizzie turned to Emma. "There's one other thing you should know."

KELSEY

"Is it weird, living in the house where your dad killed himself?"

Kelsey's grip on her water bottle tightened. What was weird was the fact that Felicity Wells was in her house. That she felt welcome here. That she had the gall to say something like that.

"He didn't kill himself, Felicity!" one of her friends said, gasping, but laughing. "It was an accident."

Felicity's eyes trailed over Kelsey's bare shoulder to the door between the kitchen and the space that had formerly been the garage. She and her friends were huddled around the keg, alternately gaping at Hunter's hot friends and peppering Kelsey with inane questions.

"But doesn't it freak you out, just being here?" Mychaella Carson asked. "I'm creeped out and I've only been here ten minutes."

Kelsey turned around and left the room without a word. The usual chorus of *freak* and *loser* and *weirdo* following after her. But she didn't care. Tomorrow she would kill her audition, and then she'd get through the rest of the semester and she'd never have to deal with these people again. Also, she'd just realized that she hadn't seen Willow in a while, and that couldn't be good. Slowly, Kelsey made her way through the house, slipping from room to room unnoticed as she expected to, being a lowly freshman and all. Half the people here probably didn't even know this was her house—didn't realize Hunter had a sister. As much as she railed against it in her daily life, sometimes being invisible had its benefits.

God, please let me get into Daltry, she thought, stepping over the outstretched legs of a couple who were making out with their backs up against the living room wall. *Please get me away from these people.*

Upstairs, Hunter had locked their mom's room, thank God. Otherwise, Willow probably would have already made off with half her jewelry. Four boys in backwards baseball caps were gathered around the Xbox in Hunter's room playing Fortnite. A couple was going at it in the guest room, but neither of the amorous parties was Willow. Her room was still, mercifully, locked. That left the basement.

Hunter had told everyone as they came in that no one was allowed in the basement. "It's a construction zone," she'd heard him telling people, the lie sliding off his tongue like ice on a hot day. "I don't want anyone down there." The tenor of his voice had left no room for arguments. If Hunter Walsh told you what he wanted or didn't want, the people abided by his wishes.

It must be good to be king.

Kelsey slipped downstairs, opened the basement door, and heard movement. She closed the door behind her and tiptoed down. The storage room lights were out, but the door to her dad's museum was open, and it blazed like an arena on concert night. Kelsey walked over and found Willow, on her knees, shoving her father's things into a garbage bag.

"What the fuck are you doing?" Kelsey demanded.

Willow whirled around, saw Kelsey, and relaxed.

"Taking what's mine."

She went back to her task as if Kelsey weren't there. As if Kelsey were a smear of dog crap on the bottom of her shoe.

"You can't just take that stuff," Kelsey snapped. "The lawyers—"

"Like I give two shits about the lawyers," Willow said, and scoffed. She got up and slung the black bag over her shoulder like Santa Claus.

"They're your mom's problem, not mine. None of them even know I exist. *Our* father made sure of that."

"Give it back!" Kelsey snapped, and made a grab for the bag.

Willow swept her arm wide, knocking Kelsey aside with such force that Kelsey slammed into the wall. With the wind knocked out of her, she crumpled to the floor. Her vision swam, then crystallized, her jaw clenching so tightly she heard a crack. Willow was laughing.

"Your dad was right," she said, looking down at Kelsey. "You are worthless."

Kelsey had told her that in confidence. The fact that Willow felt it was okay to throw it back in her face made her vision turn purple. She pushed her hair out of her eyes and grabbed the nearest baseball bat.

EMMA

The box contained one football, two baseballs, and a golf glove, all auto-graphed, all in their protective casing. It also contained James's cell phone.

Emma reached in and pulled it out. "It *was* Willow on the other end of the line."

"Apparently," Lizzie said. "It's dead now. I tried to turn it on."

"Of course you did," Gray said.

"You know, your way of doing things is not the only way of doing things," Lizzie said.

"Well, *your* way of doing things isn't any sane person's way of doing things," Gray replied.

"Ladies!" Emma shouted.

They both fell silent. The three of them were standing in Lizzie's bedroom, the box open on her bed. Emma had no idea where Willow was or if she was going to walk through the door at any moment.

"Why would Willow have picked up when Emma called? The caller ID would have shown it was her," Gray said.

"No. It wouldn't." Emma pressed the phone between both hands. "He had me in there as TLL."

"What does that mean?" Lizzie asked.

Emma flushed. "The little lady." Gray snorted. "I know. It was a personal joke between the two of us. A long time ago. Anyway. It doesn't matter."

She sighed, avoiding meeting their eyes.

"Lizzie, where did Willow get all this stuff?" she said, gesturing at the box. "And how did she get his phone?"

"The phone is a long story," Lizzie said, tucking her hair behind her ear and plucking out one of the baseballs. "The rest of these things were packed in separate boxes with addresses all over the country. I think she was maybe selling it?"

Suddenly, Emma remembered Kelsey's computer, open to eBay, but not to her own account. She turned around and sat down on the bed, still holding James's phone in one hand.

"I know where Willow got the phone. She stole it," Gray said. "Probably right out of James's pocket."

"Gray," Emma said, exasperated.

"What?" Gray said. "She's been picked up by the cops for shoplifting more than once."

"How do you know about that?" Lizzie was pale.

"I'm president of the town council, remember? People talk."

"Okay, fine. It's true. But she's not going to do it anymore. We're working through it." She blushed when she looked at Emma. "But, yeah, she did steal his phone."

"What?" Emma demanded. She thought back to the email exchange between James and Willow—the one she'd read entirely the wrong way—and it hit her. "Oh. At the coffee shop in the city."

"I don't understand. When did Willow even find out that James was her father?" Gray asked. "How long has she known?"

Lizzie rubbed her face with both hands. "Honestly, the whole thing was kind of a mess. For her eighteenth birthday, Willow decided to get herself a DNA test. I didn't think anything would come of it, but as it turned out, she talked a bunch of her friends into it, too, including

Hunter. When it came back, the test indicated that they shared fifty percent of their DNA."

"Her birthday last month," Emma said, then gasped. "Oh my God, does Hunter know?"

Lizzie nodded. Gray threw up her hands and turned her back on them, as if trying to keep herself from physically exploding.

"Does Kelsey?"

"I think so. They've been spending so much time together . . ."

Emma nodded. She'd thought that was odd, and this would explain it. It would also explain why Kelsey was clearly helping Willow with her eBay enterprise.

"So, even though I told her not to, Willow reached out to James. He mostly ignored her, but finally, I guess, he replied and told her to back off." Lizzie took a breath. "But my daughter is tenacious. Backing off is not in her nature."

Just like her father, Emma thought.

"I asked her about the phone after I found it and Willow told me that the day James died, she and Hunter skipped out of school early and went into the city," Lizzie said, her voice picking up speed as if she just wanted to get it all out. "Willow met him at some coffee shop or something and it did not go well. She told me she snapped and swiped his phone. I don't think she was thinking straight. I think she was devastated, and it was the only thing she could think to do to get back at him." She shot Emma an embarrassed and apologetic look.

"This is unbelievable," Emma said, turning the phone over and over in her hands. Hunter had known about this all this time. He and Kelsey had both kept this huge secret from her. It was impossible to fathom. What must they be thinking? How did they feel about all this? "I can't believe I thought he was having an affair." Gray clucked her tongue and Emma looked at her. "I mean I *know* he did have more than one affair, but that *woman* who picked up when I called his phone was *Willow*." She stood up, unable to sit still a moment longer. "I wish she'd just said something. For the past three weeks I've been losing my mind, running all over the place, trying to track down this mistress, and it was her all along. His *daughter*."

Emma brought her hands to her temples, the phone clutched in one of them, and groaned in frustration. "I can't believe this is happening." She dropped her hands and looked at Lizzie. "So is this why we're friends? Did you move out here just to spy on us? To get close to the wife of the man who fathered your kid?"

Lizzie glanced at Gray. It was pretty clear she didn't want to have this conversation in front of her, but Emma didn't much care at the moment what Lizzie wanted.

"Lizzie?" she prompted.

"Yes, at first."

Emma shook her head, incredulous.

"Of course, I was curious. And part of me wanted James to see Willow. I wanted him to see *me*," Lizzie said, her voice throaty. "I didn't want to just be some footnote to him, some random slut that didn't matter. I thought that if he knew we were living close by, he wouldn't be able to forget about us. But then—"

"But then, what?" Emma demanded.

"But then I met you," Lizzie said, her voice cracking. "You became my family—you and Hunter and Kelsey—right when I needed one most."

Emma wiped tears from her eyes. Try as she might, all she could see when she looked at Lizzie was her friend—the person who had been there for her for the past ten years, making her laugh, making her see the beauty in the everyday, giving her an outlet for her photography. She couldn't even imagine the girl that Lizzie had once been—the one who'd been sucked in by her enigmatic husband. She was just Lizzie. And for better or worse, they *were* family.

Lizzie had lied to her, yes, but Emma had kept secrets, too.

"Did you and James ever talk?" Emma asked. "All those times you were at our house . . . all those parties . . . did he ever even acknowledge you?"

Lizzie shook her head and looked away. "I tried a couple of times. In the early days. But he told me to fuck off. He told me if I said anything to you, he'd kill me."

"Jesus," Gray whispered.

Emma let out a half sob, half laugh that she couldn't find the strength to hold in. "I'm sorry, I . . . I don't even know what to say."

"You don't have to say anything," Lizzie said quietly. "I understand if you hate me."

"I don't . . . hate you." Emma let out a shaky breath. "But I'm going to need some time. To process all of this."

Lizzie nodded. "I get that."

"Are you serious?" Gray said. "You're going to *forgive* her?"

Emma ignored her. "Where is Willow, anyway?" she asked Lizzie. "I feel like we should talk."

KELSEY

"I am not worthless!"

Kelsey turned and swung the bat at the nearest glass case so hard she felt a shoulder muscle tear. The front of the case exploded, raining shards all over the floor and pelting her face. She barely felt the sting of the cuts, and closed her eyes to swing again.

"Kelsey, stop!" Willow cried.

Somewhere nearby a phone began to ring.

EMMA

"She's not picking up," Lizzie said.

"Do you know where she is?" Emma asked, blowing her nose in a tissue.

Lizzie shrugged. "I think she said she was going to your house."

"No. I told the kids they couldn't have anyone over while I was away."

"Like that matters," Gray said.

Emma raised her eyebrows.

"God, Emma, it's like you were never a teenager."

Emma's phone rang and she fished it out of the back pocket of her jeans. It was Hunter. She shot Gray a triumphant look. "Here's my son calling to check in, just like I told him to do." She picked up.

"Hunter?"

"Mom? You'd better come home right now. It's Kelsey."

Emma's heart dropped like a plane plummeting toward Earth. She was already moving toward the bedroom door and the stairs beyond. "What's wrong?"

"Emma?" Lizzie said, alarmed, as she and Gray scurried after her.

"We . . . I'm sorry, but I invited some people over and I was in the living room when people started screaming," Hunter said in a rush. Emma could hear it now. The commotion in the background—a guttural screeching that sent chills down her spine. "Kelsey's, like, snapped or something. She's in the museum with a bat and Willow's stuck in there with her."

Emma got to the bottom of the stairs. She met Lizzie's eyes and blanched. There was another scream and a cry of what sounded like pain.

"Shit. Just come home!"

And the line went dead.

———

WHEN EMMA PULLED her car into the driveway fifteen minutes after Hunter's call, there were still party stragglers milling about. They scattered when they saw her, a wild-eyed adult in primal protector mode. She found Hunter crouched on the floor of the museum next to Kelsey, who had curled herself into an egg shape on the floor. There was glass everywhere. Blood dripped from a cut on Kelsey's leg. Willow was in the corner, sobbing.

"Mom?" Hunter said.

"Is she hurt?" Emma asked, crouching over her daughter.

"Not really, I think. I don't know."

"What about Willow?" Emma said.

"She won't talk to me," Hunter replied.

Through her sobs, face to the wall, Willow said, "Where's my mom?"

"She's coming. She was right behind me." Emma turned back to her daughter. "Kelsey? Kels?"

No response. Nothing.

"Let's get her upstairs."

"She won't move."

"You'll have to pick her up."

At the top of the basement stairs, they were met by Lizzie and Gray. Gray's hands flew up to cover her mouth.

"Willow?" Lizzie said, the word strangled.

"Downstairs," Emma told her.

They got Kelsey to her bedroom by way of the back stairs, her arms and legs wrapped around Hunter like a baby monkey. The door to Kelsey's room was locked, so they took her to the guest room. The second Hunter laid her down, she curled back into a fetal position and started to cry, smearing the sheets with blood. Emma sat next to her daughter and slowly, carefully checked her over. There were nicks and scrapes everywhere, but nothing that was more than superficial. She sat back and smoothed Kelsey's hair away from her sweaty, blood-streaked face. She leaned toward her daughter's ear and whispered.

"Shhhhh, my baby girl. It's going to be all right."

Gray appeared with a cool washcloth, and Emma used it to clean Kelsey's face and cool the back of her neck.

"Lizzie told me to tell you she's taking Willow home and that she's okay," Gray said, hovering in the doorway. "She'll call you later."

"Thanks."

Gray left them alone. Eventually, Kelsey drifted off to sleep. Emma met Hunter in the hallway.

"What the hell were you thinking?" she hissed to him, clicking the door closed quietly. "A party? What would you have done if the cops came? What about Duke? The baseball team? You put everything in jeopardy, including your sister."

"I'm sorry. I didn't think it would get that big. And Willow   "

"Willow what?" Emma snapped.

"I mean . . . it was her idea."

"Don't try to shirk responsibility here, Hunter," Emma said. "That girl may be your sister by blood, but this is your house—*our* house. We do not—"

"Wait. You know about Willow?" Hunter asked.

Emma shot him a steely look. "I know about a lot of things."

Hunter rubbed his face with two hands. "I don't think I even want to know what that means."

"We can talk about it later. Tell me what happened with Kelsey," she said, looking at the closed door to the guest room.

"I honestly don't know. I heard all this screaming and banging and then Joey came running upstairs and said *Kelsey's losing her shit*, and when I came down, all these people were in the basement and she was swinging a bat around."

"She *what?*"

"I know. It was intense. But then she just sort of stopped and went quiet and, like, deflated. That's when I called you."

"Did she say anything?"

"I don't know—it all happened in five seconds," Hunter said. "I know she was screaming at people to leave."

"What people?" Emma asked, the tiny hairs on the back of her neck rising.

"People. I told you, they were watching her."

"Hunter . . ."

He went pale at the strain in her voice. "What?"

"Were any of those people filming?"

EMMA

The video was difficult to watch. Kelsey was like a tornado of grief and misery and anger, blazing a whirling trail of destruction through her father's sacred space. Thank God Willow had had the sense to hit the floor and crawl into a corner. If that bat had caught her in the right spot in the wrong way . . . Emma didn't even want to think about it.

Emma forced herself to watch the footage again and again and again. She forced herself to really look at her daughter, to truly see her. By the time the sun started to turn the sky pink and then purple outside her window, she felt she knew, for the first time, what living this life had done to her little girl. The last few times she watched the clip, she couldn't stop her eyes from trailing the arc of the bat.

Around six o'clock in the morning, eyes dry, the skin around her mouth tight, Emma put the computer aside and went to her daughter's room. She used her own key to get inside; Kelsey was still asleep in the guest room. Her daughter's bed was perfectly made, her laptop closed on one pillow. On her desk was the stationery set James's mom had sent her from France all those years ago, the blotter off-center and crooked. Emma walked past the desk to the bed, still looking awkward to her in its new position under the bay window.

She now understood why Kelsey had placed it there.

Emma crouched at the end of the bed, hooked her fingers around the baseboard rungs, and pulled. The legs against the wood floor made a screeching sound as they inched forward. She glanced over her shoulder, but there was no movement in the hallway. It took her thirty seconds to pull the bed far enough away from the wall. Her stomach felt coiled like a spring as she found the wonky board and pressed it with her toe. The board creaked, as she knew it would.

She remembered when James had discovered this flaw. The Realtor had said it would be easy enough to fix, but James had pried the board up to peek beneath and said no way. It would be the perfect spot for one of their future kids to hide their stash. She and James had both laughed.

Emma thought of the look in Kelsey's eye in the video clip. She thought of her daughter, swinging that bat. As she slowly crouched in the sunlight, she could still hear James's laugh, echoing back through the years.

She tugged up the floorboard.

KELSEY

All she was going to do was grab the box of her dad's crap that Willow had told her to stash in the garage. She'd said she was going to pick it up this afternoon. That this would be their last *score*. She loved using that word, like they were drug addicts or something. Like being like drug addicts made them cooler. Willow had no fucking idea how the world really worked.

Kelsey knew. She knew that if she didn't put this stuff back where it belonged before her father noticed, she was going to get her ass handed to her. Earlier, in the light of day, she'd felt brave, defiant, like she didn't give a shit what her dad did. But now . . . now it was getting late and he'd be home any minute, and the cold sweat of terror prickled her spine. The later he was, the drunker he was. And the drunker he was, the meaner he was.

She didn't bother to flick on the lights. She ran to the corner and tugged out the box. The Jeter bat stuck out the top at an odd angle and got snagged on a tarp. She yanked, and it was that half second that cost her. There was a click and a groan. All the lights blazed on and the garage door began to open.

Kelsey froze. She could run, but then he'd find the box sitting here in the middle of the garage floor. Or worse, he'd run over it and crush its precious contents. By the time the flight half of her reflexes really took hold, it was too late. The door was fully open. He stopped the car at the top of the steep driveway and got out. Kelsey could see right away that the situation was not good. Her father stepped sideways, one foot crossing in front of the other, and steadied himself on the open door. His hair stuck up on one side. There was something wrong with his face.

He loosened his tie and tugged it off, almost knocking himself off balance as he tossed it into the bushes. Then he unbuttoned the top button on his shirt and rolled his neck around, as if the collar had been choking him.

Somehow, his eyes focused. He saw her.

"What the fuck is this?" her father shouted.

He half-shuffled, half-stumbled down the driveway and paused unsteadily in front of her. One eye was all purple and swollen shut. The other eyeball quivered.

"What the fuck are you doing out here so late?"

He hadn't noticed the box yet. Maybe he wouldn't. Maybe he'd go inside and she'd have time to fix this. But then, as if he could read her mind, his gaze trailed down. His head tilted as his addled brain tried to make sense of what he was seeing. Kelsey thought about running out through the open garage door, but where would she go? By the time she was halfway up the hill, he'd be back in the car, chasing her down. She could easily imagine him running her over, purposely or by accident; either scenario was completely believable. How fucked up was her life, that she could 100 percent fathom her father purposely mowing her down with his car? This was what she was thinking as he turned on her. And then, all supposition went out the window. There was a crusted-over slice of blood across his cheek. He was going to kill her.

The hunch of his shoulders, the redness of his face, were feral. But it was the look in his one good eye that told her it was true.

"You little piece of shit." Spittle hit her cheek. He was on her so fast, she couldn't even comprehend it. She backed into the shelving on the wall and a box tipped. Golf balls rained down around them. "I knew you were stealing from me! I fucking knew it!"

He grabbed the wire shelf above her head and yanked it forward, pulling it from the wall and driving it into the back of her skull.

"Daddy, stop!"

She hated herself even as she said it. Hated the whining, begging tone of her voice. Hated that she was crying. Hated that she'd called him *Daddy* like some pathetic little girl. Like she expected that to work. Nothing worked. To him, she was garbage—not his daughter, not even a human. He yanked again and she felt the cut at the back of her head, heard the shelving groan. He was going to take the whole side of the garage down on her skull. But she couldn't get past him. He was too big, too fast, too angry. So she did the only thing she could think to do. She hit the floor.

That was when she saw the bat, still sticking out of the brown cardboard box. Her hand closed around the shaft. She crawled awkwardly two steps and stood up.

Her father took a second to refocus, and when he did, he saw the bat, and he laughed.

He *laughed*.

"You don't have the guts," he spat.

She lifted the bat, holding it just how Hunter had taught her when she was trying out for Little League. She knew he was right. She knew in her heart that she didn't have it in her. But maybe, just maybe, if she could get in a swing, just a glance, she could surprise him enough to get away. And maybe if that happened, things would change around here. He would know he couldn't mess with her anymore. Maybe just standing up to him would earn her something. Some tiny morsel of his respect. He'd made it beyond clear he was never going to love her—that she didn't deserve his love. But he'd always respected people who stood up for themselves. Those who took charge. That was what Kelsey was doing right now. She was taking charge.

Until he wrapped his fingers around her neck. In half a second she knew she was screwed. Her windpipe closed as her father's thumbs pressed into it. She stared at him, tried to make him see her, see what he was doing, but it was as if he was looking right through her. Looking past this moment into a world where he was finally free of her.

This was it. She was actually going to die. And the last thing she was going to see was the grotesque mask of battered flesh that was her father's face. Panic set in and her grip on the bat began to loosen.

There was a bright flash of light. Her father stumbled. Kelsey sucked in air. He threw up a hand against the glare and she lifted the bat, something inside of her understanding that this was the moment in which she would live or she would die. She swung as hard as she could.

The force of the blow jarred her arms and the bat clattered to the floor half a second before her father's head hit the step to the kitchen. She heard a sickening crack.

"Hey!"

"Hunter?" He was backlit by the Jeep's headlights as he ran down the driveway. Her father, eyes closed, mouth gaping, neck snapped. And then, her brother was there.

"Dad? Oh my God. Dad!"

"He was going to kill me. You saw, right? He . . . he was trying to kill me."

Hunter was on the floor next to their father, shaking him. No response. He held his hand under their father's nose, trembling.

"Shit. Shit, shit, *shit*."

"I'm sorry, Hunter. I'm sorry. I didn't—"

He got up and came at her and she flinched, but he put his hands up. "Are you okay?"

Tears squeezed from her eyes and she stepped into him. His shirt smelled of cigarette smoke and sweat. When he pulled back, his eyes trailed to her neck. Her fingers fluttered up. It was already tender.

"He was going to—"

"I know. I saw. Holy shit." He turned to look at the body again. "What the fuck are we going to do?"

"We have to call the police," Kelsey said.

Hunter turned. He looked larger than life to her in that moment. His broad shoulders, his squared jaw, the very strength of him, when she felt so insignificant and worthless. There was a sureness in his eyes as he said, "We don't call the police."

"But I killed him."

"Stop saying that!"

"But . . . but it was self-defense."

"Kels, we can't call the cops. Everyone will know about him. They'll find out everything. And they'll arrest you. What if we can't prove it was self-defense? What then? Do you want to go to jail? Do you know what that will do to Mom?"

It was the word *Mom* that finally brought Kelsey back to some semblance of consciousness. She reached out and gripped Hunter's wrist. "Then what?" she said. "What do we do?"

All those nights clutched together while their parents fought. Her brother's arm around her. Hunter reading her to sleep. Letting her borrow his favorite doll. Curling up in her bed when it was really bad.

"We cover it up," Hunter said.

EMMA

Her children told her the story together, sitting at the kitchen island. The game-used, Derek Jeter autographed bat—flecked with blood—on the marble surface between them, like a line drawn in the sand. Her kids on one side, their broken, guilt-ridden, horrified mother on the other. They told her how they put the roof down on the car, used a hand truck to put his body back in his seat, and some grabbing tool from the garage wall to place his foot on the gas. They were surprised, they said, by how fast the car sped down the driveway, and when it crashed into the back wall, surprised again that it collapsed the way it did.

So she'd been right all along—someone *had* been there that night. But that someone had been her daughter, and later, her son.

They had called Willow, who had picked up Kelsey at the corner and taken her back to Lizzie's, and later convinced Lizzie—who always went to bed early on Fridays—that Kelsey had been there all night. Hunter went inside, changed into clean clothes, and went to his mother's room, where he pretended he had no idea what had happened.

By the end of the story they were all crying. Emma got up and walked around to her daughter, pulling her off her stool and hugging her as tightly as she'd ever hugged anyone.

"I'm so sorry, Mom. I'm so sorry."

"Shhh. It's my fault," Emma said. "I should have done something. I should have left him. Or made him get help. I should have—"

Hunter got up and Emma reached for him. He stepped closer and wrapped them both up in his arms.

"He never would've gone, Mom," Hunter said. "He wouldn't have. He would have had to admit he was wrong . . . that he was sick. He never would've done that."

"I'm just so sorry," Emma said into Kelsey's hair. Her chest felt as if it were being crushed by a vice. She'd turned her daughter into a killer. She'd never stop making this up to them. But for now, she had to start helping them heal. Therapy. Therapy was definitely in their future. Her father would be so proud. And if she'd learned anything from her dad back in the day, it was that all good cleansing rituals began with a symbolic act.

She pulled back and wiped her eyes. "Hunter, get showered and go pick up some bagels."

"Um . . . what?" Hunter said, and laughed nervously. He clearly thought she was losing it.

Emma picked up the bat and Kelsey flinched. "Your sister and I are going for a little drive, and we're going to want breakfast when we get back."

THEY DROVE OVER to the cottage first. Kelsey had only been there once. The crew was busy taking down the rickety deck in the backyard, using a bulldozer to knock it down. From the passenger seat, Kelsey seemed transfixed.

"What if we moved in here when it's done?" Emma suggested.

"Really?" Kelsey said, turning wide eyes on her.

"I feel like a change," Emma said. "It's a little bit closer to Daltry, anyway. Cuts fifteen minutes off the drive."

"If I get in," Kelsey said. "Are they really going to take someone who looks like this for her audition?"

She flipped down the visor and opened the mirror to inspect the tiny scratches and cuts on her face and neck.

"You'll get in," Emma replied. "I'll call and tell them you have the flu and we'll get it moved to next week. All of that will be healed up by then."

"Yeah?" Kelsey's voice was so hopeful it made Emma melt.

"Yes. I do have one question, though. Why were you and Willow selling those things?"

"I wanted to raise money for my application fee." Kelsey looked down at her hands. "Since Dad wouldn't pay for it."

Emma almost smiled. "Poetic."

And Kelsey, though she tried not to, *did* smile. For half a second.

"But then she didn't want to stop. She's kind of out of control, Mom. With the stealing thing." Kelsey looked at her lap. "I think she's pissed that we have what we have and she . . . doesn't. I think she and her mom are having money problems."

"Not anymore," Emma said.

They drove through downtown, where families strolled and couples window-shopped, clutching their coffees from Ben's in one hand, the leashes on their tiny dogs in the other. Up into the hills where the roads were winding and skinnier, the houses set farther and farther back from the streets. When they'd first moved out to Oakmont, James had only wanted to look at houses in the hills. This was where the wealthiest of the wealthy lived, after all. It was where Darnell and Gray lived now, having moved out here a few years after James and Emma had. But then he'd found the house in the valley—the largest, most private piece of land in town. Privacy. James had wanted privacy. And besides, their house had been just as big, just as ostentatious, as any of these.

"Where're we going?" Kelsey asked, staring out the window at felled trees. This neighborhood had been hardest hit by the hurricane, the force of the winds up here nearly four times as fierce as they'd gotten in the valley. One of Gray's friends had lost half her roof. Another, who owned acres, had lost more than fifty trees. As Emma continued to drive, they passed crew after crew of workers—there were wood-chipping trucks everywhere.

"I want you to know that you mean more to me than anything else in the world," Emma said as she took another turn, climbing higher into the hills. "You and Hunter."

"Mom. You're starting to freak me out."

"Sorry, it's just . . . everything you and your brother just told me . . . no one should ever have to go through something like that, and it kills me that you did. It doesn't matter what Hunter says. Life with your father . . . that wasn't the life I wanted for my kids. I let it go on for far too long, obviously."

"Mom—"

"It's my fault, Kelsey. I'm your mother. I'm supposed to take care of you guys. I should have left him years ago. And I'm sorry that I didn't. I'm sorry that, because I wasn't strong enough, you went through all the things you went through."

She found what she was looking for then. A truck-sized wood-chipper, running at the side of the road. The crew nowhere in sight, probably off grabbing coffee or taking a pee break. She looked at her daughter. Her face was red with embarrassment or pleasure or both.

"From this moment on, I'm going to take care of you." She unbuckled her seat belt. "Get out of the car."

"Mom."

"Kelsey, just trust me. Get out of the car."

She stepped out herself, walked around, and popped the trunk. Kelsey joined her hesitantly a moment later. They both looked down at the bat.

"Mom?"

"I thought you should do the honors," Emma said, and tilted her head toward the wood-chipper.

Kelsey stared at her. She stared at the bat. Emma hoped she was getting her point across. That she would never tell anyone what she knew. That she forgave her daughter. That she wished she had been there, that she had stopped it, that she had protected her child, but that she was proud of Kelsey for protecting herself. Emma knew she couldn't say these things out loud—not without her voice cracking or her eyes tearing up. Not without saying it wrong or having it taken out of context. Because she meant all these things, but she was also sickened and disappointed and confused and terrified about what came next. The only thing she knew for sure was that they had to destroy this bat.

"What're you going to tell the lawyers?" Kelsey asked. "The Baseball Hall of Fame?" There was a touch of sarcasm in her voice.

Emma lifted her hands. "How am I supposed to know what James did with the damn bat?"

Kelsey smirked. She reached into the trunk and picked up the weapon with two hands. Then she walked over to the chipper, paused, and tossed it inside the dark maw. Emma closed her eyes as the mechanism groaned and grated, chewing up the only physical thing left on the planet that could tie her daughter to her husband's death. Then they got in the car and drove away.

GRAY

There was nothing Gray Garrison loved more than a job well done, and the James Walsh situation was no exception. As she and Emma and Kelsey sat back in their cushy pedicure chairs that Saturday afternoon in December, she knew there was only one thing left to take care of. Luckily, as always, she knew a guy.

"Taylor and his crew are coming out next week to start construction," she told Emma as she dipped her feet into the warm footbath. On Emma's far side, Kelsey typed away on her phone. She'd just learned of her acceptance to Daltry a few days ago and was busy making friends at her new school.

"They'll work the week before Christmas?" Emma asked, flipping a page in her magazine.

"They'll work whenever as long as the price is right."

In fact, it had been a bitch to get Taylor to agree to the timeline—a holiday-shopping week when the sky threatened snow and the temperatures were dipping below freezing—but she owed Emma a new garage, and she was going to make damn sure her friend got one. Emma was putting the house on the market in the spring, and giving part of the proceeds to Lizzie to help pay for Willow's college. This was not a move

Gray agreed with, but she wasn't about to fight that battle. She'd done enough already.

"Lizzie! Over here!"

Emma waved and Lizzie spotted them, weaving through the manicure tables to the back of the shop. She took the chair next to Gray and placed her gingerbread coffee on the small table between them.

"Sorry I'm late. I was with Ben and I lost track of time."

"Not a problem," Gray said and smiled. This was her only loose end. Lizzie and Ben Thackery. That Lizzie and Ben had struck up a relationship so soon after she'd manipulated him into switching out those security cameras was unfortunate. But if it hadn't come up in conversations between the lovebirds yet, would it ever? Even if it did, would those two dim bulbs have the imagination to put two and two together? Gray thought not. She would never forget the night she had that epiphany to tell Ben that Alex Markakis had never brought his cameras up to code. It was true, of course, but the council had been letting it slide for two years. Getting Ben to put in the work order and have the cameras off for that weekend in September, though, was the only way she felt comfortable doing what she needed to do.

Using Emma's spare key fob, which she'd lifted that day from the mudroom, and Emma—bless her heart—had never missed, to get into James's car and pop the hood. Mixing the bit of brake fluid left in his tank with water. It had taken less than three minutes, but she only felt comfortable doing it knowing there would be no lasting evidence that she'd been there. If someone had walked out of the bar, she would have either hidden behind the car or ignored them—she was just a woman taking care of her own automobile. But no one had come near her, and the whole thing had taken less than five minutes.

Of course, she had hoped that his brakes would fail on the winding roads between town and the Walsh home—had never considered that he might put the car through the back of his own garage. She hated that it had happened on Emma's property—that she and Hunter had been the ones who had to find him. She also hated that it meant she'd had so much more evidence to deal with—not just talking Emma into getting the body cremated and letting Gray take control of having the car towed, but there was the garage to deal with as well. Gray had taken forensics classes in law school. She knew what the right team of investigators could figure out based on the minutest of details. Which meant the garage had needed to go.

Which was why she owed Emma this last favor. She couldn't sell the house without a garage, and it was Gray's fault she had none. Ergo, Gray was ordering up a new garage.

She had murdered James Walsh. She had formulated a plan and executed the plan and saved her husband's business, her sons' futures, and her best friend from countless more years of misery at his hands. She knew Emma would never have left him on her own and the insanity had gone on long enough. Gray had believed that for a long time and had fantasized about getting rid of him for Emma for years. But it was his threatening *her* family, their livelihood, their reputation, that had tipped the scales. The day Derek had come to her and told her what Zoe had found out—what James planned to do—she knew she had only one option. And now, it was finally done.

"You're not paying for the garage. You know that, right?" Emma said. "We have insurance, and even if we didn't, we have plenty of money."

"It's all taken care of," Gray told her as Kelsey giggled at some text on her phone. She turned on the massage feature on her chair and let the rollers knead out the knots in her back. "This is what I do."

Acknowledgments

Thank you from the bottom of my heart to my friend Jen Calonita, without whom this book you're holding would still be a file on my computer with no agent, no editor, and no publisher. Jen, your faith in this book and your constant cheerleading pulled me out of the gutter and this story into the light, and for that I will be eternally grateful.

I'd also like to thank my agent, Holly Root. The very fact that you "got" this book from the very beginning still makes me happy and grateful and all the things. Thanks also to Alyssa Moore and everyone at Root Literary who make being part of their family both easy and tons of fun. And to Jackie Cantor, my editor extraordinaire, who always knows the right words to say to make me stop feeling like a poseur and start feeling like an author again, thank you for seeing the worth in this story and for all your advice along the way.

To everyone at Gallery Books, including Jennifer Bergstrom, who refused to let this book have a weak title, and Molly Gregory who answers emails lightning fast, thank-you for everything. And to the rest of the Gallery team, including Jen Long, Aimee Bell, Alysha Bullock, Lisa Wolff, Caroline Pallotta, Davina Mock-Maniscalco, and Lisa Litwack, thank you so much for supporting my work and for making this book look pretty and read well.

Thank you to my early readers, Aimee Friedman, Lynn Weingarten, and Britt Rubiano, who took time out of their busy lives to read and offer notes and advice (and many exclamation points via text—you know who you are).

To everyone I've worked with in this nutty industry we call publishing, I couldn't possibly list you all, but know that I'm thinking of all your smiling faces as I type this. Whether you edited me, I edited you, you agented me, you publicized or marketed my books, or you worked alongside me on editor's row, please know that each of you has taught me something along the way and that those many somethings are what got me to where I am. And I like where I am. So, thank you.

To those die-hard fans of my early career who still connect with me on social media, you have kept me going through so, so, so, so, much. I see you and I appreciate you. Special shout-out to Dyondra, Jennah, Jacklynn, Erica, and Aislyn.

To my brother, Ian, and my sister, Erin, I love you. It's my year to run down the stairs first.

To my extended family of Violas and Scotts, and to my oldest and dearest—Wendy and Shira—as well as all the other friends who have reached out when I have book news or who have come to launch events or festivals or fairs (hey, Sabina!)—here's hoping we can party by the time this book comes out, but if we can't, this is me clinking whatever glass you're holding with my tumbler full of ginger ale.

To my husband, Matt, and my boys, Brady and William, thank you for giving me time behind closed doors to do what I love. And apologies for the grumpy I-got-no-work-done days. (But you're welcome for the I-wrote-8,000-words chocolate cakes.)

To my father, who I recognize instilled the earliest love of reading and writing in me, and who I have succeeded in spite of, I hope your rest is peaceful.

Finally, to my mom, who was not perfect, but was perfect to me. Thanks for getting sober. Thanks for being there. Thanks for loving me unconditionally. Thanks for being in my head cheering me on every day. I miss you and I hold your pride in me deep in my heart.